WHERE THE
LIGHT GLOWS

Visit us at www.boldstrokesbooks.com

WHERE THE LIGHT GLOWS

by
Dena Blake

2017

WHERE THE LIGHT GLOWS

ISBN 13: 978-1-62639-958-7

THIS TRADE PAPERBACK ORIGINAL IS PUBLISHED BY
BOLD STROKES BOOKS, INC.
P.O. BOX 249
VALLEY FALLS, NY 12185

FIRST EDITION: MAY 2017

CREDITS
EDITOR: SHELLEY THRASHER
PRODUCTION DESIGN: SUSAN RAMUNDO
COVER DESIGN BY SHERI (GRAPHICARTIST2020@HOTMAIL.COM)

Acknowledgments

Thanks to Len Barot and Sandy Lowe for bringing me into the BSB family and letting me fly. You've given me the most precious gift of all, validation.

To Shelley Thrasher, my editor extraordinaire, for cleaning up my sentence structure and making this book flow so eloquently.

To Sheri for a gorgeous cover and knowing exactly what I wanted even when I didn't.

To the rest of the BSB crew for making the publishing process seamless.

To Robyn for reading all my manuscripts, correcting my grammar, and always reminding me to write the happily ever after.

To Kate for patiently waiting while I finish just one more line and giving me honest, practical feedback without shattering my ego.

To my kids, Wes and Haley, for just being there and always having faith in me. You'll never know just how much your encouragement means.

To my family for loving me no matter what and for tirelessly cheering me on each step of the way.

To my parents who never had the opportunity to see this book, but whom I hope would be proud.

Last, but never least, thank you to all of you who will read this book and, hopefully, all my books to come. Without you, my passion would never be realized.

Dedication

For Kate, who makes the impossible seem anything but.
I love you.

Chapter One

Izzy jumped when Angie slammed through the kitchen door and dropped the dirty dishes into the sink.

"That bitch is here again with a table full of people." Angie grabbed her hips and spun around. A vein pulsed in the middle of her forehead. "She's pissed because her usual table is taken. They have a solution for that. It's called res—er—vations," Angie spouted in a no-brainer rhythm.

"Did you find her another table?"

"Of course I did. You think I want to have her standing there breathing down my neck for the next twenty minutes? It took two tries, but I finally found one the princess would accept." She filled six water glasses and set them on a tray. "Not a thank you or a kiss my ass. Nothing."

"Settle down before you go back out there, Ang. I don't want any problems tonight." Izzy's hot-tempered little sister wasn't very good at serving people. She also wasn't good at holding her tongue when she thought she was right, which was all the time.

Izzy peeked out the door behind the bar and watched Angie deliver the glasses of water to the table. She smiled and took out her order pad. *So far so good.* Izzy glanced around the dining room. Almost every table was full. When she'd seen the reservation list for the night, Izzy had regretted giving Gio the night off. But he had what he called "a date with the girl of his dreams" tonight, and Izzy had given in and let him go. Her little brother had more than a few of those dates, but the excitement in his eyes always won her over. It had been a while since she'd had a date like that, and for now, she was glad she had the restaurant to occupy her time. She'd just finished plating another party's order when Angie rushed back into the kitchen.

"I need a cup of minestrone, three Caesars, and two house with vinaigrette on the side." Angie filled a metal bowl with romaine lettuce and freshly mixed Caesar dressing. After tossing the greens with the tongs, she plucked them out into individual bowls before taking the soup and salads back to the dining room.

Tony glanced over at Izzy. "She seems to have settled down."

She stuck up two fingers and crossed them. Angie was already pissed because Izzy had called her in on her night off to help out the four wait staff already scheduled. Her sous chefs, Carlos and Miguel, were keeping up with the prep in the kitchen, and she and Tony were right on spot with the dishes going out.

The kitchen door slammed against the wall. *So much for wishful thinking.*

"Unbelievable!" Angie said, barreling back into the kitchen. "She wouldn't take the plate from me. I had to squeeze between the chairs and put it down in front of her."

"That's what you're supposed to do, Angie. We've talked about this before. Mrs. Thomas is a longtime customer. Take care of her."

"I know, but she doesn't have to be so smug about it. Sitting there, tapping her finger on the table."

"Why don't you let one of the other girls take the table?"

"If she didn't tip so damn well, I would."

A few minutes later, the door swung open and the woman was in Angie's face. "This is the *wrong* salad. I said mixed green with NO onions."

Izzy watched Angie's jaw tighten. She slipped in between the two of them before Angie let loose on the customer. "I've got this." She grabbed Angie's shoulders and spun her around. "You go out back for a minute." Angie glared over her shoulder, jaw clenched, ready to spout something. Izzy pointed to the door and said, "Now!" She turned back around, took the salad from Mrs. Thomas, and set it on the counter. "I understand you're upset about the salad. I'm sorry. She's doing the best she can."

Cool, shuttered eyes zoomed in on Izzy's. "If that's her best, she needs to find another career."

"I'll take care of it right now." *Out of my kitchen!* Izzy took the woman by the elbow and guided her to the dining area.

She yanked her arm free from Izzy's grip, spun around, and dug in with both heels like she was steeling herself for battle.

"I'll have your salad out in just a minute," Izzy added, waiting for the retort she knew was ready to spew out of the woman's mouth.

Mrs. Thomas sucked in a deep breath as her frigid gaze held Izzy's. "I'd like a new waitress," she said, her voice low and even.

"Of course." Izzy pinched her lips together and counted to ten in her head. "I'll have that salad right out."

Izzy watched Mel Thomas speed back to her table before she glanced around the dining room to see if any of her other customers had been disturbed. She hurried back to the kitchen, prepared a new salad, and sent it out with one of the other waitresses.

"Is it rude to toss a Xanax into someone's mouth while they're talking?" she said to her brother, Tony, who had taken over the cooking when Izzy left the stove to deal with the woman who had burst into the kitchen.

He let out a big belly laugh and Izzy grinned. She dropped her smile and headed out back to talk to Angie. "What the hell happened out there?"

"The woman acts like she's my only table. She's waved me down five times already. Plus she's so picky. Everything has to be perfect for her."

"She's the customer, Angie. I'd like everything to be perfect for her or she may not come back."

"Good riddance." Angie swung her arm backhandedly.

"How many people are at that table, Ang?"

"Six."

Izzy scrunched her face and glanced at the dark sky. "Okay, six times twenty, plus twenty more for appetizers and around sixty for wine. That's about two hundred bucks." She glared back at Angie. "You want me to take that out of your check?"

"Well, no." Angie's eyes widened, and Izzy knew she was getting her point across. How long she would remember it was yet to be seen.

"Then get your shit together and start being nice to the customers."

"Fine." Angie pulled her order pad from the pocket in her apron and tore off a page. "She wants the shrimp scampi. Remember light on the garlic or she'll send it back." She slapped it into Izzy's hand.

"I remember."

Izzy slid the last dish for the table of six under the warmer, and Angie started loading the dishes on her arm. "No, you don't. I'll take the order out." Izzy took the plates from her.

Angie dropped the last plate she was holding onto the counter. "Whatever. Her husband has been looking me up and down all night anyway."

Izzy had delivered all of the meals except for the one for the unhappy customer, who sat tucked in close to the wall. She slipped between the two tables and was just about to set the dish in front of her when, in a quick swift motion, the man behind her pushed back in his chair as the woman swung her hand up in conversation. Time froze for Izzy as she rocked backward and then forward, her movement sluggish as if in slow motion. She reached out but couldn't stop. Her cranky customer enjoyed a delicious serving of shrimp scampi with angel-hair pasta served right into her lap. Light on the garlic, of course.

Izzy's eyes bounced from Mrs. Thomas's shocked expression to her lap and then back to her widened eyes. It seemed like the longest minute *ever*.

"Oh my God!" Her eyes narrowed and her voice erupted in a low, angry rumble. "I can't believe you just dumped that on me!"

Shit! I can't believe it either! "I am so sorry." Izzy picked a handful of pasta from her lap and put it back on the plate. "Let me get you a towel." She raced into the kitchen, the door smacking against the wall behind it. "I need towels. Now!" Tony threw her a couple. "Start another order of scampi."

She rushed back out to the dining room with Angie on her tail. They got all of the pasta cleaned up, and Tony brought out another dinner for her. In the meantime, the women at the table had all gone to the bathroom, and Izzy's unintentional target was much calmer when she returned. Who knew how long that would last. She seemed to be holding her tongue in front of her friends.

"Jesus fucking Christ!" Izzy leaned against the counter in the kitchen and rubbed her forehead. "Comp the meal."

"Everything?" Angie gave her a crazy look.

"Yes. The whole meal."

❖

"It was an accident, Mel. Let it go," Jack said as he got out of the car.

"It was ridiculously embarrassing." Mel continued to stare at the large oil spot in the middle of her Armani dress. "This is never going to come out."

"I think everyone got a good laugh out of it."

"Exactly." She blew out a breath. "Not the impression I like to make in public."

"Everyone doesn't have to think you're perfect, Mel." Jack, always the gentleman, held the door for her as Mel entered their condo.

"I never said I was perfect." She just didn't like them to see her lose her composure. She had certainly done that tonight. She headed for the stairs and Jack moved to the bar. She stopped at the bottom step. "Are you coming up?"

He shook his head. "I have work to do."

She took in a deep breath and proceeded up the stairs. She always asked, and he always gave her the same response.

The room was Mel's sanctuary. It was decorated with two linen wingback chairs near the window and antique cherrywood dressers covering each wall. A king-sized, leather-padded sleigh bed centered the room with matching tables on each side.

Mel crossed the room to the bathroom, kicking off her shoes on the Oriental rug covering the wood floor. Glancing at herself in the mirror, she unzipped her ruined dress and let it drop to the floor. The loss of the dress didn't really bother her; it was the embarrassment that hurt. And the look of disdain Jack had given her stung the most. She finished undressing and stepped into the shower. The steaming jets hit her from all sides.

She heard Jack come into the bathroom. The drawer rattled open and closed, and then he was gone again. Once in their marriage he would've come into the shower with her uninvited, but those days were long gone. He regularly slept in the guest room now, with the excuse of the constant news-monitoring he did during the night. Being married to an international news reporter was glamorous but had many drawbacks.

When had she become so driven by other people's opinions? Mel had never aspired to keep up with the Newhouses and the Murdochs. After all, she had her own marketing and public-relations firm that had been successful for quite some time. Maybe if she'd succumbed to Jack's requests for her to stay at home and be satisfied with what he provided, they would've been closer.

She turned the knob on the shower and sighed as she stepped out. He would have been happier, yet she could never have been fulfilled that way.

Izzy found herself at one of her usual haunts on a barstool sitting next to a beautiful brunette she'd met for the first time only an hour before. She filled her glass as well as the brunette's with the last of the wine from the bottle of merlot she'd ordered.

"I'll be right back," Izzy said, motioning to the restroom. She glanced at the woman's backside as she got up. The woman had an irritating voice similar to the sound made by rubbing your hand on a balloon, but her knockout body made up for it in spades.

"I'll be waiting."

When Izzy returned, the woman sipped her wine and gazed over her glass at her. She gazed back at her smoky, dark eyes and knew immediately where this was going. "You want another glass of wine?"

"I think I've already had too much. Would you mind giving me a ride home?"

"Not at all. Just let me settle the tab." She waved the bartender over and handed her a couple of twenties. "Keep the change, Terry."

Terry gave her a wink. "Thanks. You two have a good night."

"We will," the brunette said over her shoulder as she took Izzy's hand and led her out.

❖

Izzy dropped her keys on the entry table and grabbed a bottle of water from the fridge before she went out on the deck. She flopped down into a chair and took in the welcome sight of the ocean. The night sky was clear. The moonlight shimmered across the water as the waves rolled up on the shore. She probably should've gone straight home after the restaurant closed tonight, but she was too keyed up. The pasta fiasco had sent her adrenaline skyrocketing, and she knew she wouldn't be able to relax. The brunette had been a nice distraction. She took in a deep breath and smiled. The familiar face that popped into her mind when she'd peaked was certainly unexpected. As was her body's heightened response to the image.

What was she going to do about her problem customer or, more still, her problem sister? Angie's heart just wasn't in it. The blood that ran through her veins was different than Izzy's. Angie didn't feel the pull of the restaurant like she did. It was clear Angie didn't want to be there. Her mind was always a million miles away in cyberspace. No matter how many times she told her, Angie couldn't seem to grasp the idea that the customers were the ones who paid her salary. For someone who spent the majority of her time in school or communicating with a laptop, that wasn't surprising.

The thought of another talk with her made Izzy's stomach turn. It would be another bitch session she didn't want to have. The thought of letting her go made it even worse. But if she didn't rein her in, she would lose a customer who spent a considerable amount of money in the restaurant on a regular basis. She didn't know how to get her point across to Angie without making her feel threatened.

She pushed out of her chair and went into the house. Tomorrow was going to be a big day. First off, she would call her regular to apologize again and offer to pay her cleaning bill. She couldn't afford to lose her business, no matter how much of a bitch she was.

CHAPTER TWO

The mountains of Marin County were brown from lack of water. There had been only a smidgen of rain this summer. Izzy was thankful to have the beach in her backyard. She put all of her nagging thoughts of yesterday behind her as she soaked up the beautiful view on her drive to work.

Summer was almost over, but surf camp was still in full session. Camp ran from nine to four daily until mid-September. Black wetsuits filled with kids as young as six dotted the shore, eager to learn how to tame the choppy waves of the Pacific. The sight brought back good memories for Izzy. She'd learned to surf on this very beach when she was a child, and to this day, she still kept the friendships she'd made with many of her surf buddies.

The cars were sparse at this time of the morning. Whatever traffic there was on Highway One had already gone, except for a sporadic group of motorcycles. Izzy loved not having to commute into San Francisco. She didn't care too much for the city and absolutely hated traffic. She'd had enough of that when she was in culinary school. The forty-five-minute trip downtown she drove five days a week had lost her close to two hours a day in traffic, easy.

Now her morning commute to the restaurant lasted only about thirty minutes. That included the detour to her parents' house in Mill Valley. She was living the dream and only wished she could find someone with whom to share it.

She pulled up in front of her parents' house and collected the daily paper from the driveway as she stepped onto the porch. She gave the door a light tap and let herself in. Bella was sitting at the kitchen table still in her housecoat waiting for her, as usual. She'd made the coffee and already had a cup in front of her.

"Hey, Momma." Izzy bent down and kissed her on the cheek. "How are you feeling today?"

Bella patted her on the hip as she responded. "Today is a good day, I think."

"Well, that's good to hear, Momma." She dropped the paper on the table in front of her. "What are you in the mood for this morning?"

"Pancakes."

Izzy grinned at her mother. It *was* a good day if Bella wanted pancakes. "Plain or blueberry?"

"Blueberry, but only half the amount this time. You got carried away with them last time."

"The doctor said they're good for you."

"I know, but I want to taste the pancake too."

Izzy grinned. Bella knew what she wanted and wasn't afraid to tell her. She fixed them both a plate of pancakes and ate with her mother. They talked about the weather, politics, and the pope.

Bella really liked this new one. He seemed to understand more about the people than others had in the past. Izzy wasn't a religious woman any longer, but on this subject, she agreed with her mother. It had taken far too long to choose a pontiff who had compassion for every human being.

Izzy cleaned up the dishes and sat back down to finish her coffee.

"Your sister tells me you gave someone their whole meal free last night."

"Yes, I did, Momma."

"You did this because?" Bella lifted a brow while waiting for Izzy to answer.

"I spilled a plate of pasta in her lap." She didn't mention that Angie had words with the customer also.

"I see. Have you called her to apologize?"

"Not yet. I'll do that this morning."

Bella reached over and patted her hand. "Good girl." She smiled and sipped her coffee.

Customers were business, and Izzy knew how to keep them happy. Even when they were really unhappy, she could usually turn the situation around. Typically, all it took was a sincere apology and a free dessert. But this particular one might be a little more difficult.

"Your youngest daughter can be a challenge to work with. She doesn't want to be there."

"She'll settle down. I remember a time not long ago when you were just like her. Wild in your ways, never agreeing with anyone."

Izzy laughed. "Then I realized how much I need you."

Bella's lips tipped up. "Angie will realize that about you someday."

"This is different, Momma. She's not a cook. She likes technology."

"You mean computers?"

"More than just computers. She wants to change the world. She probably will. She's so much smarter than I ever was at her age."

Bella's brow furrowed. "Not smarter, dear. Just different."

"I'm going to cut back her hours at the restaurant so she can focus on her college courses."

"If you think that will help her."

"I do." Izzy took the last swig of her coffee and put her cup in the dishwasher. "I love you, Momma. See you tomorrow." She kissed her on the cheek.

"I love you too, sweetheart." Izzy turned to the door and Bella said, "Don't forget to pick up the cleaning bill for that customer." Izzy smiled at her mother's persistence. Even though Izzy had taken over the restaurant years ago, Bella still never failed to remind her of what to do.

"Don't worry, Momma. I'll take care of it."

Izzy drove the short distance to the market to buy some fresh fish and meat for the specials. On tonight's menu, she would offer a small roast pork chop with garlic-mashed potatoes as well as prawn fettuccine with marinara.

She drove to the restaurant thinking about how she would apologize to Mel Thomas. She fully expected to get another earful when she did and needed to be prepared to respond without becoming angry. After all, even though it was an accident, it was her fault that she had stained her dress. She couldn't deny that.

The kitchen was already clean and Carlos was doing food prep when Izzy arrived. Tony had the sauce started, and the first lasagna of the day was in the oven. Once everything was set for the day's business, she would slip into the office and place the call she was dreading.

She had mixed emotions about Mel. There were times when Izzy found her to be very likeable, but when she was unhappy, she could be a mega-bitch.

❖

Mel was running late for lunch with her mother. She'd planned to get out early but had gotten hung up at the office, as usual. It was her mother's turn to choose, and she'd selected her favorite restaurant on the pier in Tiburon. This was the only day this week she could break away to see her. Tomorrow Mel was doing a lunch presentation on email and Internet safety at the senior center, and she usually used her Friday lunch hour to catch up on work. Mel had stopped to drop off her dress at the cleaners on the way. She wasn't counting on getting it back without the stain.

Mel knew when she arrived her mother would already be seated outside on the deck enjoying the sun. Cecilia Collins was always punctual. She wouldn't fuss about Mel's tardiness, and that's why she hated to be late.

"I'm sorry, Mom." Mel slid down into the chair adjacent to Cecilia. "I had to stop at the cleaners on my way over."

"It's the middle of the week. Don't you usually do that on Friday?"

"It was unavoidable. I had a plateful of pasta dropped in my lap last night."

Her mother chuckled. "That must have been a sight."

"It's not funny. I was livid." She unfolded her napkin and slipped it onto her lap.

"Of course it is, dear. Stop being so pretentious. I didn't raise you that way."

Mel could see a twinge of disappointment in her mother's eyes and felt it deep in her gut. Her mother had taught her to always be compassionate and to remain aware of other people's feelings. Growing up, she'd always hated it when some of the girls in her group had made the less-fortunate girls within it feel different, like they were unworthy in some way of having the same things the rich girls had.

"I guess it was a little funny." Mel let her lips slide into a smile. "The look on the chef's face was hysterical." *Surprise and horror all jumbled together.*

"I'm sure it was an accident. Was it at the Italian place you like so well?"

"Yes. She comped the whole meal." Her voice wisped up slightly.

"You do throw quite a bit of business their way, don't you?"

"I do, but even though I love the food, I think I'm going to steer clear of it for a few weeks. It was very embarrassing."

"That may be difficult, dear. I planned a nice little birthday party for you there this weekend."

"Mom, I told you I don't want a party. Jack and I are planning to spend the weekend together."

"Well, it's already paid for. So you'll just have to start your weekend after the party Saturday." Cecilia arched an eyebrow. "Since when are you and Jack getting along?"

"I'm giving it one last shot."

"How many times is this?"

"Mom, let it go." She blew out a heavy breath. "I know you don't like the way he treats me." Mel opened her menu and gave it her full attention.

"Never mind that *I* don't like it. *You* shouldn't like the way he treats you."

Mel could feel her mother's eyes bearing down on her as she scanned the menu.

"Look at you. Beautiful. Successful. You've done that all on your own. My God, Mellie, you're a grown woman. You don't need to please anyone but yourself. Jack hasn't worried about anyone but himself for quite some time."

Mel ignored her mother's comments. She didn't need to be reminded of her husband's roaming eye. She'd gotten enough of that last night at the restaurant every time the cute little waitress came to the table. She'd felt like she was back in high school when her beautiful best friend had enticed her first serious boyfriend away.

After that painful experience, Mel had promised herself she would never become close friends with any woman again. She'd only broken that promise once in college. That was another story altogether and hadn't worked out the way she'd planned either.

Mel glanced up when the waiter brought two drinks and put one in front of each of them. "I ordered you an iced tea," her mother said.

"Are you ladies ready to order?" the waiter asked.

Mel spoke up, thankful for the interruption. "Yes. What are the specials today?"

The waiter rattled them off, describing each one in delectable detail while also offering his opinion on which was the tastiest. Mel decided against them all and ordered a Cobb salad. Cecilia opted for the same, as well as a small cup of tomato basil soup.

"You know what you need to do, Mellie," her mother said, gazing out onto the water.

Mel was silent, contemplating her next question. "What's the difference between my situation and yours? Why did you stay with Dad?"

Cecilia's gaze snapped back to Mel. "That was different. I had you and your brother to raise."

"But you might have been happier with someone else."

"Maybe so, dear. But where would I have gone? You and Michael would never have had the education and opportunities you received growing up if I had left."

The waiter delivered their salads, and that was the end of the conversation. Mel knew her mother was right; she wasn't happy. She hadn't been for a long time. The thought of leaving Jack had crossed her mind more than once over the years, and the thought of not having him around didn't really upset her anymore. But the thought of being alone for the rest of her life terrified her.

The salad was delicious, yet so large Mel left half of hers uneaten, as did her mother. She apologized to her for being disrespectful, questioning her as she had. Cecilia had done what she thought best for her family, and it was probably at her own expense.

They left each other on a good note, her mother looking forward to the birthday party she'd organized for Mel on Saturday. She wasn't quite as thrilled, but her mother had gone out of her way to do something special for her. She would go and put on a good show for her family.

When Mel got back to her office, the red light was blinking on her phone. She hit the speakerphone button and dialed her voice mail. The sound of the head chef from Bella's Trattoria filled her office.

"Good morning, Mrs. Thomas. This is Izzy from Bella's Trattoria. I just wanted to apologize again for last night. If you'll bring me the bill, I'd like to pick up the cleaning tab for your dress. I'm here most days, or I can come by your office and get it if you prefer." There was silence for a moment. "Again, I'm so sorry for everything that happened last night."

Mel pushed the replay button and listened to the soft, husky voice again. Izzy sounded sincere enough, not a twinge of nervousness in her voice. Mel felt a little ashamed now. She'd been embarrassed and reacted badly last night. She wouldn't let Izzy pay for the cleaning. Comping the entire meal last night was more than she'd expected and altogether unnecessary. A nice bottle of wine would have sufficed.

She would see the chef again next week at the birthday party her mother had planned for her. It would be uncomfortable at first, but Mel appreciated the apology and wouldn't take the issue any further.

"Hey." Izzy scowled when she caught Angie hanging around in the kitchen with their brothers, Tony and Gio, who was bragging about a recent date. "I thought you had class tonight."

"I do. Web design."

"Are you nervous about it?"

"Are you kidding? I am *so* looking forward to it."

Izzy smiled at her sister's enthusiasm. It was nice seeing her excited about something. "Learn it all. Then maybe you can build a website for this place and bring Bella's into the twenty-first century."

"You'll let me do that?"

"I'll not only let you. I'll pay you to do it."

"Really?" Her eyes grew wide.

Izzy nodded. "Really."

Angie glanced at the clock on the wall. "I gotta go or I'll be late. I'll see you guys later."

"Okay, learn lots." Izzy watched her rush out the door.

"What are you doing? Getting her all excited like that." Their older brother, Tony, pushed the kitchen door open to see if she was gone. "What if she doesn't get the hang of it?"

"She's a smart girl, Tony. I have no doubt she'll do great." She crossed her arms and leaned back on the counter. "Have you talked to her lately about anything to do with technology?"

"Why would I? I don't know anything about the subject."

"Maybe if you did, you'd learn something. Or even better, get a cell phone."

"What do I need one of those for? I got a phone right here." He picked up the receiver from the wall phone and dropped it back onto the cradle. "I got one just like it at home. Speaking of phones, did you call Mrs. Thomas and apologize?"

"Yep. Called her first thing when I got here this morning."

"You think she'll come back?"

"She'll be back."

"Oh yeah? How do you know?"

"Her mother has a birthday party planned for her on Saturday."

"I guess that's a good thing. You'll get a chance to win her over."

"I just have to keep Angie away from her."

"You have to admit, she's pretty uptight."

"I don't have to admit anything, Tony. I just have to keep her coming back." Not only did she bring in a fair amount of business, but she was also very easy on the eyes.

Angie joked with her friend, Doug, as she waited in the hallway for the classroom door to open. She was making fun of his Croc flip-flops, and he was critiquing her new home-dyed ombre hair color. She and Doug had been friends since middle school, when they'd ended up in a few classes together. Doug helped Angie get through English, and she did the same for Doug in history class. They both aced computer fundamentals and immediately knew they wanted careers in information technology. They'd decided to go to the College of Marin before moving to a four-year college. It would be cheaper, and they could take all of their classes together.

The teacher's aide pushed through the waiting students, unlocked the door, and propped it open. "Okay everyone, let's not leave any empty seats up front. You're here to learn."

Angie and Doug took seats in the third row. The instructor came from the back up the middle aisle to the front of the classroom and turned around.

"Hello, everyone. My name is Mel Thomas, and I'll be one of your instructors for this class. Nancy Dolan will be the other. We'll switch off teaching every couple of weeks. Also, on occasions, we will both be here teaching the class together." She leaned back against the desk and crossed her legs. "I own an advertising and public-relations firm called 365 that specializes in web design. Nancy is a very talented designer who works with me."

"Holy shit." Angie sank down in her seat, hiding behind the computer monitor on the desk.

"What?" Doug quirked up an eyebrow. "You know her?"

"Yeah. Remember the crazy lady at the restaurant I told you about the other day?"

He nodded.

"That's her."

"Holy shit." He chuckled "This is gonna be so good." He grinned and returned his attention to the instructor.

"The first thing we're going to do is go around the room and introduce ourselves. That means, your name, what program you're in, and why you're taking this class. Who wants to start?"

Doug threw his hand up, and Angie tried to bat it down.

"Okay." The instructor pointed to Doug. "Go ahead."

"My name's Doug Haskell, and I'm in the computer-science program. I'm taking this class because it's one of the requirements."

"Hmm." She touched her finger to her lips. "So you're only taking this class because it's a requirement. What do you plan to do with your computer-science degree after you complete college, Doug?"

"Be an application developer."

"That's fair. How about the young lady next to you?"

Angie peeked around the monitor.

"Yes, you." Mrs. Thomas motioned for her to sit up.

Angie sat up and immediately saw recognition in the instructor's eyes.

"Go ahead. Tell us about yourself."

"My name's Angie Calabrese. I'm in the computer-science program too. I'm taking this class because I want to create beautiful places for people to visit on the web."

Mrs. Thomas nodded slowly. "Have you taken a web-design class before, Angie?"

"No, this is my first, but I've created a couple of websites on my own." Angie shifted nervously in her seat as the woman moved toward her and tilted her head curiously.

"Do you think you can learn something in this class you don't already know?"

"I wouldn't be here if I didn't," she shot back.

Mrs. Thomas gave her a ghost of a smile and strolled back to the front of the classroom. "Good. We'll see if we can help you improve on what you've created." She fixed her eyes on the girl sitting next to Angie and dipped her chin, motioning for her to speak next.

"You are so screwed," Doug mouthed to Angie, pumping his fingers into the side of his fist with a huge grin on his face.

"I'm going to kill you," she mouthed back, narrowing her eyes and dragging her finger across her neck.

After they'd finished the introductions and had thoroughly reviewed the syllabus, it was nine o'clock. When the instructor dismissed the class, Angie grabbed her book and flew out of the classroom. She didn't want any more one-on-one interaction with Mrs. Thomas.

Izzy jumped when Angie tossed her book onto the counter and flopped onto one of the stools in the kitchen. Doug followed her in and sat down next to her.

"How was class?" Izzy asked.

"I am so fucking screwed."

"Watch your mouth."

"She's right. She's screwed." Doug grabbed a slice of sourdough bread and bit a chunk off.

"It's only the first night. What happened?" Izzy dropped some pasta into a couple of bowls and ladled sauce over them.

"That crazy customer. The one you spilled pasta on the other night."

Izzy nodded. "What about her?"

"She's my instructor."

Izzy stared. "No way." She slid the bowls of pasta in front of them.

"Yeah. It was great." Doug laughed as he twirled spaghetti on his fork. "Angie got all cocky with her. I thought the lady was going to grind her gears right there in front of everybody."

"That's priceless." Izzy laughed.

"It's not funny. She's going to hate everything I create."

"No, she won't. I've seen what you can do. She'll love it."

"You just had to go and spill pasta on her."

"It's not like I did it on purpose. I called and apologized."

"You did? But she was such a bitch."

"She still didn't deserve to have pasta tossed in her lap. Maybe a little salad."

"That's your opinion." Angie raised an eyebrow.

"And that's what counts around here, right?" She pinched her lips together, holding back a grin.

"Yeah…right," Angie said as she let out a huge laugh.

"Dougie, get her out of here." Izzy chuckled and snapped a kitchen towel at her. "Go do some homework or something." Izzy turned to Tony after they left. "You don't think she'll hold it against her, do you?"

"Maybe." Tony's voice rose slightly.

"Shit. I hope not, or I'm going to have to do some serious groveling."

"Humph." Tony grinned. "A little humility might be good for you."

CHAPTER THREE

Mel's stomach gurgled loudly as she and Nancy drove from McDonalds to Arby's, and then to Starbucks. They'd been working all morning on a last-minute project, and her stomach was making it painfully clear she'd skipped breakfast this morning. The project had been thrown their way by a long-time acquaintance and current competitor who couldn't seem to handle the load. They had barely taken a break to go to the bathroom since seven this morning, let alone eat something. She certainly couldn't complain about the referral, but it would have been nice if she'd had more notice.

Mel thought she'd never get Nancy out of the car. She had to have a burger from McDonalds, curly fries from Arby's, and a frappuccino from Starbucks, all of which had cost Mel close to twenty bucks.

Nancy carried the food into the conference room and divided it while Mel put straws in the drinks. "You know you shouldn't accept referrals this late in the game. This project should've been done weeks ago." Nancy unwrapped her burger and took a big bite.

"I know, but we can always use the business." Mel took the top bun from her burger and scraped the massive amount of catsup from it. She ate about half her burger and tossed it back into the bag. "This food is terrible." Bella's would've been so much better for lunch and probably cheaper.

"It's not that bad." Nancy took another bite and continued to talk in between chews. "You want to grab a drink later? We can go to the microbrewery. They have great burgers there."

"Another burger?"

"Then you choose."

Despite how she felt about going back to Bella's, the food called her, thoughts of linguine Bolognese floating through her head. The phone call she'd received from the head chef, Izzy, yesterday had thrown Mel off guard. She'd asked Mel not to judge Angie by her behavior the previous weekend. She'd admitted her sister was a hothead and didn't control her tongue well, but she hoped Mel wouldn't let that impact her assessment of Angie's schoolwork.

"No, the microbrewery is okay," she remarked.

The fact Izzy had risked losing Mel's business to look out for her little sister provoked a bit of admiration in her. Putting family first went a long way with Mel, and it tugged at her heart just a bit. She hadn't let anyone new into her life in a long time and the thought of letting this strong, compassionate woman in scared her more than she wanted to admit.

❖

The bar was busier than they'd expected. Nancy pushed through a few people and found them a couple of seats at the end of the bar.

Mel waved down the bartender and ordered two glasses of chardonnay. She always felt a little funny ordering wine in a microbrewery, but she wasn't in the mood for beer tonight.

"This day seemed twice as long as it needed to be," Nancy said.

"I know, but isn't it exhilarating knowing we still work so well under pressure?"

Nancy lifted a brow. "That's not the way I like to work."

"Thanks for pitching in and helping me get it done." Mel reached over and squeezed Nancy's hand. Nancy was Mel's best friend and biggest ally. She had been ever since college.

"You're buying dinner." Nancy grabbed the menu from the holder and flipped it open. "Will you order me a cheeseburger and fries? I need to run to the ladies' room."

Mel had just put in the order for a grilled chicken sandwich and a cheeseburger with a large order of fries when a young body dressed in a charcoal skirt and jacket slid onto the stool next to her.

"Hey." The woman smiled and flipped her long blond hair over her shoulder.

"Uh, hello," Mel said when she realized she was talking to her.

"I haven't seen you here before. Are you new to the area?" She leaned back and crossed her legs, letting her skirt pull up and expose a good portion of her thigh.

Flattered, Mel held back her grin. "No. I just haven't been here in a while."

"My name is Ashley." She held out her hand.

Mel took her hand, surprised at how soft it was. "Nice to meet you Ashley. I'm Mel."

"Is that short for Melanie?"

"You're very intuitive, Ashley." She smiled, not wanting to burst the young woman's bubble. Nancy would take care of that. She could see the look of amusement on Nancy's face as she approached. Nancy loved to play the role of the possessive girlfriend whenever Mel attracted an unwanted suitor.

"I think you're in my seat," Nancy said firmly, prompting the perky twenty-something woman's smile to vanish. "That's right. She's with me," she said, and the girl slid off the stool.

The girl laid a business card on the bar in front of Mel, then leaned in and whispered in her ear, "Give me a call sometime."

"Seriously?" Nancy stared her down as she left. "The audacity these girls have now is beyond me."

"She did mention she'd been waiting for you to leave so she could sit down." Mel chuckled as she egged her on.

"She and I are gonna have a talk." Nancy flipped her red hair back on her shoulder and turned to go after her.

Mel grabbed her arm and held it. "You're taking this a little far, aren't you?" She raised an eyebrow. "Considering we're not actually a couple."

Nancy let out a short breath. "She doesn't know that."

"Sit down and finish your wine. Your burger will be here soon." She watched Nancy as she assessed the perky blonde who had since taken a seat at the table from where she'd come.

"She's still checking you out." As were the rest of the girls at the table.

"Please?" Mel let the word out slowly. "I'll put my arm around you and rub your back to make it look good." Her voice turned sugary sweet.

"Fine, but what's with that?" Nancy slid onto the stool, and Mel put her arm around her just as she said she would.

"What's with what?"

"You have the girls lined up and I've got nothing." She threw up her arms. "It's not even a gay bar."

"It's like being the girl who doesn't like cats...the cat always wants to be in her lap."

"I don't think that analogy works in your case." Nancy bumped her shoulder. "Face it, Mel. Whether you like it or not, you still give off a vibe."

❖

"Jack, you shouldn't have." Mel opened the Harry Winston box, took out the two-carat diamond pendant necklace, and let it dangle for all to see. Everyone's eyes flew wide at the jewel. Mel hid her indifference as best she could. She couldn't get excited about Jack's gifts anymore. They were just one more substitute for what she really wanted from him...his time. He was leaving on another trip Monday but had promised her his sole attention for the weekend. That was the only birthday present she was looking forward to: a chance at getting the passion back between the two of them.

"You deserve it for putting up with me." He took it from her hands and fastened it around her neck. It hung midway down her chest between the spaghetti straps of her black silk dress. "It doesn't do you justice."

She smiled, but his compliments didn't have the same effect on her as they had in the past. She'd heard one too many of them over the years as he went out the door headed to another assignment. His work was still the most important thing in his life, and she'd grown tired of competing. She would never be enough to keep him home.

They were just bringing out the fruit-filled birthday cake when Jack's phone buzzed at his waist. Watching his hand pull it from the sheath, Mel heaved a sigh and tossed her napkin onto the table. "Jack, you promised."

"I'm sure it's nothing." He shrugged, pressing the phone to his ear as he got up from his chair.

"Then don't answer it," she said when the waitress set the cake down in front of her and lit what seemed to be a million candles. She waited for her family's rendition of "Happy Birthday" to end and took in a deep breath before blowing out the candles. The waitress started cutting the cake.

Jack came back to the table, and the waitress handed him a large piece.

"Can't." He raised a hand in refusal before leaning down and kissing Mel on the cheek. "Sorry, honey, I've got to go," he said, without a twinge of regret in his voice. "We're taking off earlier than expected."

"But I thought we were going to spend the weekend together before you left." She couldn't hide her disappointment. Ignoring her plea, he grabbed his suit jacket and headed for the door.

Mel popped up out of her chair and followed him. "Jack, it's my birthday."

"I gave you your present."

"I don't want this present." She fingered the necklace hanging from her neck. "I want you."

"Mel, don't do this." He pinched his lips together.

"Do what? Ask for a little bit of your time? Time that you promised me?" Her anger began to build inside.

"We'll have plenty of time to spend together when I get back," he said with such nonchalance, she couldn't stand it.

"What? One or two days before you get called out again?" The restaurant was quiet, too quiet. She could feel everyone watching them.

"It's my job, Mel. You know how it goes."

"I hate it." *And I hate you for loving it so damn much.*

"I have to go straight to the airport. We're leaving in a couple of hours." He pushed through the door.

Then it dawned on her. He was packed and ready to go. "You already knew about this." She shook her head. "You had no intention of spending the weekend with me."

"I'll see you in a couple of weeks." She rebuffed him when he stepped back inside and tried to kiss her on the cheek. "I'll call when I can."

Mel waited by the door as it slowly closed, then glanced back to the table. Her family quickly veered their wide-eyed gazes to their plates of cake. She wanted to bolt right then. She was suffocating. The happy façade was becoming too much for her. She would make an excuse for Jack, as usual. But they wouldn't accept it, and she wasn't up to defending him again.

She had to get out of there, if only for a few minutes. She weaved through tables in the dining room and headed for the bathroom. As she passed the side door to the kitchen, she saw the open back door and slipped out into the alley.

Izzy spotted Mel going out the door and followed her, wondering what was going on. "You shouldn't be out here."

Mel didn't turn. "I just need some air."

"The air quality is probably better out front." Izzy lifted the lid of the garbage bin and tossed a bag inside, grimacing as the rotten smell floated into her nostrils.

Mel swung around, swiping the tears from her cheeks with the back of her hand. "I can't go out front. He went out there."

Shit. This is all I need. Izzy tried to ignore the woman's tears. She turned to go back inside but couldn't leave her like this. Mel might be a bitch, but Izzy wasn't heartless. "Are you okay? I mean, can I get somebody for you?" Izzy stuttered. She wasn't good at this kind of stuff.

"No, I'm fine." She looked up, and Izzy was taken by the vivid green eyes she'd tried to ignore in the past. They shimmered with tears but were still captivating.

"You don't look fine." Izzy reached into her pocket, pulled out a cloth napkin, and handed it to her.

Mel took it and smiled slightly. "It's just a little overwhelming in there right now."

She smiled back. "It must be nice to have so many people who care about you."

Mel let out a low sob, fell into Izzy's arms, and began to cry uncontrollably.

"Double shit," Izzy said, reluctantly holding her. "Guess that was the wrong thing to say." *What the hell are you doing here, Izzy? You sure as shit don't want to be this chick's shoulder to cry on.*

"I'm so sorry," Mel uttered, still sobbing. "I was so awful to you the other night."

"It's okay." She let her fingers trip lightly up her back and then patted her softly. *I am so fucking screwed.*

"You must think I'm crazy." She pressed into Izzy's shoulder. "The way I acted before, and now this."

"Not totally." Mel pulled back slightly. When Izzy saw her soggy green eyes again, she felt a familiar pang inside. *I'm the one who's crazy, letting you get to me like this.* She led her to the edge of the concrete barrier by the loading dock and sat with her arm around her until Mel got control of herself. "I've had one or two of these days myself." Thoughts of her recent break-up flashed through her mind as she took the napkin from Mel's hand and blotted her tear-streaked cheeks.

"How's your mother?" Mel asked softly.

"She's doing all right," Izzy said, a little surprised by the question. When Bella first got sick, customers asked about her all the time, but in recent weeks, not too many still inquired. "Thanks for asking," she said reluctantly as the sadness crept up her throat, stealing her voice.

Bella used to greet all the customers personally. It was one of her joys in life. Then about six months ago, she was diagnosed with lupus. Now because of her swollen joints, the Italian matriarch rarely came into the restaurant. Even though Izzy visited her mother daily on her way to work, she missed her presence at the restaurant immensely. Her long hours in the kitchen weren't quite the same without her mother's constant uninvited, yet loving, advice.

"Next time you see her, tell her I miss her smiling face."

"Now you have to suffer with mine?" Izzy regained her composure and pulled her lip into a cocky half-smile.

"Suffer isn't quite the word I'd use." Mel smiled, and the startling glimmer Izzy remembered shone in her emerald-green eyes again. It was a glimmer that had entranced Izzy from the very first time she'd seen her walk into the restaurant. She was definitely a handful, but a beautiful one.

"Better now?" Izzy let her arm drop from Mel's shoulder.

She nodded, tucking a strand of her dark-auburn hair behind her ear. "I should probably get back inside," she said, blowing out a short breath.

"Hang on a minute." Izzy blotted the napkin under her eyes to remove the runs of mascara staining her cheeks and slid the dress strap that had fallen back onto her shoulder. "That's better."

"I'm really sorry. This isn't me." Mel smiled and her eyes sparkled again. "I don't randomly pour my heart out to people. I'm just a mess tonight."

"You're fine. Just tell them your allergies are acting up." Izzy winked. "That always works for me."

"Thank you," Mel said as she got up and headed for the door.

"Oh, and—" Izzy drew her brows together, trying to find the right words of reassurance regarding her jerk of a husband.

"It's Mel, Mel Thomas." She swung around and offered her hand. Izzy took it, squeezing her soft, manicured fingers lightly. "Mel." Izzy smiled as she spoke. The woman's unpretentiousness surprised her. She was spoiled and demanding, yet, even after frequenting the restaurant for the past year, she didn't assume Izzy knew her name. "If you ever need to talk, I'm here pretty much every night." She kept the comment she felt like making about her husband to herself. It was really none of her business anyway.

"Thanks." Mel took a deep breath, straightened her shoulders, and strode into the dining room again.

Mel had just gotten back to the table when the waitress brought the usual apology from Jack, a snifter of cognac. Whenever he left her stranded, it always seemed to appear at her table after he left.

"A birthday wish from the chef."

Mel glanced toward the kitchen, where Izzy stood leaning against the doorjamb. She smiled and lifted the glass to her. Hesitating before taking a sip, Mel realized Jack had never sent the cognac at all. The woman whose shoulder she'd just cried on had. The woman she'd reamed out the other night.

She glanced down at the napkin wrapped around the bottom of the glass. Happy Birthday was printed in all capital letters across the top, and a phone number had been written in just underneath. She flushed with embarrassment. It wasn't like her to be so weak. She folded the napkin and slipped it into her purse, then picked up a glass of ice water from the table and took a long drink. She set the glass back on the table and raked her cool hand across the back of her neck. Suddenly the room was very hot.

Izzy waited in the kitchen doorway for a few minutes, making sure everything at the table was running smoothly. She glanced at Mel, who was dressed to impress as always. Tonight she wore a turquoise cap-sleeve dress cinched at the waist. Izzy had noticed how well it loved her shape as she followed her back into the restaurant. Dark hair, long eyelashes, full lips. The woman was beautiful, but she was also a big pain in the ass. Izzy wasn't expecting her vulnerability to jab at her the way it had earlier. She threw her a wave and slipped back into the kitchen.

"What was that all about?" Tony asked as he tossed a pan of pasta into the air.

"Yeah, what the hell was she doing back here?" Angie's eyes narrowed. She was clearly still upset about earlier in the week.

"Her husband took off on her again."

"Serves her right. She's a b.i.t.c.h." Angie loaded an order on her arm.

"Knock it off, Ang." Izzy pushed the door open for her.

"Just sayin'. Who would want to be married to someone like that?" She snarled and strode back into the dining room.

Tony crossed the kitchen and looked out the doorway with Izzy. "She tell you her husband left?"

"No. She's been coming in for a while. He does it a lot." She let the door close. "She hasn't realized she'd be happier without him yet."

"Don't even think about it." His brows pinched together. "You'll only get hurt."

She rolled her eyes. "I'm not thinking about anything." *Except what's underneath that silky turquoise dress.* Alarmed by the vision, she shook her head to erase it from her thoughts.

Tony swung his arm around Izzy's shoulder and squeezed. "I'd believe that if she wasn't so hot."

"You think she's hot?" Izzy moved around to the bar door and pushed it open, catching another glimpse of the tall, dark-haired beauty. *Definitely hot.* Izzy had seen that the first day she came into the restaurant last year. "I guess she is kind of attractive. With all the blubbering she was doing, I hadn't noticed." She read the order hanging from the ticket holder and took a knife from the block. "She asked about Mom."

"She did?" Tony dropped a glob of butter into a pan, and it sizzled as he swished it around. "Hmm, a hot woman with a heart. She might be worth a look."

"Maybe." *Damn right. She's worth more than a look. For a night anyway.*

"You get her number?"

She took an onion and sliced the knife through it. "I gave her mine." She gave her big brother a wink.

CHAPTER FOUR

When Mel got home, she went straight into her bedroom, stripped everything off, and studied herself in the mirror. *Why doesn't he want me? Is something wrong with me?* She brushed her hands up her flat stomach to her B-cup breasts. She didn't look so bad for thirty-seven, did she? After carefully scrutinizing her well-toned body, she let out a heavy breath and pulled on an old, comfy T-shirt. She brushed her teeth but didn't wash her face tonight; she was mentally and physically exhausted. Flopping into bed, she rolled over and felt the cool sheet covering the empty space next to her. She should've known Jack was going to cut out on her this weekend. That was what he did best.

When Mel had arrived home from work earlier, she'd gone into the bedroom to change and had actually thought about making love to Jack. The thought hadn't entered her mind in months, and it had excited her. But when he came into the room, he'd barely acknowledged her. Even with her standing in front of him totally naked, he hadn't given her a second look, and the desire to be intimate with him had left her as quickly as it had come.

Sex between them was nothing like it used to be. When they were first married, there was never any question of his desire for her. He frequently stripped her naked and made love to her all night, and she'd enjoyed it. Had there ever really been anything else between them? The sexual attraction had always been so strong it had never really mattered before. When had they stopped wanting each other? The last time they'd made love was months ago, with no romance, no foreplay, and no orgasm—again. She didn't know what was wrong with her. She used to have orgasms every time—sometimes twice. She wanted so much for it to be different, but now sex had become more of a duty than a pleasure. These past few years with Jack traveling so much had been hard on them both. When he was gone, all she did was work, and when he was home all she did was try to please him. *God, my life is pathetic.*

She rolled over to look at the picture of Jack on her dresser. Was he sleeping with that hot little reporter who traveled with the crew? Did she even care? Mel had been living this way for so long it didn't really matter anymore. When he was gone, she was alone. When he was home, she felt alone. He was too locked up in his own world and wouldn't let her in. When, exactly, had her fairy-tale life gone to shit?

Izzy pushed open the front door and headed straight for the shower to wash the restaurant smells off her. Between the garlic and onions, no deodorant in the world would make her smell better tonight.

As she lathered her body, she thought about the scent of the beautiful brunette she'd held tonight. She wasn't a fan of jasmine, but it certainly smelled wonderful on her. The woman was so out of her league, not to mention married. Her heartbeat quickened and she shuddered, wondering if Mel had noticed its rapid rhythm when she'd fallen into her arms earlier. Tonight she'd gotten too close.

She'd seen Mel head out the back door and couldn't help herself. She had to follow. Izzy didn't want to comfort her; she didn't want to go anywhere near her. But she couldn't stand to see a woman cry. What was Mel doing right now? She closed her eyes and plunged her face into the shower stream. *What the hell am I thinking? The woman is straight.* She scrubbed at her face with the washcloth, then wadded it up and threw it against the shower wall. Pushing the image of her crying from her mind, Izzy let the hot spray of water pulse on her face.

After her shower, she pulled on a pair of shorts and a tank top before heading to the kitchen. She took an open bottle of chardonnay from the refrigerator and poured herself a glass. On her way out to the deck, as she rounded the counter, she noticed the light blinking on the message machine. She pushed the button, and her skin prickled at Dana's sultry voice as it rang through the speaker.

"Hi, it's me. I was wondering if maybe I could come over tonight and we could talk or something. Call me."

"Fuck, no!" Izzy shouted, slapping her glass to the counter. She pulled her sweatshirt over her head. "We're never doing *something* again." She yanked open the glass door. It flew down the track and stopped with a thud when it reached the end. At least the damn thing hadn't broken this time. She grabbed her glass and the wine bottle from the counter and stepped out onto the deck. Apparently, Dana hadn't gotten the message yet. Izzy was through playing games with her. She set the wine on the table between the loungers and moved to the railing. Gripping the wood in her palms, she took in a deep breath of sea air, trying to make the ache in her heart disappear. After all these months, it still hurt. When was it going to stop?

It was her own fault. She'd gone into the relationship knowing full well Dana had never been faithful to anyone. Yet, she still dove in headfirst. *Stupid! Stupid! Stupid!* She swung back around, swiped her glass from the table, and gulped down the rest of the wine. She had to stop letting Dana get to her like this.

She flopped into one of the lounge chairs and took in the beauty of the night sky and all its stars to clear her head. Her body tingled again as sparkling emerald-green eyes invaded her thoughts. The beautiful face of her familiar customer had been invading her thoughts for some time now. She'd stopped trying to elude it long ago. Mel Thomas could definitely help her get over this heartache. Then again, she could quite possibly just give her another one.

The morning flew by. Mel finally finished the preliminary design for Rick Daniels's new website around eleven fifteen, and it was pretty damn good. The intro was flashy, but not too wild. The site included lots of promo pictures and links to all of his DVD movie titles on Amazon as well as placeholders for current box-office movies. This baby should net some profits for him. Now all she had to do was shoot him the link, so he could review it and give her some feedback.

She started typing a nice professional email to send, then decided to call him instead. She glanced at her watch, picked up the phone, and punched in his personal cell number. Rick had probably finished shooting for the day and was possibly still in his trailer getting ready to leave the set. He was on location for his new action movie, and the last time they'd talked, he'd mentioned they were shooting scenes at sunrise this week. Mel wanted to make sure he reviewed the website as soon as possible just in case he wanted any changes made. His latest film was due to be released in theaters next month, and she didn't want any last-minute panic attacks.

"Hi, Rick. It's Mel."

"Hello, beautiful," he said, his voice low and sexy.

"I've finished the preliminary design on your website."

"Great. I can't wait to see it."

"Check your email. I'm sending you the link as we speak. Same password as last time."

"I'll take a look and give you a call back tomorrow."

"I'll only be here until about six tonight." She smiled to herself.

"Big date?"

"Not really. Just some good Italian food."

"I love Italian. You'll have to take me there when I get back in town."

"Sure. Just let me know when." She pulled Izzy's number from her purse and rubbed the napkin between her fingers. "I don't think you'll be disappointed."

"Nothing you do disappoints me, sweetheart."

"We won't know that until you look at the site, now will we?" She chuckled.

"I'll give it a look and let you know what I think."

"Thanks, Rick. You know I appreciate you."

"Not as much as I appreciate you." His voice lowered again.

"You're sweet. I'll talk to you later," she said, ending the call and dropping the receiver into its cradle.

Rick had always been Mel's number-one fan. They'd been high school sweethearts, and everyone assumed they'd get married someday. Then Rick skyrocketed to stardom and Mel married Jack. She wasn't happy with her current situation, but the other choice would have been a disaster.

❖

Izzy pushed the back door open and found Bella sitting at the kitchen table. "Hi, Momma." She leaned down and kissed her on the cheek. "It's good to see you up and around."

Her mother seemed well today. Bella was holding up pretty good for a seventy-five-year-old woman with an autoimmune disease. She didn't take the amount of steroids the doctor prescribed because she claimed they made her puffy, but Izzy had stopped fighting with her about it. She didn't like her decision, but she didn't want her days with her mother to be filled with resentment either. She wanted to share every moment they could, letting her know just how much she loved her.

She peeked through the doorway into the living room. "Where's Pop?"

"You just missed him. He's gone to the post office."

Sadness pinched her. It didn't hurt as much as it used to, but she still hoped she'd walk in one day and he'd be sitting at the table, happy to see her. She didn't like the way things were between her and her father, but then they'd never really seen eye to eye on anything. When he'd found out she was gay, he'd pulled away completely. In turn, she'd rebelled, deciding they could no longer continue even the strained father-daughter relationship they'd once shared. She'd finally decided to avoid him altogether. No relationship was better than the unforgiving one he was offering. In recent years, with the news of her mother's illness, she'd rethought that decision.

"What's for breakfast today?" She pulled open the refrigerator. "We've got fruit, eggs, and, ooh…how about French toast?"

"Whatever you want, dear. I don't have much of an appetite."

"You will when you smell this." She took out the milk, eggs, and butter and set them on the counter before fishing around in the cupboard for a bowl.

"Have you started dating again?" Bella crossed the kitchen and took the Italian bread from the pantry.

"What?" Izzy reached up in the cabinet above the stove for the vanilla and cinnamon.

"Since you broke up with that woman."

"You mean Dana?" She cracked an egg in the bowl and whisked it around.

"Yes, her."

"No."

"What?"

"No. I haven't dated anyone since Dana."

"Oh." Her mother observed her curiously. "I have this friend, a lovely young woman. I think you two would get along nicely."

"I appreciate the thought, Momma, but I can find my own dates." She took a frying pan from the broiler drawer, set it on the stovetop, and ignited the fire under it.

"But you just said you haven't dated." Bella was very supportive of Izzy. It was quite possible she knew Izzy was gay before Izzy did. By the time she'd turned nineteen, she realized she preferred women and her mother was already trying to fix her up with women.

"Because I don't want to right now." She dredged a piece of Italian bread through the mixture and plopped it in the pan. "I'm a little too busy with the restaurant to worry about that kind of stuff."

"Oh." Her eyes flickered back and forth between her hands and Izzy. "But you might want to meet this woman. She's very pretty, and she has a warm soul."

"Bella. I said no." She warned her again.

Her mother sat back in her chair and crossed her arms. Izzy always called her Bella when she meant business, and her mom knew it.

"Maybe I don't want French toast this morning." Bella did a little sing-song tone with her voice.

"I'm still going to make it, whether you eat it or not." She flipped the bread to brown the other side. "I'm hungry."

"You're being selfish. Can't you make an old woman happy before she dies?"

"Wrong daughter. That guilt doesn't work with me like it does on Angelina, remember?" She sliced off a pad of butter and spread it across the toast before sprinkling powdered sugar on top and sliding it in front of her mother. Izzy smiled, watching as Bella picked up her fork and took a small bite. "See, you were hungry."

"Not really. I'm just eating to please you."

"I'm still not going to let you set me up."

"Stubborn and bullheaded."

"Just like my mother." Izzy fixed her own plate and sat down across the table from her. "Now eat."

"Perhaps I could invite my friend for breakfast sometime."

"Bella." Her voice was stern.

"She's a little thin. I thought maybe you could fatten her up."

"Everyone's a little thin in your eyes. If you had your way, I'd be waddling across the kitchen."

"That's not enough to feed a bird." She poked at Izzy's toast with her fork. "There's nothing wrong with having a little extra on your hips for your special someone to hang on to. Your father loves my curves."

"That's enough, Bella. I don't want to hear any more of that." Bella had never made it a secret she prided herself on being able to keep and satisfy her husband for fifty-plus years.

"There's nothing wrong with having a healthy sex life."

"Stop." She dropped her fork and pressed her hands to her ears. "Kids aren't supposed to know what their parents do in the bedroom." The sound of her own voice echoed in her head.

Izzy heard the muffled sounds of protest through her hands. When she saw her mother's lips tip up, Izzy removed her hands and picked up her fork.

"If you'd like to invite your friend for breakfast," Izzy cut a piece of French toast and snaked it through the flakes of powdered sugar scattered across the plate, "I'd be happy to fix it for the two of you, but I don't want any matchmaking." She stuffed the bite into her mouth.

After Izzy finished her breakfast, she cleared their plates.

"Did Dad eat?"

"He'll probably get a roll while he's out."

Izzy reheated the frying pan and threw a couple more slices of drenched bread into it. "I'll cook these last two slices for him."

"He'll appreciate that."

"You think so?" She glanced back at her mother as she slid them out of the pan and onto a plate, then buttered them before covering them with aluminum foil and leaving them on the counter for her father. He might not love her right now, but she hadn't stopped loving him.

"Of course he will."

"I've got to go now, Momma." She leaned over to give her mother a kiss on the cheek. "When Dad gets back, all you have to do is warm those up in the microwave and sprinkle a little powdered sugar on them."

"Thank you, sweetheart." Bella took Izzy's face in her hands. "He may not show it, but he does love you, Isabel."

"It would be nice if he actually spoke to me once in a while." She hated to admit it, but she missed her conversations with her father, even if they always turned into debates.

"He'll come around."

She shot out a short breath. "It's been five years, Mom."

"I'm working on him."

"Thanks, Momma." She choked back the tears as she pressed her lips to her mother's head. "I'm going to the market to pick up the makings for the special today." She made a mental note. *Steak, crab, asparagus, bread.* "You need anything?"

"Bring me some fresh mozzarella and tomatoes for salad." Bella pulled open the refrigerator and rummaged through the vegetable drawer. "My friend is coming for lunch tomorrow."

Izzy opened the door before turning and raising a brow. "Your friend?"

"Yes, the one I was telling you about."

"Oh." She pushed the door back slightly. "Does she come to the house a lot?"

"A few times a week."

Halfway out the door, she hesitated, wondering about her mother's mystery friend. "What's your friend's name?"

"Mary Elizabeth."

"Mary Elizabeth what?"

She pushed the drawer in and let the refrigerator door close. "She told me, but I can't remember."

"Hmm," Izzy said, thoughtfully. "You have fresh basil?"

"No. I'll need that too."

"Okay. I'll see you in the morning." She headed out the door, pulling it closed behind her. *And maybe I'll drop back by for lunch.*

Izzy loved the local market. Family-owned since 1929, Mill Valley Market was a landmark in town. There were newer, larger markets that many shopped at, but none compared to this one when it came to fresh, homegrown products. The store was filled with good memories for Izzy. When she was younger, her mother had taken her there often. She got all the best cuts of meat because she knew all the butchers from the old neighborhood. Most of them had their sons working with them now, even a few Izzy had surfed with.

Izzy had been a tomboy and hung out with the guys most of the time growing up. Then she'd discovered girls—pretty girls who were attracted to other pretty girls. She fell head over heels in love with one of her culinary instructors. The relationship was short-lived, and Izzy was stricken with her first broken heart at the age of twenty. That was a defining period in her life because she knew from that day forward she would never be happy in a heterosexual relationship.

"Basil, tomatoes, she'll want mozzarella too," Izzy mumbled to herself as she wandered through the produce. "This looks good," she said, picking up a couple of bunches of young asparagus and heading toward the butcher counter.

"Hey, Joe," she called to her regular butcher. "You got any nice tenderloin steaks back there?"

"You bet, Izzy. How thick you want 'em?"

She held up a bunch of asparagus. "About an inch, inch and a half maybe. The special tonight's gonna be steak Oscar."

"Don't tell my wife. She'll drag me down there for dinner." He smiled.

"I'd love to see her. What's her number again?" She pulled out her cell phone and slid her finger across it.

"Don't you dare. The basketball game is on tonight." He headed in the back to cut her steaks.

She shouted after him. "Okay, Joe. I'll take that excuse."

She thumbed through her text messages as she waited for him to come back. Delete, delete, delete. Dana just wasn't getting the message.

Joe returned through the door and slid the package of meat across the top of the case. "Here you go."

"I'll see you and Rose on Saturday night, then?"

"As usual." He gave her a wink.

Mel's stomach growled. Thoughts of spaghetti Bolognese, sourdough bread, and Isabel Calabrese flew through her mind. Boy, that woman could cook. The image of her standing in the doorway with that grin on her face invaded her thoughts, and her stomach flipped.

She shook her head. *What the hell is that about?* She took a ten from her wallet and headed out of her office to run to the corner deli for a sandwich. Mel had opened her public-relations firm years ago and had leased the same office space within a multi-tenant building because she craved the daily interaction with others. When she first started the business, she had worked from home and found it to be a very lonely experience. Renting space downtown in one of the newly restored buildings worked well for her. As she'd added other services like web design, social-media promotion, teaching, and blogging, she had room to expand the office. Plus, she respected and got along well with the business tenants, which made her life not so lonely.

"Hey, where you going?" Nancy said, increasing her pace to catch up with her in the hallway.

"Down to the corner to get something to eat."

"To the diner? Why don't I go with you, and we can sit down and grab a bite together?"

"I was just going to get a quick sandwich at the deli." Mel continued her pace. She'd tried to slip out without anyone noticing to avoid exactly what was happening.

"I really, really want a cheeseburger. Please don't make me eat it alone."

"I've still got an awful lot of work to do and am trying to get out of here early tonight."

"Come on. It'll take an hour max." Nancy gave her a sad, puppy-dog face.

Mel smiled and blew out a breath. "All right, but no more than an hour."

"Great. Let me grab some cash."

"Grab a lot. Lunch is on you," Mel said, following her back into the office.

The waiter seated them in a booth by the window and told them the specials. Mel ordered the chicken salad, and Nancy got the biggest cheeseburger on the menu.

"So what's going on tonight?" Nancy asked.

"Nothing."

"Don't lie to me. You never cut out early unless there's a reason."

"Just dinner at Bella's." Mel focused her attention out the window, watching the cars as they passed.

"Is Jack back in town?"

"No. He won't be back for a while."

"Then who are you going with?"

"No one, just me."

"What's the occasion?"

"I finished the prelim for Rick's website."

"Boy. You banged that out in record time."

"I had a little more time to work on it this weekend than I expected."

"You and Jack were supposed to go away together." She picked up a fry and trailed it through the catsup before biting off the end.

"Didn't happen."

"Why?"

"Same reason."

"I'm sorry, Mel."

"Don't be. It gave me some time to think."

"About what?"

"About what I want."

"And?"

"I think I want out." Saying it lifted a huge weight off her chest.

"Wow. Just like that?"

"It's been coming for a long time."

"You certainly hid it well. I thought you two were the perfect couple."

"We do put on a good show, don't we? I'm tired of faking it."

"Hey. Why don't I join you for dinner tonight?" She shot Mel a huge smile. "And you can tell me all about it."

"That's okay, I'm fine." Mel took a drink of her water. "You probably already have plans." She didn't want to explain everything to Nancy right now.

"Nope. Ann's got spin class tonight." She flopped back in her chair. "Come on. It'll be fun."

She let her lips tip up. "All right, but just dinner. Don't try to drag me out for a drink afterward."

"I won't. Ann's coming over after class, and I have plans to cuddle up on the couch with her and watch some hospital drama she likes."

"Are you sick?" She reached over and touched Nancy's forehead. "I thought you only liked that reality stuff."

"I do." She laughed and her face lit up. "But you have to give a little to get a little, if you know what I mean."

"So are you guys a couple now?"

"No, but she's fun to be with."

"Oh, I see. She's not ready yet."

"I don't think either one of us is."

"Sooner or later you're going to have to trust someone."

"Not until someone reciprocates."

CHAPTER FIVE

Mel pulled into a space not far from the front door of Bella's Trattoria. "You're going to love this place. Their spaghetti Bolognese is out of this world."

"You come here a lot?" Nancy asked.

"Once or twice a week. You know I don't have much time to cook."

Nancy grinned. "You weren't all that good at it either, as I recall."

"I've gotten a whole lot better since college. Besides, I wouldn't call mac and cheese and ramen cooking." She hit the button on her key fob, the headlights blinked, and the horn chirped.

"You're not supposed to eat fast food all the time either."

"Thank God we had your mother." Mel chuckled.

"She is a good cook."

"So why didn't you pick up any of that?"

"I do all right."

"Couldn't prove it by me."

"Maybe I'll show you sometime."

"I bet you could show me lots of things." Mel lifted a brow and pulled her lip up into a suggestive smile.

"Are you flirting with me?" Nancy's eyes grew wide.

Mel slapped her hand to her mouth. "Oh my God, I think I am." She chuckled. "I really need to get laid."

"You know, I really could help you out with that."

"That was a long time ago, Nance." She drew her brows together. "I wasn't very good at it, remember?"

"And I was?" Nancy laughed. "You've grown a lot since then." She laced her fingers in Mel's and shot her a sly smile. "We both have." She squeezed Nancy's hand and returned her smile. Mel *had* grown a lot since then, but her feelings for Nancy hadn't. They were nothing more than platonic.

Mel had been Nancy's first love. They were in the same public-relations program in college and were always seeing one another in class. They became fast friends and ended up pulling a lot of all-nighters studying together. That's where it began. The harmless banter and locked gazes between them were frequent. They had been for quite some time.

She remembered the first time it happened. They had been studying at her place on the couch. It was close to three in the morning when Mel woke from a drowsy sleep and heard the rhythm of Nancy's heartbeat beneath her ear. Her book still on her lap, she'd slid into the crook of Nancy's shoulder and was resting nicely on her left breast. She remained still for what seemed like hours until she felt Nancy kiss the top of her head. Mel glanced up to see the desire clear in Nancy's smoldering brown eyes, and that was all it took. Soon their late-night studying sessions were filled with more than just books.

Mel was crazy about her, but Nancy was out and never worried about what anyone thought. Mel, on the other hand, had been raised in a strict Catholic family and couldn't overcome the guilt that plagued her. Their whole relationship existed exclusively behind closed doors. Nancy hated it. When Nancy got tired of hiding their relationship, they had so many disagreements, they finally decided to call it quits. It was a painful breakup, but they both had managed to move on. Well, at least she thought they had. After college, Mel met Jack at one of many parties her parents threw at their house in Tiburon while Nancy slept her way through a string of loveless relationships.

For a brief time they didn't see each other. Thankfully, they were eventually able to work through the hurt and the awkwardness, and the two of them had remained close ever since. Somewhere along the line, times had changed, *Mel* had changed. She'd been able to dispense with the Catholic guilt, and now she often remembered those days with Nancy affectionately. But she would never get intimately involved with her again. She couldn't. No, she wouldn't risk losing her best friend by letting her believe they could be anything more than friends.

Nancy pushed the door open and Mel stepped inside, letting her hold the door for her. Seemed like Mel always had someone holding the door for her, and she liked it that way.

"Ooh, I love the ambiance. Rustic Italian décor."

Mel glanced around the restaurant. She loved the warm, cozy atmosphere here. Large, unfinished redwood beams stretched across the ceiling, and antiqued, glazed walls met stone window and door wrappings. Pendant lights hung high throughout to give just enough light to enjoy the company and see the food. The fireplace that doubled as a cooking oven was more modern, surrounded by rock, and had a criss-crossed firewood holder underneath that extended from floor to ceiling next to it.

The bar seemed as though it was centuries old. Directly ahead as you entered, it ran the expanse of the south wall. Behind it sat a collection of liquor that would impress any bartender. Tables were elegantly draped with white cloths and finished with small amber glass candleholders in the middle. And the intimate booths in each corner of the restaurant were elegant, flanked with long curtains hanging from the ceiling at each booth's entrance that could be pulled for privacy.

Nancy nodded, zoning in on the corner booth. "With just enough candlelight for romance."

"Or for a secret liaison." Mel winked. Her heels clicked on the swirl-stained concrete floors as she followed the hostess to the table.

"I like the sound of that." Nancy took the room in again, letting her gaze fix on the bar this time. "Who's the babe behind the bar with the beautiful dark hair?"

Mel glanced back over her shoulder.

"That's Izzy, the chef slash owner."

"She's cute." She glanced over at her again. "Is she gay?"

"I don't know." She rolled her eyes at the usual question Nancy asked whenever she saw an attractive woman. "Why? Is she checking out your ass?"

"Not mine. Yours."

"Really?" Mel's smile widened. "Well, at least she's got good taste." They reached the table, and Mel glanced back over at Izzy, giving her a slight wave. Izzy gave her a nod before pushing through the door behind the bar.

❖

When Izzy saw Mel come through the door in that royal-blue Anne Klein suit, fitted perfectly to her figure, a searing jolt had attacked her stomach. God, she was unbelievably sexy tonight. She couldn't tear her eyes away as Angie led her and her friend to a table. The curves, the lines, the way the skirt hugged her body made Izzy shiver. After the conversation they'd had last week, she'd been sure she'd call. If only for a little support, but now she understood why she hadn't. She already had someone for that.

She pushed the door behind the bar open a crack and watched them as Angie forced a smile and took their order. She met Angie in the kitchen as she came in. "Who's that with—"

"With the bitch?" Angie growled. "I don't know why I have to wait on her."

"Because she's a customer, Angie. She brings us a lot of business." Izzy shot back.

"Well, she's not doing business tonight. The conversation sounds pret-ty comfortable." Izzy knew Angie would never get a thick-enough skin to let customer actions and comments roll off her back. Izzy peeked out the kitchen door again. *She has a husband, yet she was holding hands with this woman.* A beautiful woman with fiery red hair who appeared to be about the same shape and size as Mel, but a little thicker, more athletic. She dropped a handful of pasta into the sauté pan, poured two ladles of Bolognese sauce over the pasta, and mixed it with the metal tongs. "Pasta for two," she mumbled, letting it slide onto the dish and twisting it up nicely before dusting the top with Parmesan cheese.

"What?" Tony asked.

"Angie's busy. I'm going to deliver this one." She unfastened the top few buttons of her chef's coat and let the flap fold down to hide the food splatter, then sucked in a deep breath. She had to know who this woman was and why they were so friendly. She picked up two plates as she hurried out of the kitchen. She had just about reached the table when Mel leaned back in her chair and crossed her long, lean legs. Izzy paused and let her gaze follow the smooth, white thigh up past the line of her skirt. She continued past the ivory silk shell under her suit jacket and made eye contact with beautiful green eyes. They locked with hers and...*Sizzle.* Heat ran up her neck when Mel caught her staring. Her neck was on fire, but she couldn't break the connection. Apparently, neither could Mel.

"Wow, that looks delicious," Nancy said. Her gaze danced between the two of them.

Mel pulled her eyes away and cleared her throat. "Yes, it does. Umm...thank you, Izzy."

Izzy slid the pasta on the table and set an empty plate in front of each of them.

"Wow, this is special. I've never had the chef bring my meal out personally before," Nancy remarked.

"Well, they know me here," Mel said coyly.

"Besides, she and my little sister didn't get off on the right foot the last time she waited on her." Mel snapped her head up, and Izzy was immediately caught by sparkling emerald-green eyes. "But in any case, I'm happy to attend to you personally anytime." *Did I just say that? Jesus, what a stupid line.*

"That's sweet, but unnecessary." Mel's voice came out in a whisper as her eyes darted from Izzy to the food and back again.

"Is there anything else I can do for you?" Izzy said, holding Mel's gaze and tipping her lips up slightly.

"I can think of a number of things you can do for me." Nancy's voice was low and sultry, but Izzy didn't shift her attention from Mel.

"No. I think we're fine for now."

Izzy watched as the heat seemed to transfer from her own face to Mel's. "Enjoy your meal, ladies." She broke the connection and glanced over at Nancy.

Izzy turned and strolled back to the kitchen. The need for another look at the woman with the beautiful green eyes pressed her. She glanced back over her shoulder and found Mel watching her. *Yes!* She pushed through the kitchen door and moved directly to the bar door, pushed it open a crack, and peered out. All Mel had done was look at her, and her heart was beating so fast it was about to explode in her chest. It wasn't just any look. Something had happened between them. She wasn't sure what it was, but it was definitely something. She glanced at the woman sitting with her. Not a bad looker, she thought, but subtlety didn't seem to be her best quality.

❖

Nancy's eyes widened. "What the hell was that?"

"What?" Nancy was scrutinizing Mel with her glare as she veered her eyes to her plate. She'd known Nancy would have lots of questions after Izzy left the table.

"The 'I'm happy to *attend to you* personally anytime,' that's what."

"Just a little harmless banter."

"That was more than banter, missy. That was an invitation."

"No, surely not." Mel watched Izzy as she left the table. Dressed in a red, short-sleeved chef's coat and black cargo pants, she had an unbelievably sexy confidence about her as she crossed the room. Izzy turned back momentarily and shot her a sexy smile before heading into the kitchen. *Zing!* There was that feeling again. *Was it an invitation?*

"Uh, yes, it was. Now what are you gonna do about it?" Nancy's full attention was on her as she pressed for an answer.

Mel rubbed the back of her neck, trying to suppress the flaming heat rushing over it. "Nothing." *Absolutely nothing.*

"Because of Jack? We both know how that's working out for you." Nancy picked up her fork and twirled her pasta against the spoon. "You should hightail it into that kitchen and get her number right this minute."

"I already have her number." Mel sipped her wine, batting her lashes as she looked over it at Nancy. "She gave it to me last week."

Nancy let out a low growl. "A woman like that gives you her number and you don't use it? Okay, now I know you're crazy." She slid a forkful of pasta into her mouth. "And she cooks too. This is delicious. If you're not interested, maybe I'll ask her out."

"Oh," Mel lifted a brow as she ripped off a chunk of sour dough bread. "Did she give you her number too?"

"Ha, you're so funny. I think we need to have lunch again tomorrow so you can tell me more about your personal chef."

"Can't. I'm busy tomorrow." She motioned for Nancy to pass the butter.

"With work again? You can't keep skipping meals. You're already practically skin and bones."

"Well, thank you for that wonderful compliment. But I won't be skipping any meals. I have plans tomorrow with a friend."

"Another new friend?"

"One of the ladies from the community center invited me to lunch." She wasn't about to tell her it was Izzy's mother. That would add a whole new pile of complications to the conversation.

"Then how about Wednesday?"

"I'll be eating at my desk Wednesday. I have a conference call with Rick I can't miss."

"Hmm, he calls you beautiful all the time, she wants to attend to you…it must be nice to be so wanted." Nancy gave her a sly smile. "So, what are you gonna do?"

"I told you, I'm not going to do anything. Now stop quizzing me and let me eat my pasta while it's still hot."

Mel locked the deadbolt behind her as she entered her house and then dropped her keys on the entryway table. Her shoulders were tight and her feet were sore. It had been a long day. She'd thought Nancy would never finish eating. She kept dragging the evening out, cross-examining Mel between each bite. She felt like she was being interrogated about something she had no inside intel on. Thankfully, Ann called looking for her, and she realized how late it was. The next time they went to dinner, she planned to meet Nancy at the restaurant rather than ride together. That way she could make her escape from the inquisition more easily.

She slid into her empty bed and closed her eyes. She was exhausted, but she couldn't sleep. All she could think about were those piercing blue eyes staring at her earlier. The familiar feeling hit her midsection. Izzy Calabrese had left an impression on her tonight, and Mel wasn't quite sure what to do about it. She ran through the evening again in her head. The way Izzy had stared at her was definitely intentional and had made Mel very anxious. The way her body had reacted made her freak out. She'd never had thoughts about a woman like this before and was totally confused. It wasn't that she didn't notice attractive women, but this dizzy feeling was like nothing she'd ever experienced before. The way the heat rose in her body, she'd been barely able to keep her composure.

She thought about her ten-year relationship with Jack. She'd never had that feeling with him. The thought of divorcing Jack had crossed her mind more than once over the years, but it always faded. She was fairly certain it wouldn't disappear this time.

CHAPTER SIX

Izzy took a deep breath and let it escape her lips slowly. She didn't get out of the car; she'd been dreading this all morning. It had been a while since she'd been alone in a room with Dana. More than three months to be exact. Emotions fired rapidly inside her. Anger, hurt, sadness, then anger again. She wasn't quite sure she could handle it. "It's now or never."

She stepped through the door of Gustoso to find Dana waiting at the bar. "You said you had some of my things?"

Dana strutted behind the bar and hoisted a box on top. "Can we talk for a minute?"

"You can talk all you want." Izzy picked up the box.

"Izzy, can't you just be civil for once?"

She dropped the box back down on the bar and thought about giving Dana an earful of civility, but it would just make her feel worse. "You've got ten minutes."

"Will you at least sit down?"

"I'd rather not."

Dana moved around the bar. "I miss you."

"What do you want, Dana?"

"I made a mistake. I want to come home."

"I don't think so. You made what you wanted pretty clear. Now that you have your own restaurant to run, you can see how much time it takes."

"Please, Izzy. Just give me another chance. I'll give you half my share of this place, and we'll have two successful restaurants."

"What about Jess?"

"I'm going to break it off with her."

"But you haven't yet."

"I can't very well get rid of her. She's put a lot of work into this place."

"If you want any part of me, she has to go."

"So, if I let her go, you'll give me another chance?"

"I didn't say that."

"Then what did you say?"

"I didn't say anything about another chance. I just asked what you were willing to give up. As usual, you're not willing to sacrifice anything that matters."

"That's not fair. As I recall, you weren't willing to compromise on anything that mattered to me."

"You know I can't run a restaurant without being there."

"You can't be the chef at both places, and you know she does all the cooking here. This restaurant can't survive without her recipes."

"You mean *my* recipes."

"She may have started with yours, but she's tweaked them enough to make them her own."

"That's a laugh. She would've never been able to make any recipe her own if I hadn't taught her how to cook."

"You can't fault her for being a good student."

"No, but I can fault her for fucking my girlfriend."

"Damn it, Izzy. Does it always have to come back to that? I'm sorry. I fucked up."

"That's the one thing we agree on."

The door flew open and Jess rushed in. "Sorry I'm late. I hit traffic on Miller." She stopped when she saw Izzy. "Hey, Izzy. What's going on?"

"She just stopped by to pick up a few of her things." Dana glanced at Izzy. "Right?"

Un-fucking-believable. One minute she was begging for Izzy's forgiveness, and the next she was silently pleading with her not to tell her girlfriend. "Right." Izzy pinched her lips together and brushed by Jess. "I gotta go."

Dana followed her to the door. "So, you'll think about my offer?"

"You have got to be kidding."

Visions of Dana and Jess together flashed through Izzy's head. It was partly her fault for not paying enough attention. But she didn't have forgiveness in her yet and didn't know if she ever would. The smiles. The flirtations. She should've seen it. Everyone else did. Izzy was so wrapped up in keeping both restaurants running, she'd had no clue.

She pulled open the back door of her SUV and tossed the box inside. Was she ever truly in love with Dana, or was it the embarrassment that stung so much? She didn't really know the answer to that, but now that Dana was her competition, she was even more determined to keep Bella's a success.

❖

It was seven thirty, and Mel sat behind her cherrywood desk looking at the crystal clock perched on the corner as the seconds ticked away. She'd been watching it for at least twenty minutes, dreading the thought of going home to a big, empty house. The office was silent; Nancy and the rest of the staff had gone home hours ago.

She rummaged through her purse to find her keys and came across the napkin Izzy had slipped her last week. It appeared to be her home or cell number; it wasn't the number for the restaurant. Mel knew that one because she'd called it many times. She reached for the phone and hesitated a minute before picking it up and punching in the number. She flattened the napkin on the desk in front of her and reasoned with herself. It was just a phone call. What could it hurt?

Four rings and no answer. Izzy was probably working tonight. She put in the first three numbers of the restaurant and then hit the reset button. *God, this is stupid. I shouldn't listen to Nancy. There's no way a beautiful woman like Isabel Calabrese is interested in me.* She slapped her laptop closed. *And what the hell am I doing even thinking about it?* She let out a sigh as she fanned her fingers out and stared at the wedding ring strangling one of them.

She thought about her ordinary life. She thought about Jack. Why was it so hard to leave him? Because he was safe. She knew what to expect both when he was gone and when he got home. There were no surprises, no lingering emotions to tamp down. Without the first two, no hidden desires lurked deep in her soul. After ten years, she'd fallen out of love with her husband.

In the midst of feeling sorry for herself, she yanked her laptop out of the docking station. Though she dreaded going home to her empty house, she knew she could at least get some more work done this evening. Work always made the weekend go faster.

❖

Saturday, Mel spent most of the day at her kitchen table in front of her laptop reviewing the new website contract Nancy had been working on. It was coming along well, but Nancy still needed a history write-up from the owner and a few more pictures to get the website started. She shot off an email to Nancy with her thoughts and closed her laptop. She'd told Nancy she didn't need to run contracts by her anymore. She was very capable of making decisions without Mel's input, but Nancy still asked her anyway. She supposed it was a courtesy Nancy extended since Mel was the owner of the company and technically her boss, even though she never pulled rank on her. Mel hadn't eaten since she'd grabbed a couple of sticks of cheese for lunch around noon, and by eight o'clock, she was starving. She rummaged through the refrigerator for something to eat, but of course, she found nothing except cheese, cheese, and more cheese. She could do only so much with that. She tossed it back onto the shelf. Time for a grocery run. Mel loved to cook when she had time, but to even attempt it, she needed food.

She intended to go to the store but somehow found her car on autopilot headed for Bella's Trattoria. Before she knew it, she was standing in the alley behind the restaurant and knew she wasn't here just for the food. She'd done her best to stay away for the past few days, but she wanted some company tonight. Was it a crime to want to have a conversation with someone? To share a smile? To feel good about something? She leaned against the brick wall thinking—no, hoping Izzy would wander out the door. Two boys on skateboards flew by, and she suddenly felt foolish. Lurking around the workplace of this woman like she'd developed some kind of schoolgirl crush. *Get a grip, Mel! What are you, fifteen? Go home. Izzy doesn't want to see poor, pitiful you.* Just as she popped away from the wall, the metal door clanged open, startling her.

"Hey." Izzy smiled as she came out the door. "What are you doing out here?"

"I was going to fix myself something to eat but realized I didn't have any food in the house. I got busy working and forgot to go to the grocery store."

"I didn't see you come through the front."

"I parked and walked around. I'm not really dressed for the restaurant tonight." She motioned to her black yoga pants and white cap-sleeved T-shirt.

"You look great." Izzy grinned as she swept the length of her body with her gaze. "You were still working this late?" She lifted the lid of the dumpster and heaved a bag of trash into it.

"Deadlines."

"What do you do at work?" She strolled to the concrete barrier, hiked herself up onto it, and patted the spot next to her. She smiled, and Mel fixed her gaze on the adorable dimples denting her cheeks.

"I handle public relations and do a little custom website design here and there." Mel planted her palms on the concrete and lifted herself up next to Izzy.

"That sounds complicated." She pulled her brows together.

"Not really, once you get the hang of it."

"I probably couldn't do it." Izzy bumped her shoulder, and Mel couldn't help the giddy feeling that came over her. *Jesus Christ. I am fifteen.*

"I probably couldn't make pasta like you do either," Mel said, looking down at her feet as they bounced against the concrete.

"So we're in agreement?" Izzy held out her hand. "You won't go in to the restaurant business, and I won't go in to PR and web design."

"Agreed," Mel said, shaking her hand.

Neither of them released her grip right away. Mel found herself captured by a pair of dark-sapphire eyes. She watched as Izzy's gaze skittered down to her lips and back again, and her stomach flip-flopped. Mel kneaded her lip between her teeth, fighting the urge to move closer. After an awkward moment, Mel drew her hand back. "I almost came by last night, but I figured you were probably busy."

"Weekends are always busy."

"Right." She slid off the concrete. "You're probably just as busy tonight."

"No, wait." Izzy hopped off the wall and grabbed her by the arm.

Mel stood speechless as the tingle from Izzy's touch zapped through her.

"I'm glad you're here." Izzy didn't release her arm.

A flash of heat rushed Mel. Her heart thumped loudly as she decided to step closer.

"Ay, Iz, we've got some orders in." Mel jumped, stepping back when a man stuck his head out the doorway and shouted.

"I'll be right back." Izzy brushed the back of Mel's hand with her fingers before heading back into the kitchen.

What the hell are you doing here, Mel? She breathed in and out quickly, dizzying herself. She was just about ready to hightail it when Izzy came back through the doorway with a glass of red wine.

"Here, you wanna come in?" Izzy motioned through the door to the bustling kitchen behind her. "I'll just be a few minutes more."

"Uh, no. I'll wait here." She took a couple of sips of wine and settled back against the concrete, enjoying the moonlight and the tempered light of the old nautical copper lanterns mounted on the building.

After more than just a few minutes, Izzy came back through the door "Sorry, had a four top," she said, leaning on the concrete next to Izzy.

"These old lanterns are beautiful." Mel wandered over and examined the patina that had formed on them. "How old are they?"

"They're the original lanterns on the building."

"Really?" The excitement rang in her voice. Mel was a big fan of keeping history in place no matter where it happened to be. That passion often got her in trouble with the planning commission because she was never cautious with her tongue.

"Yeah, my pop was in the navy. That's one reason my folks chose this old building for the restaurant." Izzy leaned against the wall under the lantern. Her face took on the soft romantic glow of the light, and Mel was lost in the depth of Izzy's sapphire eyes.

Izzy cleared her throat. "So tell me…why is a woman with such good family and friends…" She waited for confirmation, and Mel answered with a nod. "All alone on a Saturday night?"

"I've just got a lot on my plate right now." She knew Izzy could see right through her, but she couldn't very well tell this woman, whom she barely knew, about her marital problems.

"Is that all?" She frowned. "What about the argument between you and your husband the other night?"

Mel took another drink of wine. "I'm afraid that's par for the course these days. I'm in a relationship with a man who's in a relationship with his job."

"If I had a girlfriend as beautiful as you, my job would never come between us."

Mel shuddered. She'd waited so long to hear someone tell her that. The only thing was, she'd thought Jack would be the one to say it.

"What about all those people who were here on your birthday? Aren't they any help?"

"My family? I can't talk to them about Jack. They would all say 'I told you so.'" She took another swig of wine, emptying her glass. "I've been putting on the façade for too long, trying to make them think everything between us is perfect."

"Okay...but it's not, is it?"

Mel shook her head, and Izzy took the empty glass from her hand. "Come on." She grabbed her hand and pulled her toward the kitchen. "Let's get you something to eat before that wine kicks in."

She didn't need the wine to kick in to make her dizzy. Her head started spinning the moment Izzy touched her.

Izzy pulled a stool over to the long metal table in the center of the kitchen. "Sit," she said, sliding a basket of sliced sourdough bread and a butter knife in front of her. "Butter's in the fridge."

Mel searched the Sub-Zero and found a plate with an industrial size hunk of butter on it among the steaks, fish, and veggies.

Izzy refilled the wineglass and took a drink before dropping a basket of angel-hair pasta into the hot water. "You like shrimp, right?"

"Love it."

"Light on the garlic, right?" The pan sizzled when she tossed in a handful of shrimp.

"Yes, please." She smiled at Izzy remembering her other favorite order.

Angie came bursting into the kitchen. "I need a chicken parm and a piccata." Her face dropped when she saw Mel. "What the hell is she doing in here?"

"Angie, don't." Izzy started across the kitchen to intercept her.

"It's okay." Mel stood up and moved closer to Angie. "I'm sorry about the way I acted the other night. I was upset with my husband and took it out on you." Mel could see the skepticism in her eyes. "I hope you can forgive me."

"Yeah, sure. I understand." She broke eye contact. "I've had nights like that myself." She seemed stunned as she moved to the refrigerator and pulled out a couple of salads. "You know, you really need to dump that guy."

"That seems to be the consensus."

"The what?" Angie asked.

"Everyone agrees," Izzy said, heading her back through the door in the dining room. "Sorry about that. She has no filter."

"No. I'm the one who's sorry." Mel remembered how her husband had gawked at Angie and cringed inside. "Jack was inappropriate with her, and I was an ass about it." Izzy gave her a look she couldn't quite read.

"I'm sure she appreciated the apology. Honesty goes a long way with her." Izzy turned back to the stove, and in a matter of minutes she'd set a plate of scampi on angel hair in front of Mel and taken another for herself. Mel hadn't realized how hungry she was until her stomach growled at the marvelous aroma that floated to her nose.

"So you gonna tell him how you feel?" Izzy said, pulling up a stool and sitting across from her.

"I already have." She let out a heavy sigh. "Too many times." She set down her fork and reached for the wineglass that seemed suddenly empty again. "He doesn't seem to care."

"So what's next?" Izzy picked up the bottle of wine, and Mel slid the glass over for her to refill it.

"I don't know." She took a swallow and pushed the glass back to Izzy, who took a drink. The intimacy of sharing a glass didn't even faze her. Mel finished the rest of her pasta and realized she'd left her money in the car. "I'll have to go out and get my purse. What do I owe you?"

"Dinner's on me tonight." Izzy took her plate and set it in the sink. "Can you close up tonight, Tony? Only a few tables are left."

"Sure." He pulled his lip up, and she pushed her fist into his side.

"Thanks." She took off her purple chef's coat, revealing a black tank top with turquoise bra straps peeking out underneath. "Come on. You can give me a lift home." She tossed the soiled coat into the laundry bin. "You parked in the lot?"

"On the street."

"Close enough." She took Mel's hand and led her out the back door.

❖

They turned the corner, and Izzy observed the three cars parked on the street. A white Chevy Suburban, an ivory Mercedes, and a midnight-blue BMW. She couldn't see Mel driving the monster SUV, so it had to be one of the other two. The Mercedes was pretty flashy, so she was banking on the BMW. When the car chirped and the lights flashed on the BMW, Izzy smiled.

As they neared the car, Izzy heard Tony shout from the back door of the restaurant. "Hey, Iz. Dana's here."

"Shit," Izzy mumbled. "Go ahead and get in. I'll be right back." She turned and jogged back across the street and into the kitchen. Dana met her mid-kitchen and slipped her arms around her waist. "Stop." Izzy grabbed Dana's wrists and removed her too-familiar arms.

"I'm going to get a glass of wine from the bar to go with the pasta you're going to fix me." Dana kissed her on the cheek and spun around toward the door.

"I'm not fixing you pasta, Dana. Tony, can you help me here?"

He shook his head. "She's your girlfriend. You take care of her."

Izzy glared at him. "You can be such an ass sometimes." She turned around, and Mel was standing in the doorway. "Sorry, I need to take care of this."

"Anything I can do to help?"

Dana stopped when she heard the voice. "Who's this?"

"Just one of the customers." Izzy whirled around and grabbed Dana's hand. She pulled her through the doorway into the dining room and led her to a table. "Sit and stay." She threw her hands up in front of her.

"I'm not a dog, Izzy."

Izzy let out a sigh. "Please. Just stay here. I'll make you some pasta."

"Then we can talk?"

Izzy didn't answer as she shot back into the kitchen. Mel was gone. *Fuck!* She raced out the back door and saw the red glow of the BMW's taillights headed down the street.

"What the hell was that all about?" Dana said as she came back through the kitchen doorway.

"How about you tell me." Izzy turned and Dana stood right behind her. "What are you doing here, Dana?"

"I miss you, baby." Dana's lips pulled together into a pout.

"I'm not your baby."

"Don't say that. We're good together."

"Stop. We're neither good. Nor are we together. Now go home."

Izzy knew she'd just lost a chance to get to know Mel better and might never get another. She'd just have to wait and see if Mel Thomas ever set foot in her restaurant again.

CHAPTER SEVEN

Nancy flipped through a handful of file folders as she strode into Mel's office. "The web-design class seems to have a few shining stars in it. What do you think about throwing a few of these projects to the students and seeing what they come up with?"

"That's a great idea. We might be able to get a couple of interns out of the class. We could have a contest, see how they do. Maybe even give them a little experience and let them in on the pitch to the clients."

"Yeah," Nancy said thoughtfully. "Any preference on which ones? We've got a few products, some local businesses, a cruise line, and a couple of restaurants."

"No, you pick. But look at some of the more agreeable clients. We'll have to let them know what we're doing, make sure they're on board with it."

"We could pitch it as kind of a work-experience program. I might need to tap your persuasive powers if they're hesitant."

"Sounds like a plan." Mel smiled. "I knew there was a reason I kept you around."

"Only one?"

"Maybe two or three." Mel grinned while Nancy stood silently as she waited for Mel to continue. "There are those design skills...oh, and that knack you have for advertising comes in handy once in a while too." She flopped back into her chair. Mel knew her company wouldn't be at the level it was today without Nancy. She might have been able to provide the financing, but Nancy was a stellar graphic designer and had an inherent creativity when it came to tag lines and slogans.

"I'm glad you appreciate me for something." Nancy dropped the files on the edge of Mel's desk and sat down in the chair on the other side. "So are you gonna tell me about the hot chef?"

"There's nothing to tell."

"Uh, you need to open your eyes, honey. There's more going on in that woman's mind than you realize."

"Duh. I'm not blind." She tossed her pen onto the desk. "It's not like I can do anything about it."

"But you've thought about it." Nancy raised her eyebrows. "Wow. That's a milestone."

Thoughts of her tumultuous relationship with Jack flew through her head. "I have to figure things out with Jack."

"Mel, when are you going to start thinking about yourself first? He doesn't make you happy anymore. He hasn't in a long time."

"It's that obvious?"

"Probably not to everyone else. But to me, it is."

"It doesn't really make any difference. She has a girlfriend." *A beautiful girlfriend.*

"How do you know that?"

"I was at the restaurant the other night when she showed up."

Nancy scrunched her face. "Oh, now I'm confused. The way she was flirting with you, I would never have thought she was involved with anyone."

"Welcome to the club."

Nancy got up and plucked the files from the corner of the desk. "I'll take a look at these and let you know which ones will fit the best."

"Okay. Sounds good."

Nancy took a few steps toward the door and turned back. "I still think you should dump Jack."

"Got it." She gave her a backhanded wave. "Shut the door on your way out, please."

Mel was impressed with Nancy's resourcefulness. She would've never thought to get the students involved in designing actual client websites. If they could bring in a couple of students as interns, they could teach them the process the way they wanted it done as well as save them money.

She'd thought about making Nancy a partner in the company more than once but had never acted on it for one reason or another. Maybe it was time to let up on the reins and share some of the responsibility. It would certainly give her more free time.

❖

Mel sat at her desk, exhausted. She swung her chair around and stared out the window at the streetlights. Another Friday night working late. The sun was beginning to set, and soon it would be another night of fast food and going home alone. She hadn't been back to Bella's since last week when she'd found out Izzy had a girlfriend. Tony's voice still rang clearly in her head. "She's your girlfriend."

That night, Mel had driven around the block and pulled into a different space along the curb, farther away from the restaurant, debating whether to go back inside. It wasn't long before she saw Izzy and the woman come through the back door and cross the street to a silver Mustang. She watched Izzy open the passenger door for her. Her stomach knotted as the woman gave her a quick kiss before she ducked into the passenger seat.

How could she have been so stupid? She let her head fall back against the seat. It was plain that Izzy had a girlfriend, and nothing would ever happen between the two of them. She probably had that reality check coming. She was still married to Jack and had no way of letting him know she wanted out until he was back in town.

She heard a light tap on the door and spun her chair around. "Come in."

Nancy entered the office with her purse slung over one shoulder and her laptop bag over the other. "I'm heading out."

"How did your meeting go with the new client today?"

Nancy dropped her bags into one chair and sat in another. "Really well. She seems to know what she wants, and it looks like they have a great menu."

"Oh yeah? What kind of food?"

"Kind of nouveau Italian. I know you're partial to Bella's, but it looks good. We should try it sometime."

"Yeah, sure." Mel didn't relish the idea of going somewhere else, but after acting like such a fool, she didn't want to go back to Bella's in the near future.

"Well, I'm leaving." Nancy pushed out of the chair and pulled her bags onto her shoulder. "I don't have anything going on tonight. You want to grab a burger?"

"Really? Another burger?"

"I'm up for anything. Let's go."

"No. That's okay. I'll just grab something when I get home."

Nancy let her bags slide back into the chair. "Call the order in. I'll go pick it up."

Mel drew her brows together.

"At Bella's. Do it now or I'm leaving."

Mel smiled. She really missed Izzy's cooking. "Do you want anything?"

"Get me a chicken Caesar salad, extra dressing."

Mel picked up the phone and called. "Twenty minutes."

"Finish up, so you can go home when I get back." Nancy grabbed her bags again and rushed out.

❖

Izzy pushed open the bar door and peeked into the dining room. Mel hadn't been in for dinner all week. She was disappointed but kind of knew it was too good to be true. It wasn't smart to set her sights on a married woman unless it was just for a good fuck. Even then, it was a bad idea. She was already way past that stage. Mel had gotten into her head and was slowly seeping into her heart. *Not smart, Iz.*

It was just after ten o'clock and the restaurant was slowing down, when Angie came hustling through the kitchen door. "Hey, I need an order of shrimp scampi on angel hair to go. Light on the garlic."

Izzy swung around and took the ticket from her hand.

"Yep, it's the bitch."

So she would get a chance to see her again, after all.

"She's not a bitch."

"Not to you." Angie growled. "She said she's been swamped at work." Angie took a large Caesar salad out of the refrigerator and transferred it to a Styrofoam container before she wrapped some sourdough in foil and put it in a paper bag. "This needs a chicken breast." She pointed to the salad. "I told her it would be ready in twenty."

Izzy had it all packed up and in the bag waiting for Mel. She'd told Angie to leave it in the kitchen and send her back when she arrived. She was cleaning the grill when she heard the door open.

"Hey, stranger. I've missed seeing you this week." She didn't turn around.

"If I'd have known that, I would have come by sooner."

Izzy spun around when she heard someone else's voice. She must have noticed the surprise in Izzy's eyes.

"I'm Nancy. Mel's at the office." She smiled. "She's working on a project. Deadlines, you know." Nancy rummaged through the bag and pulled out the salad and dressing. "Can I have another bag?"

Izzy pointed to the shelf behind her with various to go containers stacked on it.

Nancy reached back into the bag, found some plastic utensils, and moved them to the separate bag with the salad. She must have sensed Izzy watching her. "The salad is for me."

"You're not working late tonight?"

"God, no. I've had enough for the day. I'm just going to drop this off before I head home. She'll probably be there for a few more hours, and if I don't take her something, she won't eat." She tilted her head slightly. "Hey, do you guys deliver?"

Tony spoke up. "No delivery, only takeout."

Izzy raised a hand, motioning Tony to be quiet. "I think we can make an exception." Izzy took the bag from Nancy's hand.

"Are you sure?"

Izzy nodded. "You go on home. I'll make sure she gets it."

"Wait. Are you going to take it?"

"Probably."

"That's okay. I'll do it." She grabbed the bags from the counter.

"It's not a problem. I got it." Izzy ignored the intensity of her stare and took the bag from her hand.

She narrowed her eyes and pressed her lips together tightly before she spoke. "Don't flirt with her if you're not available."

"Okay." Izzy let the word slip from her lips slowly.

"Are you? Available?" Nancy rolled back onto one heel, crossing her arms across her chest.

"Last I checked, I am." Izzy was confused. First, why would Mel's friend think she wasn't available? Second, why would she care?

"Okay, then. The address is fifteen hundred Kingston, and she's in suite B." Nancy wrote it on an order pad and slipped it into the bag. "I'll call the security guard at the front desk and tell him you're delivering so you don't have any trouble getting into the building. She keeps the door to the suite locked, so you'll have to knock when you get there. I'd say thank you, but she's gonna be pissed at me for this." She gathered up her salad and rushed back out the door, leaving Izzy wondering what the hell she was talking about.

"It was enough with the extra portions and the feeding her in the kitchen, but now you're delivering to her?" Tony grumbled. "That girl is going to be the end of you."

"Apparently there's something I need to straighten out with her."

"Yeah, whatever, but I'm not working late tomorrow night. The Warriors are on."

"I think you can cut me some slack, Tony. Seeing as how I work late almost every night."

❖

Mel leaned back in her chair, hardly able to keep her eyes open. She should go home but hated being there alone. The phone rang, startling her out of her drowsy state. She looked at the caller ID and picked up the phone. "Where are you?"

Nancy's voice rang through. "I'm almost there, but I can't find my key."

"Again?" Mel blew out a breath.

"Just come out to the reception area, so you can hear me when I knock."

"Can't you just call me when you get here?"

"Do you want me to drop your dinner while I'm juggling the phone?"

"Fine, but hurry up." It was only a few minutes after she'd hung up and gone to the front of the office when she heard the knock on the door.

"I can't believe you lost your key again."

"I don't think you gave me a key," Izzy said, tugging her lips up into a smile and producing those irresistible dimples.

She looked different tonight. Her dark hair wasn't tied back; it was wild and thick around her face. Mel bit her bottom lip as she let her gaze sweep the length of her. Dressed in skinny jeans topped with a charcoal T-shirt fitted just enough to accentuate the curves of her breasts, Izzy was propped casually up against the doorway with the bag of food swinging from her fingers. She was sexy as hell.

"Oh...I thought Nancy was bringing that."

"Since it was out of her way, I offered. I thought since you've been to my place of business so many times, maybe I should come to yours for once."

Mel didn't move. "That really wasn't necessary."

Izzy tilted her head. "Well, now that I'm here, can I come in?"

"Uh...sure." She moved aside and let Izzy though the doorway. "I'll get my wallet."

"No need. Nancy took care of it. This is a nice place." Izzy scanned the office. "Do you have a table somewhere?"

"I was going to take it home."

"It'll be cold by then. We should eat it now."

"We?"

"I brought some for myself. I didn't want you to have to eat alone. Is that all right?"

"Okay." She relented, leading Izzy into the small conference room in the suite. For a woman involved with someone else, Izzy was being pretty presumptuous.

"Wow, this place is bigger than it looks." Izzy pulled out a couple of containers, setting one in front of Mel and one in front of herself.

"This is awfully sweet of you, but don't you need to get home to your girlfriend?" Mel sputtered.

"No." She shook her head slowly. "No girlfriend."

Mel crossed her arms. "Last week, I clearly heard Tony say that woman in the kitchen was your girlfriend."

Izzy seemed thoughtful for a moment. "I guess he did say that."

"Well? Who is she?" Mel could see Izzy's lip quirk up a bit. She was sure it was perfectly obvious she was jealous. Mel had no idea why, but she was.

"Why don't you sit down and eat your pasta before it gets cold, and I'll tell you all about it after we're finished."

Skeptical, Mel sat down, folded back the foil edges, and took the top off her container. She wasn't going to let Izzy leave tonight without telling her about this woman. Why would Tony say she was Izzy's girl-friend if it wasn't true?

Mel took a bite of pasta and let out a groan. "This is so good."

Izzy buttered a piece of bread and handed it to her. "So what are you working on that's keeping you here so late?"

"I've got two major projects and many more updates that all need to be done yesterday."

"Do you have anyone to help you?"

"Nancy offered to take some of it, but she has her own work to do."

"I say, between you and Nancy, you write it all down and prioritize it. Then the two of you can knock it out together."

She smiled. "I guess I would be able to get it done a lot faster if she helped me with the style pages."

"I have no idea what those are. But if it will take some of the pressure off you, then you should let her do them."

Mel's heart warmed as she watched the slow smile creep across Izzy's face. She'd missed more than the pasta. She kept her eyes glued to her food as she finished eating, determined not to let Izzy soften her up.

"So, who is she?"

"Is that why you left last week?"

Mel shrugged and wiped her mouth. "You seemed to have your hands full with her."

"And the reason you haven't been in all week?"

"No." Mel shifted in her seat. "I've just been busy here at work."

"But you thought she was my girlfriend." One side of Izzy's mouth pulled up.

"Well, that's what Tony said. What was I supposed to think?" She pushed her empty food container aside. "Tell me differently."

Izzy picked up the containers and slid them back into the bag. "Dana *was* my girlfriend. We haven't been together for a while."

Mel saw the turmoil on Izzy's face and got a sick feeling in her stomach. This story wasn't going to end well.

"I caught her with someone else."

"Oh my God." Mel sat forward in the chair. "That must have been horrible."

She nodded. "It was certainly a surprise." Izzy stared into space for a minute, and Mel knew she was reliving the experience. She watched her closely as she waited for her to continue.

"So I let her go."

"But she still comes around?"

She blew out a short breath. "Oh, you don't know the half of it." Izzy shifted in her seat. "She acts like it never happened."

"Is she still with the other woman?"

Izzy rolled her lips together and nodded.

"Does she know she still comes around?"

"I'm not sure. I've thought about telling her, but I don't want to be pulled back into that situation. She probably wouldn't believe me anyway."

"I'm so sorry, Iz." She reached across the table and covered Izzy's hand with hers. "No one should have to go through something like that." Mel was seeing a whole new side of Izzy. It seemed as though the tough girl who made light of every situation had a hurtful past. She had a soft, vulnerable side Mel hadn't seen before, and it made Mel feel so much closer to her.

"I'm sorry. I shouldn't have dropped all of that on you."

"No. I'm glad you told me. That's what friends are for." Mel squeezed her hand, and they shared a gaze before Mel broke away and fixed her eyes on her watch. "Oh my. I had no idea how late it is. We should go."

"I'll walk you to your car."

"Let me get my things." Mel locked the door to the suite and waved to the guard as they left the building.

Izzy opened Mel's car door for her. "You know, someone like you could make a girl forget all about what happened in the past."

"Well, I don't know about that, but I'm certainly willing to help out." She pressed her lips to Izzy's cheek before sliding into the driver's seat. "Thanks for bringing me dinner."

Izzy raised her hand to her cheek, stunned and unsure of what exactly Mel had meant. If it was anything remotely close to what Izzy was thinking, she needed to act on it now. Her heart raced as she caught the door before it closed. "Do you think maybe we can get together next week sometime?"

Mel smiled widely. "Yeah. Sure. Just give me a call." She rattled off her cell number, and Izzy repeated it over and over in her head as she watched Mel drive away. The grin on Izzy's face felt frozen. She kept Mel's car in sight until it was out of view. A passing set of headlights brought her back to reality. She got into her car and put Mel's number in her cell-phone contacts before she fired the engine.

Izzy thought about the look on Mel's face when she'd asked her about Dana. Her expression wasn't just inquisitive; it was demanding. Izzy had been confused as to why she even cared until she detected the jealousy in her tone. It was clear now what she'd thought when Dana had showed up at Bella's, and she'd stayed away this past week because of it. *Where do we go from here?* She was still married, not happily, it seemed, but married just the same. Izzy had never knowingly crossed that line before.

❖

"All right, class, I want a website proposal from you all by Friday. You can work individually or in groups of two. If you need a partner or a company to create a website for, come see me after class."

After whispering with Doug, Angie stepped to the front of the class to talk to Mel. "If it's all right, I thought Doug and I would create a website for Bella's."

"That sounds like a great idea. Did you run it by your sister?"

"Yeah. She's all for it."

"Good. You'll need to write up the proposal first."

"Already did that." Angie slid the proposal onto the desk in front of Mel.

She read through it, made a couple of corrections in the verbiage, and handed it back. "Looks good. Just make the changes I indicated and submit it through the online drop box.

You'll need to create a flowchart next. If you take a blank writeable DVD to the test lab, you can trade it for a student copy of Visio. Let me know if you need any help installing it."

"I will." She turned to return to her seat.

"Angie." Mel called her back. "What's your plan?"

"We're going to have a main page with links for each menu and pictures for each one of the dishes."

"I mean for the future. Are you going to work at the restaurant, or are you serious about being a web designer?" Mel continued when Angie's eyebrows pulled together. "Because you really have a gift for it." Mel probably shouldn't have told her that, but it was true. She'd viewed the other sites Angie had created, and they were good, really good. She had talent.

Angie slid down in the chair next to the desk. "You think so?"

"I do. And if you work really hard, I think you have a good shot at getting the internship."

"I will."

"If you get stuck on anything, I'll be happy to help you work through it."

"Okay, thanks."

Mel held back her grin as she watched Angie walk back to her desk out of the corner of her eye. It was a bit strange having Angie in class; the resemblance between her and Izzy was uncanny. Her hair had been colored, fading from dark to light, but she had her sister's Mediterranean features and her beautiful blue eyes. Her stunned expression when she left Mel's desk was still on her face when she sat down next to Doug.

Angie whispered something in Doug's ear, and her lips spread into a wide smile. It was clear Angie had no interest at all in working at Bella's. Izzy seemed to be aware of Angie's interest in technology, judging by her earlier phone call, but did she have any idea how passionate her sister really was about it? And was she willing to let her find her own path outside of the restaurant?

Izzy hummed while she skimmed through the produce at the market, picking up fresh vegetables to add to the special for the night. Her daily ritual was extra enjoyable today, because tonight she was planning a special meal just for Mel: beef Wellington with mashed red potatoes and roasted baby carrots. It was going to be perfect. She'd made herself wait a couple of days before calling, but she'd had the date all planned out the next day. She would hold the little booth in the corner, one of the romantic ones with a curtain. Add some good food and wine, and the night will be perfect. When she rounded the corner to the butcher counter, she heard a familiar voice. It was Jack Thomas, holding a bouquet of roses, waiting on one of the butchers to wrap a couple of steaks for him.

"There goes my night." She let out a sigh. His trip must have been cut short. She waited until he left the meat counter to get her order.

"Izzy, sweetheart, I've got your order right here." Joe called to her and then checked the order. "Hang on. It looks like we're short that extra tenderloin you requested." He turned to go into the back. "I'll cut it right now for you."

"Forget the tenderloin, Joe. My special party for tonight canceled."

"Oh, well, that's too bad. They don't know what they're missing."

"Thanks, Joe. Tell Rose I said hello."

"Tell her yourself. We'll be in tomorrow night."

Izzy smiled and turned to go, then turned back. "Joe, how did you make Rose fall in love with you?"

He moved to the side of the counter and motioned her closer. "You really want to know?"

"Yes, I do. When she looks at you all I see is love."

"I wasn't the first guy she fell in love with, you know." He raised an eyebrow and seemed to become lost in a memory. "He was a looker. Big and handsome, played all kinds of sports. I was never like that."

"What are you talking about, Joe. You're adorable."

"Well, maybe a little bit." He smiled. "But that's not what got her. Patience and persistence did the trick. I never went away. I always stayed close with her and her family." He shrugged. "And then one day the other guy was gone and I was still there, waiting. So, you see, I couldn't *make* her fall in love with me. She had to do that herself." He grabbed her shoulders softly. "If she's worth it, be patient."

Izzy gave Joe a thoughtful look. "Thanks, Joe. Dinner's on me tomorrow night." She gave him a quick hug and headed toward the checkout.

"If I'd have known all it took was a little advice to get free dinner, I would have given that to you a long time ago," he shouted after her.

On the way to the restaurant, Izzy thought about what Joe had said. If Mel was really worth it, she would wait as long as it took for her to realize her life could be better. She pulled up to the back of the restaurant, got out of the car, and banged on the back door. The door swung open, and Tony came out as she was getting a couple of bags of food out of the backseat of her car. He took the bags from her, and she followed him into the kitchen.

"Carrots, rib eye, snapper." Tony inventoried her food choices as he put them into the refrigerator. "Where's the tenderloin?"

"Not gonna happen tonight."

"Why not?"

"Her husband is back in town."

"She tell you that?"

"I saw him at the market."

"Oh." He moved the sourdough-bread delivery to the other counter. "You talk to him?"

"No. Just saw him picking up steaks." *And flowers.*

"Don't you think that's odd?"

"What?"

"Him coming all the way down here for steak."

"What's odd about that? He comes here to eat."

"Yeah, but the airport is in the city. You'd think he would stop a little closer to home."

The phone rang. "Bella's," Tony said, pressing the receiver to his ear. "Hang on just a second." He cupped his palm over the mouthpiece and motioned to Izzy. "It's for you."

She scrunched up her face. "Who?"

"Dunno." He lifted his shoulders. "She just asked for you."

She took the receiver from him and slipped it up against her ear. "This is Izzy."

"Hi, Izzy." Mel hesitated. "I wasn't sure if you'd be there yet."

"Oh yeah. I'm always here early." Izzy figured she was calling to cancel tonight since Jack was back in town.

"Just wanted to check and see if we were still on for dinner tonight."

"Oh, I wasn't sure." Izzy's voice rose. "I thought you'd be with Jack."

"That would be difficult since he's still out of town."

"But I—" She stuttered, rubbing her face. "I thought maybe he was back?"

"No. He won't be in town for another week."

"Oh." Izzy pictured him in her head. Six feet tall, sandy blond hair, cut short around the ears and flopped into a naturally curly mop on top. An athletic type with a pretty-boy face and a sophisticated air about him that didn't quite seem deserved. She was sure it was him she saw at the market.

"So, I'll see you around tenish, okay?"

"Okay, sure. That sounds good." Izzy hung up the receiver and turned to Tony. "She doesn't know he's back."

"Who?"

"Mel. She doesn't know her husband is back."

"You think he ever left town?" Tony asked.

"Doesn't look like it, does it?" *The bastard.*

"You gonna tell her?"

"Should I?"

"Maybe you should stay out of it."

"Wouldn't you want me to tell you?"

"Of course, but you and I are always straight with each other."

"I feel like I should be that way with her too."

"What if she doesn't believe you?" Potatoes thudded against the metal sink as he dumped the sack into it. "Then you end up being the bad guy."

"I don't know, Tony. I think I should."

"Ahh, Izzy." He frowned. "You're the only one who's gonna get hurt if you get involved in this." He wrapped his big arms around her and held her in a tight hug. "How long have you known this woman? Do you know anything about her?" He rested his chin on her head.

Tony was right. She'd spent only a short amount of time with Mel, but she felt so comfortable, like they'd been friends forever. "Long enough to know she's straight." *And long enough to wish she wasn't.*

"And you're gonna chance it anyway?" He released her from the embrace.

"I really like her, Tony." She lifted her shoulders. "She's different."

"What if she just wants to be friends?"

"That's all we are, Tony. I told you she's married."

"I've seen that look in your eye before, Iz." He tightened his lips. "I hope she doesn't break your heart."

"Yeah, me too," she whispered.

The community center was busy today. It was the seniors' monthly birthday and anniversary party. They had chosen a luau theme, so everyone aged sixty and above was dressed for fun in the sun. There were Hawaiian shirts, muumuus, and even an occasional grass skirt worn by a few of the bolder women in the group. Everyone was adorned with a multicolored lei hanging from their neck.

Mel had created the webpage announcing the party, and it had brought in more than the usual number of seniors this month. She scanned the crowd for Bella, who had asked for additional help after her lesson on email and Internet safety last month. Mel had purposely come early to make sure she'd understood what they'd discussed.

Bella came bustling across the room. "Mary Elizabeth, I'm ready to learn how to write to my cousin in Italy."

"Wonderful. Just let me set up my laptop, and we'll get started." She moved to a table in the corner of the room.

"It's so sweet of you to help me. I don't know anything about computers."

Benito pulled out a chair for Bella before he plopped into the chair next to her. "Our youngest Angie is a whiz, but she won't ask her."

"She's busy with her classes. Besides, I want to make sure I can do it before I surprise her, Benny."

"Of course you can do it." He smiled broadly. "Do you think she got her computer skills from me?"

Bella gazed lovingly back at him and gave him a soft smile. "My cheering section."

"You two are so funny. If I didn't know better, I'd think you were in love." Mel winked.

"Anyone want punch?" Benito asked.

Bella spoke up. "We'd love some, dear."

Benito smiled and squeezed Bella's hand as he left the table.

Mel's heart swelled as she watched the exchange. Even though they'd been married for forty-plus years, the love between Bella and Benito was solid yet still fresh in some way. He waited on her and complimented her as thought they'd just met the week before. He was still courting her after all these years. In all the ten years of her marriage, Jack had never looked at her that way, and she doubted he ever would. Sadness crept in and tears welled in her eyes. She would never have a love like that.

She felt Bella's hand on her own. "Are you okay, dear?"

"I'm fine," she said, focusing on her computer screen. She pinched her eyes closed before looking back up at Bella. "How do you two do it? How can you still be so in love after being married so long?"

"We've had some wonderful times, but it hasn't always been easy. The difficult times are when you need to remember how good it can be. You always need to keep the light glowing." She laid her hand across her heart.

"What if you've never had that light?"

"Then maybe you're with the wrong person." She squeezed Mel's hand. "You should come to family dinner sometime and meet my children. I think you would get along well." Bella assessed her for a minute. "And they're all single." She winked.

Mel chuckled. "I, however, am not." There was no question she'd get along well with one of them.

"Time will tell," Bella quipped with a broad smile.

Benito came back with two glasses of punch and set them on the table. "While you do this, I'm going to catch a little of the Giants game in the rec room."

"Don't stay too long." Her voice rose sweetly. "You're number one on my dance card."

He shot her a wink. "I'll only be a few minutes."

After creating a free email account and showing Bella how to access and create a message to her cousin, Mel watched Bella and Benito dance to famous crooners from earlier decades. She imagined herself doing the same, only it wasn't Jack holding her close on the dance floor. It was Izzy. She sucked in a deep breath and tried to clear the image from her mind but couldn't seem to shake it. Maybe Bella was right. Maybe time will tell where her heart belonged.

Izzy tried to play it cool as Mel watched her work in the kitchen. All she needed was a sliced finger to deal with.

"Sorry about the beef Wellington. We had a mix-up with the butcher." She pulled open the fridge and reached inside. "But I have a couple of nice steaks I can cook."

"That sounds good, but pasta would be fine if it's easier."

"Okay." She slipped the steaks back onto the shelf and reached for a different package. "How about some scallops?"

"I'm sure anything you make will be delicious."

"Well, I'm not so good at Chinese."

Mel let out a deep belly laugh. "That's okay. I know a great place for takeout."

Tony took the package of scallops from her and replaced it with the steaks. "Why don't you take the steaks home and grill? Show your friend here the view from your deck." He turned to look at Gio. "We can handle it tonight. Right, Gio?"

Gio nodded. "Yeah, sure."

Izzy turned to Tony. "You're actually volunteering to work alone with Gio?" The two worked well as brothers, but not so good as co-chefs. Tony was always giving advice, and Gio was always rejecting it.

"We've done it before." He waved her off. "Better get out of here before I change my mind."

"You want to?" Izzy could sense Mel's hesitation. "Oh, wow, what was I thinking?" She touched her fingers to her forehead. "You probably have other plans later."

"No, no plans. I'd love to see your view." She shot her a subtle smile.

"Okay then." Izzy took off her lime-green chef's coat and tossed it into the laundry. "Let's do as Tony says and get out of here before he changes his mind."

Izzy walked with Mel to her car and opened the door for her. "Just follow the black Jeep." She pointed toward the mid-sized SUV parked farther down the street.

"Lead the way."

The thirty-minute drive seemed shorter tonight, and it certainly wasn't enough time to prepare herself for being alone with Mel. She should've run the first time she saw her, but she couldn't. The gravity surrounding her was too strong to resist.

CHAPTER EIGHT

Mel pulled into the driveway at the side of the house next to Izzy. She could see as she drove up that the house was shaped like an H from the front, a wing with a large window on each side. Not unlike that of a William Wurster design, Mel thought. Red cedar shingles covered the structure all around. Flowerpots lined the walkway, mixed with a variety of herbs and flowers. It seemed as though Izzy had a way with plants as well as with cooking. Izzy unlocked the front door, slid it open, and waited for Mel to enter before her. She dropped her keys on the table just inside, and Mel followed suit.

She stood in the entryway for a moment, in awe of the living room. Large sets of sliding doors matched the adjoining windows exactly the same on both the front and back of the house. The living room was engulfed in the middle between them, creating an amazing outdoor experience. She followed Izzy in farther and noted the fir wainscot that covered the floors and butted up to the bluestone fireplace, flanked by bookcases filled with books.

"You like to read?" She moved to the bookcase and took in the wide variety of authors. Izzy had classic works by Henry David Thoreau, Oscar Wilde, Ralph Waldo Emerson, Willa Cather, and even Darwin, as well as contemporary fiction by Stephen King, John Grisham, Nora Roberts, David Sedaris, and Alice Munro.

"I do. It helps me relax." Izzy slid the back doors open, and the sea air flooded in as she stepped out onto the redwood deck.

"Tony was right about the view." As the sun peeked just above the water, Mel turned and caught Izzy's gaze. "This is positively radiant."

She stopped, studied Izzy for a moment. With the fiery red, burnt-orange colors of sunset reflected on her face, *she* was positively radiant. Mel wanted to go to her, pull her in close, and kiss her right then. *God, I shouldn't have come.*

"I just wish I could spend more time here," Izzy said.

Mel cleared her throat and strolled to the edge of the deck. The beach stretched as far as she could see. "I think I'd have to work from home if I lived here." She let out a soft sigh. "No. I would have to work from home." She turned around and caught Izzy checking out *her* view. Izzy's cheeks pinked as she slipped around the grill to turn on the gas and ignite it. After that, she stepped back inside to the kitchen. Mel spent a few more minutes taking in the sunset before she followed her in.

"What can I do to help?" Mel noticed the bowl filled with fresh greens on the counter, a bottle of homemade dressing behind it.

She pointed to the open bottle and glasses on the table. "You can pour the wine."

"I certainly can." The cabernet nosed nicely as she poured. Mel picked up the glasses and took them into the kitchen, where she handed one to Izzy. Mel raised the glass to her lips but stopped midway and clinked it against Izzy's. "Cheers," she said, fighting the dangerously strong urge to lean close and touch Izzy's full lips with her own. Izzy took a sip, holding her gaze before setting the glass on the counter and focusing her attention back on the steaks. Mel watched her season them with salt and pepper on one side, then flip them to do the same on the other. Long, thin fingers, lovely petite hands, tanned arms and shoulders, long, beautiful neck. *How soft would it feel under her lips, and just how sweet would it taste?*

Avoiding her gaze, Izzy handed Mel her glass. "Would you mind?" Mel took it from her as Izzy gathered the plate of steaks and a pair of tongs. Her feet wouldn't move. She was stuck, still in a daze thinking about what it would be like to touch her. Only when Izzy motioned to her did she snap out of it and follow.

Mel handed Izzy her glass and stood beside her at the grill. "Can you show me how you get your steaks so crisp on the outside and tender inside?"

"Sure." Izzy gave her a soft smile. "First you preheat the grill and get it really hot—500-degrees hot."

Mel raised her eyebrows. "Wow."

"Yeah. You have to be careful." Izzy lifted the corner of the steak. "You see how it comes off the grill easily?"

Mel nodded.

"It only takes a few minutes, but you need to wait for that." Izzy handed her the tongs. "Go ahead, flip them."

Mel took the tongs and flipped both the steaks. "Now what?"

"You do the same on the other side."

"And then they're done?" Mel scrunched her nose up.

"If they're thick like these, just move them over to the other side of the grill and close the lid for a minute or two so they can cook with the indirect heat." Izzy wrapped her hand around Mel's, picked up one of the steaks, and moved it to the other side of the grill. The wave of heat was instant and blazing, radiating from Mel's hand up through her shoulder. She didn't speak; she just nodded as Izzy released her hand.

Izzy picked up the empty plate and said, "I'll be right back." Then she went into the house and came out again with a clean one.

"How do I know when they're done?"

"That's why you have me."

Is that why I have you? Mel watched her walk into the house, then gazed up at the darkening sky and took in a deep breath. The sun had gone down below the water now, and only the glow of violet remained in the sky. Being here with Izzy in this beautiful place was like a dream, a dream Mel didn't want to wake up from. Izzy appeared next to her again, opened the grill, and moved the steaks to a fresh plate.

"Now we just have to let them rest for a few minutes to let the juices settle." She took Mel's hand and led her to the edge of the deck. "No matter how many times I see the sunset it always amazes me." She pointed to the sky. "Look at the way it reflects in the clouds, the twilight hues billowing together like soft waves fading into the darkness."

Izzy's low, velvety voice filled Mel's senses. Her soft, sensual passion provoked incredible feelings in Mel, feelings she'd never felt before.

"You ready to eat?" Izzy said.

Mel cleared her throat. "I am."

Izzy pointed to the table that had somehow been set in the meantime with cloth place mats and napkins, along with a small amber lantern in the middle.

Izzy filled their wineglasses and held hers up. "To you, earth, and life, till the last ray gleams."

"Walt Whitman," Mel said with a smile as she clinked her glass against Izzy's.

They sat quietly adjacent to each other as they ate. The air between them was thick, somehow charged with awareness and sensuality. Mel's body was sizzling; even the cool breeze from the ocean had no effect on her. She concentrated hard on her dinner, which was delicious, but didn't come close to capturing her attention like the beautiful woman sitting next to her. She watched as Izzy slid a knife into her steak. Mel knew she was in serious trouble.

She helped clear the plates, but Izzy insisted she just leave them in the sink for later. Izzy closed the sliding doors, and they moved into the living room on the couch. Still able to see the beautiful view of the ocean, Mel watched the surf through the glass doors.

"How did you end up here, in this house?"

"It was my grandfather's. He left it to my mom and dad, but they didn't want to leave the old neighborhood. They offered it to Tony first, but he doesn't like isolation. He likes living in the city within walking distance of everything." She took a sip of her wine. "I was just lucky enough to be next in line."

Mel raised an eyebrow and drained her glass. "Not the usual luck of the second child."

"No, I guess not." Izzy chuckled, bending forward to refill Mel's glass. "Listen. I need to tell you something." Izzy settled back and shifted on the couch facing Mel.

"I hope it's that you have some of that wonderful cheesecake from the restaurant." She said it lightly, but her stomach tightened from thinking it might have to do with the tension between them.

"I do have that, but that's not it." There was a seriousness in her voice.

"What is it?" Mel said quietly.

"I saw Jack at the market today."

"Oh, really?" Mel's voice was low and even.

Izzy nodded, seeming to notice that the news didn't surprise her.

Mel shifted on the couch, looking past Izzy. "I know."

"You know?" Izzy's voice rose, confusion filling her blue eyes.

She put her hand to her forehead and pinched it. "He's having another affair."

"*Another* affair?"

"He had one last year." She shook her head. "Maybe more than one. I don't know. Hell, it's not like we share the same bed anymore. He's been sleeping in the guest room for almost a year. When he's home, that is."

"So why do you stay with him?" The question from Izzy seemed honest, nonjudgmental.

"I don't really know." She ran through all of the same reasons that didn't seem to be valid anymore, considering where she was sitting right now. "I guess it's just convenient. I'm not good at change."

"Sleeping in separate rooms? It sounds like you've already had a major change. Don't you think there's more out there for you than convenience?"

"We just got into a routine and…between his work and mine, we saw less and less of each other. I always thought it would get better."

"But it hasn't."

"No. You actually have to make an effort for that to happen." She blew out a slow breath. "We don't talk. We don't have sex. We don't connect at all anymore. We haven't in a long time." She tossed the pillow she'd been absently holding to her body away. "I feel more connected to you than I ever have to him." She bolted up and paced the room. "And probably more connected to this bottle of wine too." She picked it up and clanked it back down to the table before swiping her keys off the counter.

"Well, that's great. I'm as good as a bottle of wine." Izzy grumbled, getting up to follow her.

Mel turned back to Izzy and shook her head, tears on the verge of spilling out. "That's not what I meant."

"You shouldn't drive." Izzy took the keys from her hand.

Mel felt a tear run down her cheek, and Izzy wiped it away with her thumb. Mel fell into her arms. Izzy's warm body pressed up against her, and then a hand rubbed her back gently.

"Maybe you should—"

"No. I can't stay, Izzy." She pushed away. Looking deep into Izzy's dark-blue eyes, she knew Izzy understood why.

"Come on. I'll drive you home." Izzy took her by the hand.

❖

Izzy fished Mel's keys out of her pocket and set them on the entryway table with her own. She'd absently slipped them into her pocket after unlocking Mel's front door and letting her inside. Mel had invited her in, but after stepping into the darkened foyer, Izzy had thought twice about it and decided taking the night any further was a bad idea.

She raked her hand across her face and eyed the clock. It was after midnight. It had taken her an hour round trip to drive Mel home. Five minutes into the ride, Mel had passed out mid-sentence. Izzy was impressed when she pulled up to the condo, which had a well-landscaped yard and backed up to a golf course. She wondered which of them played golf, Mel or Jack. *Jack.* The name rang in her head. Mel had taken the news about her husband in stride and hadn't given the slightest indication of jealousy. The anger bubbled in her chest. Izzy didn't understand why a strong, beautiful woman like Mel would let someone treat her that way.

She stripped off her clothes and climbed into bed, thinking about their conversations during the evening. It had been clear from the moment they entered the house there was something between them. Mel seemed to have more than a passing interest in her, or was that just wishful thinking? She'd caught Mel watching her more than once—starting the barbecue, cooking the steaks, during dinner. And then that embrace at the end of the night. No, it was definitely there. She'd have to watch how much wine she gave her in the future. Considering the sparks flying between them all evening, taking her home had been the right decision. Asking her to stay would have been begging for trouble.

Izzy had noticed Mel the first time she came in the restaurant, tall and slender, with dark amber locks that bounced upon her shoulders as she moved. Mel carried herself like a woman with confidence. That made Izzy tingle. Crushing on a married straight woman wasn't practical, so she'd done her best to keep her distance. She'd managed to do just that the first few times they came in, but then one night Mel's husband had requested an appearance from the chef. She'd tried to send Tony out, but he wouldn't go since Izzy was the one who usually prepared their meals. She couldn't just ignore them; she had to go. It would be rude not to respond to the request. She remembered being really nervous at first, but they were both so warm and pleasant, her anxiety quickly passed.

They'd had a short exchange, which entailed compliments on a wonderful meal from Mel and her husband, as well as an offer from Izzy to prepare them the specialty of their choice the next time they dined at the restaurant. All she needed was a day's notice, and she would prepare them anything they wanted on or off the menu. They had taken her up on the offer, requesting a traditional formal Italian dinner with all the courses, known as a *cena* in Italy. The menu at Bella's listed a few family-style dishes, but nothing that compared to a traditional Italian cena. Izzy knew the basics from the many family gatherings of her childhood but had to consult her mother on some of the not-so-well-known traditions to assure it was authentic.

Izzy remembered the night well because it didn't go as smoothly as planned. Mel's husband had invited another couple along. Mel had apologized profusely, but Izzy had assured her there would be plenty of food. Somewhere between the second piatto and the dolce, Izzy knew she was in trouble—not with the dinner, but with one of her guests. Along with being gorgeous, Mel Thomas had a wicked sense of humor. From overhearing their dinner conversation, Izzy could see Mel knew exactly when to give a jibe or a one-liner as well as a compliment. She was definitely the kind of woman Izzy could fall for.

It had been a long and expensive evening, but she had promised them anything they wanted, so that's what they got. While her husband, as usual, hadn't touched his wallet, Mel tried repeatedly to give Izzy her credit card, which Izzy refused each time. Later that night after their party had left, Izzy found four one-hundred-dollar bills in one of her pockets. Mel must have slipped in somehow while she was serving. After that night, Mel had made several weekly recurring appearances at the restaurant, with and without her husband.

CHAPTER NINE

"Hey there, early bird," Nancy said as she came through the suite doorway. "What's gotten into you? You're never here before nine." She hung her jacket on the hall tree and headed to the break room. Stopping briefly, she turned back to Mel. "Do you want some fresh coffee?"

"No, thanks. I've already had more than enough this morning. A bottle of water would be nice, though." Mel had taken a cab to pick up her car from Izzy's before six. She didn't want to risk waking her and had felt bad about Izzy having to drive her home last night. She'd pick up her other set of keys later and grab dinner to go. She was sure Izzy was sick of her and her problems by now.

Nancy dropped off the bottle of water, then strolled back to her desk and logged on to her computer. "You want to grab some lunch today?"

"I can't. I'm really behind."

"How about dinner then? Maybe at your favorite restaurant?" She lifted a brow, waiting for Mel to answer.

"I was just going to grab something to go."

"Come on, Mel. You have to take a break sometime."

She did have to pick up her keys. Taking Nancy along might pre-empt any awkwardness she and Izzy might share because of her emotional meltdown last night. She'd have to make sure to keep that little tidbit of information from Nancy.

"Okay, sure, but I probably won't be done here until after eight or so."

"We'll see about that." She took the few steps over to Mel's desk. "How about I take a few of these things off your hands?" She gathered up a few file folders.

"But I…"

"Don't worry. I'll let you check it all when I'm done."

"Wait, Nancy. Sit down for a minute."

"Uh-oh, what'd I do?"

"You didn't do anything. In fact you do just about everything to keep these projects on track."

"I do what I can."

"I've been thinking about making some changes around here. With us considering bringing in some interns, I'm going to need help. How would you like to come in as my partner?"

"I'd love it." Nancy gave her a broad smile.

"Being a partner has some pros and cons." Mel pushed back in her chair and crossed her legs. "You'd get a pretty good raise right now because we're doing well. But if business went down, you'd have to shoulder some of the financial responsibility."

"Where do I sign?"

"That's what I hoped you say." She walked around her desk and gave Nancy a hug. "I'll have the papers drawn up."

"Are you going to have your father do it?"

"No. My brother. My father will try to talk me out of it." *Besides, I'm not in the mood to be reminded of how inferior I am today.* She remembered their last dinner conversation well—his stilted presence, his harsh voice. They'd loomed in her thoughts constantly over the past few days.

"When you take on a partner, you give up control. What about work equity? You're working all the time. Is she? Vision, does she share your vision for the company?"

"You mean your vision, don't you?"

"I did help you get started."

"As I recall, when I asked you for help, you sent me packing."

"And you were more successful because of it." *He glanced up from his plate at her.*

Teetering between anxiety and anger, she bit her tongue and shot her mother a please-help-me look.

"Richard, do we have to do this at dinner?" Cecilia said, her voice low and firm.

"These are important details she hasn't thought about, Cecilia." He set down his fork, picked up his glass of wine, and took a drink.

"Of course I've thought about the details. I have a written business plan."

"What about the most important factor? You'll have to split the profits." His voice rose, laced with skepticism.

It always came down to money with her father. She wished he trusted her judgment as much as he did her brother's. She was older and more successful, but that didn't seem to make a difference in her father's eyes. Emotions swirling in her head, she'd excused herself from the table and left the house without another word.

"Well, I certainly don't want your father to try to talk you out of your decision." Nancy's voice emerged through her thoughts, and she felt her lightly touch her shoulder. "Mel, are you all right?"

She reached up and patted her hand. "Yeah. I'm fine. I'll call Mike and we'll get it all set up."

❖

Izzy rolled out of bed and went to the bathroom. She ran her fingers through her hair to get it out of her face. She scrutinized the reflection in the mirror and smiled; she was going to see Mel this morning. What a great way to start her day. After brushing her teeth, she flipped on the stereo and danced into the kitchen. She filled the electric hot-water kettle before dipping two scoops of coffee into her French-press decanter. When the water was ready, she filled the decanter to the top metal band and let the coffee steep for a few minutes before pushing the press to the bottom. Her brother kept trying to get her to buy one of those fancy single-serve coffeemakers, but she was happy with this old-fashioned French press she'd bought years ago. She reached up into the cabinet for her favorite coffee mug and poured herself a cup. She'd need more than one cup today after that late night with Mel. She smiled again and headed back into the bathroom.

She took a shower and got dressed before grabbing Mel's keys and heading out the front door. "Oh, shit!" She stopped, panic streaking through her. The car was gone. She swung around to go back inside. Then she saw the note taped to the pane of her front door.

Izzy,
Thanks for dinner. It was wonderful. I can't tell you how much I appreciate it. Sorry you had to drive me home last night. I usually don't drink that much. You can just leave the house keys at the hostess stand of the restaurant, and I'll pick them up later today.
Thanks again!
Mel

"Nope." Izzy tossed the note on the counter as she headed out to her Jeep. If Mel Thomas wanted her keys back, she was going to have to get them directly from her.

Izzy didn't spend much time with her mother this morning; she wanted to get to the restaurant to make sure she was there when Mel showed up. Her mother told her about her lunch with her friend Mary Elizabeth. Still trying to set something up between them, she practically talked the whole time about her being such a nice girl. Izzy was sure she was nice if her mother liked her, and it would probably be wise for Izzy to forget all about Mel Thomas and meet the woman. But who knew if she was gay. It wasn't like her mother had very good gaydar. Nice wasn't exactly what Izzy was looking for right now. She wanted someone exciting who made her mind swim and her belly tingle. That was Mel Thomas.

When she reached the restaurant, Izzy started preparing the sauce for the dinner crowd. She smashed and chopped a head of garlic, then turned her knife over and scraped it from the cutting board into the pot with the onions and fresh basil sautéing on the stove. She added a hunk of butter, letting it melt in the middle before adding the browned veal. She smiled. Her Bolognese sauce was obviously Mel's favorite because she ordered it at least twice a week. Never the same pasta, but always the same sauce.

It was a good thing lunch had been slow, because Izzy's mind hadn't been on cooking today. She thought about the way Mel had felt in her arms last night, and her body warmed. She was trying to pace herself, but damn, it was hard to be around that woman and not want to kiss her senseless. If she came by again tonight, Izzy promised herself, she would control her urges. But then she thought about the way Mel's green eyes had darkened when their gazes met and knew she wouldn't. She wanted this woman, and she wanted her badly. She would probably get carried away; she just hoped she didn't scare her off.

The day had flown by, and with Nancy's help, Mel had finished her work much earlier than she'd expected. It was just about seven when they pulled into the parking lot of Bella's Trattoria. Mel met Nancy at the door, having made sure they'd driven separate cars this time.

"After you brought me here the other day, I get why you come here so often," Nancy said, pulling the door open and filing in after Mel. "I'd been wondering when I could convince you to bring me back. The food is so fabulous I've been having dreams about it."

"Nancy, I know it's good." Mel chuckled. "But having dreams about it? You must be missing out on something else at home." She gave her a suggestive look. "Has Ann been holding out on you?"

"No. She pretty well keeps those fires burning." She blew out a slow breath "When she's around."

The hostess led them to Mel's usual table, away from the door and close to the fireplace.

"Still not exclusive, huh," Mel said as she sat down.

"Nope. I'm not sure I want to be exclusive. I mean the sex is great, but when we're not having it, she's not really concerned with what I want. We watch the movies she picks out, and we go to her favorite restaurants. Heck. We even eat eggs the way she likes them."

"Have you talked to her about it?"

"I'm not really sure how."

"Just tell her you want your eggs scrambled." Her voice was louder than she expected, and Angie gave her a funny look when she came to take their drink order.

"How do you like your eggs, Angie?" Mel asked.

"My eggs?" she asked, obviously confused.

"Yes, your eggs. How do you like them cooked?"

"I like them over easy. Why?"

"Say your boyfriend served them to you scrambled every time he fixed them. Would you eat them?"

She rocked her head back and forth. "I'd probably eat them the first time because he fixed them for me. But after that, I'd tell him how I like them."

"And if he scrambled them again?"

"I'd take over the egg-making."

Mel raised an eyebrow and shot Nancy a look. "See?" She glanced back at Angie. "Thanks, Angie. We'll have a couple of glasses of the house cabernet and…" She turned to Nancy again. "You want what you had last time?"

She nodded.

"Two orders of linguini Bolognese."

❖

"I need an antipasto tray," Angie blurted as she came through the kitchen door. "The Thomas woman is here again and wants the Bolognese times two."

Izzy's ears perked up. "Is her husband with her?"

"No, thank God. She's with some lady, and she's asking me all kinds of crazy questions."

Izzy peeked out into the dining room. She was with the flirty woman she'd brought in a couple of weeks ago. Nancy, she thought. She'd hoped Mel would come alone so they could spend a little more time together. She ducked back into the kitchen and started to work on their orders.

"How's it going out there?" Izzy asked Angie when she came back in to pick up another party's order.

"Busy!"

"That's good news." She picked up the pasta orders for Mel and Nancy. "I'll deliver these for you so they don't get cold."

"Thanks. Don't forget the cheese."

"I won't." Izzy hadn't always been the chef. In her younger days she'd waited tables in the restaurant while her mother cooked.

"Good evening, ladies," Izzy said as she approached the table. "I have a pasta Bolognese and a pasta Bolognese." She smiled as she slid the plates in front of the women. "Would either of you like Parmesan?"

"I'd love some," Nancy answered.

"Yes, please," Mel said.

She gathered the cheese and grater from the wait stand and grated a generous amount on both dishes.

"Can I get you ladies anything else right now?"

Izzy slipped her hand into her pocket and rubbed Mel's keys between her fingers. "I'm sorry. I left your keys at the house. I can bring them with me tomorrow or...maybe you can come by and get them later tonight?" Izzy could practically hear the wheels turning in Nancy's head.

"I'll probably just get them from you tomorrow. If that's okay?"

"Sure." Izzy smiled. "I'll make sure to bring them. Enjoy your meal." She backed away from the table, then turned and strode back into the kitchen. She probably shouldn't have done that, but Izzy was still a little miffed she'd taken her car this morning without knocking. From the look on Nancy's face, she and Mel were going to have some interesting dinner conversation.

"Oh my God, you and her?" Nancy squealed, barely waiting until Izzy was out of earshot to start peppering Mel with questions.

"Stop. I told you nothing is going on between us."

"Then why does she have your keys?"

"I just had a little too much to drink last night, and she gave me a ride home."

"You closed this place down last night?"

"Something like that." Mel evaded eye contact.

"You have to tell me. Spill. Now."

"I was upset about Jack." She put her fork down. "She saw him at the market down this way yesterday."

"So he's back?"

"Looks that way, but when I called him he said he wouldn't be home for at least another week."

"That bastard! You really need to get rid of him."

"I don't want to talk about that right now."

"Okay then, tell me more about last night. So you got drunk here and she took you home."

"I was actually at her place. She cooked dinner for me."

"I was right all around." Nancy chuckled as she sipped her wine. "Jack's an ass and the lady chef wants you."

"Well, Jack *is* an ass, but I don't think Izzy wants me. I'm a married straight lady to her." She took a bite of bread.

"We both know better than that. You're not going to be married much longer, and just because you've been in a relationship with a man for the past ten years doesn't mean you're straight. I can remember a time when—"

"That was a long time ago, Nance."

"It's never too late to find your soul mate." Nancy nodded toward the kitchen. "She's keeping an eye on you."

Mel glanced toward the kitchen and saw the door close quickly. It was all making sense now. The cognac, the phone number. *God, I'm dense.* It was becoming very apparent Izzy didn't just want to be the friend to whom Mel told her troubles. It seemed she might have been waiting her out for some time now.

Izzy seemed happy to see Mel waiting in front of her house when she got out of her car. "Sorry about tonight. I mentioned I was going to come by and get dinner, and Nancy kind of invited herself."

"That's okay." She unlocked the door and slid it open. "I know you work with her."

"We're also friends. Been that way for a long time."

"So why haven't you been spilling your guts to her instead of me?" Izzy dropped her keys on the entry table along with Mel's set and headed into the kitchen. Mel smiled, noting that Izzy hadn't really left her keys at home. She'd had them in her pocket all along.

"She's been kind of busy lately. She's got a new girlfriend."

"So I'm a fill-in, am I?" Izzy pinched her lips together and winked.

"No, not at all," she said, concerned Izzy was upset. "She likes to tell me what I should do. You just listen."

"You ever go out with her?" She poured two glasses of wine.

Mel hesitated, wondering if it would make a difference to Izzy. "Yes." She accepted the glass of wine Izzy handed her and took a sip.

"Just yes?" Izzy's brows rose, creating a small wrinkle across her forehead.

"It was nothing really. We went out for a while in college." She took another sip of wine. "It didn't work out."

"Why not?"

"She's just not my type."

"What *is* your type?"

"Independent, outgoing, funny." *Someone like you.* She picked up her glass and took a gulp of wine this time.

"Like Jack?"

"I thought so." Mel found herself watching Izzy's movements as she strolled across the room to retrieve the bottle of wine from the counter. Her walk was smooth and confident, way beyond sexy. She swept the length of her with her gaze. Small shoulders led to toned arms. A long torso that wasn't cut with much of a waist. Her pants hung low on her hips, sliding against them slightly as she moved. They looked as though they were hanging on for dear life. All it would take to lose them was one swift tug. *Stop it.* She yanked her gaze away but couldn't help letting it drift back slowly as Izzy turned. She shouldn't have come, but she just couldn't stay away.

"What are you thinking?"

Can't tell you. Mel glanced up to catch Izzy's deep-blue eyes and chugged down the rest of her wine. Izzy offered more, and Mel held her glass out. Izzy filled it with a mere twist of the bottle.

"I was just thinking how sweet you are…I mean to invite me over like this and listen to my ramblings."

Izzy poured the last bit of wine into her own glass and set it on the end table next to Mel, along with her glass. When she slid down on the couch next to her, Mel's pulse went into overdrive.

"I don't really mind, but I wouldn't characterize myself as sweet. If I'd had tickets for tonight's Warriors game, you'd have been out of luck." Her eyes darkened, and when their legs brushed against each other, Mel's stomach fluttered. She had to look away—now. She wasn't ready for this, whatever it was.

"I'd better go." She stood up.

"You just got here." Izzy popped up after her.

"I've got an early meeting. I just wanted to pick up my keys and apologize about earlier."

"You never have to apologize to me for someone else's behavior."

"Thanks for being so understanding." Mel hesitated and then gave her a short hug.

Izzy took the opportunity to wrap her arms around her, pulling her body close. The jolt in Mel's midsection unnerved her. She didn't know what was going on; she'd never had such a strong physical reaction with anyone. Locked in her arms, she felt Izzy's warm breath on her shoulder and the tender touch of her hands roaming up and down her spine. Mel backed up slowly, their cheeks brushing against each other's. When her eyes met the dark pools of blue, she didn't have a chance. Their lips met and her body was on fire. She pushed as Izzy pulled, one warm body against the other. Tongues clashing, the taste of wine mingling between them, everything went hazy. *God, this woman can kiss.* Mel could literally stay here all night like this, just kissing her.

Izzy's hand roamed up her side, and she ripped her mouth away, took a ragged breath trying to settle her body, and Izzy did the same. Izzy's eyes were dark, clear with desire. Mel's pulse raced and she was hot, so hot. She couldn't remember when she'd ever been this turned on. *Get out of here—now.* She weaved as she moved to the door. Her head was spinning, and it wasn't just the wine that made it happen. Again, she was in no shape to drive home.

"Whoa, hang on. Are you all right?" Izzy held her by the shoulders.

"I shouldn't have had that last glass of wine." *I shouldn't have had any wine.*

"Come on. You can stay here tonight." She took her hand and led her down the hallway.

Was that some kind of invitation? The thought sent Mel's nerves jumping. "I can call a cab." She twisted to go back the other way.

"No, you don't." Izzy wrangled her back around. "I have a guest room. You can sleep in there."

"Oh, okay," she said, relieved yet oddly disappointed.

Izzy put her arm around her and took her down the hallway. "The bathroom's here." She pushed open the partially closed door. "And your room is at the end of the hall on the left."

Mel headed to it, glancing into the master bedroom just across the hall before turning in. *Queen-size bed, just enough room for two.* She shook her head. *Stop it right now. You are not a free woman.*

Izzy brought her an over-sized T-shirt with AC/DC WORLD TOUR printed across the front. Looking at the T-shirt, Mel chuckled. "Oh my God! I think I went to this concert."

"I had backstage passes. It was pretty wild as I recall."

"I would've never pegged you for a hard rocker."

"Nor I you," Izzy said with a tilt of her head.

"Well, I guess we'll have to swap stories about it sometime."

"Definitely." Izzy leaned up against the doorjamb. "I'd enjoy learning more about your past."

"I have many things in my past you might not expect."

"As I already found out tonight."

"Oh yeah, sorry." Mel's cheeks warmed. "Just give me a little wine and I share way too much."

"I'll have to remember to buy more wine." Izzy twisted her lip into a half smile and handed her the T-shirt. "Stay as long as you like," she said, and closed the door.

Mel pulled off her clothes and slipped on the T-shirt. She ran her hands across her breasts and down the front of the shirt. There was something very intimate about sleeping in another woman's clothes, especially a woman who made her body sizzle the way Izzy did. She slid between the sheets of the queen-size bed and wondered whether Izzy ever slept here. She pressed the side of her face into the soft down pillow. When she was with Izzy, she didn't have any cares. But tomorrow she would still have to deal with Jack. She pushed the unwelcome reminder from her mind and thought about her beautiful hostess as she quickly fell asleep.

❖

Dana drove by the house, went to the end of the block, turned around, and drove by again. *Who the fuck's car is that? The same one was here last night.* She pulled up to the curb and slowly rolled to a stop. She cupped her hand and squinted to see through the car window on her way to the door.

She knocked on the door and Izzy pulled it open immediately. She must have heard the engine.

"Why are you here?"

"Two nights in a row?" She motioned to the car. "Who is she?" She tried to push her way inside.

"That's none of your business." Izzy stepped outside and closed the door. "Stop driving by my house."

"Are you seeing her just to get back at me?" A hundred random thoughts whipped through her mind. "Is it that brunette from the restaurant? Did you fuck her?"

"Why do you care?"

She moved in close and whispered in Izzy's ear. "Of course I care, baby." She put her arms around her neck, pulled her head down, and kissed her hard. She heard a groan escape Izzy's lips and backed her up against the door, pressing the full length of her body against her.

Izzy yanked her hands from her neck and shifted to the side. "Stop." Her voice was low and ragged. "We are *not* getting back together."

"Please just let me come back home. I know you miss me." She tried uselessly to free her wrists from Izzy's grip. "I bet she can't make you come like I did."

"I can't do this with you again." Dana's shoulder burned as Izzy pulled her to the Mustang parked on the street. "Now go home."

Dana yanked her arm free and slid into the driver's seat. She watched Izzy walk back to the porch and wait for her to leave. "You can fuck every girl in town and you'll never be over me."

Her cell phone rang the special tone for Jess. "Hey."

"Hi. Are you on your way home?"

"Yeah. I'll be there soon. I had to stop and get gas."

"Okay, love you."

"Love you too." She threw the car into gear and hit the gas. The tires squealed and the Mustang fishtailed down the street.

CHAPTER TEN

Izzy lifted her hand to knock on the guest-room door but let it fall to her side instead. She slowly turned the doorknob and cracked the door slightly. Mel lay on her side, dark hair mussed around her face, lips partially open. Almost the same position she was in the night before when she'd checked to see if Dana's rant had woken her. She watched her for a few minutes before she pulled the door closed and moved on down the hall to the kitchen.

She set the coffee next to the French press, then scribbled a couple of words on a notepad and left it in the middle of the counter. She would pick up a cup on the way into the city. She needed to get out of there as quickly as possible. Izzy didn't know if she had the strength to resist Mel this morning.

Izzy drove up Mount Tamalpais and parked, then sat in her Jeep with the windows rolled down and watched the sunrise. The mountains were exceptionally beautiful today. Mount Tam, in all its glory, peaked majestically above the rest of the landscape. Sprinkled with forests of redwood, fir, and eucalyptus, it seemed to be permanently green. She took in a deep breath, a hint of eucalyptus floating into her nose. The crisp, unique scent made it known that the mountain was a living sliver of beauty between the ocean and the densely populated region of Mill Valley.

Last night had been perfect until Dana showed up. Izzy's body had betrayed her, making it clear the attraction was still very much there. When Dana had kissed her, she'd had to create some much-needed space between them to keep it from taking over. The kiss had been hard. Demanding. Tumultuous. Just as their relationship had been. She was not going back there again.

On the other hand, Mel's kiss lit every one of her nerve endings. The sensation blazing through her system was new; she'd never felt something so intense before. She'd gone further than she'd planned last night, but she couldn't resist the chance to feel Mel's soft body pressed against hers. When she'd stroked her back, she'd felt Mel's breath catch. In her wildest dreams, she'd never imagined the kiss that came next. Soft, slow, and deep, Izzy had become lost in it, but then Mel was out of her arms as quickly as she'd fallen into them. She didn't care if she was gay or straight. Izzy wanted to do unspeakable things to her body, wake up next to her, and do them all over again. She shook her head. It was way too soon for that.

Torture. That's what it is. Pure torture. She should keep as far away from Mel Thomas as she could. Instead, she'd asked her to stay just a few steps across the hall. *What am I gonna to do about this?* She fired the engine and drove back down the mountain.

Izzy reached into her mother's refrigerator and took out a carton of eggs. "You want pancakes this morning, Momma?"

"No. Just eggs. I'm getting a little thick in the middle."

"Ah, Momma. You've never been thick in your life."

"That's what Mary Elizabeth says. She thinks I should put on a few pounds." She waved her finger in the air. "I still have eyes. I can see in the mirror."

"This Mary Elizabeth seems pretty observant. Maybe I should meet her." She cracked the eggs and dropped them into the pan.

"You may be too late. I think she may have found someone. She's seemed very happy lately."

"Well, then maybe it just wasn't meant to be." She slid a plate of eggs and toast in front of her mother and plated another for herself. "You want another cup of coffee?"

"Just a little warm-up, dear."

She refilled her mother's cup as well as her own. "So, tell me. Where did you meet your friend Mary Elizabeth?"

"At the community center."

"Oh? What was she doing there?"

"She and another woman came around with the director and took some pictures. She stayed and asked some of us for our opinion of the place during lunch."

"Like an interview for the newspaper?"

"Yes, like that."

"So, how did she happen to take such a liking to you?"

"Just lucky, I guess. She said she's been to the restaurant a few times, and the food is always delicious."

"You told her about the restaurant?"

"Of course, dear. Why wouldn't I? I'm very proud of what you've done with it."

"Bella, you can't just go telling strangers all about your business."

"She's not a stranger, Isabel. I've known her for months."

"Momma, you just have to be careful. I don't want anyone taking advantage of you."

"Don't worry, dear. She's a nice girl. She would never do anything to hurt me."

Izzy just shook her head. Bella had no idea how charming people could be when they were conning someone. "I'd still like to meet her." Izzy wasn't going to let up on meeting this Mary Elizabeth. She needed to know who this woman was who might be influencing her mother. "Do you remember her last name?"

"I'm not sure, dear. You can ask her yourself, if you want to come back later. She's coming by for a visit this afternoon."

"Okay. Call me when she gets here, and I'll come over." Izzy hoped it would be before the dinner crowd, so she could break away for a little while. Once she found out her last name, it might be worth a Google search to check her out.

Izzy rinsed the dishes and loaded them into the dishwasher. "I've got to get moving. I need to go to the market." Izzy bent down and kissed her mother on the cheek.

"Okay, dear. Be careful."

"I will. Don't forget to call me this afternoon."

Izzy threw her Jeep into park and ran around the back to get the groceries. She'd spent too long at her mother's and had totally underestimated her time at the market this morning. She rushed through the back door of the restaurant and dropped everything on the prep table. "Did you start the sauce?"

"Of course I started the sauce. It's after ten. Where have you been?" Tony didn't sound happy.

"I went by and fixed Mom some breakfast before I went to the market."

"How is she?" Tony took the bag of groceries and put them in the refrigerator.

"I'm worried. Apparently, she has a new friend visiting her a couple times a week."

"When did that start?"

"According to her, it's been going on for some time now."

"I had no idea."

"Maybe you would if you stopped by and saw her once in a while." She knew that was a low blow, considering their strained relationship. Tony's relationship with Bella mirrored that of Izzy and her father's minus the gay issue.

"Don't start, Iz."

"She's still your mother." She glanced over her shoulder at Tony, who had a funny look on his face and nodded toward the door. "What?" She whipped her head around and saw Mel standing in the doorway, gorgeous as always. She wore a sleeveless, black button-up blouse matched with gray-cuffed dress pants. "Hey. What are you doing here?"

"You were gone when I got up."

"I went to see my mother. I thought I'd let you sleep in."

Tony chuckled, and Izzy pulled her aside out of earshot. "Besides, you seemed so peaceful. I didn't want to wake you. Did you find the fruit in the fridge?"

"Yes." She smiled. "And the coffee too. Thanks."

"Good. I wasn't sure if you knew how to use a French press."

"If you keep treating me like this, I'm going to want to move in." Her cheeks flushed as though she'd suddenly realized what she'd said. "Listen, about last night. I'm sorry you had to sit through all my sad stories again."

"They weren't all sad." Izzy lifted her chin with a finger. "We had a couple of laughs, didn't we?"

"After the third glass of wine."

"Now we know where to start next time."

"Or when to stop."

"We didn't have to stop." Izzy jerked her lip up to one side.

A blush rushed across Mel's face, and Izzy's insides flipped. She didn't know how anyone, man or woman, could ignore a woman as vibrant and beautiful as Mel Thomas.

"I don't have to work late tonight."

"You coming by for dinner?"

"Can I eat in here...with you?"

"I'll reserve you a stool."

Mel's lips tipped up. "Then I'll see you tonight."

She nodded and Mel turned. She couldn't help but check out her ass as she strolled out the door. Her slacks hung perfectly from her flawlessly rounded rear.

"Late because of Mom, huh?" Tony gave her a sly grin. "Sounds like you had a late night with your new lady."

"She's just a friend, Tony."

"Oh?"

"We had a couple glasses of wine and talked. That's all." Her mind wandered to the kiss they'd shared.

"A friend today, but maybe something else tomorrow, eh?"

"She's married." She hung her jacket on the hook and slipped on a royal-blue chef's coat. *Straight and married.*

"And H.O.T."

"Shut up, Tony." She tossed a dishtowel at him. But he was right about that. She was definitely hot—and after last night, Izzy wasn't really sure about the straight part. "She just needs a friend right now."

"You'd better remember that."

"Don't worry. I will." *I've been reminding myself every minute.*

"I suppose you'll want to take off early tonight."

"No, but Mom's supposed to call me when her friend comes over, so I'll need to step out to go meet her."

❖

Mel parked her car in the lot. Strolling along the sidewalk, she gazed into the distance, not having the slightest twinge of guilt for being late this morning. She'd put in enough twelve-hour days to justify taking the morning off. As she waved at the security guard, she glanced at the clock on the wall above his desk. It was almost noon.

Her nights with Izzy had somehow lightened the load she'd been carrying for the past year. Her problems with Jack didn't seem so important now. If the man didn't love her anymore, why should she waste her time and energy on him? Izzy was right. Mel needed to focus on herself for a while. Looking out for number one had just moved to the top of her to-do list.

Nancy met her at the door. "Where have you been?" Her tone was low, yet urgent.

"I overslept."

"You what?" She pulled at her shoulder. "You missed the meeting with Perry Electronics this morning, and all you can say is I overslept?"

"You handled it, didn't you?"

"Well, yes."

Mel smiled. "Thanks for covering for me."

"What the hell is wrong with you? Why are you so happy?" Her eyes widened. "Did you get laid last night?"

"Jack hasn't come home yet. Besides, that rarely happens anymore."

Nancy's expression was thoughtful. "Then what happened this morning?"

"I told you. I overslept." Mel held her tongue. "I'll have all the details finalized by this evening." She smiled. It didn't even bother her that she was going to have to work a little late. She would see Izzy afterward and...and what?

"Great. After that, you can pick up Rick and discuss the changes he wants done to his pages. I told him you'd take him to dinner. He's expecting you around seven."

"I thought he wasn't going to be here until next week?"

"He had a break in filming."

"Can't you take him to dinner?"

"I can't tonight. I already have plans. Besides, he doesn't want to go to dinner with me."

"What if I have plans?" She didn't try to hide her irritation as she rounded the corner and went into her office.

Nancy eyed her suspiciously. "You did get laid."

"I did not."

"So, then what?" Nancy said, closing the door.

"I went by Izzy's house last night."

"After we had dinner?" Nancy's eyes widened. "I knew something was going on with you two."

Mel smiled and felt the burn as it rushed over her cheeks. "We've been kind of hanging out together the last few nights."

"Oh, my God. I never thought I'd see the day when straight-laced Mel Thomas fell for another woman." The giddiness in her voice was as plain as the smile on her face.

"I wouldn't say I'm falling for her. I just like her, that's all."

"Whatever you say."

"Knock it off, Nance. She's a good listener." *And she makes me feel good about myself.*

"And I'm not."

"Between bits about your own life crisis."

"Sorry. I guess my life has been a little crazy lately. I guess I can go to dinner with Rick, but he's not going to like it."

"No worries. I'll go. Just let him know I'll pick him up in the usual place."

"You want to get a drink later?"

"Can't. I have plans."

"With who?"

Mel smiled and shook her head.

"Your new lady friend?" Nancy asked in a sultry tone. "And you said you weren't into women."

Mel let out a short breath. "You're making way too much of this, Nancy."

"So then, tell me. What makes her so special?"

"I don't know." That wasn't a question she'd asked herself, but Izzy *was* something special. "We just seem to click. She gets me, you know?"

"Maybe that's what she wants?"

Mel drew her eyebrows together.

"To get you."

"Maybe she does." She winked. "It's nice to have a little attention once in a while, even if it's from a woman. Especially a sexy, beautiful one, who literally cooks my socks off." She flopped down into the chair behind her desk. "Now, if you don't mind, I have work to do."

"You're not getting off that easy. Sooner or later you're going to have to spill."

"Not today. Now go." She lifted her hand and shooed her away. "And close the door on your way out."

She picked up the phone and first cancelled her lunch plans with Bella and then dialed Izzy's cell number. No answer, just voice mail. She left an apology about canceling dinner, explaining about Rick, and said she'd be bringing him to the restaurant for dinner. There was no way she could blow him off. Rick had been one of her first clients when she'd started working independently. They'd known each other since they were kids. She'd taken over as his publicist and designed his website when he was still trying to launch his acting career.

Somehow, between the B movies and his skyrocketing to stardom, his agent had persuaded him to leave her and go with a competitor instead. Bigger always meant better, according to the money-hungry go-between. She guessed fate was looking out for her, because the other agency had botched the new site, and Rick had insisted they bring her in as a consultant to fix it or he was walking. That didn't come cheap either.

❖

Mel pulled up to the gate and punched in the code. It would be good to see Rick's parents again. She hadn't seen them since he was in town the last time, which was a few months ago. She pulled into the circle drive and went to the door. It pulled open almost immediately, and Rick was waiting for her with a huge grin.

"Hey, Mellie." He grabbed her up into a bear hug. "I've missed you."

"I've missed you too." She squeezed him back. "Where are your mom and dad?"

"They're out on a date night."

"A date night? Seriously?"

"Yeah." His smile widened. "Apparently they've decided their life has grown too boring. Now they go out dancing a few times a week." He grabbed her, pulled her close, and danced her around the room.

She chuckled. "At least someone's taking the bull by the horns."

He swung her out of his arms, and she spun briefly. "Just let me run upstairs and get my jacket."

"I'll meet you in the car."

Mel sat in the car tapping the steering wheel nervously as she waited in front of the house. "Come on, Rick, hurry up. I've got a— what do I have tonight?" She smiled. "A date with Izzy, that's what I have." She started the car when she saw him saunter out.

"Where are we going?" Rick asked as he slid into the passenger seat.

"To my favorite Italian restaurant. The one I told you about on the phone."

"The food's good?" He raised a brow, giving her a skeptical look.

"The very best." And she wasn't just saying that because she was partial to the chef.

"I'll be the judge of that," he said in a teasing tone.

But Mel knew he wasn't kidding, Rick was a hard sell. When she'd first started her business, it had taken a lot of convincing for him to let her design and maintain his website. In the end, Rick knew he'd gotten the good end of the deal.

Mel pulled into the restaurant lot and searched for a parking space. It was busier than usual for a weeknight. She hoped they could get a table since she hadn't thought to make a reservation. She checked in with the hostess, who said there was about a fifteen-minute wait. The two of them elected to get a drink at the bar rather than wait by the door.

❖

"Looks like your friend is back again." Angie motioned to the dining room.

"She's supposed to eat back here," Izzy said.

"She's not alone, sis. They both can't eat in the kitchen. We're gonna get a code violation."

"What?" This morning, Mel hadn't said anything about bringing anyone with her. She pushed the door open a crack and stole a look at the dining room. Seeing the tall, handsome man seated across from Mel, her gut twisted. "Who the hell is that?"

"It's Rick Daniels," Angie shot back. "You know. The movie star," she added when Izzy gave her a blank stare.

"Rick Daniels?" She let the door swing closed.

"Oh my God, Iz. I can't believe you don't know who he is. He's only one of the hottest movie stars ever. He grew up right here in the Bay area." She chuckled. "You really need to get out more."

"Maybe I do." She had no idea what was going on. Mel knew she was expecting only her, so why would she bring this dude along? "Bring their order to me, okay?"

"Here." Angie handed her the ticket. Izzy glanced at it and reached for the red-pepper flakes. Mel's new Casanova was going to get a helluva tongue burn tonight.

❖

The food was excellent, as usual, but Izzy hadn't come to the table, and Mel hadn't seen her look out the door once. The place was busy, but Mel thought she'd at least poke her head out of the kitchen and give her a wave. Had she done something wrong last night? She shouldn't have kissed her, and she honestly didn't know why she had. Well, that was a lie. She'd kissed her because each and every one of her nerve endings had fired when Izzy hugged her.

Mel hated canceling on her for dinner tonight and hadn't had the chance to sneak back and apologize in person. Hopefully she hadn't been too disappointed when she got the message. *Oh, God, maybe she wasn't disappointed. Maybe she was relieved.* She thought about last night and her body warmed. *No, it had to be disappointment.*

Even though it was just a casual meal in the kitchen, it was all Mel had thought about since she'd left her this morning. She was looking forward to seeing Izzy again—alone. But this detour wasn't about her; it was about work and couldn't be avoided. Panic shuddered through her. She sounded just like Jack and his excuses. She knew how it felt to be on the other end of that statement and didn't want Izzy to think she'd been second choice tonight. She flopped her napkin on the table and pushed her chair back.

"Will you excuse me a minute?" Mel slid out of her chair.

"Are you going to see the chef?"

"After the ladies' room."

"Let her know that I agree with you. She *is* the best Italian chef in town."

"I will." She gave him a soft smile.

Izzy startled when Mel touched her on the shoulder. "Hey." Mel let her hand drift down her back.

"Hey," Izzy said, without turning to make eye contact. "I see you're getting right back out there."

"What?" Mel clenched her fingers as her hand left Izzy's back. Izzy glanced at her. "A movie star, yet. *"*

Mel let out a chuckle. "You didn't get my message, did you?"

"Message? What message?" She pulled her cell phone from her pocket and hit the voice-mail button. Mel's voice rang through the speaker explaining how she had to take her client to dinner. "He's a client?"

Mel nodded. "We had to go over some changes to his website." She blurted out a laugh. "I'm sorry, Izzy, but you should see the look on your face."

"I thought he was your date."

"You thought I was dating Rick Daniels?" She gasped.

"Yeah, why not? You're a beautiful woman."

"You think so?"

"Absolutely." Mel felt the heat rise in her cheeks. She turned away, relieved when Izzy peeked into the dining room. "I hope his dinner wasn't too spicy."

"Was it spicy?"

"The man's taste buds must be dead. I put enough red pepper in the sauce to burn a hole in his tongue."

"Really? I did notice the four glasses of water he drank." She moved closer to whisper in her ear. "For a minute there, I thought your sister was going to bring the pitcher and pull up a chair." Her lip jerked up into a smile. "And for your information, he's not interested in me. He likes his women hot, just like his food."

"That's what had me worried." Their eyes met and Izzy held her gaze. There it was again. *Zing!*

Mel broke eye contact and cleared her throat. "Listen. I have to take Rick to his house. Is it all right if I come back after I drop him off?"

"Sure."

Mel gave her a light kiss on the cheek. "Thank you."

"What was that for?"

"For impressing Rick in spite of trying to fry his taste buds." She slid her hand down Izzy's arm. "And for being so good to me."

"Well, why don't you get back out there? I'll send him out a complimentary plate of cannoli."

"You don't have to do that. This dinner is a business expense."

"It would be my pleasure." She grinned. "After all, I did just try to burn the man's mouth."

❖

Izzy looked up as Mel led Rick into the kitchen.

"Rick Daniels, this is Izzy Calabrese. The best Italian chef in town."

Tony cleared his throat loudly, and Mel smiled. "Oh, and this is Tony. He's pretty good too."

He took her hand between his. "I didn't believe her until I tasted your Shrimp Diablo."

"I hope it was to your liking."

"It was magnificent."

Definitely dead taste buds.

"Well, we'd better get going." Mel motioned him toward the door.

"You want to go someplace for a drink?"

"Oh." Mel seemed surprised that he asked. "I can't tonight. Too much work to do on that website of yours." She shot Izzy a smile. "I can drop you somewhere if you'd like."

"There's a nice little bar at the hotel my agent uses when he's in town. How about you have one drink?"

"I really shouldn't."

"You can't leave me there alone. The paparazzi will be all over me."

"And you think I want my picture plastered across every rag in town?"

"It's good publicity. You'll have every star in town calling."

She pinched her lips together. "Okay, one drink."

"Have fun," Izzy said.

Mel turned momentarily and mouthed, "I'll be back." She pointed at her watch and held up one finger.

Izzy flinched when Rick put his hand on the small of Mel's back to guide her through the restaurant.

❖

Mel couldn't wait to get out of the bar and back to Bella's. The bar was loud and crowded. She didn't think they'd gotten through a whole conversation without being interrupted by a fan or someone in the business who wanted a minute of Rick's time. She was delighted when he'd taken an interest in someone else and she was able to sneak away.

She tugged at the restaurant door, but it was locked. She could clearly hear music coming from inside so she walked around to the back. The door was open, so Mel let herself in. She followed the sound of the music into the dining room, slipped just inside, and leaned against the wall. All of the tables had been moved out of the center, and the restaurant crew was dancing around the dining room to some classic rock song. Angie was with Dougie, and Gio was with a girl Mel didn't recognize. She scanned the rest of the room and immediately zoned in on Izzy, dancing alone by the bar. Mel was content just to stand back and watch her as her hips swayed back and forth to the beat.

Angie squealed when she spotted Mel. "Come on. Dance with us." She grabbed Mel's hand, pulled her out into the middle of the room, and began dancing with her. "Come on. sis. Let's dance."

"Yeah. Come on, Iz." The guys cheered, and Carlos switched out with Angie.

"No. I'm good right here." She leaned up against the bar and smiled.

Mel could see Izzy's gaze roll over her body like a slow burn. Suddenly she felt like she was dancing just for her. Mel felt somebody come up behind her. Relief washed over her when Izzy bolted across the room and pulled her from between Carlos and Miguel. She hadn't planned on being sandwiched between the two of them.

"No, you don't, boys." She swung Mel around into her arms. "Sorry about that. They're harmless, but they get carried away sometimes." Izzy pulled her close and whispered in her ear, "I didn't think you wanted Miguel grinding up against your ass."

"Grinding…no." Mel smiled, thinking she would much rather it would have been Izzy.

"This generation has no boundaries."

"They do that even if they don't know each other?"

"They do it especially if they don't know each other." Izzy shoved her out, twirled her under her arm, and pulled her back in close. "Just stick with me, beautiful. I'll keep you safe." She gave her a wink and released her when the song ended. "All right, everybody. Let's get something to eat and get outta here."

They all headed into the kitchen, and Angie scooted in next to Mel. "What happened to your hot date?"

"Not a date. A client."

"Oh, so you can introduce me?"

"I'm right here," Dougie said.

"I'm not sure you'd like the exposure." She thought about the mob scene at the hotel. All of the flashes had practically blinded her. "I only had one drink with him, and there must have been a hundred pictures taken."

Mel peeked over Izzy's shoulder into the pan. "What're you cooking?"

"Linguine Bolognese."

"My favorite." She reached over and stole a string of pasta. "I just can't get enough of it." She held it up and let it trail into her mouth. "You knew that though, didn't you?"

Izzy bit her bottom lip and nodded. "Hey, Carlos. Throw this into the warmer for me?" She tossed her sous chef a loaf of bread.

Turning to Miguel, Carlos grinned and spoke to him in Spanish. "The pretty lady is back again tonight. Maybe I should ask her out for a drink."

"Or better yet, take her home for one," Miguel responded.

Noting Mel's lack of reaction to the comment, Izzy responded in the same language. "Knock it off, Carlos."

"But she has such a nice—"

"I said stop." Izzy glanced at Mel as she reached up to get a glass. "No one's going to ask her out."

"Ohhh. I think the boss lady is calling dibs on this one, Miguel." He laughed. "You see the glimmer in her eye?"

"I see it. Maybe she's going to try and turn the straight lady." Miguel chuckled.

"Never mind what I'm going to do." She wadded up a towel and threw it at Carlos. "Go have a smoke or something." She glanced over at Mel and smiled.

"If it doesn't work out, let me know," Carlos said, giving her a huge grin as he took his pack of cigarettes from the top of the Sub-Zero and headed out back.

"Not a chance in hell, Carlos." She glanced back at Mel again. *I'm going to do my best to keep this one around.*

"What were they talking about?" Mel set the glasses on the table and pulled the cork from a bottle of red wine.

"He wants to take Saturday off. He was giving me grief because I told him no. I'm taking it off."

"Oh? What are you doing on Saturday?"

"I don't know yet. You have something in mind?"

Mel grinned. "Now that was a set-up if I've ever heard one."

Izzy took off her royal-blue chef's coat and leaned back against the counter. Mel handed her a glass of wine and propped herself next to her.

"You want to come over to the house? I could fix us a lunch cooler, and we could hang out at the beach for a while."

"How about we go for a hike first?" Mel took a sip of her wine.

"Exercise on my day off?" Izzy widened her eyes and rocked her head back and forth comically. "Sounds exhausting."

"After all the carbs you've been feeding me, this body needs some activity." She nudged her with her shoulder. "Come on, just a short one. It'll be fun."

"Okay, as long as you promise it'll be short. Then when we get back we can hit the beach." Izzy couldn't help but smile at the thought of the many other calorie-burning activities she would love to experience with her, but hiking would do for now.

CHAPTER ELEVEN

Izzy snapped the blanket and spread it out on the sand before unfolding the beach chairs and setting them side by side, facing the water. She couldn't wait to sit her tired butt down; her calves were killing her.

Mel had failed to mention the little hike she planned to take her on was up and down the Dipsea Steep on Mount Tam. It was short, less than four miles; she had to give her that. But it wasn't for beginners. It went from trail to stairs to trail to more stairs. However, the beautiful view had made it all worth it.

"I'm exhausted." Izzy flopped into a chair.

"Oh, come on. It wasn't that bad," Mel said, her smile tinged with a bit of a frown.

"Maybe not for you, but my legs feel like spaghetti." She stretched them out in front of her. "I've got a knot right here." She bent her leg and winced as she pushed her thumb into the center of her calf.

"Let me see." Mel squatted next to her and kneaded it with her fingers. "Take a nice hot bath later, and you'll feel better."

"Can't do that. My tub's out of commission."

"Your tub doesn't work?" A mix of surprise and disappointment rang in Mel's voice.

"Something's wrong with the jets. The motor whines, but they don't blow. It was like that when I moved in, and I just haven't gotten around to having it fixed."

"I could never live without a tub." She pressed a thumb deep into Izzy's thigh, and she squirmed. "Even if the beach was my backyard, I'd have to fix it."

"Well, you can still shower."

"That's true. Then I can take a bath when I get home."

"So, you would shower here and still go home and take a bath?"

"Probably." Mel closed her eyes and took in a deep breath. "A nice glass of wine, a couple of candles, and a good book. It's the only time I get to really relax."

The look of contentment on Mel's face entranced Izzy. "Wow. I never thought taking a bath could sound so good. I'll have to try it sometime."

"You can borrow mine anytime."

Izzy jerked her lip up into a twisted grin. "I knew there were perks to hanging out with you. Kind of odd ones, but perks nonetheless." She laughed and scanned the beach. Her neighbor Dolores was sitting in the sand at the edge of the water watching her grandkids ride the small, rippling waves to shore. She watched a couple of guys throw a football back and forth. One of them threw it way long. As she watched the other guy run after it, she saw an all-too-familiar face.

"Shit," she said under her breath.

"Does that hurt?" Mel said, easing up a little on her leg.

"No."

Mel followed her gaze down the beach to the beautiful blonde tossing a beach ball around with two little boys. It was the woman from the restaurant a few weeks before. *She's your girlfriend. You take care of her.* Tony's words flashed from her memory. Mel had to know who she was. "Who is she?"

"My ex."

Mel snapped her head around to get a better look. "She has kids?"

"Her sister's." She smiled.

Izzy flipped open the cooler. They'd stopped at the corner store on the way back from their hike and picked up a couple of sandwiches, some fruit, and drinks. Izzy tried to slip in some chips a couple of times, but Mel made her put them back.

"You want a sandwich?"

"Just half." She nodded, moving into the chair next to her. "How about a water too?"

Izzy handed her a bottle of water and half a sandwich, taking the rest for herself. Keeping one eye on Dana, Izzy sat back in her chair and nibbled on her sandwich.

"Your ex, huh," Mel said softly as she popped a grape into her mouth. "Were you in love with her?"

Izzy shifted her gaze to Mel and then to the ocean. "I thought so."

"I'm sorry, Izzy." She touched her hand lightly. "Do you want to go back to the house?"

"Not a chance. I'll be damned if I'll let her run me off my own beach."

"Do you think she'll bother us?"

"Oh, she'll bother us all right." Izzy stiffened. "Here she comes now."

"Come here." Mel motioned with her fingers. "You've got something on your face." She leaned close and gently brushed her thumb across Izzy's cheek before touching her lips lightly with hers. Soft and warm, Mel's lips parted slightly. Izzy took the opportunity to dip her tongue inside. It was met by another—exploring, touching, baiting. Everything got a little fuzzy for Izzy at that point, and she let out a quiet groan. She tore her mouth away when she heard an obvious cough behind them, and just like that, it was over. Looking breathless, Mel gave her a long, mystified look before she turned her attention to Dana.

"Hello, Izzy."

"What are you doing here?" Izzy said, using her hand to shield her eyes from the sun.

"The kids wanted to come to the beach." She threw her the usual flirty smile.

"You should've picked another one."

Dana ignored Izzy's comment. "I haven't seen you out here in a while."

"I've been busy."

"I can see that." She turned her attention to Mel. "Who's this?"

"Oh, this is—"

"Mel Thomas." Mel stood up and extended her hand. "And you are?"

"Dana Monroe." She shook Mel's hand. "You look familiar. Have we met?"

Mel shook her head. "I don't think so."

Dana tilted her head, studying her.

"How do you know Izzy?" Mel asked.

"She and I are partners," Dana said.

"Oh." Mel's brows furrowed, and her head snapped back to Izzy. "She owns half of Bella's?"

"No. Another restaurant venture we started together," Dana said, without giving Izzy a chance to answer.

"Oh. Well, I'm sure I haven't been there." Mel smiled at Izzy. "I'm pretty partial to Bella's these days." She took off her Ray-Ban sunglasses and dropped them onto the blanket. "I think I'll go for a swim and let you two talk."

"You don't have to go," Izzy said, popping up and clasping Mel's elbow. She was much more interested in discussing that kiss than talking to Dana.

"It's all right. I need to cool off anyway." Mel gave her a wink and jogged to the water.

When Mel reached the waves, she dove in headfirst, letting the icy Pacific rush over her. *Well, shit. Why did I do that?* She swam out a few yards where she could still stand and turned to watch Izzy and Dana on the beach. The jealous twinge had hit her so suddenly, she couldn't control it. Mel could see right away Dana wasn't finished with Izzy. *Why didn't she just come right out and say it?* Her stomach knotted at the thought of that woman worming her way back into Izzy's life. *This is crazy. Who am I to be jealous of Izzy? No one, that's who. She's just my friend.* But a few moments ago, when Izzy's warm tongue had brushed across her lips and dipped into her mouth, Mel had not only let it happen, but she'd enjoyed it. She had shuddered, feeling a surprisingly wonderful tingle. Mel didn't know what to think. She'd kissed Izzy to send Izzy's ex a message, never expecting the kiss to excite her the way it did. Her heart raced at the memory, and she wanted to do it again.

She watched Dana on the beach as they talked. Tall, long blond hair, great legs. No wonder Izzy had fallen for her. Their body language was on opposite ends of the spectrum. Dana kept moving in closer, but Izzy kept her arms crossed firmly across her chest, rebuffing any attempt Dana made to touch her. The contrast between them was striking: Izzy with her dark hair and complexion, Dana with her blond hair and fair skin. They probably drew plenty of attention when they were together. She saw Dana reach up and touch Izzy's face and had to close her eyes. Leaning back, she slipped under the surf. She couldn't watch the woman get any closer.

❖

What the hell was that? Izzy touched her lips with her fingers and tried to douse the raging inferno Mel had ignited. She watched her walk down the beach, hips swaying back and forth in a cute little royal-blue bikini. She dove into the water while Izzy stood stunned, wondering why Mel had kissed her like that. For whatever reason, she *had* kissed her, and it sent a jolt through her that was still lingering low in her belly. She hadn't felt that in a very long time. Did Mel really know whether she was straight or not? But she was still married.

"Hello. I'm over here." Dana waved a hand in front of Izzy's face. "I see you've replaced me with a beauty."

"Can't say I regret it."

"Since when do you have time to hang out on the beach?"

"Since I met her." She watched Mel floating in the water.

Dana glanced at Mel and then back at Izzy. "Maybe if you'd had a little more time when we were together, we—"

"Don't put that on me, Dana. You made your choice." She glanced over Dana's shoulder. "By the way, where is Jess?"

"She's at the restaurant. I needed a break."

Like I didn't know that was going to happen. "Not getting what you need from her? I thought you were looking a little thin." Izzy smiled in satisfaction. "Is it just you and the boys today?" She changed the subject, not wanting to rehash their whole breakup.

"My sister is over there under the umbrella." Dana motioned down the beach.

"They sure have grown. How are they?"

She turned her head and glanced behind her. "Ask them yourself." Josh and Jamie plodded across the sand. "Aunt Izzy."

"Hi, guys. How are my favorite boys?" She knelt down and scooped each of them into an arm for a hug.

"Can you play with us?"

"I'm afraid not today, guys. Izzy is busy playing with her new friend," Dana said, her jealousy ringing through.

Izzy glanced up and shot her an evil look. "We'll have to do it another time."

"When?" they said in unison.

"I don't know. I'll check my schedule and let your mom know."

"Oh-kay." The disappointment in their little voices tore Izzy up.

"Go on back over to your mom, boys." Dana swatted them lightly on their butts. "I'll be right there."

"I really miss those guys." Izzy stood up and gave Dana's sister, Tracy, a wave as she watched them run back to her.

"You should come over and see them sometime. They miss you." She touched Izzy's cheek. "I miss you."

"We're done, Dana." Izzy removed her hand. "How many times do I have to tell you?"

"Can you honestly tell me you don't think about me anymore?"

"As a matter of fact, I don't." She watched Mel floating in the surf. "She's all I think about now." She wasn't lying about that. She pulled her shorts from her hips. "Now if you don't mind, I'm going for a swim."

When Mel felt the hands under her back, she ripped open her eyes and let her weight drop.

"Sorry. I didn't mean to surprise you," Izzy said.

"No. I'm sorry. I surprised you before, didn't I?" *Kind of surprised myself too.*

"Little bit." She gave her a nod, her dark hair slicked back from the water.

"I don't really do that. I mean…kiss women I barely know. I just thought it might be easier to get rid of her if she thought you were involved."

"I think she got the message, and it certainly took my mind off her." She smiled lightly.

Mel sank into those deep-blue eyes and got that feeling again. Izzy leaned down and brushed her lips softly against Mel's. The jolt zipped through her and made her knees weak. She slid her hands up to capture Izzy's face before plunging herself full into the kiss. Her mouth opened freely as Izzy's tongue slipped between her lips. She let out a gasp when Izzy slipped her arms around her waist and the length of their bodies met. Her heart thundered so loudly she barely heard the laughter from some teenagers as they swam by. *What the hell am I doing?* She ripped her mouth away and felt Izzy's uneven breath on her lips. God, she wanted more, so much more. She shuddered and dropped down under the water. *Get control of yourself, Mel.*

She raked her hair back as she emerged. "I'm so sorry. I don't know what's come over me." She floated with her shoulders just below the surface to keep some distance between them.

"No worries." Izzy dropped down next to her and searched for her hand, then laced their fingers together and squeezed. "Thanks for being concerned about me."

"You're welcome." *Jesus, Izzy. I should be thanking you.* She'd never been kissed like that before.

After an awkward silence, Izzy stood and gazed back to shore, where Tracy was playing with the boys in the shallow water.

"You okay?" Mel asked.

When Izzy's eyes started to well, Mel planted her feet in the sand and took her in her arms. It was obvious she still had feelings for her ex. Why else would she have remained partners with her?

"I loved those boys like they were my own. Now, because of her, I can't see them anymore," Izzy mumbled into her shoulder.

Mel let out a quick breath as relief shot through her. So, it wasn't about Dana after all.

"Why don't you ask her sister if you can take them to the zoo or something?"

"Dana would never let that happen."

Mel took her face in her hands, wiping the tears away with her thumbs. "They're not her kids. Maybe she'd at least let them come hang out with you at the beach once in a while."

"I doubt it. Dana and Tracy are pretty tight."

"Couldn't hurt to try."

Izzy glanced over at the blanket where Dana was sitting.

"Go on. Do it now while Tracy's in the water with the boys."

Mel watched Izzy as she swam to shore and headed for Dana's sister before she got out of the water and skittered across the hot sand to their own spot on the beach. She watched Izzy splash down next to Tracy and the boys in the shallow water before she put her sunglasses on and leaned back into the chair.

❖

Dana's temper soared as she watched Izzy and the beautiful brunette in the water. Izzy had never taken a Saturday off when they were together. She was going to pay for replacing her so soon after their breakup. She took her cell phone from her bag and changed the setting to block her caller ID. Then she looked up the number of the *San Francisco Examiner* on her smartphone and pressed the call button in the listing.

"Good morning. *Examiner*. This is Karen. Can I help you?" Who said it was a good morning? The woman was so cheerful, she wanted to scream.

"Hello, yes, Karen. I need to speak with Jonathan, the food critic, please." She waved at Tracy and the boys in the water while the line rang through.

The receptionist picked up again. "He's not answering, ma'am. Would you like to leave a message?"

"Yes, I would. Tell him he may want to dine at Bella's Trattoria this evening. The head chef has been out for a couple of days, and the sous chef is filling in for her."

"I'll give him the message when he checks in."

"No, wait. Could you please call him and let him know?"

"That's not our usual process."

"I'll be happy to give you a few complimentary meals at Gustoso for your trouble."

The woman didn't answer right away, and Dana worried he wouldn't get the message.

"I'll see what I can do."

"Thanks so much, Karen. What is your last name?"

"Anderson."

"Great. I'll leave your name with the hostess at Gustoso. You can come anytime."

❖

Mel hoped Tracy would have her children's best interest at heart and agree to let Izzy visit them now and then. If those boys loved Izzy as much as she loved them, what could possibly be wrong with letting her see them?

The warmth of the sun put Mel into a sleepy daze, and she closed her eyes.

She felt the softness of Izzy's lips brush hers and opened her eyes. It was already dark, and they were alone on the beach. Her lips continued down her neck to the valley between her breasts. She felt the gentle touch of her fingertips as they brushed across the fabric covering her breast, circling in on her taut nipple. They walked their way across her belly to the ridge of her bikini. She shuddered as they dipped beneath it.

"Hey, you awake?" Izzy's voice rang through her dream, and Mel shot forward in her chair, hoping Izzy didn't notice the heat flooding her body.

"Yeah." She wiped the moisture from her forehead. "How'd it go?"

"She said yes." Izzy grinned as though she'd just discovered ice cream.

"Wow. That's great."

"Yes, it is. Thanks for suggesting I talk to her."

"You're welcome."

"She said I could see them anytime." She glanced back at the boys. "Maybe we can do it sometime next week."

"We?"

"Of course. I want you to get to know them. They're great kids." She frowned. "You're not a kid-hater, are you?"

"No." Mel shook her head. "I don't hate kids. As long as I can send them home at the end of the day."

"I'm with you there." Izzy narrowed her eyes as Dana strutted out to the water. "I hate it that she uses them to get to me." She flopped back into her chair. "I remember when they were born." She hesitated for a minute, and Mel could see the light in her eyes. "We were halfway through dinner when Tracy called. She'd waited until the last minute, of course. She was already in full-blown labor by the time we reached the hospital." Her face broke into a broad smile. "They were so tiny I was afraid to touch them." She watched the kids playing in the water. "I guess a couple of good things came out of that relationship."

Mel sat back in the chair. "So, you're part owner in her restaurant?"

"No, not any more. I got out of it as soon as we broke up." Izzy reached into the cooler and took out a soda.

"That was smart thinking."

"Smartest thing I ever did besides breaking it off with Dana." She popped open the can and took a swig.

"Is it an Italian place?"

"I'm not sure what it is, but I wouldn't call it Italian."

Mel glanced over at Dana, who was still keeping a close eye on her and Izzy. "Has she been coming here looking for you?"

"I've seen her here on the beach a few times."

"She wants you back." Mel watched the waves washing in and out on the beach. She didn't want to pry, but she wondered what was so special about Dana that had made Izzy fall in love with her.

"I just want to forget about her." Izzy took her hand and laced their fingers together. Mel's temperature soared again. She didn't know what the hell was going on with her body, but she couldn't control the new sensations flooding it. "You okay?" Izzy sounded concerned. "You look like you've had a little too much sun."

"I'm fine. It's just my fair skin. I pink up a little faster than you do." Mel could feel the heat on her face.

"You're really red. Let's go back to the house." Izzy got up and folded up her chair. "I'll get the cooler and the chairs if you'll get the blanket and the bag."

Mel slid the sunscreen into the bag, then got up and shook the sand off the blanket before folding it. "Did we get everything?" She scanned the area.

"Looks good," Izzy said, motioning in front of her with her hand. "After you, beautiful."

Mel smiled and followed the pathway woven among the scattered patches of tall grass. She was unsure of what might happen when they got to the house and how she was going to handle it. She'd set something into motion, and now she didn't quite know how to stop it.

❖

"The towels are in here." Izzy tapped on the cabinet door in the guest bathroom "And you'll find shampoo and body wash in the shower. Let me know if you need anything else."

Izzy headed into her room and swung the door closed. She got in the shower and stripped her suit off, tossing it into the corner. Izzy could sense Mel's anxiety as they walked to the house. She hadn't mentioned anything about the kisses they'd shared. She smiled. They were certainly very nice and totally unexpected. Izzy decided to let whatever it was run its course on its own. It wouldn't be easy, but letting Mel figure out what she wanted was probably the best way to go. The warm water felt good on her sore muscles. She thought about what Mel had said about the tub; right now it sure would be nice to soak in a hot whirlpool. She'd have to see about getting hers fixed.

Mel was already out on the couch when Izzy came out of her room. "Can I get you something to drink? A glass of wine?"

"No wine, thanks. A bottle of water would be great, though."

"Water it is." She grabbed a couple of bottles out of the fridge and handed one to Mel before plopping down on the other end of the couch. "You want to watch a movie or something?"

"I'm so tired, I don't know if I'd last through a movie."

"Good. The Warriors are on, anyway." She shot her a grin.

"So, you were just being polite when you asked about the movie?"

"Something like that." She winked.

"I should probably go."

"Why? You have someplace to be?"

"No," Mel said, twisting her lip up.

"Then stay." She patted the couch. "Put your feet up and relax."

Mel leaned back into the corner of the couch and pulled her knees up. Izzy reached over, slid her hand behind her ankles, and pulled her feet onto her lap. Mel groaned when Izzy pushed her thumb into the ball of her foot.

"I should really be rubbing your feet after the hike I took you on."

"Don't worry. I'll be sure you make it up to me." She kneaded her thumbs up and down the arch of Mel's soft, manicured feet. Her toes, nails painted pink, wiggled with each press of Izzy's thumb.

"You're going to spoil me."

That's the plan. Izzy smiled and then focused on the game. Mel was asleep by the first basket. Her head dipped to the left, thick chestnut tresses mussed around her face. Small breasts rose and fell as she took in slow, even breaths. Izzy felt the impact of her beauty in full force. It took everything she had to look away from the beautiful view. She slid out from under Mel's feet and went into the kitchen without looking back. She felt a little empty inside. It had been such a long time since she'd met anyone who listened and responded with coherent thought, someone who held her interest for more than a week. There was only one problem. She was off-limits.

❖

Mel forced her eyes open. The ball game was still on, but Izzy wasn't there. "What smells so good?"

"I didn't mean to wake you," Izzy shouted from the kitchen.

"How could I sleep through that? It's like an aromatic alarm clock."

"I sautéed a couple of chicken breasts. Come on in and get a plate." Izzy took a couple of dishes from the cabinet and plated the chicken. "You like broccoli?"

"Love it."

She added a few trees to each plate. "Want some lemonade?" She handed Mel a plate and pointed to the pitcher on the counter.

"That sounds good." Mel picked up the pitcher, poured herself a glass, and refilled Izzy's.

"I think the game's back on." Mel sat down on the couch.

Izzy rushed back into the living room, set her plate and glass on the coffee table, and pulled it closer to the couch.

Mel finished her dinner and slid back into the corner of the couch and watched the game. When her eyelids became heavy, she didn't fight it. It wasn't food that woke her the next time; it was Izzy.

"Beautiful even in your sleep." She heard in a soft sexy voice so close to her ear she could feel the warm breath upon it.

"Hmm?" She stirred awake.

"Mel, honey." Izzy was kneeling by the couch, nudging her shoulder. "Wake up and come to bed."

"Okay," she said, still half asleep as Izzy led her into the bedroom.

She slid between the soft, cool sheets and moved up against the warm body lying next to her. Mel had been thinking about this for weeks. She ran her hand the length of Izzy's body, her skin so soft. She didn't know why she'd resisted for so long. God, she felt good. She heard the door click shut and opened her eyes. Wide-awake and cold, she slid her hand across the cool sheet. She was in Izzy's guest room. Alone.

CHAPTER TWELVE

Mel rolled over and slid her hand across the cool sheet. Still alone. She let out a low growl. She'd had such a beautiful dream last night. It was so real she almost felt guilty. She faintly remembered Izzy telling her to come to bed and thought she'd even called her honey. She lifted the sheet. Where were her yoga pants? More importantly, how had they come off? This wasn't good. She needed to cool these feelings she was having for Izzy.

After a light knock on the door, it opened slowly. The scent of coffee wafted into the room.

"Mel? You awake?" Izzy asked softly.

"Hmm...what time is it?" She stretched an arm behind her head.

"A little before noon."

"Jeez. I haven't slept this late on a Sunday in ages." She scooted over and patted the bed. "Come sit for a minute."

Izzy seemed hesitant at first, but then crossed the floor to perch on the edge of the bed. "You okay?"

"Yeah. I'm fine." She leaned against the fabric-covered headboard and pulled the sheet up across her chest. "I was so tired that I'm a little fuzzy about what happened last night."

"Well, first off, it was a little difficult to hear the game over your snoring."

Mel smiled. "I'm sorry. I wasn't aware of that."

"It's okay. Once I squeezed your nose a couple of times, you rolled over and stopped."

Now Mel knew she was teasing. "So that's why my nose is so sore." She reached up and touched it.

"You want some breakfast?"

"I feel like I've already taken advantage of your hospitality."

"I'm going to fix it whether you eat or not."

"Okay, but you have to let me cook."

Izzy's brows shot up. "You can cook?"

"As a matter of fact, I can." She hitched her lip up into a smile.

"Then it's a deal." Izzy popped up off the bed. "Meet you in the kitchen."

"I need eggs, mushrooms, tomatoes, bacon, and potatoes. Oh, and orange juice," she shouted as she snatched her yoga pants from the chair and pulled them on quickly.

Mel had already diced the potatoes and started them frying before she dropped the blended eggs into the pan. "What time are you going to the restaurant today?"

"I'm not." Izzy plucked the crispy prosciutto out of another pan with the tongs. Apparently, she didn't keep bacon in the house. Thankfully, prosciutto was a close second.

"Is it okay to be away from the restaurant two days in a row?" Mel sprinkled the cheese, tomatoes, and mushrooms on top of the partially cooked eggs and flipped the two sides into the middle.

"Sundays are kind of slow, and Tony and Gio need to learn to work alone together."

"They look like they get along well." Mel lifted the pan and, with a twist of her wrist, flipped the omelet up in the air. She caught Izzy's lip quirked up to one side as the omelet landed on the other side in the pan. So she shot her a wink as she picked up the potato pan and did the same.

"Plates?" Mel asked, scanning the counter.

Izzy took a couple from the cabinet to her left, handed one to Mel, and set the other next to the stove. "Most of the time they get along, but they're both very hardheaded. Tony wants the kitchen run his way, so he shoots down any idea Gio might have for a new dish or improvements to the kitchen."

Mel slid the enormous omelet onto the plate, then cut it across the middle and moved half onto the other plate. "Even if it's a good one?"

"Yep, but he eventually changes his mind without admitting Gio was right."

"Wow. Does he do that to you too?" She carried the food to the table as Izzy brought the juice and silverware.

"Oh no. He doesn't mess with me. He knows I'll sic Bella on him. If nothing else, she did teach him to respect women. Besides, when we were growing up, he could see how the family worked. Bella was the one who did the books, made the sauce, and took care of the family."

Mel smiled at the influence the Calabrese woman held. "She sounds like a very strong woman."

"She always has been, but lately she's been...she's been tired." Mel could see something, maybe sadness in Izzy's eyes as she broke eye contact and reached for her fork. "Anyway, that's why I leave them to work alone. I won't always be around to buffer them." She cut off a piece of the omelet and scooped it into her mouth. "Wow, this is delicious."

"Thank you."

"Do you cook a lot?"

"Not as much as I used to. You can probably tell that by how often I come to your place."

"Life gets busy. If it didn't, I'd be out of business."

"I only cook a few things I really like, so I've gotten pretty good at them."

Izzy pushed back from her empty plate. "Well, I'm impressed. That omelet was exceptional."

"I only wish we'd had some crab. Mix that with a little Parmesan cheese, and you'll never want anything else." Mel closed her eyes and licked her lips.

"Well, that settles it. We're going to the wharf to get some crab."

"Izzy, as much as I'd like to spend the day with you, I need to go home." She grabbed the bottom of her T-shirt and pulled at it. "I've been wearing these clothes for two days." *Plus, I'm way behind on this project I've been working on.* She picked up the plates and took them into the kitchen.

"Let me get those." Izzy jumped up and followed her. "You can't tell me about something like that and then not fix it for me." She took the dishes from her and set them in the sink. "Tell you what. We'll swing by your place first so you can change and then make a quick run into the city, grab a couple of crabs, and you can make dinner tonight."

The thought of it sounded really good to Mel. If she got home early enough, she could put in a few hours on her project. "Okay, but I'll fix dinner in my kitchen."

"Okay then." Izzy gave her a big smile. "Let me get these loaded into the dishwasher and change. Then we can hit the road."

"You don't need to change." Mel let her gaze sweep over Izzy, assessing the black flip-flops, khaki shorts, cream tank top, and black zip-up hoodie. "You look great." She smiled as the color in Izzy's cheeks deepened. Then she reached over and straightened the collar of her hoodie, letting her hands drift across her shoulders when she was finished.

They were headed out the door when the phone rang. Izzy looked at the caller ID. "It's the restaurant. Just give me a minute."

"Hey, what's going on?" she said, pressing the receiver to her ear. "Jonathan who?"

She seemed confused.

"From the *Examiner*?"

Her smile immediately vanished.

"Holy shit!"

She grabbed her forehead.

"Why didn't you call me?"

She listened intently, pacing the room.

"What did he order?"

This was not good news.

"And?"

Then, after a moment, she threw her head back, put her fist into the air, and said, "Yes!"

Now *Mel* was confused.

"I guess he'll think twice about protesting the next time Gio has a new recipe, won't he?"

Her smile returned even bigger than before.

"I bet! That's great news, Ang. Now I don't feel so guilty about taking off."

Hmm, it's Angie, Mel thought. Something had happened at the restaurant.

"That's great, tell them both, I'm very proud of them."

She listened for another moment.

"I will. See you tomorrow."

Izzy slid the receiver onto the cradle, pulled Mel into a tight embrace, and swung her around in place.

"What happened?" Mel said, sharing Izzy's excitement.

"You know, Jonathan, the food critic from the *Examiner*?" She released her embrace and took Mel's hands.

"The guy that tore the Balboa Cafe apart from top to bottom?"

"That's the one."

"Oh my God, Izzy. What happened?"

"He came in last night and ordered one of Gio's additions to the menu, rigatoni boscaiola. Angie said Tony nearly had a heart attack."

"And he loved it?" Mel could tell from Izzy's excitement the news had been good.

"Yes, and Tony actually gave Gio a pat on the back after Jonathan left."

"So your plan is working, huh?"

"Seems to be." She pulled her out the front door. "Come on. Let's go celebrate."

Izzy followed Mel to her condo and waited as she pulled her car into the garage. When she motioned to Izzy to come into the house, she killed the engine, tossed her aviator sunglasses onto the dash, and met Mel at the door. She trailed her inside through the kitchen to the living room.

"Just give me a few minutes to change, and I'll be right back." She picked up a remote, pushed one of the buttons, and a TV appeared from behind a mirror above the fireplace. "I have all the sports channels if you want to check out the highlights from last night." She handed her the remote. "Try 983."

Izzy set the remote on the coffee table. The condo was beautiful, filled with art and landscape photography from the likes of Ansel Adams and Brett Weston. It was an extensive collection, yet not pretentious. Just like its owner. The artwork went well with the modern decor. Pictures of her family were scattered sporadically throughout the room, but Izzy saw none of Mel and her husband. She wandered back into the kitchen and gaped at the beautiful Viking six-burner with two large ovens. Also, a huge porcelain sink and a granite center island were perfect for meal prep and rolling dough. Izzy fingered the pots hanging from the rack above it and slipped one off the hook to feel its weight. She was way out of her league with this woman.

"I thought you might be in here." Mel had changed into a pair of white capris and a royal-blue V-neck shirt that enhanced her figure perfectly.

"You really do know how to cook, don't you?"

"I like to, but I don't know how good I am."

"Well, I guess we'll find out later." Izzy slid the pot back onto the hook.

"Yes, I guess we will." Mel smiled tentatively and led her to the front door. "Do you mind if we stop by my parents' house? I told my mom I'd drop off these shoes I picked up for her last week." She locked the door on their way out.

"No, not at all."

"It's just across the highway."

"In Tiburon?" Izzy slid into the driver's seat.

Mel nodded. "On Spring Lane. It's easy to find."

"I know where it is. Is that where you grew up?"

"Uh-huh."

"Are your—"

"Yes, my parents are rich," Mel blurted.

Izzy pulled up one side of her lip. "I was going to ask if your folks are members of the yacht club."

"Oh." She spoke hesitantly, as though she was embarrassed. "Yes. They're very active in the local boating community."

"It's a nice place. I used to work in the kitchen there."

"It is, but I didn't spend much time there."

"Why not?"

"I was too busy with school activities, and then there was college."

Mel pointed the house out as they went up the hill, and Izzy pulled into the cobblestone circle driveway. It wasn't the smallest house on the hill, but it wasn't the largest either.

Mel got out of the car and headed to the door, then jogged back to the car and leaned down to look in the open window. "Come in with me."

"I can wait here."

"No, really. Come in. My dad's probably not home, but I want you to meet my mom." Mel waited for her to get out of the car.

"Okay." She followed her into the house but stopped at the edge of the living room. The whole room was glaringly bright. The walls, the furniture, the rugs, the lamps were all white, and with the sun shining through the floor-to-ceiling windows she felt snow-blind.

Mel turned and saw she wasn't following. "I know. I'm always afraid to touch anything in this room." She walked back across the room, took her hand, and led her into the kitchen. "Mom, are you home?" she shouted.

"I'm out back, dear." The voice resonated through the screen door.

"I just came by to drop off your shoes." She lifted the bag and then set it on the cedar table. "Izzy, this is my mother, Cecilia. Mom, this is my friend Izzy."

"Nice to meet you, dear." Cecilia tilted her head curiously. "How do you know my daughter?"

Izzy stood at the edge of the deck, amazed by the view. "I cook for her a few times a week." Izzy swung around and grinned, amazed at the resemblance between Mel and her mother. The lines in her face were a little deeper, but Cecilia was a beautiful woman too.

Mel smiled and bumped her with her shoulder. "She owns Bella's."

"Oh. Well, my daughter has good taste. The food there is wonderful."

"Thank you. You have a beautiful place here. I'd love to have a view like this."

"What are you talking about? You have a great view." Mel rolled her eyes. "Stinson Beach is literally her backyard."

"I guess I can't have them both, can I?"

Izzy could see Cecilia's gaze fix on her daughter. "What are you two up to today?"

"We're going to the city to pick up some fresh crab," Mel said.

"Mel is going to show me the proper way to cook an omelet." She arched a brow and shot Mel a playful smirk, instantly rewarded by Mel's dazzling smile.

"Stop." Mel's cheeks pinked as she glanced back to her mother. "Do you want us to bring you some crab? I know how much you love it."

"No, dear. Don't worry about that. You two just have a good time."

"Okay. Then we'll go now." Mel bent down and gave her mother a kiss on the cheek.

"It was nice to meet you," Izzy said with a wave.

Mel's mother smiled. "Come back anytime, Izzy."

Izzy followed Mel out the door to the car. "You must have something special," Mel said as she slid into the passenger seat.

"Why do you say that?" Izzy got into the car and fired the engine.

"You got an invitation to come back."

The conversation in the car was easy, like they'd been friends for years. Izzy enjoyed seeing the fun, spirited side of Mel. She talked about her family and how she'd teased her tag-along brother when they were younger. How she and her friends had skipped school to take trips into the city when she finally got her license. Izzy was intrigued. She was learning that Mel wasn't quite as straight-laced as she seemed to be.

They were lucky enough to find a parking space in the garage near Pier 39. Izzy would have normally just tried to find a one-hour meter on the street within walking distance to Fisherman's Wharf, but she wanted to spend every moment she could with Mel.

They walked Pier 39, window-shopping as they strolled until they stopped to watch a juggler tossing pins into the air.

"I learned how to do that when I was five," Izzy said.

"Really?"

"No, but it would make a good story, wouldn't it?" She grinned. "Couldn't you just see little bitty me with my tiny hands throwing around those big pins?" Izzy motioned juggling with her hands. "Dodging them when they came falling out of the air at me?" She darted to the side, comically avoiding the imaginary pins.

Mel jabbed her in the ribs with her elbow. "I can clearly see one hitting you on the head."

"Oh, is that why I'm like this?" She tilted her head and crossed her eyes.

"Stop." Mel gave her a shove and headed toward the musicians playing in the plaza. "I suppose you can play saxophone too."

"God, no. You have to be full of a lot of hot air for that."

"You probably wouldn't have any trouble then, would you?" Mel chuckled.

"And your point is?" Izzy's brows rose.

"No point, just an observation." Mel raised an eyebrow too and cocked her head to the side.

They wandered over to K-dock to see the sea lions. Some were sunbathing, but a few were entertaining the crowd. They barked loudly as they bobbed their heads back and forth. Watching Mel bark back at one of the larger sea lions was hilarious. She moved down the walkway, and the large ball of blubber paralleled her on the pier.

"He's barking at you." Izzy howled.

"He is not." Mel moved farther down the pier, and the sea lion continued to move with her. "Maybe he is." She ran down farther and watched as he dove into the water and jumped back on the pier across from her. "Oh my God, he is," Mel squealed.

"I think he wants you to be part of his harem." Izzy was laughing so hard, she could hardly get the words out. "It must be your irresistible bark."

"I think we should get the crab now." Mel grabbed Izzy's hand and pulled her along behind her.

"Should we pick up a couple of pounds of squid for your boyfriend?"

Mel grinned and shook her head. "I've been hit on by some unusual characters, but that one's a first."

"Well, at least you know you've still got it." Izzy chuckled.

They headed over to Alioto's and bought a couple of cracked Dungeness crabs wrapped to go.

"I'm kind of hungry after all that barking. How about you?"

"Flirting always makes me hungry," Mel quipped.

"Come on. I know a place where we can get a great sandwich."

When they reached the parking garage, Izzy put the crab into the small cooler she'd placed in the trunk before she left her house. Then they got in the car and headed up to Ike's Place on Sixteenth Street. Ike was an old friend of the family and had the best sandwiches in town.

Mel scanned the large menu on the wall as the line moved just inside the door. "Oh, my. How do you decide what to get?"

"Do you like turkey and avocado?"

"Yes. That sounds good."

A familiar face came from behind the counter. "Izzy." He drew her name out as he put his arms around her. "How's the family?"

"Hey, Ike. They're good. We haven't seen you in a while."

"Yeah. I've been kind of busy with this place. How's Tony? Is he still working on his old Chevy?"

"Yep. He loves that car."

"Too much, I think, huh?"

"You still living at the beach?"

"Yep. Lots of people in the snappers out there today."

"Seen any A-Frames lately?"

"Yeah. The surf's been looking pretty sweet. You should come out sometime."

"I'll see what I can do and let you know." He turned to Mel. "And who is this lovely young lady?"

"This is my friend Mel. I promised her the best sandwich in the city."

"Iz, you're too kind. What are you having today?"

"I think we're gonna get a couple of Barry Zs to go."

"Well, all right then." He smiled and moved back behind the counter. "Two Barry Zs to go, on the house."

"Ike, please let me pay for them."

"Not gonna happen. My mother would never forgive me." He slid the wrapped sandwiches across the top of the deli case. "Grab some chips and a couple of sodas on your way out."

"Thanks, Ike." She grabbed the sandwiches. "I'll tell Tony hello for you."

"You do that. In fact, tell him I'm gonna call him. I wanna see that car of his."

On the way to Tank Hill, Izzy explained to Mel that an A-Frame is the perfect wave that breaks really nicely, and snappers aren't fish but the small waves on the shore. Izzy climbed out onto the rocks and extended her hand to Mel as she followed. They settled in on the edge of a rock and gazed out at the city. The view stretched from ocean to bay and as far north as Point Reyes.

"Is this payback for the hike we took yesterday?" Mel said, breathlessly.

"The thought crossed my mind, but no. It's just someplace I thought you might like to see." Izzy had been to Tank Hill many times before but had never shared it with anyone. She'd never had the slightest desire to do so until now. Somehow, she felt it would no longer be special if she let someone in on it who didn't appreciate its beauty the way she did.

"Wow. You can see the whole city from here." Mel sounded almost giddy as she took in the beautiful view.

"It's one of my favorite places." Izzy smiled at her reaction and then took a bite of her sandwich. It was exactly what she'd hoped for.

"I can't believe I've never been up here before."

"It's kind of a locals' place. There used to be a water tank up here that was built in the late eighteen hundreds and torn down sometime in the fifties. The city finally bought the land from private investors in

1977 and turned it into a protected space to prevent the area from being developed."

Mel finished her sandwich and tucked the trash into the empty bag, then shoved it under her leg to keep it from blowing off the rocks. The view of the city from Tank Hill was beautiful, and within an hour, the sun would slowly ease down, leaving an indescribable glow across the blend of urban structures that made up San Francisco. The Hill never failed to display the most beautiful sunsets.

Mel linked her arm with Izzy's as they sat in silence, just taking in the view. After a short while, Mel leaned her head on Izzy's shoulder. "This is absolutely breathtaking," she whispered. "I don't know how you do it, Izzy, but you make me see the world in a totally new and different way." She let out a long sigh and laced her fingers with Izzy's like it was the most natural thing in the world.

Izzy's body warmed at Mel's touch and the subtle jasmine smell of her hair flowing across her shoulder. Something had stirred deep inside her when she met Mel. She didn't know if it was how Mel had opened up to her that night behind the restaurant or the way she listened intently to everything Izzy said. It was as though her next thought hung on her every word. The personal boundaries she'd held for herself had unlocked, and she'd known Mel would appreciate the marvel of this place just as she did. She would have no regrets about bringing Mel here to her special place.

❖

The sun was long gone by the time they got back to the house. The ride home had been long, lengthened by Mel's heightened sensitivity. Sitting on the hill watching the sunset together, so closely, almost intimately made her brutally aware of her essence. It had unlocked something deep inside, something that craved Izzy in every way.

Mel's hand trembled as she tried to put the key in the lock. Izzy's warm hand wrapped around her own, and Mel gazed up into endless pools of blue. Still trembling, she turned to look at Izzy and let the bag of groceries drop to the ground. Her eyes dark, gaze steady, all Mel could do was focus on Izzy's mouth, her full lips parted slightly. She reached up, ran her thumb across Izzy's bottom lip, and wasn't surprised at all when she felt Izzy's hand hook behind her neck and pull her in for a soft kiss. She pulled away slightly, saw her deep-blue eyes filled with desire, and kissed her again.

Izzy pressed her to the door, eliminating all space between them. Mel grabbed her shirt, pulled her closer. Izzy's mouth opened, and Mel didn't wait for an invitation. She pushed her tongue deep inside. She'd expected it to be good, but this kiss was long, slow, and erotically sensual. Every nerve ending in her body tingled, and she lost her bearings for a moment. Mel had never been so aroused. She felt the warmth of Izzy's hand under her shirt and broke away. She pushed the door open, picked up the bag of groceries, and pulled Izzy inside. As they made their way through the living room, Mel saw light coming from the kitchen. She didn't remember leaving it on when they'd left earlier. She turned the corner into the kitchen, ran smack dab into Jack, and shrieked.

"It's just me," he said.

"Oh, my God. You scared me." She slapped her hand to her chest, the shock zapping her out of the erotic haze she was in.

"Sorry, babe. Not my intention." He pulled her into his arms and gave her a soft peck on the lips.

"I thought you were going to be gone until next week?" Her evening had just been ruined.

"Change of plans. I finished up early." He glanced over her shoulder.

Mel spun around, heart still thundering. "You remember Izzy, don't you?" She stuttered. "The chef at Bella's?"

"Oh, yeah. Great food there. Great food."

"Thanks," Izzy said, setting the bag of groceries on the counter, her cheeks flushed, lips swollen. Mel put her hand to her mouth, knowing hers looked just the same.

Jack put his hand on Mel's arm and brushed it with his thumb. "I had a long flight today. I'm hungry and beat. What's in the bag?" He didn't wait for an answer before emptying its contents out onto the counter. He picked up the package of crab and tilted his head at Mel.

"Izzy was going to show me how to make crab omelets." She moved toward the sink.

"Sounds great." He observed Izzy. "Make yourself at home."

"Actually…" Izzy pinched her lips together. "I need to get to the restaurant and make sure everything's running smoothly."

"I know what you mean. You can let someone else fill in, but you can never let go." He reached for a bottle of wine from the rack and then searched for the corkscrew in the drawer. "Mel can probably handle the omelets. Can't you, babe?"

She turned to Izzy and saw her reaction to the distance she'd put between them. "Are you sure you can't stay?" she asked and immediately saw the wall go up. She'd changed from the sweet, sensitive woman she'd just kissed to an aloof stranger. Mel instantly regretted her words.

"No. I really need to get going."

Jack gave Izzy a nod. "Nice to see you again."

"Yeah. Nice to see you too," Izzy said.

"I'll walk you out." She brushed past her through the living room and opened the door.

She waited to say anything more until they were outside on the porch. "I'm so sorry, Izzy. I didn't know he was going to be here." A pang of disappointment hit her deep inside. She'd had a wonderful day and was looking forward to cooking for Izzy tonight. Suddenly everything felt stilted and awkward.

"No problem," she said stiffly. "He *is* your husband."

Mel reached to touch her face, but Izzy turned and headed down the walk. "I really am sorry."

Izzy threw her a wave as she slid into her Jeep and closed the door. Izzy didn't give her another glance as she backed out of the driveway. Then she was gone. *He* is *your husband.* Her reality hit her square in the face. Mel turned around and pressed her head to the door as the thought resonated in her head. *That is going to change.*

Jack was leaning back against the counter casually when Mel came back into the kitchen. "It's too bad your friend had to leave. She's cute. Do you see her often?"

"It's not like that, Jack." She twisted the wedding ring on her finger. "Unlike you, I believed in those vows when I took them."

"What makes you think I didn't?" He tossed the package of crab from hand to hand.

"The fact you've been in town since Friday and I haven't seen you until tonight. Were you with her again?" She intercepted the package and put it back in the bag, following it with the eggs and cheese.

"With who?"

"Don't patronize me, Jack. I've seen the way she looks at you. And the way you look back." She blew out a breath. "You used to look at me that way."

"What do you want me to say?"

"I want you to tell me the truth."

"Yes, I was with her."

"Every time you sleep with someone else, it chips away a little more of my heart."

"I've never lied to you, Mel."

"Because I've always been afraid to ask."

"You don't respond to me, not like—"

"Don't you dare say like her." She fought to hold the tears back.

"You don't respond to me, not like you should. I want a woman who can't keep her hands off me. Who doesn't have to drink a half a bottle of wine for her to feel comfortable having sex."

A sob threatened to escape, and Mel slapped a hand to her mouth. Her heart began to pound. He was right. She couldn't remember the last time they'd made love when she hadn't been drinking. She'd always thought it made it better, but now she could see it just made it easier.

"Maybe it wouldn't be like that if I wasn't afraid of picking up some kind of STD whenever we have sex," she shot back.

"Don't do that, Mel." He shook his head. "I'm not trying to hurt you. I just want more." He pushed away from the counter and paced across the kitchen. "I deserve more. So do you."

"That's it? Ten years and just like that? You're done?" She felt the tears spill out, and Jack moved toward her. "No." She threw up a hand to hold him back. "You're right. I can't do this anymore. It hasn't been a picnic for me either. *I'm* done." She grabbed the bag from the counter and rushed out of the kitchen, looking for a way to escape. Somewhere, anywhere but here. She heard Jack come after her from the kitchen. She grabbed her keys and flew out the door to her car.

CHAPTER THIRTEEN

Mel stood at the door of Nancy's house and raised her hand to knock. She pulled back and wiped the tears from her eyes, but it did no good. Every time she cleared them away, they filled her eyes even heavier. When she finally thought she had herself under control, she knocked. She saw Nancy in the doorway and the floodgates opened again. "He doesn't want me anymore, Nance," she choked out.

Nancy put her arms out and Mel fell into them. "Oh my God, come here." She led her into the living room and sat her down on the couch.

Mel sobbed uncontrollably, then tried to pull herself together. Nancy reached across her to the side table and pulled a wad of tissues from the box. Mel took them from her and blew her nose.

"I'll get you a glass of wine." Nancy got up to move past her to the kitchen.

Jack's words echoed in her head. *Someone who doesn't have to drink a half a bottle of wine for her to feel comfortable having sex.* She grabbed Nancy's hand. "No. No wine."

"Okay...coffee? Tea?"

"Tea." Mel blew her nose again as Nancy disappeared into the kitchen. She scanned Nancy's living room. The place was so clean, almost clinical. Mail stacked neatly on the entry table, matching throw pillows in exactly the right spot on the couch. Even the TV remotes were lined up perfectly on the end table. Everything was in its place, but no pictures, no comfort, no love filled the house. This was what it was like to live alone.

Nancy reappeared with two cups of tea and handed one to Mel. "You want to tell me what happened?"

Mel nodded. "Jack was at the house when Izzy and I got home from the city."

"Oh. You were with Izzy today?" Nancy's voice rose, and Mel could hear the question in her tone.

She nodded. "We drove in to get some crab so I could show her how I fix my crab omelets." She wiped her nose with the tissue. "Anyway, when I saw Jack, I got nervous and acted like she was just there to show me how to cook."

"So she left. What did Jack say about the two of you?"

"He didn't come right out and say it, but he wanted to know if I was seeing her."

"And you said?"

"I said no, of course. We're just friends."

"Okay..." Nancy shifted on the couch to face Mel, skepticism in her face.

"He told me he'd just gotten back in town, but he's been here since at least Friday night—with that reporter."

"How do you know that?"

"Izzy told me Friday night she'd seen him at the market."

"Hmm...so you were with Izzy again?"

"I was with her all freakin' weekend, okay," Mel blurted, and Nancy's brows flew up. "It wasn't like that. She lives at the beach and invited me out for...and we...I just hung out there with her...and... shit!" *It was like that.* She hopped up and paced the room, kneading her forehead with her fingers. Mel had kissed Izzy multiple times and wanted to do it again. She'd finally admitted to herself she'd gone way past the friend stage weeks ago.

"Yeah, shit." Nancy nodded. "I'm not condoning what he's done, but you clearly have eyes for someone else."

Mel relayed the rest of the conversation she'd had with Jack about their sex life.

"Jesus, Mel. Half a bottle of wine?"

She nodded. "I didn't realize it, but I do when I think back." Mel blew out a short breath. "This whole time, I just thought he was sleeping with other women because he couldn't keep it in his pants, not because of me."

"So what are you going to do now?"

"I don't know." Mel shrugged. "I always thought I'd be the one to break it off."

"Well, I guess you have a decision to make, but it's pretty clear to me who you want to be with." She squeezed Mel's shoulder. "Let's get you something to eat." Nancy picked up their cups of tea that were long cold by now and took them into the kitchen.

Mel retrieved the grocery bag she'd left in the entryway and followed. She slid the bag onto the breakfast bar and took a seat on one of the barstools.

Nancy picked up the bag, emptied it, and held up the white, butcher-papered, package. "Crab?"

Mel nodded. "I wasn't about to leave it for Jack."

"So, you want an omelet?" Nancy's mouth hitched up on one side. "Sorry. I couldn't resist. Salad or grilled cheese?"

"Do you have avocado?"

"Let me see." Nancy pulled open the refrigerator door, put the crab along with the eggs and cheese onto the shelf, and then pulled open the produce drawer. "Yep. Tomatoes and cucumbers too."

"Then salad."

Nancy washed the tomato and cucumber and set them on the counter next to the avocado. She picked up a cutting board, took a knife from the block, and then slid them in front of Mel along with the washed vegetables. "Cut, please."

Mel did as Nancy asked, then divided the vegetables into each bowl of lettuce as Nancy rounded the counter and took the seat next to her. She put two bottles of dressing in front of her. "Your choices tonight, my dear." Mel reached for Italian, and Nancy took ranch. They sat eating quietly for a while until Nancy broke the silence. "So are you gonna tell her?"

"Who?"

Nancy's eyes widened. "The woman you've been crushing on for the past few weeks."

Mel stared blankly at her salad and pushed the lettuce around in the bowl. "I think maybe I should take care of things with Jack first. I don't want to give him any ammunition if he decides not to be amicable."

"That's probably a good idea." Nancy scooped up the last bit of salad onto her fork and slid it into her mouth.

"Yeah, probably," Mel said. The hard part was actually doing it. The pull she felt from Izzy was stronger than anything she'd ever experienced before. But what if Izzy moved on before she'd taken care of things with Jack?

"The bigger question is how are you going to do without all of that wonderful food?" Nancy cleared their plates and set them in the sink.

"I need to cut back on my carbs anyway." Mel got up and helped her clean the dishes.

Nancy took her by the hand and led her to her bedroom. "Come on. You can stay with me tonight."

Mel slowed as they passed the guest-room door. "Uh, I can stay in here."

"No, you can't. I've been sorting through my closets. The bed's covered with clothes, and I'm not going to move them. You'll have to sleep with me." She opened the door, showed her, and closed it again before she turned to Mel and quirked an eyebrow up. "So you'll need to keep your hands to yourself."

Mel chuckled. "Oh, okay. I'll try."

Izzy sat in her Jeep in front of her parents' house, staring at the amber light in the window. Her dad must be out somewhere. Bella always left the small antique brass lamp turned on when Benito was away as a sign she was inside waiting for him. Bella had performed the ritual since he'd gone to war right after they were first married. Whenever he was away, the light was on. Benito was proud of that fact too. When he was out with his friends and had to head back home, he never failed to tell them he was going where the light glows. To him this meant he was going home to the woman who held his heart. Someday Izzy hoped to have someone hold her heart that way. Chasing a married woman certainly wasn't the way to make it happen.

When Izzy entered the kitchen, Bella was playing gin rummy at the table with her Aunt Julia. "Where's Pop?"

"With your Uncle Rennie at the Giants' game." That was one of the good things about being part of a large Italian family: there was always someone to go to the game with.

"Oh yeah. I forgot they were playing at home tonight." Izzy's dad had been a season-ticket holder for more than thirty years and rarely missed a game. When she was a kid, Benito had five tickets, one for himself and each of his kids. Izzy loved going to the ballgames.

"Have you found yourself a new girl yet?" Julia blurted.

"Julia, she isn't ready to start dating so soon after her breakup with whatshername. Right, Izzy?" Bella said.

"Her name is Dana."

"That's not important." Julia threw her hands up. She was a physical talker who didn't pull any punches. "What matters is you need to get out and be social. Meet someone new." Her voice became louder, her Italian impatience flaring.

"Actually, I thought I had, but I don't think it's going to work out."

Both women dropped their cards to the table and gave Izzy their full attention.

"Tell us what the problem is, dear." Bella's eyes were wide with curiosity.

"Yes, tell us." Julia scooted her chair closer to Izzy. "We don't need all the details. Just the facts."

Bella disagreed. "What are you saying? Of course we want all the details."

"The fact is, she's married."

"Oh my, Isabel," they said in unison, disapproval ringing through. "That's not good."

"Don't get all crazy on me. Nothing's happened between us. But she's not happy with her husband."

"Then you must let their path run its course," Julia declared.

"If it's meant to be, she'll free herself," Bella insisted. She motioned to Julia and they both nodded.

"That's what I did so many years ago. Then I met your Uncle Rennie." Julia beamed.

"Now that was meant to be." Bella smiled widely.

The two sisters had the most annoying yet uncanny way of reading each other's thoughts. Where one left off, the other began, as though they shared the same mind.

Mel was spooned against Nancy's back when she woke up, and it took her a minute to realize where she was and who she was spooning.

She also realized she had Nancy's breast cupped in her hand. Before she could move it, she heard a soft groan and Nancy said, "Are you gonna do something with that hand, or are you just teasing me?" Mel chuckled and rolled to her back. Nancy grumbled. "Not the choice I was hoping for."

"Sorry. I'm a cuddler."

"I remember." Nancy rolled over to face her, and Mel saw something different skitter across her face. "You know you wouldn't be so difficult to resist if you hadn't gotten so damn beautiful." She brushed a stray strand of hair from Mel's face and tucked it up behind her ear. Nancy was silent for a moment, seemingly lost in the past. "Why couldn't you have gotten ugly or something?"

"Would that change things?" Mel lifted a brow.

"No." Nancy rolled her eyes and shook her head. "I'd still want you."

"I wish I could change the way I feel." Mel gave her a soft kiss on the cheek.

Nancy let out a growl. "If I didn't love you, I'd definitely take advantage of this situation."

"I know." She flopped her head to the side. "I'm sorry I was such a mess last night."

"You were a fucking mess." Nancy laughed. "Which is a switch. I'm usually the one with all the drama."

"I don't know what to do, Nance."

"First things first. You need to call Mike and get the ball rolling on your divorce." Nancy pushed out of bed, took the cordless phone from the nightstand, and tossed it to the spot she'd just vacated. "I'm going to jump in the shower." She moved through the bathroom doorway and then peeked back out at Mel. "Wanna wash my back?"

"Go." Mel rolled her eyes and shooed her with a backhanded wave.

Nancy was right. It was no use trying anymore, and she certainly didn't want to live like she had been with Jack for the rest of her life.

Her whole weekend with Izzy—the beach, the wharf, that beautiful sunset—had been so perfect. She'd been excited about bringing her home, sharing dinner, a bottle of wine, and who knows what else with her. It had been clear when they'd returned home to find Jack in the kitchen that Mel had put the cart before the horse. She still had issues to deal with before any of that could happen. Her ten-year relationship with Jack was over but not quite finished.

They had to deal with legal matters. Mel wanted out, but she needed to be smart about it. If Jack had any inkling she might be seeing someone else, which he might have after last night, he could make the financial split long and arduous. Her mother had warned her, and Mel now knew she should have never agreed to merge their financial portfolios without a prenup. At the time, she'd never doubted that her relationship with Jack was permanent. Today she would call her brother, Mike, who was also her attorney, and get the paperwork started. Soon Jack would be free of her, and she would be faced with the cold reality of starting over.

What the hell am I doing? Mel flashed a look over at Nancy belted into the passenger seat next to her as she weaved in and out of traffic. She'd gone to bed with a knot in her stomach last night and hadn't slept nearly enough to be faced with her dilemma again so early this morning. She needed to apologize to Izzy and let her know everything she'd seen last night was a perfectly choreographed show Jack had perfected over the years to fool anyone who cared to take an interest in their relationship.

"Mel, are you listening to me?" Nancy asked.

"What?" she said, snapping her attention back. "Of course I'm listening."

"Where are we going? You just passed the Mexican restaurant." Nancy grabbed the oh-shit handle above the window when Mel threw her blinker on, jerked into the right lane, and took the next exit.

"Bella's. I thought you might like to eat there again."

"So much for my input." She flopped her head back against the headrest.

"I really need to apologize to Izzy for last night."

"A phone call would probably do."

"You don't think I should do it in person?"

"I'm not so sure it's a good idea."

"Why?"

"Remember our conversation last night? I thought you were going to stay away from her until you took care of things with Jack."

"I changed my mind."

"Are you sure she's not seeing someone?"

"I've spent enough time with her recently, I'd know that."

"True. You've spent so much time with her, I thought *you* were seeing her."

Without another word, Mel whipped the car into a parking space between two Ford trucks. "Come on. You love the food here."

"If you say so." Nancy got out of the car and followed her into the restaurant.

Angie wasn't at the hostess station, so Mel reached behind it and grabbed a couple of menus before finding them a table. "Did you see the special on the board when we came in?"

"No. I didn't notice."

"I wonder where everyone is." Mel glanced toward the kitchen.

"It's only eleven o'clock. They're probably not all here yet."

"Will you excuse me for a minute?" Mel didn't wait for an answer. She dropped the menus on the table and headed across the restaurant and into the kitchen.

"While you're in there, find out what the special is."

"Hey, Tony."

"Hey, beautiful." His blue eyes creased at the sides as he smiled.

"Where's everyone?"

"Angie's running late, as usual, and Izzy's gone to the market."

"I thought she always went to the market before you opened." She pulled open the Sub-Zero, and it was full.

"Don't know, sweetheart. She must've forgotten something." He peeked over her shoulder into the refrigerator. "I'm just telling you what she told me."

She started back into the dining room, then stopped and turned. "Tony, will you tell me about Dana?"

"How do you know about her?"

"We ran into her at the beach the other day."

He shook his head slowly. "That one is pure trouble."

"Were they together for a long time?"

He scrunched his face up and squinted at the ceiling. "About six years on and off."

"Six years." She snapped her gaze back to Tony.

"Maybe I should let Izzy tell you." He gave her a wary look, seeming to realize she really didn't know the whole story.

She blew out a short breath. "She told me what happened, Tony."

"Dana, that—" Tony took a sauté pan from the stack and slapped it to the stove. "She won't leave her alone."

"What do you mean on and off? Weren't they exclusive?"

"That would depend on which one of them you asked."

"Oh, I see. Do you think Izzy's done with her?"

"I hope so. She doesn't care about anyone but herself."

"Thanks, Tony." Mel's voice weakened as she started out of the kitchen.

"What do you want to eat?"

"Oh, just give us a couple orders of linguine Bolognese with house salads." She pushed back through the swinging door.

Nancy's eyes were fixed on her as she crossed the restaurant. "What's the special?"

"Izzy's not here."

"Where is she?"

"Tony said she's at the market."

"She'll probably be back before we leave."

"If not, we can go find her."

"Listen, Mel. Apologizing to Izzy at her restaurant is one thing, but don't you think hunting her down at the market might be a little awkward?"

"Oh, yeah. I guess that would be kind of weird."

"What's the special?"

"They have a daily special, pasta with soup or salad. I ordered the Bolognese for you."

"Oh...okay."

"You liked it last time, didn't you?"

"Yes, but I'd like to try something else on the menu sometime."

"I'm sorry. I'll let you decide next time. You're getting a house salad also, by the way." Mel stretched her lips wide, giving Nancy a toothy grin.

❖

"What are you doing out here?" Izzy jumped at the sound of Angie's voice behind her. She let go of the restaurant back door and threw herself against the cold metal as it closed.

"Mel Thomas is in the kitchen with Tony."

"Umm...why don't you want to see her all of a sudden? I thought you guys were—"

"We're not. She's married, and I don't want to get in the middle of it."

"She was married last weekend when you took her home, wasn't she?"

Izzy blew out a heavy breath. "I know, Angie. That was a mistake." *A huge mistake.*

"I'm glad you've come to your senses. That woman's a little whacky anyway, if you ask me."

"Just let me know if she's gone, okay, Angie?" Izzy hid behind the door as she pulled it open.

"She's not in the kitchen."

Izzy slipped around the door and followed Angie inside.

Tony shot Angie a look. "Where the hell have you been? I've got two house salads and a bruschetta that need to go out."

Angie waved him off as she picked up the salads and took them through the kitchen door. Tony waited until Angie went into the dining room before turning back to Izzy. "What the hell was that all about?"

"I'm sorry, Tony. I just need to stay away from her for a while."

"I told you she was trouble."

Izzy slipped around and peeked out the door behind the bar. Mel was dressed in a charcoal pantsuit with a black shell underneath. Her hair was twisted into some kind of knot behind her head, revealing the length of her neck. *God, she's beautiful.* She let the door close, then slid up against the wall next to it and shut her eyes. Tony was right on point with that one. Izzy could see herself falling hard for Mel Thomas.

CHAPTER FOURTEEN

Mel knocked lightly and then pushed through the door. "I brought crab salad for lunch."

"That sounds wonderful, dear." Bella took the salad from Mel and spooned it on top of the lettuce beds she arranged on the plates.

"Not too much for me. I had a late breakfast." Mel had forgotten about her lunch date with Bella until the reminder had popped up on her phone. She'd dropped Nancy back at the office and had just enough time to run by the house and pick up the crab salad.

Bella set a plate on each of the three placemats, then stepped to the hall doorway and shouted. "Benny, lunch is ready."

Benito's voice resonated as he came through the doorway. "This is a nice surprise. I didn't know we had company." He pulled out Bella's chair for her and took the seat across the table. "Mmm, crab salad. Did you make it?"

"Mary Elizabeth brought it."

"It looks delicious."

"Thank you. I picked it up at the wharf yesterday." Her day with Izzy flashed through her mind, and she smiled.

Benito dug into his food, eating two helpings of crab salad before dousing the remaining lettuce with bleu cheese dressing.

"You look tired. Have you been working too much?" Bella asked between bites.

"I've been putting in a lot of extra hours lately to stay on schedule."

"Your parents must be very proud of you."

"My mother is very supportive, but my father always seems to want more."

"How do you know that?"

"No matter what I've accomplished, my father has a way of making me feel like I could've done better." The salad was wonderful, but suddenly her previous lunch began to rumble in her stomach. She took a gulp of lemonade.

Benito raised a brow. "Sounds like he has very high standards." He crunched the iceberg lettuce loudly as he chewed.

She nodded. "Unreachable."

"Have you ever told your father how it makes you feel when he dismisses your accomplishments?"

She set her fork down and gave Benito her attention. "No. I've always thought he'd think I was whining."

"You seem to have your life together."

"I thought I did until recently."

"Your business is successful, eh?"

"Yes. That's one thing going well right now."

Bella patted her hand and got up.

"You've certainly got no reason to be ashamed," Benito said. "I'd be proud to have you as one of my daughters. You should talk to him."

"Are we playing do as I say, not as I do today?" Bella talked into the refrigerator as she reached inside to get the pitcher of lemonade.

"What do you mean?" Benito's voice rose just a tad.

"You just told her a father should listen to his daughter. Maybe you should take your own advice. You are proud of your daughters, aren't you?"

"Bella. You know I am. Izzy has accomplished more with the restaurant than I ever did. She cooks, handles the ordering, and does the books. Angie hasn't quite found her path yet, but she's in school, and I know she will soon."

"Have you told them how you feel?" Mel asked, concerned. Izzy hadn't mentioned any tension between her and her father.

He pushed back in his chair and got up. "Sometimes we fathers don't articulate what we're feeling very well. You should talk to your father. He may surprise you."

She gave him a soft smile, thinking how nice it would be to have her father behind her. "How about we make a deal? I'll talk to my father, if you'll talk to your daughters."

Bella set the lemonade on the table and wrapped an arm around Benito's waist. "That's a fine idea. It's about time you loosened those principles of yours and made peace with Izzy."

Benito narrowed his eyes. "Bella, don't push me."

"No matter what kind of life she chooses for herself, she's still your daughter." She veered her gaze from Benito to Mel. "Don't you agree, Mary Elizabeth?"

She nodded. "A daughter always needs the love and support of her daddy."

"I'll think about it." Benito grunted and went back down the hallway. "The Giants are up by three. You wanna come watch?" he said, turning back momentarily.

"Can't today. I have to get back to work." Mel helped clear the dishes and kissed Bella on the cheek. "Can we get together again soon?"

"Anytime, dear." Bella followed her to the door. "Let me know how it works out with your father."

The lunch crowd had been thick today, but Izzy finally slipped out to take her mother some food. As she made the short drive, she ran through the weekend in her head and kept returning to the kiss on the beach—hot, wet, soft, and completely unexpected. Izzy had been imagining it for weeks. Seeing Mel earlier today only made her want her more. It was going to be difficult to stay away if she came back to the restaurant.

Her mother met her at the door as she came in.

"I brought you some lunch."

"We already had lunch, dear."

Her dad bustled through the room to the refrigerator. "It's almost four," he grumbled as he swung the door open and took out a soda. "Too late for lunch."

"Well, then this can be dinner."

He peeked into the bag and then up at Izzy. "Smells good." He headed back into the den, where Izzy could hear the TV blaring.

"What was that?" She stood stunned.

"What was what, dear?"

"He talked to me. He never talks to me." She stared down the hallway toward the den.

"Oh, yes, he does."

"Not voluntarily."

"Then I guess that's progress, isn't it?"

"Yes…yes it is." Izzy smiled. He'd even said thanks. She had no idea what had made him end his silence, but she was happy he had. "So, what did you have for lunch?"

"A nice crab salad."

"Oh, yeah? Where'd you get the crab?"

"Mary Elizabeth brought it by."

"Did she make it?"

"Yes, and it was delicious. I've never seen your father eat so much."

"Huh," she said thoughtfully. "Pop ate a salad for lunch?" Something was definitely going on. Her father had always required something much more filling for lunch in the past.

"Yes. He and Mary Elizabeth sat and talked for a long while today."

"Really? About what?"

"Sports, computers, cars. You."

"Me?"

"She's a very insightful young lady." She glanced down the hall. "She's had some issues with her father in the past. I think she's made him realize what he's missing by choosing not to be a part of your life."

Izzy sank down into the chair at the kitchen table. "I guess I really am going to have to meet this girl."

"I wish you would. I think she's a little lonely."

"I don't know if I'd be good for her, Momma."

"She's like you in a way." She tilted her head. "She hasn't been able to find the kind of love she needs to make her happy."

Izzy grinned. "I hope you haven't been giving her advice. A lot of things have changed since you and Dad met."

"I told her to find where the light glows."

"I wish it was that easy."

"It is if you look into the right heart."

Izzy smiled at her mother's optimism. It actually gave her hope that someday she would find the woman who would hold her heart.

❖

Jack came strolling into Mel's office with the receptionist protesting as she trailed behind him. "I'm sorry, Mrs. Thomas. He didn't give me a chance to let you know."

"It's okay, Jenny."

"Can I get you anything?"

"A cup of coffee would be nice." Jack flashed Jenny the boyish smile Mel had seen him use too many times.

Mel nodded to her assistant as she got up and closed the door. "Again, a call would be nice."

"But I like surprising you."

"You mean keeping me off guard, don't you?"

He shot her the usual charismatic smile as he sat down in one of the club chairs in the corner of the office. Keeping her distance, Mel sat back down behind her desk.

"Listen, Mel. I'm sorry about the other night."

"Don't be. You're right. I do have a hard time being intimate with you." She threw the jab at him, even though she wanted out of the relationship. "The thought of coming down with some disease is pretty off-putting."

"Really, Mel. Is this the way you want to do this?"

"What do you want from me, Jack?"

"I want half."

"Half of what? The condo?"

"Half of everything."

"You have got to be kidding. You put absolutely nothing into my company."

Jenny came back through the door with a cup of coffee and handed it to Jack.

"Thank you, darlin'," he said in a sugary-sweet tone and winked at her.

Watching him in action made Mel's stomach turn. "Seriously, Jack?"

"I was there, supporting you while you created it. My attorney says that's all it takes." His voice was still low and sweet.

"You are a bastard, Jack."

"Yes, but you've known that for a long time." The smile never left his face.

"I can't give you that, Jack, and you know it."

His grin vanished as he leaned forward. "There is one solution. All you have to do is give me the 401k."

She blew out a short breath. "You expect me to pay for your infidelity."

"I'm pretty sure we've both been unfaithful in this relationship."

"I've never slept with anyone else. You, on the contrary, have slept with many."

"You may not have done it yet, but you want to."

"What do you expect, Jack? I've been sleeping alone for years."

"Oh, come on now. Don't put that all on me. You never really were very responsive."

"Did you ever think it might take a little more than wham, bam, thank you, ma'am to get me going?" It was always all about him, the narcissistic prick.

He chuckled. "No, not really." He got up from the chair. "Anyway, if you agree, you can be free to see that little chef of yours. If not, it will take a lot more time and cost a lot more money. I promise." He took a last swig of his coffee and set it on the table. "You have my number. Think about it and let me know." He winked at her as he pulled the door open and strolled out of her office.

Mel had no choice now. She closed the door and picked up the phone.

❖

The scent of burning pinion wood filled Mel's head. The brisk temperatures of fall that had swept in with full force. Leaves blanketed yards with vibrant changing colors, signaling the death of summer. Neighborhoods were scattered with tall, green pine trees, some with brown needles that wouldn't see another spring.

Mel had made several trips to the townhouse to pick up her warmer wardrobe to help combat the chill in the air and had arranged to put the home on the market. In the meantime, she'd settled in quite easily living with Nancy. After a week of unfulfilled temptation sleeping in the same bed, Nancy had finally cleaned the clothes from the one in her spare room. Jack couldn't get anything on her now, because, although she'd thought about it many times, she hadn't seen or talked to Izzy in weeks. She knew he wouldn't give up his bread and butter so easily, and recently he'd been exceptionally nice. She got the impression he was trying to woo her back, but she knew him too well and wasn't having any part of it.

She and Nancy were getting along well, living in the same space but, as Nancy put it, living as friends without benefits. Nancy had spent several nights out but hadn't mentioned Ann or anyone else. Mel knew she was in the way. She'd kept her mind occupied during the day with work, but at night, when she was alone in bed, her thoughts always made their way back to Izzy.

Mel and Nancy were leaving on a week-long trip to LA next week, so maybe a little more distance would make the interminable feelings for Izzy fade a bit. She doubted it, but seeing her in her dreams every night and not telling her how she felt were getting more difficult every day.

"So, how was your day?" Nancy broke the train of thoughts clouding Mel's mind.

Mel got a glass from the cabinet and filled it with water before leaning back against the counter. "Jack came by to see me today while you were at lunch."

"What's going on, Mel?" It was clear Nancy could sense her resolve weakening.

"He says he wants to talk about things."

"You're not falling for that, are you? What about reporter girl?"

"I don't know." She rubbed her forehead. "He wants to discuss things over dinner tonight."

"You can't be considering going back to him after everything he's put you through. You don't love him."

"Of course I love him."

"You don't *love* him." She let the words tumble out slowly. "Not the way you should."

"What difference does that make?" Nancy was right.

Nancy pulled her brows together. "Really? Do we have to go over this again?"

Mel shook her head and avoided eye contact.

"Jesus Christ, Mel. I'm having a hard enough time letting you go for another woman. I'm certainly not going to sit around and watch you go back to him." Nancy grabbed her hand and pulled her out of the kitchen. "You need to go see Izzy. Remind yourself of what you want."

Chapter Fifteen

Nancy dragged Mel out of the car and into the kitchen at Bella's. "You two need to talk." Izzy opened her mouth to say something, but Nancy didn't let her get the words out. "She's thinking about going back to that slimeball husband of hers."

The stunned expression on Izzy's face dissolved, and she turned to the dish she was cooking. "And you brought her here because?"

"Jesus. Not you too." She grabbed Izzy's hand and pulled her away from the stove.

"Hey, I can't just—"

"Yes, you can." Nancy looked over at Tony. "He can take over for you, right?" Tony nodded. She opened the back door and shoved them both outside. "Now talk."

"What the hell!" Izzy stumbled out the door, then spun around and was face-to-face with Mel.

She shrugged. "I'm sorry about this."

"It's good to see you." Izzy's grimace melted into a soft smile. "How have you been?"

"Okay. Just working a lot."

"Yeah, me too." She took Mel's hand and led her to the concrete barrier they so easily used as a bench. Mel propped herself up on it, and Izzy stood in front of her. "So you've decided to make a go of it with your husband?" Izzy's tone was soft, and Mel could hear the vulnerability coming through.

"Possibly." Mel watched her feet as she bounced them off the concrete.

Izzy raked her hand down her face. "Why in hell would you do that?"

Startled by Izzy's unsteady voice, Mel snapped her gaze back to Izzy's.

Mel opened her mouth, but nothing came out. She had no words to explain the inner battle she was experiencing.

Izzy raked her teeth across her bottom lip. "Can I ask you something?" Izzy spoke softly again and didn't wait for an answer before she moved closer and took Mel by the shoulders. Mel flinched at the heat of her touch. "Does he make your nerve endings tingle every time he looks at you?"

Mel stared into her darkening blue eyes. *No. That would be you.*

Izzy fired the next question at her. "Is he the first person you think of in the morning and the last person you think of before you go to sleep at night?"

Again, you.

She leaned close to whisper in her ear. "Do you get wet just at the thought of touching him?"

Mel felt the heat of her breath, and liquid gushed to her panties. *Only you.*

The warmth of Izzy's cheek pressed against hers sent a hot, arousing jolt through Mel. She didn't know how much more of this she could take. She shrugged out of her grasp. "I don't see you out there getting any of that."

"Apparently, you don't see much." She took Mel's face in her hands, and the familiar ache afflicted her belly as Izzy's gaze flickered from her eyes to her lips. "I don't want any of that from anyone else. I want it from you."

The softness of Izzy's lips touched hers, and she felt them part slightly. That's all it took. Mel had been longing for this ever since she'd kissed her that day at the beach. When Izzy's tongue slid across her lips and dipped into her mouth, Mel was lost in her. She pulled her closer, pressing herself against Izzy as she twined her legs around her. Her hips ground into her as Izzy rocked against her. God, this felt so good. Mel couldn't stop the moan from escaping her lips as Izzy's hand moved up her side and her thumb slid across her nipple. The cloudy haze lifted slightly, and Mel ripped her lips away.

"I can't do this."

"Then tell me you don't want me." She trailed her tongue down Mel's neck and back up to meet her lips again, kissing her hard, possessively. Mel let her eyes flutter closed as Izzy's hand cupped her breast, her thumb flicking the nipple. She knew just what to do to her. Izzy pulled the shirt from Mel's pants and slipped her hands underneath. Her fingers sizzled against her skin.

The sound of a skateboard scraping against concrete yanked her back to her senses. "Stop." She shoved her away and pulled her shirt down. "For God's sake, Izzy. Stop touching me like that." She pushed herself farther back on the concrete, trying to clear her head. "Don't you know what it does to me?" The heat lingered on her lips. It was too much, too fast.

"I thought so, but then why would you consider going back to Jack?"

"I have to get this stuff with him settled." Mel could hardly breathe, and she could see the speed of Izzy's pulse from the throbbing vein in her neck.

"But you want me."

"I can't be with you while I'm still married to Jack."

"You and me." Izzy waved her hand between the two of them. "We could be really good together."

"Not like this." Mel couldn't deny she wanted her, but no matter what Jack had done, she couldn't be with Izzy while she was still tied to him. "I'm sorry, Iz. I wish things were different." Legs shaking, body tingling, Mel slid from the concrete. "I have to go." Mel didn't look at her. She couldn't. She could hardly walk. She felt literally kissed senseless. The wave of raw need coursing through her was more powerful than anything she'd ever imagined.

"Figure out what you want, Mel. But don't take too long. I won't wait forever."

She rushed through the restaurant, avoiding all the strange looks shooting her way. By the time she reached the car, Nancy was right on her tail. Mel yanked on the car door handle. "Unlock the door." She yanked again. "Now...please!" Her eyes welled, tears threatening to spill out.

Nancy fumbled with the key fob she took from her pocket and clicked the button. The BMW beeped twice and the door unlocked. Mel pulled open the door and slid into the passenger seat.

Nancy slipped into the driver's seat. "I'm sorry. I honestly thought talking to her would help."

Mel saw Izzy coming out the front door. "Just get me out of here, please." She wouldn't be able to keep the tears in much longer, and she didn't want Izzy to see her cry.

Nancy fired the engine and shot out of the parking lot, leaving Izzy behind, standing in the empty parking space.

❖

Izzy watched the car drive away. There was nothing else she could do. They'd gone from ninety to nothing in three seconds flat. She went back in, through the kitchen, and out behind the restaurant.

The screen door slapped closed behind Tony as he followed her. "Is she going back to her husband?"

"I don't know, Tony."

"What are you going to do?"

"Nothing. Absolutely nothing."

"So you're just going to let her go?"

"She doesn't know what she wants, Tony. She needs time to think." She took in a deep breath and let it out slowly. "*I* need her to decide."

"That doesn't sound like the sister I know."

"She's different. I can't be an experiment for her. If she wants me, she'll come back."

"What if she doesn't?"

"Then I'll wish her well. Life will go on." *I'll know she didn't want me enough, and I can't just be friends with her.*

"Damn it, Izzy. I hate it when you act so grown-up."

"Yeah. Me too."

CHAPTER SIXTEEN

Mel's meltdown had been huge, and she knew Nancy felt terrible for causing it. They hadn't discussed it at all, except for Nancy's explanation of why she'd taken her to see Izzy. Nancy wanted her to remember how strong her feelings were for Izzy, and Mel had remembered all right. All of the strange, new, wonderful feelings had come flooding back with such impact, she felt like she'd been jettisoned from ten thousand feet. She hadn't gotten out of bed for two days.

Over the past week, Mel had thought long and hard about what she was going to do next and concluded she needed some space. The timing of their trip to LA couldn't have been more perfect. Hopefully, the distance would help her clear her head. She hadn't met with Jack but had made her decision about their marriage. It was done. She couldn't untangle her feelings for Izzy while she was still close enough to touch. She'd never felt like this about anyone before and seriously wondered if it was even normal.

The two of them would take some time in LA with Rick to hammer some specs out. Then she would have to decide what she planned to do about her feelings for Izzy.

"I don't understand why we couldn't take a later flight." Nancy dropped her suitcase into the trunk of Mel's BMW. "It's not even light out."

"You can sleep on the plane."

"For the half hour between takeoff and landing? I doubt it."

"Then you can take a nap at the hotel."

"Did you request early check-in?"

"Yes. Now let's go."

Mel slammed the trunk closed and got into the car.

"Are you going to tell me what happened?"

"I did something really stupid." She twisted to look behind the car as she backed it out of the driveway.

"What?"

"Izzy kissed me that day you took me to the restaurant to see her." *God, did she kiss me.* She shifted the car into drive and stared straight ahead at the road. "And I kissed her back."

"I knew it." Nancy slapped her hand to her leg in satisfaction.

"It's not that simple, Nance."

"Oh, I see. The Catholic guilt is getting to you again."

Mel shook her head. "This has nothing to do with religion. I'm just not the kind of girl who starts one relationship without ending another." *No matter how much I want to.*

"But you admit you like her."

"I don't like her. I think I'm in love with her." She slid her hand from the wheel to the gearshift. "Is that crazy?"

"No, it's not." Nancy covered Mel's hand with hers. "Love isn't something you can control. It's like a meteor that crash-lands in your heart. You just have to let it burn." Nancy smiled. "You should ease up on the reins a little and try it. You might actually like it."

"I don't know if I can." She moved her hand back to the wheel and gripped it. "I like being in control."

"And with Izzy, you're not?"

"Not even close. Just the thought of being with her makes me want to drop everything and go to her. I don't even want to work."

"Jeez, Mel. I had no idea you had it *that* bad for her."

Mel rested her head back against the seat and blew out a slow breath. "I've never felt so intensely for someone before, and I don't know what to do about it."

"If you feel this way about her, why are you running away?"

"I don't want to mess it up."

"Mess it up how?"

"By sleeping with her." Mel's voice rose, and she took the corner too quickly.

"That should only bring you closer."

"What if it doesn't?"

"Will you answer something honestly for me, Mel?"

She nodded.

"Let's see. How can I say this gently?" She planted her elbow on the console between them. "When we were together, you never really wanted to...uh...go down on me."

Mel was certain Nancy saw the horrified look on her face.

"Don't get me wrong here. You were great with your hands, but you weren't really interested in anything else."

"We were so young then, Nance." She shook her head.

"Have you thought about that? Are you going to be able to do that with her?"

"Actually, I've thought about it a lot." Mel blew out a breath. "Probably way too much."

"And?"

"Yes. I want her in every way." Even now, just thinking about it made her body warm. "But what if I'm not good at it?"

"You kissed her, right?"

"Yes."

"How was that?"

"Amazing. I've never felt so sexually charged."

"And she liked it too?"

"I think so." *It certainly felt like it.*

"Then you don't have anything to worry about, sweetie."

"Except Jack."

"That's a whole other story."

"It may be, but that's why I can't tell her how I feel. That wouldn't be fair."

"Then get it done."

Mel pulled the ticket from the machine and slid it onto the dash as she drove into the covered long-term parking lot. She found the closest spot to the shuttle stop and popped the trunk. Nancy took the bags out, and they walked the short distance to the shuttle area. They were both silent on the short ride to the terminal and as they went through security and on to the gate. The airport wasn't very crowded. Getting to the gate two hours early made for easy seating. Mel found a couple of spots across from the window and rolled her suitcase up in front of the seat next to hers.

"I need a cup of coffee," Nancy said.

"I could use one too." Mel reached for her wallet.

"I'll get it. Just black, right?"

"Yep."

"Okay. I'll be right back."

Nancy came back with two black coffees and a white paper bag. "Banana or blueberry?"

"Blueberry."

As Nancy sat down, Mel saw her glance at the brunette sitting in the seat across from them. She handed Mel one of the coffees and a blueberry muffin.

"What would you do if you weren't still dealing with Jack?"

"Honestly? I probably would have already slept with her."

"When are you going to get your divorce?"

"I told Mike to have Jack served with papers last week."

"Jesus, Mel. Why didn't you tell me?" She leaned closer. "How'd he take it?"

"He's not happy. Now he knows I'm not backing down. He can threaten me all he wants, but I haven't done anything wrong."

"He knows you know about the reporter, doesn't he?" Nancy's voice rose, and the brunette across from them glanced up from her book. "Sorry," she whispered, shifting in her seat.

"Yes. Mike said he would give him the choice whether to make it messy. He'll have to decide how he wants to move forward."

"What do you think he wants?"

"It's all about money."

"You're not going to let him get his hooks in the company, are you?" Nancy screeched, prompting the brunette to look up again.

"Not a chance. It's always been in my name." She smiled. "And now yours."

The call for first-class passengers came over the speaker, and Mel collected the empty coffee cups and bag and headed for the garbage can. On her way back, she watched the woman across from them gather her carry-on. She handed Nancy something and proceeded to the boarding area.

"What was that?"

"She gave me her card, said to call her if you needed help."

"That was nice."

Nancy continued to watch the woman as she glanced back over her shoulder and smiled.

"What else did she say?"

"She said she'd love to have a friend like me. I should call her anyway." She chuckled.

"Oh my God." Mel rolled her eyes. "You are just a magnet." Mel grabbed her bag and pulled the handle up. "Come on. You can flirt with her on your way to business class."

It was pouring down rain when they arrived. They managed to pick up the rental car without difficulty, made it to the hotel, and were checked into their suite by ten. Next on the agenda was a room-service working lunch with Nancy.

Since lunch was on the company, Nancy had pretty much ordered one of everything. Thankfully, the room included a mini-fridge, and she would be able to munch on the leftovers later instead of ordering more. After they squared away all the details for their meeting with Rick, Mel jumped into the shower to freshen up before meeting him for dinner. When they arrived, they'd had a message from him at the front desk to meet him at some sushi restaurant in Beverly Hills at nine o'clock. Mel wasn't a big fan of sushi, but usually she could find something on the menu she could stomach. Nancy, on the other hand, didn't like sushi and had complained about it all afternoon.

Mel let the hot water run down her face as she thought about the conversation with Izzy behind the restaurant the week before. It wasn't the first time today her mind had wandered there, and it wouldn't be the last. The kiss she and Izzy shared was so intense she'd been unable to think. All she'd wanted to do was lose herself in it and let all of her insecurities go for just one night. She knew Izzy was hurt. She hadn't called, and Mel knew she wouldn't after the way they'd left things. Mel sat on the couch and blotted her hair dry as she flipped through the TV channels.

She heard the beep of the door lock, and Nancy came bustling in. "This is ridiculous!" she said, setting two cups of Starbucks coffee on the table. She slipped her soaking-wet coat from her shoulders and threw it over a chair. "It's been raining since we got here."

"Thank you," Mel said, popping up to get her latte. "You'd better get moving if you're going to take a shower."

"Look at me! I've already had one."

Mel laughed. "Well, you might want to at least do something with that wet mess on your head. Especially if you're planning to see that cutie from the airport while you're here."

"Oh yeah. Where'd I put her card?" She scanned the room.

"It's right here on the table." Mel held it up in the air, and Nancy tried to swipe it from her hand.

"Uh-uh. Not until after you get ready."

Nancy grumbled and headed to her room. "Jesus. I look like Carrot Top."

"Told you," Mel said singingly.

❖

"Well, what do you think, Mel?" Nancy asked.

Mel pulled her brows together.

"The wine. Isn't it wonderful?" Nancy zeroed in on her glass.

Mel picked up her glass and took a sip. "It's lovely."

"Where did you learn so much about wine, Rick?" Nancy took a sip.

Mel heard him mention something about working in Napa Valley and couldn't pay attention to him any longer. It took too much energy to concentrate on what he was saying. Her thoughts of Izzy overshadowed the endless details of his younger days in wine country that she'd heard many times before. She couldn't wait for the night to be over so she could get back to the hotel and call her. It had been wrong to leave without phoning, without letting Izzy know she wanted to talk when she got back to town.

Rick got up from the table and stood next to a young girl for a picture. Mel felt Nancy's hand land on her leg and squeeze. "What?" she asked with a jump.

Nancy whispered in her ear. "Look. I know you'd much rather be at home eating an Italian for dinner. But since we're here, let's make the most of it, shall we?"

"Stop." Mel gasped, her face reddening.

"I'm just stating the obvious. You've got one of the best-looking guys in LA jumping through hoops to impress you. Can you at least look interested so he doesn't get a bad rap?"

"Been there, done that." She picked up her glass and sipped her wine. When Rick sat back down at the table, she rolled her eyes at Nancy and relented. "Rick, with so many choices on this menu, would you mind ordering for me?"

"Nice," Nancy mouthed to her.

Rick ordered conservatively, with rolls including shrimp, avocado, and crab, among other items. She guessed he wasn't taking any chances of her not liking what he chose. They'd just finished their delicious main course when a young woman approached the table and asked Rick for an autograph and a picture. He politely obliged and stood up next to her for the photo.

Nancy glanced toward the door and her face lit up. "Is that—" She focused on Rick when he sat back down. "Do you know her? Can you introduce us?"

"Yes, and no. See the woman behind her?"

"Uh-huh."

"They just got married last month."

Nancy's smile dropped.

"Damn, too late again." Mel patted her on the arm. "Haven't you already made other plans for later anyway?"

Her smile returned. "Oh, yeah. Are you sure you don't mind if I invite her along to go out for a little while after dinner?"

"I'll keep her company," Rick said. "Right, Mel?"

"Sure." Mel smiled. That wasn't quite what she had in mind. A nice, warm bed and a much-needed phone call to Izzy sounded so much better.

Nancy snuck out to get the car while Rick paid the check. By the time Nancy pulled up in front of the restaurant, a line of photographers was blocking their path to the car. The early evening rain had formed a large puddle in the street gutter. Mel had started out around it when Rick swept her up into his arms and carried her across. "What a gentleman! Rick, this way. Give us a smile!" The photographers cheered as they snapped their shots.

He swung around and gave them a huge smile. Mel was stunned, blinded by the lights. In one swift move, Rick dropped Mel to her feet, pulled her into his arms, and planted a nice, long kiss on her mouth.

She wedged her hands between them and pushed. "Knock it off, Rick."

"It's just a little kiss. It'll be great publicity. Once they find out you were my high school sweetheart, the new website will be hit hard. You'll need to put some pics of us from back then on it." He reached for the backseat door handle and pulled open the door, motioning her to get in before him.

Mel slid across the seat, and Rick got in after her. "That may be good publicity for you, but it's not for me. Did you ever think I might have something going on in my personal life?"

"I'm sorry, Mel. I guess I got carried away." He gave her a sullen look.

She wiped the back of her hand across her mouth. "You're going to have to come out sooner or later."

Nancy chuckled. "Look who's talking."

Mel saw Rick's brows draw together as he caught Nancy's gaze in the rearview mirror.

"She's got a crush on her favorite chef."

"The cute little brunette at the Italian place you took me?"

"I do not." Mel felt her cheeks warm and knew Rick could see the blush.

"Oh, my God. You've come over to the dark side. That settles it. We're going out tonight."

"I was intending to head back to the hotel."

"Oh, come on. I said I was sorry." He seemed concerned, but he was a good actor. "It wasn't that bad, was it? I've been told I'm a pretty good kisser." He gave her a wounded look.

"Damn it." She couldn't suppress her smile. "If you weren't so cute, you'd be in big trouble."

He grinned. "So, why don't we head on over to the W? There's a great club at the top." His grin had returned way too quickly for Mel to believe he was sorry about anything.

Nancy's eyes were wide in the rearview mirror. "You can get us in there?"

"Of course. Why don't you call your friend and have her meet us there?"

There went Mel's chance to call Izzy tonight. They wouldn't get back to the hotel for a while. She watched as Nancy swiped her finger across the phone screen. She hit one button and pressed the phone to her ear. Mel shook her head. Nancy had already put the woman's number in her phone.

Mel was up early and down in the lobby to get a cup of coffee and a paper. She couldn't help but notice the lady at the counter staring at her. When she approached it to pay, she knew why. Pictures of her and Rick were all over the tabloids in the rack on the wall. She saw the headline and knew she had to fix this—now. She couldn't believe the pictures had already made the rags. And on the cover, no less. She picked up a copy of each and took them back upstairs to see exactly what kind of damage control was necessary. She thumbed through all of the pictures and captions and sighed. Jack was going to have a field day with this.

"Good morning," Nancy said, coming out of her room.

"That depends on your perspective." Mel slid the magazines across the table.

"He really did plant one on you, didn't he?"

"Yep, he did." She shook her head. "Great publicity for him. Not so much for me."

"His timing did kind of suck. Have you called her?"

"I can't find my phone. You took it last night, remember?" Mel was on her third glass of wine when she'd started missing Izzy, and by the fifth, she was calling her. Izzy hadn't answered, and Mel had only gotten halfway through the message she was leaving when Nancy had snatched her phone out of her hand.

"Oh, shit. I forgot. I gave it to Rick, and he put it in his pocket."

"Oh no, no, no, no." Mel slapped her hand to her mouth. "What if she called and he answered?"

"Jesus, Mel. Give you a couple of drinks and you start thinking too much. I told you not to call her last night." Nancy grabbed her phone. "What's Rick's number?"

"I have no idea. I just push the button." Mel grabbed the key to the rental car from the table. "Come on. Let's go. We have work to do."

"Surely she'll understand after you tell her what happened, won't she?"

"I'm not so sure about that. I said some things I probably shouldn't have before I left. Whatever I thought I had with Izzy may be gone by the time I get home."

Izzy thought back to the morning. She'd seen the missed call from Mel's number on her phone screen, then swiped at the screen and entered her passcode. Sure enough, there was a message from Mel at 11:23. Izzy pressed the play button and held the phone to her ear. Muffled by loud music and rowdy voices in the background, Mel's voice rang through the line. "Hey, Iz. I had to leave town early this morning on business and won't be back for a couple of days. But I was hoping…well, I thought maybe when I got back we could—hey, give me that." There was a high-pitched squeal and the message ended. Izzy checked the time on the phone, Mel had left the message close to nine hours ago.

She'd pressed the call-back button and waited for Mel to answer. After three rings, a groggy voice said, "Hello." It wasn't Mel. It was a deep male voice. Confused, Izzy had pulled the phone from her ear and double-checked the number. MEL THOMAS displayed across the screen. After pressing the phone back to her ear, she'd asked for Mel. Her stomach churned as the man said, "Mel, you awake?" The line had gone silent for a minute, with only rustling sheets in the background, and then he'd said, "She's out. You're gonna have to call back later." The line went dead.

How stupid could I have been?

❖

It was already nine o'clock and they were still busy. It was a good night. They'd even run out of shrimp, so Tony had sent Angie to the market to pick up more. When Angie got back to the restaurant, she tossed a tabloid magazine on the counter. "Guess we know now why the crazy lady's been acting so odd."

"Is that Rick Daniels, the movie star?" Tony asked.

"Yep." She unloaded the bag, yanked open the refrigerator, and tossed the vegetables inside. She unwrapped the shrimp and dropped it in the colander to rinse.

"I told you to watch out for her," Tony said.

"Shut up, Tony. I don't need that right now." Izzy couldn't take her eyes off the picture of Mel and Rick locked in a heated kiss on the front page of the magazine. She snatched it up and read the caption: RICK DANIELS SWEEPS NEW LOVE OFF HER FEET. "Business, my ass." She tossed it onto the counter.

"This looks a little awkward to me." Angie twisted the paper sideways, trying to make sense of the picture. "How could they even get a picture like this?"

Tony smirked as he read the article. "The paparazzi are everywhere. They'll even sit in trees for days with telephoto lenses to get stuff like this."

"You think this is real?" Angie held the magazine up, squinting as she thumbed through it. "She looks a little stunned to me."

"Looks pretty real to me." Izzy grabbed the paper from Angie's hand and scrutinized it again. She tossed it into the trash.

"Hey," Angie said, snatching it back up. "I want to read that."

"Take a good look. You probably won't be seeing much of either one of them around here anymore."

It had been almost twelve hours since Izzy had called Mel's number and was met with Rick Daniels's groggy voice. She hadn't gotten so much as a phone call from Mel since, and after seeing the tabloid, she didn't expect she would. Izzy knew she'd blown it with her the night before she'd left. She'd never felt so deeply for anyone before in her life, but it was clear Mel didn't feel the same. The pictures in the tabloid proved that.

"Fuck this." She yanked her chef's coat off and headed for the door.

"Where are you going?"

"Out." *To get over this woman.*

CHAPTER SEVENTEEN

Izzy drove around to clear her head for a while until she ended up at one of the clubs she used to frequent. She sat at the end of the bar nursing her glass of merlot. It was still early and the crowd was sparse.

A woman slid onto the stool next to her. "I haven't seen you here in a while."

"That's certainly a shame." Izzy slipped back easily into her old charming persona. "You're still as beautiful as ever."

"I'm glad you're back." She slid onto the stool next to her. "Buy me a drink?"

Izzy waved the bartender over. "Can I get a gin and tonic for the lady?"

"How sweet. You remembered."

"I'll be right back." Izzy excused herself to go to the bathroom.

When she came out, the woman from the bar was waiting right outside. She pushed Izzy up against the wall and kissed her hard.

"I've been waiting months to do that again."

"I'm sorry I made you wait." Izzy flipped her around and pressed the woman to the wall and kissed her again. Izzy slipped her tongue in her mouth, and the woman moaned. There was no tingle, no sizzle, no heat. Her body didn't register the slightest bit of excitement. Mel's face flew through her mind. What the hell had she done to her? It used to be so easy, a different woman every night. She couldn't do it. She couldn't be with another woman when she knew how blistering hot it was with Mel.

"You wanna get out of here?" the woman asked.

"Uh…I just got here. Let's get another drink first." Izzy took her hand and led her back to the bar.

Izzy sat at the bar all evening, the woman very close, claiming her for the night. She had gone from slightly intoxicated to feeling good to totally smashed before Dana strutted in.

"Hey, baby."

Izzy shot her a look. "What are you doing here?"

"This is one of my old haunts, remember?" She nodded to the bartender. "Thanks for the heads-up, Terry." She nodded back.

"You all alone tonight?"

"I wouldn't say I'm alone."

"She's with me," the woman said.

"Yeah." Izzy smiled as she leaned back on the stool and almost fell off. "I'm with her."

"I don't think so, honey." Dana made herself a wall between the woman and Izzy as she steadied her. "Where's your girlfriend tonight? Still in LA?"

"Girlfriend? You didn't say anything about a girlfriend." The woman swirled around and popped up off the stool. "I'm outta here."

"Not my girlfriend," Izzy called out to her.

"That's good to know." Dana slid onto the now-empty stool next to her and brushed Izzy's thigh with her knee as she crossed her legs. "Buy me a drink?"

Izzy motioned the bartender over. "My ex needs a drink. Bring her something sour, like her disposition." Izzy chuckled to herself as she downed the last of her wine and motioned for a refill. "Get it?"

"You're hilarious, Iz." Dana waved the bartender off. "Don't you think you've had enough for tonight?"

"Nope. There's still half a bottle left." She gave her a wink, then turned back to the bartender. "Pour me another glass, Terry." She pulled her lips into a smile. "Please."

She let the bottle sit. "I think Dana's right. We're getting ready to close anyway."

"Did she run a tab?"

"Nope. Cash."

Dana pulled a twenty out of her pocket and slid it across the bar. "Ready to go?"

"Terry's gonna pour me one more." She winked at the bartender. "Right, Terry?"

The bartender picked the empty wine bottle up by the neck and let it swing back and forth. "All gone."

"Come on, Romeo." Dana pulled Izzy's arm up over her shoulder. "It's time to go."

"Still got half a glass to finish." Izzy wasn't slurring yet, but she was getting close.

"You don't really want the lights to come on in here and let all these women see how shit-faced you are, do you?"

Izzy glanced around at the women in the bar, many of whom she'd taken home at one time or another. She swung around on the barstool. "Take me home, honey."

❖

Dana almost had Izzy out of her car and inside the beach house when Jess drove up. *Shit. How am I going explain this?* She let Izzy slip back into the passenger seat and met her at the back of the car. "Hey, baby."

"What's going on?" Jess craned her neck to look around her.

"Terry called me from the bar and said she was in bad shape." She motioned to Izzy in the car. "I guess she's pretty upset I won't give it another shot with her."

"Yeah. She called me too."

Thanks, Terry. "I can't get her out of the car." She moved to the open door.

"Here. Let me help you." Jess lifted her legs out of the car, and they each put one of her arms over their shoulder and lifted her. Izzy was a wisp of a woman, but tonight she was dead weight. Dana unlocked the front door with the key from Izzy's pocket, and they took her inside.

After they rolled her into bed, Jess took Dana's hand. "Come on. Let's go."

"I can't just leave her like this. What if she gets sick?"

"So you want to stay here with her tonight?"

"I think I should."

Jess opened the door across the hall and poked her head in. "Okay. We can stay in here." She took off her jacket and tossed it on the chair. "I'm not leaving you here alone with her."

"I won't let her get by with anything." She kept up what she'd been telling Jess about Izzy trying to get back together with her.

"With the way she keeps calling you? Not happening." Jess pulled the blanket up over Izzy and grabbed Dana by the arm. "Come on. She'll be fine. We're right across the hall."

Dana was up early to check on Izzy. She was still passed out.

"Come on get your stuff, and let's go," Jess said.

"I have to get gas," Dana said on the way out the door.

Jess followed her to the second intersection. Dana turned right into the gas station, and Jess kept going to the highway.

She filled her tank, then got back into her car and called Jess. It went to voice mail, just as she'd expected. Even though it was hands-free, Jess didn't talk on the phone when she was driving. She found it too distracting. "Hey. My sister just called. I forgot the kids have a play this morning and I told her I'd go see it with her. I'll see you at the restaurant in a little while."

She pulled out of the gas station and drove back to Izzy's house. She'd left the door unlocked so she could sneak in again. She walked quietly to the bedroom, found Izzy still sleeping soundly, took off all her clothes, and slipped under the covers. Then carefully she did the same to Izzy before she nuzzled up close to her, gently laying her head on her shoulder. Izzy took in a deep breath and stirred slightly. Dana stilled until she settled back in and then wrapped herself around Izzy.

❖

Izzy pulled her glued eyelids open and tried to focus on the ceiling fan above the bed. She felt the warmth against her side and the weight on her shoulder. When she turned her head, blond hair blurred across her vision. *What the fuck?* She popped up in bed, and the body next to hers flopped to the side.

Dana rolled over and smiled. "Hey, baby. How are you feeling this morning?"

"What happened last night?" She put her hand on her head, trying to stop the throbbing pain. "How much did I drink?"

"I don't know. You were pretty far along when I got there." Dana planted a kiss on Izzy's lips before sliding out of bed. "I brought you home and put you to bed."

She glanced around the room and caught the trail of clothes on the floor. She lifted the sheet...naked. *How the fuck did I get here?* Flashes of the bar the night before flew through her head. *What the hell did I do?*

"Are you going to visit your mother today?"

"I visit her every day."

"I'd go with you, but you know she doesn't like me." Dana poked her head out of the bathroom and shot her a smile. "I've got a few things to do, but could we get together later?"

"Can't. I have to work." She watched the naked, line-free, bronze woman walk out of the bathroom and cross the room to pull on her clothes. Izzy cringed, knowing the drill all too well. Dinner, sex, and see-ya.

She couldn't remember anything after the first three glasses of wine, after she'd seen those pictures of Mel and Rick in the tabloid. *What the hell is wrong with me? How could I have fallen back into bed with Dana, of all people?*

The phone rang and Dana picked it up. "Good morning."

Izzy pulled the phone from her hand before she could say anything else. She wrapped the sheet around herself and shot through the house out onto the deck.

Tony's voice rang through the receiver. "Was that Dana?"

"Uh-huh." Izzy pinched her eyes closed, thankful it wasn't Mel on the phone.

"I know it's none of my business, Iz. But if you want any chance with that beautiful brunette who's been coming around, you'd better get your shit together."

"Don't you think I know that?"

"Then how the hell did Dana end up at your house?"

Izzy glanced back toward the house to see her at the kitchen window. "I honestly don't remember."

"How much did you drink last night?"

"Two bottles."

"Between the two of you?"

"I think just me."

"You'd better lay off that stuff for a while."

"No kidding."

"I just called to let you know Momma's not feeling good this morning. Pop said she's not out of bed yet."

"Okay. I'll get over there as soon as I can. I need to grab a quick shower. Call you when I get there."

Dana was in the kitchen when Izzy returned. "What the hell was that all about?" Dana said.

"You tell me."

"We did spend the night together last night." Dana's lip quirked up.

"I don't remember."

"Well, I do, and you were wonderful." Dana slipped her arms around Izzy's waist.

"Stop." Izzy grabbed Dana's arms and pried them from her waist. "If anything happened last night, it was a mistake." Izzy rubbed her forehead. She couldn't be that much of a shit.

"Don't say that. We're good together." Dana kissed her on the cheek and spun around toward the door. "Let's stay at my place tonight. Bring home some lasagna."

"I'm not going anywhere near your place, Dana."

"Okay, then. I'll come back here." She didn't wait for Izzy to respond.

Izzy grabbed a bottle of water from the fridge. "I guess I'll be sleeping at Mom's tonight." She chugged down half the bottle, then went into the bathroom and saw her reflection in the mirror. Puffy eyes and dark, matted hair sticking out in all directions. *Jesus. It must have been some night.*

❖

Mel tugged her bag down the Jetway, pausing at the entrance to the plane just long enough to see a young man heaped over the trash can puking his guts out. "Too much fun," his buddy said with a chuckle as he stood next to him, dressed in a UC Berkeley T-shirt and holding his luggage.

Her stomach rumbled. That's exactly what she felt like doing, only it wasn't for the same reason. Mel was sure Izzy had seen the tabloids by now. She'd gotten her phone back from Rick yesterday and left Izzy a dozen messages since then. Izzy wasn't answering or returning her calls. She should've trusted Izzy enough to tell her about Rick, but her contract clearly stated she couldn't divulge any personal information about him. Mel hoped she would let her explain when she got home.

❖

Mel dropped her purse in the entryway of her parents' house and strolled into the living room, expecting to find her mother in her usual chair by the window, drinking her cup of tea. Instead, she found her father in his, typically empty, chair reading the newspaper. She glanced at her watch and noted it was only a little after six o'clock.

"Hey, Dad. I didn't expect to see you home so early. Where's Mom?"

He looked over the paper at her. "She's meeting with her book group tonight."

"Oh, yeah. I forgot about that."

"What's this I hear about your picture being splashed across the front page of some tabloid rag?"

"One of my clients thought it would be good publicity."

"That's not the kind of publicity you need."

"It's actually bumped the traffic on his website thirty percent."

"Maybe you should be a little more selective about who you accept as a client. Your brother would never take on someone so brash."

"He would if the client paid the kind of money Rick pays. Besides, Rick is a friend of mine." She spun around. "Why do you do that?"

"Do what?"

"Compare me to Mike. Make me second-guess my business decisions." She crossed the room and poured herself a drink.

"I'm trying to help you make decisions that won't prevent your little company from growing. I do have a few more years of experience than you."

"My little company? You don't even acknowledge I've had any success at all."

"That's not true. I know you're successful, but you can't compare that to your brother. He's a partner in one of the most prestigious law firms in San Francisco."

"You just did it again. I was in the top of my class, Dad. I graduated summa cum laude. Mike only made magna." She flopped down onto the couch.

"They're both great honors, Mellie."

"I've got so much work at 365, I can barely keep up."

"What's 365?"

"My little public-relations company, Dad."

"Has it always been called that?"

"Yes, Dad. 'We're here for you 365 days a year' is our hook." Her voice rose an octave. "I can't believe you don't even know the name of it."

"What do you want from me, Mellie?"

"I want you to acknowledge the fact I've built a successful company that serves multiple clients. And I want you to appreciate that I'm damn good at what I do. I want you to be proud of me." Her voice faded, and the last sentence came out in a whisper.

"Why would you think I'm not proud of you?"

She threw up her hands. "Everything you just said."

"Contrary to the old saying, things *don't* come to those who wait. Success takes work. Hard work and focus. You have a husband to take care of, and someday you'll have a family."

"I'm divorcing Jack, so I won't have a husband for long, and I doubt I'll ever have a family."

"I'm sorry. I didn't know."

"Because you never ask." The words came out harsher than she intended.

"I'm not good at this, Mellie." He sat on the couch next to her. "Do you think I like working twelve hours a day, every day?" He hesitantly lifted his arm and put it around her shoulder. "Watching you come across that stage at graduation was one of the proudest moments of my life."

Her gaze snapped to his. "You were there?"

He nodded. "I slipped out to see you graduate, but I couldn't stay for the celebration. I've given up many things to get where I am today."

"Was it worth it?"

"Perhaps not, but I've been doing it for so long, it's hard to stop."

Mel studied the creases in her father's forehead. The years of stress had taken their toll. Maybe she was asking more than he could give. "I love you, Dad."

"I love you, Mellie, and I am proud of you. I've never intended to make you feel otherwise." He pressed his lips to the side of her head, and her heart warmed a bit. He'd given her some insight into why he was the way he was. It wasn't quite what she was looking for from him, but it was enough to know he cared. Enough to make a new start.

Mel had been back from her trip for a couple of days now and hadn't seen or spoken to Izzy. She'd been trying to get things settled with Jack. It had been almost two weeks since Izzy told Mel she wanted to be with her, and she still hadn't dealt with her own epiphany that she might actually want to be with Izzy too. When she parked on the street next to the restaurant, her excitement was laced with trepidation. She wanted so badly to give Izzy what she wanted but was afraid of the consequences if it didn't work out. The fallout would leave their friendship broken and her heart irreparably damaged.

She slipped in through the back door and watched Izzy work her magic at the stove. Tony said something funny, and Izzy gave him a wide, dimple-pricked smile, her deep-blue eyes showing only through the slits created as her cheeks rose. Unprepared for the intense dip her stomach took, she spun around and plastered her back against the concrete wall. *Just tell her, stupid.* Why was this so difficult? But it wasn't just Izzy's heart on the line here. Her own heart would be shattered if this didn't work.

It was now or never. She sucked in a deep breath, pushed off the wall, and went inside.

"Hi, guys." Izzy stiffened at the sound of her voice.

"Hey." Izzy rolled her lips together. "When'd you get back from your trip?"

"A few days ago."

"Oh." She poured wine over a chicken breast in the pan, tilted it into the flame of the stove, and fire surged into the air. "Been doing damage control?" Izzy sounded aloof and Mel's stomach dropped.

"Something like that. I've still got a few things to work out with Jack."

"So you're not through with him?" She slid the chicken breast out of the pan and onto a plate, letting the juices run on top.

"I am, but it's not that simple, Izzy. We have ten years of history—"

"I don't want to hear about your history with Jack." She dropped the pan down onto the stove. "You can tell that to your movie star." The plate rattled as she skittered it onto the warming shelf.

"Izzy, don't do this." This wasn't going to be easy.

Izzy held up her hands. "Far be it for me to give you marital advice." The warm blue eyes Mel loved had become frozen.

"Walking away after all these years is complicated."

"I'm sure it is—"

"I guess this was a mistake." Mel turned and walked out the door.

She'd just started the car when the passenger door pulled open and Izzy slid into the seat.

"What now?"

"I'm sorry. I'm not really good at showing people how I feel." The ice in Izzy's eyes had melted.

"I think you just let me know exactly how you feel."

"I'm still stinging from those pictures of you kissing that movie star."

Mel whipped her head around. "He did that, not me. And you're one to talk. It's not like your lips have never been where they shouldn't be." Mel focused on the rustic sign hanging on the side of the building, remembering what Nancy had said about Izzy having a reputation.

"Listen, Mel. I admit, I'm no angel. I've dated, no…" She shook her head. "I've slept with more women than I can count and…when I caught Dana cheating, I went right back to it again." Izzy hesitated. "And then I found you out back that night."

"That was months ago." She let her gaze shift to the bottom of the steering wheel, where she swept her finger back and forth across the inside of it.

"Yes, it was."

"You're telling me you haven't slept with anyone since I…?" She let her hand slip from the steering wheel to the gearshift.

Izzy shook her head. "No, I…no one." She covered Mel's hand with hers. "Do you think we can start over? Maybe you could come out to my house tonight and we can talk?"

"It won't be until later. I've got a lot of work to do."

"I won't get out of here until at least nine anyway. Why don't you bring your laptop with you and work until I get home?"

"I guess I could do that. Will you bring me something to eat?" Mel shot her a soft smile.

"You've missed my cooking?"

"Among other things."

"I'll bring you anything you want." Izzy grinned, and the familiar jolt sizzled through Mel's body. Only silence passed between them for what seemed like an eternity, but Mel was sure it was only a minute or two before Izzy said, "Then I'll see you tonight."

"Yes, tonight."

"The key is under the flowerpot on the porch, and the wireless code is on the fridge." She squeezed her hand, then got out of the car and headed back into the restaurant.

She didn't really know if Izzy truly loved her. Mel only knew she didn't want to live the rest of her life without Izzy in it.

CHAPTER EIGHTEEN

Mel found the key under the flowerpot exactly where Izzy said it would be. After placing her laptop just inside the door, she noticed a small, hand-addressed envelope on the floor. She picked it up and laid it on the entry table before she carried her bag into the guest room. She hoped she wasn't being too presumptuous, but she knew it would be late by the time they ate dinner and had a chance to talk. Not that she knew what she was going to say. It would be at least ten when Izzy got home, and Mel was usually fast asleep by then. She'd be too tired to drive home.

She changed into her yoga pants and T-shirt and then hung her beige slacks and white blouse on the hanger she'd brought. After taking her clothes out to her car, she carried in the new pour-over coffeemaker she'd bought for Izzy. It was identical to the one she had in her own kitchen, which she'd seen Izzy eyeing when they'd been at her house. Mel's plan was to get up early in the morning and set it up as a surprise. She pulled open a couple of cabinets, looking for a place to hide the fairly large box. She finally found a spot at the bottom of the coat closet.

She took her laptop from the chair and set it up on the dining table. She had work she couldn't ignore. She'd already let a few things slide the past two nights and had to finish them by the end of the week. If she wasn't ready for tomorrow morning's meeting, she might be out of a client by the end of the day. Thank God for Nancy. She'd already saved her butt several times this week.

❖

Izzy buzzed into the house with a bag hanging from each hand. "I brought you something new tonight. One of Gio's creations."

Mel glanced up. "What?"

"Chicken saltimbocca." She emptied the bags onto the counter.

"Sounds fattening." Mel followed the wonderful smell into the kitchen.

"It's Italian. It's all fattening. I went light on the butter for you."

"Smells divine." She reached for the container and Izzy tapped her hand. "I need to take a shower before we eat."

Mel smiled. She'd expected a certain amount of tension but found only the natural easiness that seemed to always exist between them.

"Then why'd you put it in front of me?"

"I want you to savor the scent." She cupped her hand above the container and wafted the scent up to her nose. She winked and shot her an incredible smile as she turned on the oven. "After the oven preheats, can you slide these in?" She took the foil containers and a loaf of sourdough bread out of the bag and placed them on a cookie sheet. "They should be warm by the time I'm done." She turned and headed down the hall.

Before Izzy was out of sight, Mel lifted the top off a container and stuck a finger inside for a taste. The chicken saltim-whatever-it-was tasted just as magnificent as it smelled. The woman was a treasure. Mel could imagine her cooking her dinner every night. She lifted the lid on the other one to find angel-hair pasta.

"Izzy, did you say to put both containers in the oven?" No answer. She pressed the lid back down and took off down the hall to the bedroom. Peeking through the open doorway into the bathroom, she shuddered at the sight of Izzy through the clouded glass doors. She knew she should turn away, but she couldn't. She looked at Izzy from head to toe and then back up again until she met Izzy's smiling eyes staring back at her.

"Yes?" Making no attempt at modesty, Izzy opened the shower door farther.

Mel froze for a minute, taking in the sight of Izzy's glistening, boyish body as she tried to form words. "Uh, the pasta. I just didn't know if you wanted me to put it in the oven as well."

"No. Just leave it. I'll warm it on the stove when I get out." She slid the glass door closed and leaned back into the stream of water.

Mel couldn't help but watch her for another minute through the glass before pulling the door closed. She rushed back into the dining room, dropped down into the chair, and stared at her computer screen. "Shit." She slapped her laptop closed. No way was she going to get any more work done tonight with that vision of Izzy burned into her mind. She hopped up and paced the room. Maybe she should just march back in there, strip her clothes off, and get it over with. No. She couldn't do that. She'd want her again and again. That couldn't happen until she was totally free of Jack.

She pulled open the patio door and stepped outside. "Why are you doing this to me?" she shouted, looking up into the darkened sky. "Is this some kind of test?" She flopped down into one of the loungers on the deck and closed her eyes. After about ten minutes, she heard Izzy in the kitchen.

"Mel, you out here?" Dressed in pajama pants and an oversized T-shirt, she came outside. Mel pulled her knees up close to her chest, and Izzy plopped herself down on the bottom of the lounger. "The tide is pretty high tonight."

Mel watched her as she watched the waves, wet, dark locks falling on her shoulders, full lips, and long black lashes. She was a natural beauty.

"I like to sit out here at night and listen to the waves whisper." Izzy leaned back against Mel's legs. "Close your eyes and listen for a minute. Do you hear them? Slow and steady, they never stop. Rushing in and out, each time stealing a small sliver of the beach. They captivate your soul with their steady chant and work magic on your mind. They make the impossible seem achievable with their subtle, unsolicited advice. The ocean's vastness makes any problem seem insignificant."

"Izzy. How do you do that?" Mel had been out here alone and had heard the waves only as white noise. She certainly hadn't heard them in any way close to what Izzy described.

"I try to look for the beauty in things." She sat up and gazed back at Mel. "Like the sunflower flecks in your eyes." Izzy's eyes were dark, full of desire. Mel broke eye contact. Izzy put her hand on Mel's knee and let it slide down to her ankle. "Hungry?"

"Umm, yeah," Mel choked out, swinging her legs to the other side of the lounger and jumping up. "I'll get the plates."

Izzy gazed up at her with her blue eyes, hazy in the moonlight. "You want to eat out here?"

"No," she answered quickly. The mood out here was way too romantic. If they stayed here by the ocean in the moonlight, she'd be a goner. "Oh, by the way, you got a card from someone today," she said, hoping to hide the obvious effect Izzy was having on her.

"Who's it from?" She headed into the kitchen and took the bread out of the oven.

"Don't know. There's no return address." She grabbed it from the counter and handed it to Izzy.

Izzy ran her finger under the flap, slipped the card out, read it, and then tossed it into the trash.

"Who's it from?"

"No one. It's just one of those time-share invitations," she said, carrying the sourdough loaf to the table. "Want some bread?"

"Of course. I'm starving." Sliding the foil container across the table, she pried the lid off a little at a time, her fingers stinging from the heat. "You'll be lucky to get some tonight."

"That would be lucky, wouldn't it?" Izzy tugged her lip up on one side, and Mel felt her cheeks heat, knowing exactly what she meant.

After putting the plates in the dishwasher, Mel collected the containers and had started to drop them into the trash when she saw the card Izzy had tossed away. All it took was one look to make Mel's insides twist.

It was really good to see you the other night. I miss you, lover...
Dana

She tossed the containers into the trash on top of the note. *Lover!* *Man, this chick has nerve.* Mel wasn't at all surprised at who it was from, just at her audacity in sending it. Dana had seen the two of them kiss on the beach; she had no reason to assume they weren't together. She headed for the living room but stopped at the doorway.

What was she doing? Izzy had thrown the damn thing away. What good would it do to let her know she'd invaded her privacy? Still, why did Dana keep coming around? Would Izzy ever get together with her again? Mel finished cleaning up before settling in on the couch next to Izzy. As the leather cushion sank, Izzy slid across the slick surface and up against her, already asleep. Mel thought about getting up but put her arm around Izzy instead, letting her tumble into the crook of her shoulder as she lay back on the couch next to her. She stole the remote from Izzy's fingers and flipped through the channels until she found a do-it-yourself show.

When Mel woke up, she focused on the bright-red digital numbers on the cable box—one thirty. She didn't want to move. Izzy had snuggled in close, with a leg draped across hers and an arm hooked around her waist. She really should get up and go to bed, but Mel wanted to just stay there wrapped up with Izzy and take in everything about her, from the soft feel of her body to the subtle scent of her skin. She'd never felt this close to anyone, especially not Jack. She stayed there entwined with her a few minutes longer, but she had to be in the office early to finish some work in the morning, and six a.m. would be here too soon. Mel tried to wrangle out from under her, but Izzy's hand moved up her side, dipped under her back, and pulled her closer.

"Stay," she murmured into her shoulder, and Mel couldn't refuse.

The next time Mel woke, it was five o'clock. She slipped out from under Izzy. Other than taking a deep breath, she didn't stir this time.

❖

"Shit." Izzy lifted her head after she thudded to the floor. She glanced up at the old clock on the mantle, which was stuck on twelve o'clock, as usual. Pushing herself up, she rested against the front of the couch and rubbed her cheek to relieve the sting from hitting the hardwood floor.

"Mel." No answer. "Mel," she shouted louder. She got to her feet, moved down the hall to the guest bedroom, and knocked. The door swung open. Gone. "Damn." She had a little pang in her stomach.

The phone rang twice before the machine picked up, and Mel's voice resonated from the speaker. "Wake up, sleepyhead. This is the third time I've called."

Izzy picked up the receiver. "I'm up."

"I was beginning to wonder if you were already on your way to the restaurant."

"Why didn't you wake me?"

"I left really early, and you looked so peaceful I didn't want to disturb you."

"I wouldn't have minded." She shuffled into the kitchen and saw the time on the microwave. Nine fifteen. *Shit!* She was never going to make it over to see her mother this morning. She needed to let her know; Bella would be expecting her any minute. "Hey, can I get back to you in a little while? I need to call my mom." She flew down the hall and into the bedroom. "Better yet, can you just come by the restaurant later?"

"Sure. Is your mom okay?"

"She's fine. I'm just running late, so I'm going to have to go see her after the lunch crowd instead of this morning. I'll see you later, okay?"

"Okay, bye."

Izzy tossed the phone onto the bed, then threw on some clothes and splashed some water onto her face. She swung through the kitchen and grabbed a protein bar from a box in the pantry, jamming it into her back pocket. She stopped when she saw the shiny red coffee machine on the counter. A half-pot of coffee was in the decanter, and a yellow Post-it note was stuck to the front of the machine. She pulled it off and read it out loud, "Your kitchen needs some color. I hope you like red." Smiling at Mel's thoughtfulness, she took a travel mug from the cabinet and filled it before she left.

As she made the thirty-minute drive to the market, Izzy ran through the previous night in her head. She'd caught Mel watching her in the shower. The woman was definitely curious. Her stutter had given her away. Izzy really hadn't meant to give her a show, but when an opportunity arises, one must take it. Izzy couldn't mistake what she'd seen in those deep-green eyes. It was pure unadulterated desire. And out on the deck when Izzy had touched Mel's leg, she'd seen it again.

Mel stood in the doorway watching Izzy work as she sang along with the radio. She was so natural and easy-going. Mel loved to cook but didn't know how Izzy dealt with the pressure of making dish after dish, all with different ingredients and all cooked to perfection. Izzy flipped the chicken breast and turned to the refrigerator.

Her lips pulled into a soft smile when she saw Mel. "Hey. You snuck out on me this morning." She pulled the refrigerator door open and took out a bowl of lemons, then chose one and sliced it in half. Squeezing it over the pan, she strained it through her fingers, catching the pits. "What time did you leave?"

"Around five."

Izzy gave her a strange look. "I don't even remember that."

"I tried to leave earlier, but you had me trapped and asked me to stay."

"Oh, yeah." She smiled. "I thought that was a dream."

"I had to go home first and change." Mel dropped her purse on the counter. "Big meeting this morning with a client." She didn't dare tell her it was with Rick Daniels.

"You shouldn't have bought the coffeemaker."

"Do you like it?"

"I love it, but it's too much."

"You feed me all the time. Let's call it even."

"Deal."

Mel's brows pinched together as she moved closer. "What happened to your face?"

"I rolled off the couch this morning." She dried her hands.

"God. I'm sorry." Mel let out a small chuckle as she brushed her thumb across the raspberry. "I would've stayed if I'd known it was so dangerous to leave you alone." She backed up slightly. "But it was probably good that I left. I might have ended up on the floor with you."

"Would that have been so bad?" Izzy lifted a brow. "The two of us tangled up together on the floor?"

"All show and no go." She stood firm, daring her. "You are such a flirt."

"You're calling me a flirt?" Izzy took a step forward. "Why didn't you just come into the shower last night? We could've cut right to the chase."

"What fun would it be without the chase?" Mel's heart thudded like it might leap out of her chest. She never was good at flirting.

"Are you chasing me?" Izzy's voice rose. She kept eye contact as she trailed her finger down Mel's bare arm and took her hand. "I can certainly make the catch a little easier."

The back door swung open. The voices of Tony, Carlos, and Miguel filled the room as they entered.

"We'll have to pick this up again later." Izzy gave her a steamy look as she pressed Mel's hand to her lips, then released it. "So, how'd it go?"

"What?" Mel murmured through the erotic fog clouding her mind. She could hardly think.

Izzy chuckled. "The meeting."

"Oh, the meeting went grea—" Mel heard a crash and snapped her head around. Carlos had dropped to the floor.

"Carlos!" Izzy rushed to him.

Mel knelt down and slapped at his face softly. "What's the matter with him?" She rolled up a dishtowel and put it under his head.

"I don't know. He was fine a few minutes ago," Izzy said.

Mel repeated the question in Spanish, and Miguel responded.

"He didn't eat this morning," Miguel spewed in his native language. "He has low blood sugar."

Mel pulled another towel from the counter and threw it at him. "Wet this and get me a glass of orange juice." She rattled off the orders in Spanish without losing a beat.

"Is he going to be all right?" He handed her the wet towel.

She blotted his forehead and he started to rouse. "Help me get him up."

Miguel lifted one shoulder as Mel got the other, and they rested him against the stove. Izzy handed her the orange juice, and she held the glass to his lips. "Come on, Carlos. Drink some of this. It'll help."

He opened his mouth and let her pour some inside.

"Good. Now another. How are the spots?" Mel said, still speaking in Spanish.

"They're gone now." He started to get up and she held his shoulder, keeping him pinned to the stove.

"Finish the juice first." She handed him the glass. "You know you can't skip any meals with low blood sugar, Carlos."

"I was running late today."

Izzy squatted down next to them. "Maybe you should take the day off. Go home and rest."

"No. I'll be fine."

She searched Mel's eyes for reassurance.

"He'll be all right in a few minutes. You should probably fix him a sandwich or something." She'd switched back to speaking English now. "My mom has low blood sugar occasionally. It's not an issue if you're prepared for it."

"Oh," Izzy said thoughtfully. "I didn't know you spoke Spanish?" Her voice rose.

"Fluently." Mel's lip pulled up. "Did I forget to tell you that?"

"Yeah. You did." A hot rush of color washed up Izzy's neck. "So you've understood everything these guys have said to me?"

Mel nodded. "And everything you've said back." She smiled and let the amusement flicker in her eyes.

Raking her hand across her neck, Izzy blew out a heavy breath.

"I'm very flattered." Mel added.

"But?"

Mel quirked one side of her mouth into a half-grin and shook her head. "No buts. Except maybe we should clarify who's chasing whom."

Izzy moved closer, and suddenly Mel wished there weren't so many people in the room. "I think—"

"I think you should make Carlos something to eat before he passes out again."

She turned to see Carlos pulling open the fridge. "Is anyone else hungry?"

"Carlos, sit down. I'll make you a sandwich."

"Will you make me one too?" Mel slid onto a stool and smiled.

"I'll make *you* anything you want." She pulled out the Italian salami and provolone cheese.

Mel reached for her purse, took out her wallet, and slid a small envelope from the fold. "I snagged a couple of tickets to the Warriors game tomorrow night. You want to go?" She held the tickets up, and Izzy snatched them from her hand.

"Courtside. These are like gold." She examined one and then the other. "Where'd you get them?"

"Just some of the perks of having Rick Daniels for a client." She smiled, totally amused at Izzy's reaction. "So, do you want to go?"

"Like there's even a question."

Mel gave her a wide grin as she held her hand out for the tickets.

"Maybe I should hang on to these," Izzy said, handing Mel the tickets and then pulling them back.

"Uh-uh. My client. My tickets." She snatched them out of her hand and put them back in her wallet. "Carlos might faint again and convince you he needs a night out."

"Not a chance."

CHAPTER NINETEEN

M el wasn't sure how Izzy would take the change in plans for tonight. She'd misunderstood Rick when he'd given her the tickets. She'd explained the situation to Nancy, and she'd agree to go, but Mel was nervous about how to explain it to Izzy. She was probably reading too much into it. She took a deep breath, trying to convince herself Izzy would be okay with it.

"Hey, Iz," she said, strolling into the kitchen.

"Hey." A smile covered her face. "What're you doing here?"

"You remember my friend Nancy, don't you?" Nancy followed her into the kitchen.

"Hi, Izzy. It's good to see you again."

"Yeah, you too." She gave her a nod. "What are you ladies up to today?"

"Give me a minute, will you?" Mel said, turning to Nancy before taking Izzy's hand and leading her out the back door. "Listen, there's a new plan for the game tonight."

"I knew I should've held on to those tickets."

"I didn't lose the tickets. Rick wants us *all* to go with him."

"But you only have two tickets."

"I guess I misunderstood him. He has four altogether and wanted me to give the extra two to a couple of friends." She took them out of her purse. "He wants to be surrounded by women. It's a publicity thing."

"And he wants you on his arm?"

"I don't know about that. But he *is* my client, and they *are* his tickets."

Izzy frowned. "Mel, you shouldn't have to do that."

"I know how much you were looking forward to the game, and Nancy loves basketball too. So, I thought we could all go together."

"Mel, I don't know—"

"Come on. It'll be fun."

"It's just one night." Mel shot her an undeniable smile. "The seats are all together."

"All right. But if it's a disaster, don't blame me."

Mel knew she'd put her in an awkward position. She also knew Izzy wouldn't hurt Nancy's feelings. "Great." Mel took her hand and pulled her back into the kitchen. "The game starts at eight." She held up the tickets. "Who's going to hold onto these?"

"I'll take them." Izzy slid them into her pocket.

"Rick will have a limo. We'll pick you up at your house at six."

"I can just meet you at the game."

"It'll be better if we all go together. The limo will take us to dinner and then to the game."

"Okay. Then just pick me up here at the restaurant."

"I'd like to meet here too, but I don't really want to drive home later," Nancy said.

Izzy handed her an order pad. "Write down your address. I'll pick you up."

"Thanks, that's very sweet of you." Nancy shot her a smile as she wrote, and Mel's stomach lurched. That meant she'd be taking her home too. *We're friends. Just friends.*

"It's my pleasure."

They held eye contact longer than Mel thought was necessary, and she cringed. She cleared her throat. "Well. I'll be looking forward to seeing you both here at six."

Izzy broke eye contact with Nancy to look at Mel. "We'll see you then."

❖

Izzy didn't like to be at anyone else's mercy to get home, but it might be nice to be chauffeured to the game. She wouldn't have to worry about traffic, parking, or even walking to the arena. Even though she'd really been looking forward to going to this game alone with Mel, tonight might not be so bad after all.

She was more nervous about the night than she realized. She must have assessed herself in the mirror dozens of times before deciding to wear an olive chambray button-down shirt with black denim skinny jeans and low-heel boots. The outfit was nice enough for dinner but also casual enough for the game.

Izzy raised her hand to knock, and the door pulled open. Nancy must have been waiting for her. "Hi, come on in. Have a glass of wine." She turned, and Izzy followed her into kitchen, where Nancy poured her a glass of red wine. "I hope you like merlot." She handed her the glass.

Izzy held it up before taking a sip. "Merlot is good."

"Make yourself at home. I'll just be a minute." Nancy set her glass down and headed into the back of the house. Izzy watched her as she left the room. She was wearing a cozy plaid-flannel top, black leggings, and black pointed flats. Casual yet sexy, Izzy noted. She had to be at least five-ten. Even wearing flats she was an inch or two taller than Izzy.

"What's it like outside? Do I need a jacket?"

"Maybe something light for later. It's nice out now."

"Light it is." She reached into the closet by the front door, pulled out a black, lightweight cotton fatigue jacket, and tossed it over her arm.

Izzy led Nancy out to her Jeep and opened the passenger door for her, then slid into the driver's seat and fired the engine. "Should be a good game tonight."

"I hope so. Have you made it to many games this season?" Nancy asked.

"Just a few. It's kind of hard with my schedule at the restaurant."

"I guess it would be. You spend a lot of time there, don't you?"

"Yep. That's what comes with owning your own business." She threw her arm behind Nancy's seat as she backed out of the driveway. "Do you and Mel work for the same company?"

"We're independent contractors. I used to work for her. She recently brought me in as her partner."

"That's great."

"It is. We work well together."

"So, what's the point of being a contractor?" Izzy asked.

"We have more creative control and can work for several different companies at the same time. Plus, we make more money that way."

"What exactly do the two of you do?"

"A lot of things. Public relations, marketing, web design." She shifted in her seat slightly toward Izzy. "I could design a website for your restaurant."

"You mean bring Bella's into the twenty-first century?"

"Something like that." She laughed.

"I think Angie's doing the website as her class project."

"That's right. Angie's your sister. She's very talented."

"You think so?"

"I do. She's got a good shot at getting an internship with us."

Izzy smiled. "She does seem to love it."

"She's a beautiful girl."

"Yes, she is."

"Just like her sister."

Izzy felt the heat in her cheeks and kept her eyes on the road as she pulled into the restaurant lot and parked. The limo was nowhere in sight. "How long have you known Mel?"

"She's been my best friend since college."

"Sounds like you're very close."

"We are. Anyone who hurts her or takes advantage of her will have to deal with me." Nancy's stare was relentless.

"Well, let's hope that never happens," Izzy said and finally broke eye contact.

"Let's hope." Nancy let her voice lilt up a bit. "Here they come." The limousine pulled up and parked on the street in front of the restaurant. Nancy pushed open the door and headed toward it. Izzy shook her head and followed.

Mel threw the limo door open and waved them in as two or three cars pulled up behind them and photographers jumped out to take pictures. "Hurry before they try to climb in here with us."

The two of them scrambled in, and somehow Izzy ended up on Nancy's lap. "Sorry," she said, sliding to her side.

"No problem." Nancy gave her a wink.

Izzy gawked out the darkened window. "Jeez, is that going to happen all night?"

"Usually just when we're getting in and out. They won't come that close at the game, even if they find a way to get in," Rick said, picking up the bottle of champagne from the chiller.

Mel could hear Nancy as she leaned over and talked into Izzy's ear. "That's why we're here. It's good publicity for Rick. Let's make the best of it, shall we?" Nancy put her hand on Izzy's knee and squeezed it lightly.

Rick handed them each a glass of champagne. "Do you ladies have a preference for dinner?"

"Anything but sushi," Nancy said.

Izzy chimed in. "And Italian."

"Mel, how about you?" Rick asked.

"I'm not particular. You choose."

"I'm glad I booked French. There's a quaint little restaurant in the city I think you'll all love."

They all agreed French sounded good. When they arrived at the restaurant, the maître d' seemed to know Rick well and seated them in a private room in the back of the restaurant. The room was small yet comfortable, furnished with a linen-covered table butted up against the wall just large enough for two people on each side. Rick pulled out each of their chairs and waited for them to sit before he seated himself next to Mel.

"I asked the chef to prepare us a few of his specialties to save time. I hope you don't mind." Rick had ordered a couple of bottles of expensive French wine, and for the first course the chef sent out truffled fromage blanc to go with the charcuterie, pâté, and a pepper tray that always accompanied the meal.

Rick picked up the fromage blanc and passed it to Mel. She sliced a small amount from the ball and spread the creamy cheese across a small slice of crusted bread.

"So, Izzy. Mel says you live at the beach. Do you surf?" he asked as the tray made its way back to him.

She swallowed the bit of bread and cheese that was in her mouth. "I've been surfing since I was a kid. I don't have as much time as I used to, but sometimes I like to hit the waves early in the morning when the beach is still quiet."

"I've always wanted to learn. Maybe you can teach me sometime."

"Sure. I'm off this Sunday if you want to come out."

"I'm afraid I can't. I have to go back to LA Friday, but thanks. I'll keep that in mind for next time."

"I've surfed a few times before, and I'm free Sunday," Nancy said.

Izzy shot her a smile. "Then you should come."

After a course of French onion soup with gruyere cheese, the chef sent out a main course of marinated grilled hanger steak with truffle butter, pommes frites, and sautéed arugula on one plate, and coq au vin braised chicken with mushrooms, pancetta, baby carrots, and whipped potatoes on another. They had more than enough for the four of them, with plenty to spare. They all took a sample of everything, and the table was silent for a short time while they all enjoyed the food.

"I like to bike ride too. How about you?" Nancy asked Izzy as she plucked the last piece of steak from her plate with her fork and slid it into her mouth.

"I love it. I've done the Ridge to Bridge a couple of times. It's a beautiful ride."

"Seriously? Me too. We've probably seen each other and not even known it."

Izzy's lips tipped up, producing those wonderful dimples. "We'll have to plan on riding together next time."

Mel watched the two of them closely as they interacted. "Maybe I could come along too?"

"When did you take up riding?" Nancy asked.

"I haven't, but that doesn't mean I can't."

"Well, you'll have to give up those whipped potatoes and do a lot of training to get ready for the Ridge to Bridge. It's a forty-one-mile ride."

Mel widened her eyes and set down her fork. "Forty-one miles. That's crazy"

"You do the forty-one?" Izzy asked, pushing her plate back and leaning close to Nancy, still talking just loudly enough for Mel to hear.

"God, no. I'm dead after the twenty-five." She chuckled. "But I thought I'd throw it out there to watch Mel freak."

Izzy smiled. "You're bad."

"I can be *very* bad." Nancy's voice was low and sultry.

Izzy raised her eyebrows and cocked her head. "Duly noted."

They all groaned when the chef brought out an assortment of desserts. Crème brûlée, warm dark-chocolate fondant, and lemon cheesecake. Nancy immediately took a bite of each.

"How's the crème brûlée?" Izzy asked.

"Delicious. Try some." Nancy spooned a taste into Izzy's mouth.

"Wow, that's wonderful," Izzy said, licking her lips.

Mel almost choked on the chocolate fondant she'd just put in her mouth. *What the hell is going on here?* She cleared her throat to get their attention. "We should probably get going soon. The game starts in an hour."

"I'll take care of the check. Just give me a minute." Rick got up and went out to the main part of the restaurant.

Mel had to use the bathroom desperately, but she wasn't about to leave Nancy alone with Izzy. "I have to use the ladies' room before we go. Anyone else need to go?" Neither Izzy nor Nancy responded, so she kicked Nancy under the table. Nancy snapped her gaze to Mel and pulled her brows together. "Why don't you join me?" She smiled.

"Okay." She got up and turned back to Izzy. "I'll be right back."

"It looks like you're having a good time?" Mel said as she entered one of the three stalls.

"I am. Izzy is awesome. I didn't know we had so much in common."

Neither did I. "She is pretty awesome."

"The biking thing isn't unusual, but I've literally never met another woman my age who likes to surf."

Mel heard Nancy flush and go to the sink and wash her hands. Then the door opened and she heard Izzy's voice. "Rick called the driver. He should be back any minute."

"Okay. I'll see you out there."

"Yep."

Mel flushed and went to the sink to wash her hands, where Izzy was standing as though waiting for her.

Izzy shook her head and took in a deep breath. "You are…absolutely stunning."

Dressed in a black, fitted T-shirt, skinny blue jeans, and leather spiked-heel boots, she had spent almost two hours figuring out what she was going to wear tonight. Those four words made it all worth it. "Thank you," she said softly, unable to suppress her smile.

"I'll be right out." Izzy brushed past her into one of the stalls.

The photographers were relentless when they got out of the limo. By the time they reached the gate, Izzy could hardly see. The gatekeeper scanned their tickets, and they headed into the arena. They had all stopped at one of the luxury suites on the way in to say hello to a few of Rick's friends. Izzy and Nancy had only stayed briefly and then gone on down to their seats. Izzy didn't want to miss the tip-off.

The seats were great—row A, center court, just behind the wood. They scooted by a few people and sat down. Izzy considered the empty seats on either side of them and figured Mel and Rick would take the two next to her, just across the center-court line. Nothing but the best for Rick Daniels.

"You want anything to eat? Nachos, popcorn?" Izzy grinned.

Nancy shot her a smile. "Are you kidding? After that dinner, I couldn't eat another bite."

"How about a beer?"

"I think I'll stick with wine. I don't like to mix."

Izzy waved the waitress over. "Can we get a glass of chardonnay and a Miller Lite, please?" Then she turned to Nancy. "So you've been friends with Mel since college?"

"Yep. Met her my first year in." She smiled as though a thought flew through her mind. "A few times I didn't think I was going to make it, but she pulled me through."

"How about you? Did you go to college?"

"Culinary school."

"From the taste of your cooking, I'd say you were a very good student."

"It's easy when you're doing something you love." The waitress brought the drinks, and Izzy paid her. Nancy offered her a ten, but Izzy waved her off. "You can get the next round."

Nancy smiled and slid the bill into her pocket, then took a drink of her wine. She cradled the glass in both hands on her lap before whispering in Izzy's ear. "I'm having a really good time."

"Me too." In fact, she was having such a good time, she was feeling guilty. She turned and scanned the stairs, looking for Mel. "I wonder where they are." She shifted in her seat to look behind them.

"Rick's probably talking someone's ear off."

When Nancy focused her attention on the pregame show on the court, Izzy took one more look around and spotted Mel coming down the steps. She'd put on a black leather jacket before they entered the arena and was absolutely gorgeous. Rick was leading, with her hand firmly in his grasp. He stopped at the row and let her go ahead of him to their seats.

"Sorry we took so long," she said, smiling as she moved past Izzy to give Nancy a hug, then came back to Izzy and drew her into her arms. "I'm so glad you're here," she whispered into Izzy's ear before dropping into the seat next to her. "With the way Rick likes to talk, I thought we were never going to make it down here."

"What time do you want to come out on Sunday?" Izzy asked, taking a drink of her beer. Izzy hadn't pegged Nancy for a surfer, but if she was willing, Izzy would go with her.

"You're really going surfing? Isn't it kind of choppy out there?" Mel asked.

"Not once you get past the shore. Do you surf, Mel?"

Nancy answered for her. "God, no. She's too prissy for that."

She narrowed her eyes. "I can come out and watch."

"Sure. Come on. It'll be early though." She turned to Nancy. "Just after sunup."

Nancy looked over her glass as she sipped her wine. "Sounds good."

"What's your number? I'll text you my address."

Nancy rattled off her number, and Izzy fired off the text and then glanced back up at Nancy. Fiery red hair, green eyes, nice smile. Maybe she just needed a good fuck to get Mel out of her head.

The arena lights flashed, and the announcer's voice boomed over the speakers before Izzy could say anything else. She sat back and watched the players shoot out onto the floor as the announcer called their names.

Izzy had a hard time concentrating on the game after halftime. Rick and Mel had gone back up to the luxury suites to mingle and had never returned to their seats. She'd received an apologetic text from Mel telling her she'd be down as soon as she could break away. All Izzy could think about was the way Rick's hand was splayed possessively across Mel's lower back as they'd headed up the stairs. By the end of the game, the arena was still full. It always was when it was a close game. They were up on their feet for most of the fourth quarter. The last three-pointer circled the rim but finally sank. The Warriors won by two.

Izzy could see Rick and Mel through the windows of the luxury suite. They were still mingling with Rick's friends. Izzy was ready to go and didn't really want to wait around while Rick hung out with his buddies, so she suggested to Nancy they catch a cab. When Nancy asked her if she wanted to get a drink somewhere, Izzy took her to a moderately busy bar near the arena that would make it difficult to become too intimate. By the time she dropped Nancy off at her house later, she'd enjoyed talking to her so much Izzy wished she'd taken her someplace a whole lot quieter. She and Nancy seemed to have a lot in common, and she'd actually had a great time tonight, despite her feelings for Mel.

❖

Mel found the key under the flowerpot as usual and let herself in the house. She changed her clothes and got comfortable on the couch. Izzy probably wasn't expecting her to be here, but Mel was having serious second thoughts about tonight. She couldn't stand the way Izzy and Nancy had gotten along so well. Everything they had in common and the food sharing. *What was I thinking?* She clicked the TV on and flipped from channel to channel until she found the highlights from the basketball game. She couldn't believe how her body had tingled when she saw Izzy staring up at her when she came down to take her seat at the game. Even after her interaction with Nancy at dinner, the look in her eyes had been unmistakable. But what was she going to do about it? She'd gone back and forth about her feelings all afternoon.

She dropped her head back onto the couch and stared at the ceiling. Her life would be so much easier right now if she didn't have these feelings to contend with. But when she saw Izzy looking up from her seat at her tonight, her body had turned to pure jelly. The woman made her feel things she didn't want to suppress. But no matter what kind of attraction she felt for Izzy, she couldn't go on letting her think there was any possibility of the two of them hooking up in the near future. She was still married to Jack, and it didn't look like he intended to let her go without a fight. It wasn't a matter of jealousy or affection; it was all about money. He wanted half of the company she'd built from the ground up, and she wasn't willing to part with it. Until they worked out some kind of settlement, Izzy was simply off limits. So why was she here in Izzy's living room, sitting on her couch waiting for her?

The camera scanned the crowd and focused on their seats. The announcer said something about Rick Daniels having a new love interest, and Mel cringed. Something piqued her interest, and she backed up the footage to watch the shot again. Izzy and Nancy were having a really good time, smiling widely as they leaned into each other, whispering in each other's ear. "What the fuck!" She clicked off the TV, slapped the remote down on the coffee table, and closed her eyes.

Mel's body shook and she pried her eyes open to look around, confused at first as to where she was. Then she saw Izzy's smile and felt the warmth of her hand on her shoulder.

"Hey. I didn't know you were coming here after the game," Izzy said.

"How was your night?" She rubbed her eyes.

"It was good."

She glanced at the clock; it was after one a.m. "The game was over hours ago. Where've you been?"

"We had a drink afterward, and then I took her home," Izzy said.

"Did you sleep with her?" She didn't know what she was thinking when she'd set this up. Nancy was so much more charming and daring than Mel was.

Izzy seemed to balk at the question. "Isn't that what you wanted?"

"No." She bolted up. Jealousy raced through her, and she suddenly felt sick to her stomach.

"Then why did you set me up with her?"

"I didn't set you up with her." *Fuck! I did set you up with her.*

"It sure seemed that way."

"I just thought the two of you might hit it off. You know, become friends."

"You thought I could have something platonic with a woman who looks like that?"

"Isn't that possible?" She pinched her forehead with her fingers. The reasons seemed unimportant now. All she could think about was Izzy and Nancy, together. She felt like retching.

"That's like trying to convince me *we're* just friends."

Mel's gaze snapped to Izzy. Had she been that obvious? She scanned her eyes. Oh, God, she had been.

"Besides, with that outfit you were wearing, I'm surprised you even made it to the game."

"I didn't wear that for him." She saw the curiosity in Izzy's eyes. "I wore it for me. I like to look nice when I go out."

"Well, you certainly succeeded."

"You think so?" Mel's voice became quiet.

Izzy shook her head. "I can't believe you don't know how beautiful you are." She sat down on the couch next to her. "Listen, Mel. I know we've both been avoiding this, but that day behind the restaurant." Izzy took her hand and fiddled with the wedding ring on her finger. "I felt my whole world shift." Her eyes skittered nervously as she gazed into Mel's eyes. "And I thought you felt it too."

She'd felt it, and she'd done her best to ignore it.

"I was really looking forward to going to the game tonight *with you*. Then you pawned me off on your friend." Izzy raked her fingers through her hair. "Your gorgeous friend. So I went. Forgive me if I had a good time."

"She's not that gorgeous." She jumped up and rushed out of the living room.

"Well, she's certainly not ugly." Izzy hopped up and was right on her heels. "Why did you leave me with her?"

"I have no fucking idea why I did it." *You weren't supposed to sleep with her!*

"What about Rick? The man is so into you, it's ridiculous."

"That would be a big surprise to his boyfriend. The guy who was having the party in the club room," she said in a sing-song tone.

"Wow." Izzy stopped short. "I didn't see that one coming."

"You actually think I would sleep with one of my clients?" Mel spun around, and suddenly they were too close.

"I don't know what to think, Mel." She snaked her arms around Mel's waist. "You keep sending me all these mixed signals."

Mel's heart pounded. "I didn't want you to miss the game, and I had to deal with Rick. I don't know what else to tell you." Yes, she did. She'd wanted to be with Izzy tonight too. Leaving her with Nancy was just crazy stupid.

"Just tell me what you want, Mel." Izzy moved closer, and their lips were so close Mel could feel her heated breath brush across them. "Is that so difficult?"

"Yes. Right now it is." She turned her head and let her cheek brush Izzy's as she fell into her. She trembled. "I don't know what I want."

That wasn't true. She wanted Izzy. If she stayed there another minute, she'd have her. "I've got an early day tomorrow." She shrugged out of Izzy's embrace, grabbed her bag, and took off out the door.

Izzy followed her out and watched her drive away. She went back inside, slid down onto the couch, and dropped her head back against the cushion. It hadn't been an awful night like she'd thought it would be. She'd actually had a good time with Nancy after the initial getting-acquainted shock wore off. She'd found she and Nancy had more than a few things in common, not the least of which were their feelings for Mel. She remembered Nancy's words clearly. "You'd better be careful with her. She doesn't let people in easily, and she doesn't sleep with people she doesn't love."

Even without the not-so-subtle warning she'd issued early in the evening, Izzy could tell Nancy's feelings for Mel were more than platonic. She'd learned a lot about Nancy; information about them both seemed to be free-flowing. Surfing, biking, she even liked to snow ski, and she seemed to know as much about basketball as Izzy. She'd had a pleasant time, but at the end of the night when Nancy had asked her to come in, Izzy had politely declined.

She'd walked Nancy to the door of her house and had even kissed her on the cheek. But while the evening had been nice, Izzy couldn't— no, she wouldn't sleep with the best friend of the woman she really wanted to be with. She didn't know what the hell was going on. All she'd wanted was to spend the evening with Mel, and it seemed like that was what she'd wanted too.

CHAPTER TWENTY

The teakettle whistled and Mel flipped off the stove. She reached up, took two cups from the cupboard, and dropped a tea bag into each one before pouring the steaming hot water into them. Mel had hibernated in her room all day Saturday and hadn't even showered until her mom had let herself into her room this morning and insisted she clean up and come down for tea. Thankfully, daylight savings time had ended, Mel had needed the extra hour to recover from her restless night.

Her mother cut two thin slices of pound cake and placed each on a plate. "Is something bothering you, dear?" Cecilia asked as she set a slice in front of Mel and sat down next to her at the table. "It's a beautiful Sunday afternoon. Shouldn't you be out enjoying it?"

"Do you believe everyone has a soul mate in life?" She twisted the fork in her cake, making it crumble.

"I believe everyone is born with the instinct to recognize their soul mate."

"Really?"

"I was young once." Cecilia lifted an eyebrow. She must have seen the look of surprise on Mel's face.

"I just never thought of you as one to leave anything to chance." She mashed the crumbs with her fork and slid it into her mouth.

"Oh, I didn't, dear. My life was thoroughly planned out. I couldn't afford to leave anything to chance. I accepted that a long time ago. Your father has been good to me. Now *you*, on the other hand, are a successful young woman. You don't need to settle for someone who doesn't make you completely happy." She blew on her cup of tea before taking a sip.

"Do you think I settled with Jack?"

"I didn't say that. But I do know life is sometimes one hurdle after another. Don't you think it would be better if you could come home to someone who helps you clear those hurdles rather than someone who watches you stumble over them?" Cecilia cut a corner of her cake and ate it.

Izzy's dimple-pricked smile filled Mel's mind. "To someone who smiles when you walk in the room and you know their smile is just for you."

"Precisely. Unfortunately, not everyone has the opportunity or the courage to act on their instincts." Cecilia covered Mel's hand with hers and waited for Mel to look at her. "We both know you're not one of those people."

"No." She shook her head. "No. I'm not. But I did something that may push someone away." She'd never really confided in her mother about her love life, and it felt odd doing it now.

"And you're regretting it?"

"I can't make any demands on anyone. I'm still married."

"But you're upset because what you did may have actually worked."

"Well…yes. I guess I am."

"How do you feel about her?"

"I'm not sure. It's still new. I just know how good it is when we're together."

"Not like how you feel when you're with Jack."

"No. Not even close." Mel drew in a deep breath and let it out slowly.

"Have you talked to your brother lately? Perhaps he can give you some assistance." Cecilia's subtle direction didn't go unnoticed as she picked up her half-full cup of tea and strode into the living room.

Mel also hadn't missed her mother's gender reference earlier. She'd said, "How do you feel about her?" Mel's anxiety had immediately vanished when she'd heard it. When had her mother become so accepting of lifestyles outside the Catholic faith? When had she become so accepting of her? Maybe she'd been that way all along. Mel had never thought to ask. She'd just assumed her mother wouldn't approve. Cecilia had always said she'd baptized her children Catholic because it was a whole lot less work to be baptized that way rather than to convert later in life. Her mother knew this from experience, having converted from Episcopal, aka Catholic light, to Catholicism before she'd married Mel's dad.

Mel took her cell phone from her purse and hit the icon for her favorites list. Mike was right at the top. She touched it and waited for him to answer.

"Mike, it's me."

"Hey, sis. What's up?"

"I want you to go ahead and have the divorce papers changed the way we discussed."

"Already done. It's a good settlement. He'd be an idiot to reject it."

"You're not going to try to convince me to work it out?"

"I've known Jack for a long time, sis. I never have liked the way he treats you. I can't, in good conscience, advise you to go back to him."

There was silence on the phone.

"You need to find someone who appreciates you, Mel."

"Someone who makes me happy," she whispered into the phone.

"Yes. Someone who loves you more than he loves himself."

Like Izzy does. Her body tingled. "I'll be by to sign them tomorrow."

She didn't care if Jack agreed to the divorce, now that she had consciously freed herself from him. She would have absolutely no guilt involved the next time she kissed Izzy.

Mel closed her eyes in the shower and let the water run over her head. She hadn't gotten much sleep thinking about the basketball game. She wanted so badly to tell Izzy how she felt, but she couldn't. She'd thought keeping Izzy occupied by setting her up with Nancy had been a good idea at the time, but now she regretted it. She'd not only let Izzy know how great Nancy was, but also that she was totally unattached. Did Nancy have a good time? Maybe she didn't like Izzy. Her mood perked. Maybe *she* had a horrible time.

Mel was still thinking about the whole situation when she got to the office. She tapped on Nancy's desk as she passed by. "Come talk to me."

Nancy trailed her into her office. "What's up?"

"Close the door, please. Did you have a good time last night?" She slid her purse into the desk drawer before crossing the room and settling into one of the club chairs in the corner.

"Sure. You know me. I can have fun with any beautiful woman." She followed Mel and sank down into the other chair.

"You think she's beautiful?"

"I'd have to be blind not to see that."

"Did you..."

"Sleep with her?" Nancy smiled. "No. I didn't sleep with her." She reached over and squeezed Mel's hand.

"Didn't you two get along?"

"We got along just fine."

"Then why didn't you go to bed with her?"

"I would never sleep with my best friend's girlfriend."

She whipped her head around. "She's not my girlfriend."

"Cut the crap, Mel. She may not be your girlfriend now, but she will be as soon as your divorce is final."

She blew out a short breath. "I tried to stay away. I really did."

"Don't stay away, honey." Nancy pulled her lips into a soft smile and shook her head. "I don't think I've ever seen you like this before."

Mel looked at her curiously.

"Your eyes light up when you talk about her. Plus, she's *all* you talk about."

"That's not true."

"'Fraid so." Nancy nodded, pinching her lips into a concerned smile. "If it's any consolation, she's certainly smitten with you."

"You think?" Her voice rose.

"Well, let's see. What did we talk about last night? You, the restaurant, you, the game, and then more you. On top of that, she didn't even make a play for this." She threw out her hands and motioned down her body. "Not to mention all the women who stopped by our table to say hello to her last night."

"How many women?"

"Let's see, there was the brunette, the redhead, and two, no, three blondes."

"Five women stopped to talk to her last night while she was having a drink with you?"

"Yeah. She seemed a little embarrassed, but she totally blew them all off." She shook her head. "She's definitely into you."

"Wow. I don't know what to do."

"What do you mean, you don't know what to do? Grab her and stick your tongue down her throat."

"God, Nancy, you're so crude." Mel's cheeks heated.

"That's what you want to do. Just admit it."

She nodded. "I want to do more than that. I want to rip her clothes off, but I can't. Jack would have a field day with it."

"You need to at least tell her the whole story about you and Jack. You owe her that. If you want her to stick around, you have to be honest with her."

"So, you're not going out with her again?"

Nancy shook her head. "No. I'm not going out with her again. I've heard enough about you."

❖

Mel told the hostess her name and that she was here to meet someone. The hostess motioned for her to follow her and led her to the table where Jack was sitting. She had been surprised when Mike had told her Jack wanted to meet for dinner and talk. The last time she'd seen him, he wasn't agreeable at all.

"Thanks for coming." He stood up and pulled out the chair for her, then sat back down. "I wasn't sure you would."

"I'm not afraid of you, Jack."

"I don't want you to be." He shifted in his seat. "I want to apologize for that day I came to your office. I was way out of line." Mel didn't know what was going on, but it wasn't like Jack to apologize for anything. "Your brother had me served with the divorce papers. I had my attorney look at them, and I'm ready to sign."

"What's going on, Jack? The other day you wanted half of everything, and today you're just going to sign the papers?"

"I was angry, and after I thought about it, I realized I was being irrational. You deserve to keep what you've earned as much as I deserve to keep what I've earned."

"Have you made some six-figure book deal I don't know about? Mike can find that out in discovery, you know." She raised an eyebrow.

"No. There's no book deal or anything else like that."

This is too easy. "What aren't you telling me?"

"Look, Mel. If we draw this out, it will just cost us both a lot of time and money and…" He pressed his lips together.

"And what?"

"And Steph and I want to get married."

"You want to marry Stephanie? What. Is she pregnant?"

"Twelve weeks."

"I thought you didn't want children."

"I never said that. The time was never right."

"And now it is? How are you going to go traveling around the world and be a father at the same time?"

"The station has offered me a permanent position on the morning show."

"But you never—"

"I know, Mel. The baby changes everything. I don't want to be like my dad. I'm not going to miss all the firsts. I want to be right there when they happen, every one of them."

Stunned, Mel didn't know what to say. Jack's eye twitched as he waited for her response. She thought about letting him suffer, making him pay dearly, but she didn't have it in her. He was so…happy. She hadn't seen him this way in years. Half of her bubbled with anger and wanted to slap the smile right off his face, while the other half wanted to throw her arms around him and tell him she was thrilled for him.

She sat quietly for a moment, watching him steel himself for her reaction. She dropped her napkin on her plate, got up, and rounded the table. He stood up, fumbling out of his chair. Mel pulled him into her arms. The smell of his cologne filled her head, and her eyes welled. She was probably never going to be this close to him again, and that was all right. Now she knew everything was going to be the way it should be.

She pushed back from him. "Okay."

"Okay?" He blew out a breath.

"Yeah, okay." She smiled and relief washed over her. Mel couldn't believe how good it felt to let him go. She slid back into her chair, picked up her glass of wine, and held it up. "To new beginnings."

"To new beginnings." He clinked his glass with hers.

Mel took a sip, set her glass back on the table, and looked across at Jack. She picked up the knife and moved it to the right of the spoon, picked up the spoon and moved it to the right of the knife, then popped back up out of her chair. "I'm sorry. I need to go."

She couldn't wait any longer to start her life with Izzy.

CHAPTER TWENTY-ONE

Izzy lay wide-awake in bed, staring at her stucco-dimpled ceiling. Her shift at the restaurant had been a disaster. She'd sent the wrong dishes to the wrong tables, chicken Parmesan went out without cheese, and she'd even forgotten to add pasta to a few plates. She couldn't get Mel out of her head. The woman was in her thoughts constantly, and she couldn't prevent it. She'd had serious relationships before, but she'd never had a woman monopolize her thoughts so completely. She'd always been able to push them away at work. Now she didn't have the slightest idea how to handle her situation.

Izzy had called Mel earlier and asked her to stop by the restaurant after work so she could come clean about the basketball game. Educated and cultured, with an elegant sophistication, Mel had politely declined. She never forgot her manners. From the very beginning, Izzy had recognized that they were from two different worlds. It was a long shot Mel would be interested in the chef at a family-owned restaurant.

Mel had told her she already had plans for dinner with Jack but said she would stop by her house afterward. Jealousy had ripped through Izzy. The shield she'd lowered had rocketed right back up again. She'd fucked it up again. She should've been straight with Mel about her feelings last night.

She couldn't stand the thought of Mel being in the same room with a man who'd touched her intimately in ways she hadn't, who'd felt her breath hitch with his caress, experienced her body wet with arousal, made her moan with pleasure. A man who'd felt her body stiffen as she'd launched into orgasm.

She heard the front door creak open and rolled over to look at the clock. *Midnight.* Her stomach knotted. Mel had been with Jack for four hours. Izzy had lost her before she'd even had her, and it was her own fault. A tear rolled across the bridge of her nose, and she wiped it clean before turning back toward the window and squeezing her eyes shut. She heard Mel's footsteps as she came to the open bedroom door.

"Izzy, you awake?" Mel whispered.

Izzy didn't answer. She couldn't let her see how much it hurt.

She heard her go across the hallway to the guest room, only it wasn't the guest room anymore. It was Mel's room now. She was no longer just a visitor in Izzy's house or in her heart.

Izzy had managed to drift off for a few hours before waking again around six o'clock. She'd lain there listening but heard no movement in the house. Izzy wasn't sure she wanted to see Mel this morning. Her anger still outweighed her sadness at this point. She was pissed at herself for putting her feelings out there too soon, and she was pissed at Mel for rejecting her. After dragging herself out of bed, she brushed her teeth, splashed some water on her face, and wandered to the kitchen for a cup of coffee. She was going to need a lot of caffeine if she was going to function today.

As she headed down the hallway, she took in the aroma of fresh coffee and stopped. Mel was up already. She sucked in a deep breath and braced herself for the confrontation she'd been dreading all night. Rounding the corner, she found Mel dressed and ready for work. Apparently, she hadn't even thought her dinner with Jack last night was worth a discussion.

"Good morning," Mel said, as though nothing happened.

"Good?" Izzy rubbed her eyes. "I wouldn't call it good."

"Coffee's almost ready."

After swiping a cup from the dish rack, Izzy pulled the decanter from the brewer and slid her cup under the stream of black liquid, letting it splash into the cup.

"That's going to be awfully strong."

"I'm gonna need it today."

"Izzy." Mel moved closer, then stopped when Izzy shot her an unrelenting stare. "Can we talk about the other night at the basketball game?"

"What's to talk about?" Izzy glanced out the kitchen window. She couldn't look into Mel's piercing green eyes any longer. "I guess you've finally made up your mind and gone back to your cheating husband."

"Somewhere in the mix you forgot I—"

Izzy zipped her gaze back to Mel. She hadn't denied going back to him. She tried to hold her tongue, but her temper got the best of her again. "Did you fuck him last night?" Izzy slid her cup out and slammed the decanter back into its slot.

"Jesus, Izzy!" She dropped back against the counter. "Do you have to be so crude?"

"That's who I am. I'm not going to change for anyone." Her voice softened. "Not even you."

"Oh, Izzy," She squeezed her eyes shut and shook her head. "I don't want you to change. I..." She reached for her, but Izzy batted her hand away.

"You should leave before I say something I'm gonna regret."

Mel's eyes widened. "There's more?"

Izzy continued to glare at her, prompting Mel to cross her arms. "Go ahead. Give me all you've got."

"Just go home to your perfect little life. Then you can fuck your husband until you can't stand it anymore."

"There's certainly no reason to stay around here." She grabbed her purse and keys from the table on the way out.

Izzy saw some papers float to the floor. She picked them up and flipped through them. *Divorce papers—signed divorce papers.* She saw the bottle on the table. *And champagne.* "Shit!" She took off out the door after her.

The car was running, but Mel hadn't left. She sat slumped over the wheel. Izzy pulled the door open. The sight of Mel's body heaving in sobs nearly killed her. "I'm an idiot." When Mel stared up at her with those glassy green eyes, Izzy sank to her knees. "The biggest fucking idiot in the world."

"Yes, you are," Mel whispered, her voice cracking. "If you'd just listen to what I've been trying to tell you."

"What, baby?" Izzy pushed a strand of hair from her face and stroked her cheek. "Tell me now."

"I don't...want to...fuck *him.*" She choked the words out between sobs.

"Oh, God, Mel. I'm so sorry. I didn't mean it. Any of it. It just makes me crazy to think about you with him." She'd never felt jealousy like this before.

"I don't know if I can do this, Izzy."

"Do what?" Panic swept through her.

"This, us." She waved her hands between them. "In my whole life…you're the only one I've ever thought about being with forever, and it scares the hell out of me."

"You've thought about it?"

Mel studied her for a minute and wiped her palm across her cheek. "Yes. I've thought about it. I've thought about it a lot, but you sure as hell don't make it easy."

Izzy took Mel's face in her hands and kissed her gently, covering her mouth with slow, soft kisses.

"I have to go to work," Mel murmured.

"Come back inside," she said, finding the key and turning the ignition off. "Please?" She kissed her again, urgently this time. Mel's response was slow at first, but as Izzy deepened the kiss, she thrust her tongue deep into Izzy's mouth, returning the kiss fully.

Mel groaned, dragging her mouth away. "I can't miss this meeting." She plucked a tissue from the box on the floorboard and dabbed it under her nose.

"Okay." Izzy took the tissue from her hand and blotted the tears from her cheeks. "Then we'll just wait a few minutes until you calm down," she said, regretting everything she'd just spewed at her in the house. She was totally in love with this woman, and the thought of never seeing her again scared the crap out of her. "Listen. I'll make dinner tonight—shit." She rubbed her forehead. "I forgot I've got to work late." She took Mel's hand and rubbed her thumb nervously across the back of it. "Tell you what. I'll make you something and leave it in the fridge. You get a good night's sleep, and we can talk in the morning."

"You don't have to do that."

Izzy's voice softened. "I want to."

"You take such good care of me."

"Because I—" She stopped herself. "Someone has to." Izzy gave her a soft smile and thought she saw a glimmer of hope in her eyes. "If you let me, I'll always take care of you." She stroked her cheek lightly with the back of her fingers.

"You will?" Mel's eyes were huge, searching, Heat filled Izzy's body.

"Uh-huh." Izzy shifted slightly at the burning tingle flooding her body. How could she have let herself get in this deep?

Mel seemed as though she was just about to say something, but her cell phone rang. She jerked it from her purse and checked the caller ID. "That's work. I've got to go."

"Okay." She kissed her on the forehead before she stood up and closed the door. "I'll see you tonight?"

Mel nodded.

"You don't have to wait up." As she watched her back out of the driveway, it felt like her universe had gone full circle.

It had been a miserable day at the restaurant. When Izzy had said good-bye to Mel this morning she saw promise in her eyes even through the tears. Mel had every right to haul ass out of there and never come back. Izzy hoped to God she was there when she got home. She didn't honestly know how she would survive without her, *if* she could survive without her.

Izzy's stomach jumped when she drove down the street and saw the beams from her headlights bounce off Mel's shiny blue BMW. Relief washed through her. Mel had come back, even though Izzy had been an unforgivable ass.

Izzy called her name softly when she came through the front door, but Mel didn't answer. She checked the guest room—empty. She pushed open the door to her room and found Mel snuggled in under the covers, asleep in her bed. Izzy fell back against the doorjamb. She wasn't expecting Mel in her bed tonight. She stood for a minute watching her take in long slow breaths. Maybe these feelings of insecurity Izzy had weren't as one-sided as she'd thought. Maybe Mel needed some reassurance Izzy wasn't going anywhere either.

She showered, dried her hair, and crawled into bed next to her. Mel didn't move. Her back was to the middle of the bed, and Izzy didn't know exactly what she should do. She painfully knew what she wanted to do. She rolled over, back to back with her, and focused on the moonlight shining through the window. Mel shifted, and Izzy felt her warm body close in against her backside. Mel pulled her closer, and the heat of her soft breasts pressed against her back nearly sent Izzy over the edge. Mel's hand brushed across Izzy's hip as it searched for hers. When she found it, she intertwined their fingers and pressed them to Izzy's stomach. The feeling was a mixture of utter pleasure and pure torture. She was in for a long, sleepless night.

"Long day?" Mel whispered.

"Very. How did your meeting go?" Izzy had managed to get all the dishes correct but hadn't been successful in keeping Mel from her thoughts all day.

"Really well."

"Good." Izzy released her hand, reached back, and patted Mel's thigh. "Is this okay?"

"Uh-huh." Mel pressed her lips to Izzy's back and sighed. Then her hand was on Izzy's breast, teasing the nipple through the cotton. With that, a gush of liquid rushed her panties, and Izzy let out a soft groan. She'd never been so aroused.

Mel propped herself up on one elbow. "Is patience still a virtue?"

"Maybe, but you should know by now there's nothing virtuous about me." Izzy twisted to gaze into Mel's eyes. Her lip jerked up to one side, and Izzy suddenly wanted to suck it between her own.

"Me neither," Mel whispered.

Izzy indulged in the softness of Mel's lips, nipping at their sweetness. The kiss began slowly at first, almost tentative. Izzy rolled to her back, letting Mel set the pace. She felt Mel's hand slip under her shirt and cup her breast. She let out a groan, and Mel pushed her tongue into Izzy's mouth, which was what Izzy was waiting for. She grasped Mel's face with both hands and kissed her deeply. She tried to take her time, to let Mel take the lead, but all rational thought was gone. She'd wanted this for too long. Mel pulled away slightly, leaving them both breathing hard.

Izzy sensed Mel's apprehension. "It's all right to be nervous."

"You're not."

She took Mel's hand and pressed it to her chest. Her heart hammered against Mel's palm, and she kissed her gently. Izzy pulled Mel on top of her, pressing her firmly to her body. She was amazed at how soft she felt.

She let her hand creep up Mel's shirt to cup her breast, and Mel tore her lips away, sucking in a ragged breath. Izzy saw what she thought was a flash of hesitation in her eyes and thought maybe she should stop. Then Mel's eyes darkened and she let out a slow growl. "I want you," she said in a breathless whisper. "I want you now."

Izzy shuddered. "Are you sure?"

Mel reassured her with another deep kiss. "I've never been so sure about anything."

Mel knelt between Izzy's thighs, slipped her hands up Izzy's shirt, and slid it over her head. Watching Mel's eyes survey her, Izzy suddenly felt very vulnerable, a little scared even, something she'd never experienced before or during sex. Izzy was always very much in control, and that didn't change in the bedroom.

"You're beautiful," Mel whispered as her mouth trailed down her neck across the ridge of her collarbone. She ventured farther until she found a nipple and sucked it into her mouth. She took her time exploring one and then the other before moving her lips down across Izzy's stomach, producing a tremor on the taut plain. She kissed the spot again, and Izzy felt her lips smile against her stomach as it quaked.

When Mel slipped a finger into the wet heat of her center, Izzy grabbed a fistful of sheet and let out a whimper of pleasure. "Oh, my God, Izzy. I have to taste you."

A guttural moan erupted from Izzy's throat as Mel trailed her tongue down the valley of her thigh, navigating around her center, coaxing the pleasure out of her. She couldn't contain the cry that escaped her lips when Mel slipped her tongue between the hot, wet folds and took her into her mouth. When she slipped her fingers inside, Izzy's stomach jerked, and she was sure her body was going to explode. Lifting her hips, she pressed hard against Mel, wanting more, *so much more.* Mel braced an arm across her belly, holding her in place as she teased the perfect spot. Izzy groaned and shoved her fingers into Mel's hair as her orgasm peaked and warm, wonderful heat spiraled through her.

Her breathing still labored, Izzy reached down for Mel and said, "Come here."

Mel crawled up Izzy's body, wrapped herself around her. "I guess that was okay, huh?"

"I'm not sure *okay* is the word I'd use." Izzy took Mel's face in her hands and brushed her thumb across her cheek.

"How about amazing? Spectacular? Earthshattering?" Mel grinned.

"All of the above."

"Then maybe I should do it again."

"Uh-uh. My turn."

"But I want to—"

"My turn." Izzy wrapped her arms around her and flipped their positions.

"God, I love it when you take charge."

Slipping her thigh between Mel's legs, she eased them apart. She lifted her thigh to meet the warm space between Mel's legs and moaned. "God, you're so wet."

"You did that."

Mel pulled her down and kissed her deeply. Izzy slipped her hand down between them, her fingers sliding through Mel's wet folds. She moaned, and Izzy's body reacted to the primal sound. She'd never felt anything so wonderful. When she slipped her fingers inside, Mel ripped her lips away and let out a soft growl. Izzy circled her thumb in her folds in rhythm with her fingers, and Mel flew into a staggering orgasm. Her hips rose, pressing hard against Izzy as the spasms rippled through her again and again. When they finally subsided, Mel dropped back to the bed and slapped her hand to her chest.

"Jesus, Izzy. I didn't think anything like that was possible." Her body jerked as Izzy stroked her inside again.

"Amazing? Spectacular? Earthshattering?"

"Oh yeah."

Izzy raised a brow, lowered her head, and rolled her tongue around a nipple.

"Izzy, I can't...not again."

Izzy slipped down between Mel's legs and went right to work. She never gave up a challenge.

"Oh my God. Oh my God. Oh my God."

Izzy glanced up to see Mel's hands gripping the pillow behind her head. "You like that?"

"Yes, please...don't stop."

Izzy slipped a finger inside and pulled the wetness up into the swollen flesh, watching as Mel's stomach surged up and down with each stroke. She felt Mel grab a fistful of her hair and knew it was time.

"Okay. Come for me, baby." She lowered her mouth to the soft folds and slipped her fingers inside. Mel let out a long cry and tightened her thighs as the orgasm tore through her.

Izzy laid her cheek against Mel's thigh. She couldn't take her eyes off her. She was absolutely beautiful as she recovered from the most breathtaking sight Izzy had ever seen.

Mel tugged at a loose strand of hair on Izzy's forehead. "Come up here so I can kiss you."

Izzy crawled up Mel's body and pressed a soft kiss to her lips before she pulled her into the crook of her arm.

"Amazing. Spectacular. Earthshattering," Izzy repeated, knowing the words were right on spot.

"Who knew?" Mel chuckled and settled into the crook of Izzy's arm, laying her head on her shoulder. She let out a sigh Izzy took as contentment. Soon Izzy could tell by her rhythmic breathing that she was asleep.

❖

It was late when Mel woke in the morning, not really late, almost nine, but late by Mel's standards, having always been an early riser. She still lay nestled into the crook of Izzy's shoulder, with her head resting on her chest and their legs tangled together. Her arm was draped lazily across Izzy's stomach, and it felt like the most natural thing in the world. She was so warm and soft that Mel didn't want to move—ever.

She'd been so nervous the night before when she'd suddenly realized she had no idea if she could satisfy her. It had been a very long time since she'd made love to a woman. Then when she'd seen Izzy's dark eyes, filled with desire, the anxiety had vanished. She'd never been so aroused. She'd wanted to touch Izzy all over, and she'd wanted her to touch her back, which they had done several times during the night.

She heard Izzy take in a deep breath as she felt her fingers brush slowly across her hip. She closed her eyes and enjoyed the sensation of her touch before speaking.

"Morning."

"Morning." Izzy kissed her on the head.

Mel couldn't resist brushing her thumb across her nipple before sliding it back down to her stomach. Izzy shuddered and let out a soft moan, sending a jolt straight to Mel's mid-section.

"Don't you have to go to work today?"

"No. Tony said he and Gio could handle it. I'm all yours until Angie's birthday party later. You want to do something?"

"Like?"

"The beach?"

Mel grimaced. Their last time at the beach had started well but had ended with Dana between them.

"I got this invite to a private wine tasting. We could check it out and then hit the party afterward."

"Wine tasting?" She lifted her head and slid her a sexy grin. "Trying to get me liquored up so you can have your way with me?"

"I don't have to take you wine tasting to do that." Izzy flipped her over onto her back and brushed her lips gently at first, then more urgently as Mel responded.

Mel's head was spinning again. Izzy's hand slid up her side. Heaving chests and rapid breaths ran together as Izzy's smoldering eyes penetrated her. She didn't have to do anything but kiss her like that again to have her way with her. Mel would gladly spend the whole day in bed exploring each other.

Izzy pulled her lips into a sideways grin, and Mel's stomach fluttered. "Besides, whenever this happens between us there will be absolutely no liquor involved. I want you to remember everything I do to you."

Mel felt the smoldering-hot palm on her breast and let out a soft moan.

"Okay. Wine tasting. Later." Mel looped her hand behind Izzy's neck and pulled her down. The kiss was long, slow, and tender. It stoked the fire in Mel's belly. She could easily stay right here in bed with Izzy forever.

CHAPTER TWENTY-TWO

Dana watched the two of them as they toured the winery. She stayed with the back of the group, making sure not to get close enough to be noticed. She wasn't thrilled Izzy had brought her new fling with her. Izzy stopped to examine one of the barrels more closely while Mel continued with the group. Dana thought she had her moment to talk to her, but then Mel came back to join Izzy at the barrel.

She had to stop herself from screaming when Mel slipped her arm around Izzy's waist. *She's my girlfriend, bitch!*

They stayed together for the rest of the tour until they reached the tasting room, and Mel left Izzy at the counter to go to the bathroom.

She moved in behind Izzy. "Hey, baby. I didn't know you'd be here."

Izzy's eyes grew wide as she swung around. "What? Are you stalking me now?"

"Hardly. The owner's a friend of mine."

Izzy glanced over her shoulder in the direction Mel had gone.

"After we spent the night together, I didn't think you'd bring her here."

"Listen, Dana. No matter how many times you say that, I still don't remember any of it." Izzy slid her wineglass back onto the counter. "If you had to get me drunk to get me into bed, doesn't that tell you something?"

"Let's not fight. I just wanted to let you know the boys haven't stopped talking about you since we saw you at the beach."

She smiled. "It seems like they've grown a mile since I've seen them."

"Tracy told me you asked her if you could come by and see them."

"Yeah. I was thinking about going by sometime before I go in to work. Then I could catch them before their nap."

"I'm sure they'd love to see their Aunt Izzy."

"I miss those little guys."

"I know. I'm sorry about that. I really didn't mean to keep them away from you."

"I'd better catch up with Mel."

Glancing over Izzy's shoulder, she saw Mel on her way back from the bathroom. She slipped her arms around her waist and pressed her lips to her mouth.

Planting both her hands on Dana's chest, Izzy broke away. "What the hell are you doing?"

"Whoops." She gave her a sly grin. "Here comes your friend now." *Mission accomplished.*

Izzy spun around, and Mel took off out of the building. "Mel, wait," Izzy shouted, following her.

Dana grabbed her by the arm and swung her back around.

"Damn it, Dana. Let go." She pulled her arm free. "Don't you get it? You aren't important to me anymore. She's the most important person in my life now. I'm in love with *her.*" *Oh my God, I'm in love with her.* She rushed outside and spotted Mel running across the grounds to the parking lot. She'd already made it to the car by the time Izzy caught up with her. She tried to pull the driver's door open, but Izzy threw her body against it, pushing it closed.

"If you've still got feelings—"

"That was all her. I swear." Standing behind her clasping Mel's shoulders, Izzy buried her head in the curls of her dark hair.

Mel didn't turn to face her. "I can't compete with her." She shook her head. "I won't."

"Please, Mel. After all the crap we've been through these past few months, you have to know you're the only one." When she turned, Izzy took her face in her hands and focused on her eyes. "I meant every word I said to you." She pressed her lips to Mel's and felt the urgency— no, the anguish in her kiss. Izzy couldn't believe how much it hurt. "Come on. Let's get out of here," she said, pulling away slightly. "I'll drive." She took the keys from Mel's hand as she led her around to the passenger side of the car and opened the door for her.

After they pulled out of the parking lot, Izzy glanced over at Mel. "I didn't know she was going to be there."

Mel sniffed back a tear. "What happened between you two?"

"That's not important."

"I need to know why she keeps coming back."

"You really want to know?"

Mel nodded.

Izzy blew out a breath. "I caught her with my sous chef." She cringed at the thought of what she, herself, might have possibly done with Dana during her drunken blackout.

Mel watched her closely.

"I caught them in my own kitchen." She shook her head. "She was my friend, and she was fucking my girlfriend. Right in my own kitchen."

Mel didn't speak.

"It wasn't all her fault. The relationship I had with Dana wasn't healthy." Izzy couldn't believe the relief she felt. The pain that used to stab her in the heart whenever she thought about it was gone.

"Izzy," she said softly. "Six years is a lot to throw away. If you think there's any chance of being happy with her—"

"Fuck." She jerked the car to the side of the road, slammed on the brakes, and threw it into park. "I don't want her." She stared into Mel's wide eyes and didn't break contact.

"I believe you."

"I wouldn't do that to you."

"I said I believe you." Mel placed a hand on each side of her face and gave her a soft kiss. "Take me home."

Izzy brushed her lips again, then laced her fingers with Mel's and rested them on her thigh before she pulled the car back onto the road.

Mel turned up the radio and watched Izzy as she drove. She sang along with the music as though all was right in her world. God, Izzy was beautiful. By the time they pulled into the driveway, Mel knew exactly what she wanted. She wanted to be part of Izzy's life—forever, and she didn't want to wait a minute longer.

Izzy met Mel at the front of the car and took her hand. "Are we okay?" She nodded, and Izzy led her into the house. "I'm a little hungry.

You want something to eat?" Izzy asked, dropping the keys on the table just inside the door before heading for the kitchen.

Mel stopped. Holding on tight to her hand, she yanked her back and closed the distance between them. She stepped forward and pressed her lips to Izzy's in an urgent kiss. She pulled back and gazed into Izzy's eyes. They were deep blue now, heavy with arousal. She kissed her again, softly at first, then deepening the kiss as Izzy put her hands around her waist and pulled her closer.

She pulled Izzy toward the bedroom. Izzy tugged her back, slipped her fingers under Mel's shirt, and slid it over her head. She stood in a daze, her eyes hooded with desire.

Mel let out an anxious chuckle. "I'm not that great." No one had ever looked at her like that before.

Izzy blew out a short breath. "Yes, you are. You're more beautiful than I ever imagined."

Maintaining eye contact, she backed farther into the bedroom, tugging Izzy along with her. When they reached the edge of the bed, Izzy leaned close, taking Mel's bottom lip between hers as her hands roamed up her sides. She crossed the underwire of her bra and continued to her breast, stroking a thumb across the taut nipple underneath.

Mel reacted with an unexpected jolt, and she let a soft moan escape her lips. "Take it off," she demanded in a low growl. She wanted to feel skin to skin now.

Izzy obliged, sliding her hand across the small plane of her back until she found the hooks. With one quick pinch, the bra was undone, and Mel let it slip from her shoulders. Izzy pulled her own shirt over her head and didn't wait for Mel to unhook her bra.

Pressing her mouth to Mel's stomach, she took in a deep breath. With short, tender kisses, she slowly worked a hot pathway to the soft skin of her breast, flicking the hard nipple with her tongue before taking it into her mouth. Mel let out a gasp, and Izzy worked her tongue against the stiff peak faster.

"Oh, God, Izzy. Do you know what you're doing to me?" she said, thrusting her fingers into Izzy's hair, pulling her closer.

Izzy unfastened the button of Mel's capris, and with one good tug, the zipper came down. She slipped her thumbs inside the top of the fabric and pushed them down across her hips, revealing black silk panties. Mel moved closer as she stepped out of them. Izzy looped her fingers under the band of the panties and slowly lowered them, torturing Mel's thighs with the soft, warm touch of fingertips along the way. Underneath was a neatly trimmed, small, brown triangle. She nipped at the skin between Mel's hip and belly button. Mel quivered, Izzy glanced up at her, shot her a steamy smile, and did it again.

Mel pushed her back onto the bed and worked the button of Izzy's jeans. After letting her yank both the jeans and panties off, Izzy scooted up to the top of the bed and waited. A rush of heat flooded Mel as she took in the perfect body lying in front of her.

As Mel trailed her tongue around the soft, black patch of hair to the inside of her thigh, the slight touch made Izzy shudder. She slipped her tongue between the hot wet folds and sucked Izzy into her mouth before dipping her tongue inside. Mel reveled in the way the sensation made Izzy's stomach quiver and brought her tongue back up to the folds as her fingers made their way inside. Izzy let out a low moan, and her body jerked. Lifting her hips, she pressed hard against Mel as the orgasm tore through her. Mel placed a hand on her belly and felt her body quake over and over again until her hips dropped to the bed.

The smell of sex filled the room.

Mel tucked herself into the crook of Izzy's shoulder. She was in heaven. She couldn't get enough of her—how she felt, how she smelled, how she tasted. "I love you, Izzy." There it was, out in the open. All her cards were on the table now. Mel had never felt so vulnerable.

"You love me?" Izzy's voice was barely a whisper.

"Yeah. I do." Mel curled her lips into a soft smile. "I think I have ever since that night you spilled pasta on me." She remembered the adorable, innocent remorse in Izzy's eyes when she'd realized what had happened.

"A little spilled pasta was all it took? If I'd known that, I would've done it *so* much sooner." Izzy trailed kisses down Mel's neck to the top of her collarbone. "I love this spot right here." She moved down to her breast. "And this spot." She took a nipple into her mouth momentarily before she trailed down to her belly button and swirled her tongue inside. "And this spot." Mel growled as the fire in her body began to heat again. Izzy crawled back up Mel's body. "But I think I love the spot that talks to me the most." She kissed her tenderly on the mouth. "I love all of you, Mel."

Mel's eyes began to well; she wasn't expecting that. It made her melt into a big puddle of emotion.

"No tears, baby. Just love." Izzy kissed the tears away, then rolled to her side and pulled Mel in closely. Mel smiled and snuggled into the crook of her shoulder.

The phone rang. Izzy ignored it, letting the machine kick on. Tony's voice rang through the speaker. "Where the hell are you? Angie's party started an hour ago."

"Oh shit. I forgot all about that."

Mel traced a finger across Izzy's belly. "It's Angie's birthday. You should go."

"I'd rather stay here." Izzy cupped Mel's chin in her hand and pulled her into another long lingering kiss. "But we should probably make an appearance."

"We?"

"Yep. Get dressed, baby. I'm not letting you out of my sight tonight."

"Afraid I'll run off?"

"Something like that."

Mel took her mouth again, enjoying this feeling she'd missed for so long.

❖

The bar was already packed when they arrived. Izzy took Mel by the hand and kept her close as she weaved through the crowd toward Angie and her friends. Getting through the mass of people was a challenge. The place was so jam-packed they could barely squeeze between the night crawlers, most of whom had passed feeling good hours ago and were well on their way to being totally sloshed.

Angie squealed and threw her arms around her sister when she saw her. "You made it."

"Wouldn't miss it," Izzy said into her ear. "I brought Mel. I hope you don't mind."

Angie backed up and lifted a brow before she pushed past Izzy and pulled Mel into a hug. Then she shouted at her friends to make room on the couch for them. The music level was earsplitting. Izzy couldn't hear a word she'd said, but Angie's friends had gotten the message.

They parted slightly and Angie motioned for them to sit. They squeezed into the small space between the twenty-somethings, sitting a step up from the main bar and dance floor, which provided a great view of the whole place. Dougie came by and said hi before pulling Angie out to the dance floor.

They sat for a while, thigh to thigh, glancing coyly at each other occasionally while chatting with Angie's friends as they rotated out of the seats next to them. A familiar song came on, and Izzy grabbed Mel's hand, pulling her onto the crowded dance floor. The area was flooded with people. Bodies floated between them, nobody dancing with anyone in particular. Izzy could feel the bass thumping in her chest. Even though she'd done it herself when she was younger, Izzy didn't know how they partied like this Thursday through Saturday of every week.

As the song ended, Mel leaned near and whispered in Izzy's ear, "I need to visit the ladies' room." Izzy followed her. On the way, Mel stopped at the end of the bar, where Angie was standing with Tony. "I'm okay. Why don't you stay here and visit with your sister?" Izzy gave her a nod and tapped Angie on the shoulder.

Angie spun around and threw her arm around her back. "Look at you." Angie laughed. "Dancing and laughing. I haven't seen you have this much fun in a long time."

"What? Can't a girl let loose and have a good time once in a while?"

"Sure, but you…" Angie's eyes flew wide. "You haven't done that since you broke up with Dana."

"That's not true."

Tony chimed in. "Yes, it is."

Izzy caught Mel's gaze and smiled as she came back from the ladies' room.

Angie's voice rose. "You're in love with her."

A smile crept across Izzy's face. "Sure feels like it."

Mel let her hand drift down Izzy's back as she eased in next to her and pushed her chin out toward the center of the room, where a few people were doing more embracing than dancing. "Do you want to try a slow one?"

Desire rumbled low in Izzy's belly. It had been only a few hours since she'd held Mel close, and she desperately wanted to do it again.

"I do. I wasn't sure you wanted to." She glanced around the room at the crowd that had somehow thickened.

"I'd like nothing better." Mel took Izzy's hand and led her to a low-lit corner of the dance floor. "It'll give us a chance to talk without the crowd."

Izzy chuckled. "You mean the spectators?"

"I didn't realize Angie had so many friends."

"More than I ever had. I think they're curious about you."

"Just about me?" Mel raised a brow.

"About us."

Mel brushed her cheek as she moved close to Izzy's ear and whispered, "I'm curious about us too."

Izzy couldn't stop the moan from escaping her lips when Mel pressed her palm to the plane of her back and pulled her close, removing all space between them. "Curiosity is a good thing." She let herself melt into Mel, giving her total control for the moment.

Mel slid her fingers into Izzy's hair, leaned back, and gave her a wicked look. "Have we been here long enough?"

A sizzling shot of arousal swept through Izzy, who took her hand and led her out the door. Before she knew what hit her, Mel had her shoved up against the building with her mouth fused to hers. Izzy's knees buckled. This was unbelievable. She'd never thought this sweet little lady could take control like this, and that Izzy would let her do it.

"Take me home," Mel whispered breathlessly into her ear. "I want to taste you again."

❖

The sun's rays sprayed through the window across the bed as Izzy lay drowsily, warmed by the beautiful body draped across her. They'd made love for hours again last night, until they'd collapsed into one another's arms and drifted off to sleep. She breathed in the woman whose arms and legs were comfortably sprawled across her. Izzy had always wondered why some women were so grateful after sex. Now she knew. She'd had plenty of good sex before, but sex with Mel was epic, mind-blowingly phenomenal. She hadn't felt anything so intense with anyone ever before. Not even Dana, and she'd truly thought she was in love with her. After the last few days, she knew it wasn't so. She'd never realized before how easily passion could ignite when you were in love. And she couldn't believe this smart, sexy woman was here with her.

The light on the clock glared six a.m. She'd have to go to work soon, but she didn't budge. There was no other place she'd rather be. She nuzzled into the crook of Mel's shoulder and took a deep breath. The spicy scent of her skin sent a rush of warmth through her body.

"Last night was amazing…" Mel's voice was low and groggy.

"Spectacular…" Izzy smiled and kissed the top of her head.

"Mmm, earthshattering…"

"Uh-huh." Izzy stroked Mel's back lightly and nuzzled closer. "Sorry I didn't let you sleep much." She felt Mel smile against her chest.

"It was a good trade."

"Do you have to work today?"

Mel nodded. "I wish I didn't."

"Can you work from here?"

"I have a meeting at ten about Rick's website."

"Rick again." She let out a groan and pinched her lips together. "Have you noticed the way he looks at you?"

"Stop that." Mel pressed her lips against the soft skin of Izzy's breast. "You know you're the only one I want."

"Mmm. Do that again."

"And he certainly doesn't have any of these beauties." Mel smiled and obliged before trailing her lips up Izzy's neck to her mouth.

Izzy rolled Mel onto her back, pinning her to the bed. "So if I hire you to do my website, will you give me the same personalized attention?"

"I'll give you a much different kind of personalized attention, and I promise to do you for free." Mel's eyes darkened with desire.

"You'll do me?" Izzy chuckled. "I like the sound of that."

Mel glanced at the clock. "I need to shower."

Izzy pressed her face into the crook of Mel's neck and took in another deep breath. "You smell wonderful."

"I smell like sex." Mel's lip hitched.

"Uh-huh." She nibbled at her lip. "I like it." She slipped her hand between Mel's legs, felt the wetness, and had to taste her again. She lowered herself down Mel's body and reveled in the cry that tore from Mel's throat when she buried herself in Mel's center. After she crawled back up her body to kiss her, Izzy was surprised when Mel flipped her onto her back and plunged her fingers inside her with such bold determination she came fast and hard. Twice.

Izzy felt Mel move out of her arms and groaned. "Don't go."

"I really do have to shower."

"You're gonna just wash me off you?" She gave her a pouty grin.

"Uh-uh." Mel planted one last heated kiss on her lips. "You'll be all over me forever."

Izzy liked the sound of that too.

When Mel finished putting on her makeup and stepped out of the bathroom, she could hear Izzy's cell phone buzzing again. The damn thing had been buzzing all morning. Thinking it was someone from the restaurant, she shouted to Izzy as she picked it up. The name Dana glared brightly on the screen. She held it until the phone stopped buzzing, and the message on the screen said six missed calls. *What the fuck? Is this woman never going to go away?*

"You miss me already?" Izzy's voice flowed down the hallway.

Mel quickly set the phone down on the bedside table, flipping the screen down. "I do." She rounded the bed to meet her in the doorway and gave her a scorching kiss that made her want to strip her clothes off and pull her back into bed. "You have got to stop looking so damn sexy, or I'll never get out of here." She trailed her finger from the hollow of her throat down to the valley of her breasts.

"Never." Izzy shot her a sexy smile.

You have no idea how natural it is for me to want to melt into you right now. Mel let out a low grumble and tugged her in for another long, heated kiss that left her breathless when she pulled away. "I do have to leave."

"If you say so." Izzy moved to the side and motioned for Mel to go in front of her.

Mel opened the car door and tossed her purse across to the passenger seat. The leather seat was cool on her legs as she slid into the driver's seat. She tapped the hideaway compartment above her head and plucked her sunglasses from the holder before starting the engine. After looking over her shoulder to back out of the driveway, she turned briefly to give Izzy a wave good-bye. The grin overtook her face. There she stood in the doorway dressed in a light-blue tank top, navy-plaid pajama bottoms, and pink, big-bear-feet slippers. *Beautiful face, long, slender body, and big-ass feet. And she's all mine.*

CHAPTER TWENTY-THREE

The barista handed Mel her triple-shot latte, and she sat down across the table from Nancy. She'd been after her all morning to get out of the office. She was having a hard time keeping the grin off her face and knew Nancy would want to know why it was there.

"You've been holed up in there all morning. I was getting worried about you," Nancy said in between blowing short airbursts into her steaming coffee.

"No need to worry. I'm fine." She glanced out the window at a woman passing by with her cocker spaniel as she took a sip of her nonfat latte. If she made eye contact with Nancy, she wouldn't be able to contain her excitement.

"Did you work all weekend again?"

"No."

"Just no?" She reached over, took Mel's chin, and pulled her head back to face her. "Your cheeks are flushed. Are you sick?" She felt her forehead.

"Stop." She pushed her hand away. "I'm not sick." She raised her cup in an attempt to cover the grin spreading across her face.

"Wait a minute." Nancy's eyes squeezed into slits as she studied her. "You got laid."

Mel covered her mouth, sputtering as she choked down the gulp of latte she'd just taken. She wiped the liquid from her mouth and cleared her throat as she scanned the coffee shop to see if anyone had noticed. "I can't hide anything from you."

"I knew it." Nancy's eyes widened.

"I've been with Izzy all weekend."

"Oh my God, you must be sore."

Mel chuckled. Nancy's thought process was always amusing. "Sore, but happy."

"You told her how you feel?'

Mel nodded.

"Stop making me quiz you and tell me how all this happened."

She described the events of the weekend. How she'd met with Jack and he'd agreed to the divorce. Izzy's unexpected outburst of jealousy the next morning. How she'd crawled into Izzy's bed and waited for her to come home that night and, without going into too much detail, the amazing things that happened after.

"I've never felt like this before." She could see the mixed feelings in Nancy's eyes and reached over, taking her hand.

"I'm happy for you, Mel. I really am." She wiped a tear away. "I don't know why I'm crying. I've got my own news to tell."

Mel raised an eyebrow. "Have you been holding out on me?"

The color in Nancy's cheeks deepened. "Remember the attorney from LA?"

"Lauren? You've been seeing her?"

She nodded. "I've been seeing her a lot."

"How? What? Where?" Mel fired off rapidly.

"Since the week we got back. She actually lives here, in the city."

Mel flopped back into her chair. "Wow. I've been a good friend, haven't I?"

Nancy chuckled. "It's okay. I can understand why. You've been tiptoeing around your dream girl for too long. I'm glad it finally happened."

Her lips quirked up into a half-smile. "Yeah, me too." She sighed. "There's only one problem. Her ex keeps calling her."

"The one you thought was still her girlfriend?"

"Yep. Tons of calls and texts all weekend."

"Did she answer her?"

"No. She kept deleting them. But there were a lot of messages, and it's getting on my nerves. Is she going to pine after Izzy forever?"

"Maybe you should pay her a visit. Set her straight."

"Maybe so. I have to go see Mike to wrap up a few things this morning. I'll stop by her restaurant afterward."

"Do you want me to come with?"

"No. I want her to know she doesn't intimidate me."

"Good girl. I'll be waiting to hear all the juicy details."

Mel had already been by Mike's office. Next up was lunch. She found herself at Gustoso for the first time. She pulled open the tall wooden door and felt unexpectedly nervous as she entered. She wasn't expecting Dana to be right up front at the hostess stand.

"Welcome to Gustoso. How many for lunch today?" Dana said, glancing up. "Oh, hello. Mel, is it?" She smiled slightly.

"Yes."

"Is Izzy with you?" Dana craned her neck to look around her.

"No. Just me."

Dana's smile faded quickly. "Are you here to eat, or talk?"

"Talk." She glanced around the restaurant. The pictures hadn't done it justice. The unique style and vibrant, multicolored tile sprinkled throughout the dining area made the eclectic figures sketched on the walls pop.

"Watching your weight?"

"Not really. Just saving my appetite for what I have at home." Mel couldn't resist the jab.

Dana's eyes narrowed before she led her to a small table next to the wall. "I'll be right back." Dana pinched her lips together and headed into the kitchen. Mel could see right off what the attraction was. She had a curvy figure and a strut that would make any woman look twice. A few minutes later, Dana came back out carrying two small bowls of pasta and set one in front of her, the other in front of her seat. "Today's special," she said before sliding into the chair across the table. "Go ahead. I didn't poison it."

The scent wafted up to Mel's nose, and she had to admit it smelled wonderful. "You have a unique menu here." She took a small bite. It tasted just as good as it smelled. "What is it? A mixture of Italian and Greek?"

"Yeah. Jess is Greek." Dana shoveled a forkful of pasta into her mouth.

"It's also a blend of Izzy's recipes. She could take you to court for that." She ate another bite.

"That's Jess's problem now. I'm working on selling my share."

"Oh, really?" She set down her fork and took a drink of water. "To whom?"

"Some corporation."

"A corporation...that's too bad." She let her gaze scan the restaurant. "They'll probably want to change everything."

"From the amount of money they're paying me, they can do whatever they want with it. But you didn't come here to talk about the menu. What do you want?" Dana pushed her bowl back.

"It appears you still have feelings for Izzy." She set her fork down and wiped her mouth with the napkin.

"Of course I do. We were together six years."

"So you're not seeing Jess any longer?"

"That's none of your business."

"Are you just going to keep calling her even though she's moved on?"

"I don't know what she's told you, but she hasn't moved on." She leaned back into her chair and flipped her blond hair off her shoulders, seeming to gauge Mel's reaction.

Mel narrowed her eyes and waited for her to continue.

"You know that week last month when you were out of town? In LA, was it?" Dana jerked her lip up into a sideways smile. "Izzy and I were together."

She felt the slash through the edge of her heart as it pumped wildly. She shook her head, hoping Dana hadn't noticed her flinch.

"She didn't tell you, did she?" Dana spoke in a low, tepid tone, success ringing through. She'd definitely caught her reaction.

"Of course she did." Her stomach tightened, and the pasta she'd eaten roiled, threatening to come back up.

"Then you should know, Izzy and I were never exclusive. We've both slept with other women. You're no different than the rest of the ones she's taken to bed. She always comes back."

The rest of the women? Blood pounded at her temples, and she couldn't think.

Dana leaned close and raised her brows. "What makes you think you're better for her than me? Or that you're the only one?"

"This isn't about me. It's about Izzy. Her mother is sick. She doesn't need the extra stress."

"Bella is sick?"

"Oh, come on. She's been dealing with it for months." Mel didn't let up, watching her as she shifted in her chair. "You don't really love her, or you would know that."

"I do love her."

"Then either get all in, or get out of her life."

"Is that all you came here to say?"

Mel nodded. "Yep. That's it."

"Then I think we're finished here."

Mel pulled out her wallet from her purse and dropped a twenty-dollar bill on the table before she pushed back from the table and stood up. "Keep the change." She turned and strode across the restaurant, doing everything she could to keep it together until she got outside.

She got into her car and flipped the A/C to high. Her pulse raced and her mind spun. The tabloid pictures, the phone, that day in the kitchen. She had no idea Izzy had been with Dana while she was in LA. Izzy had lied to her. She'd told her she hadn't slept with anyone since she saw her that night behind the restaurant.

Izzy spun around at the sound of the restaurant door slapping against the wall. "Hey. I didn't expect to see you until later." She crossed the kitchen and gave Mel a quick kiss on the mouth. She backed up when she didn't respond. "What's up?"

"I went to see Dana today." She rolled her lips in, pinching them together. "Funny story. She told me you were with her while I was in LA."

Heat rushed through her and her heartbeat faltered. Her throat constricted, strangling any words she might say. The air was thick, almost solid between them as Mel waited for her to speak. She leaned back against the counter, trying to get her bearings.

"Oh...wow. You were." Mel fell back against the wall.

Izzy moved toward her. "Mel, let me explain."

"Hold on." She put her hand up. "You didn't think that was something you should tell me?" Mel's voice cracked. Her eyes were glassy green, moisture filling them.

She closed her eyes. "Things have been so great between us. I didn't want to—"

"Fuck it up?"

Izzy's eyes flew open and she snapped her gaze back to Mel's. She'd never heard her this way. Anger, shock, more anger.

"Well, that's exactly what you've done." Mel spun around and moved to the door.

Izzy followed her, grabbed her arm, and swung her around.

"I thought I could convince her to leave you alone." She narrowed her eyes. "I guess I should've been trying to convince *you* to leave *her* alone." She shrugged out of Izzy's grasp. "Just stay away from me." She grabbed hold of the counter. Izzy watched her take in a deep breath, seeming to steady herself. "How could you fall back into bed with…with her?" Disgust, hatred, sadness, despair—everything Izzy had feared from day one appeared in Mel's eyes.

"I don't know what happened." She rubbed the back of her neck as the heat crawling up it became unbearable. "Mel, wait." Izzy grabbed her arm again, and Mel pulled loose a second time.

"Did you mean anything you said to me?" The words hissed from Mel's lungs, and her vulnerability ripped through Izzy's heart.

"I told you how I felt." She saw the pain in Mel's eyes and struggled for words. "And you left."

"So you went back to her." She shook her head slowly. "I've been an idiot. All this time I thought—" She headed for the back door.

"You thought what?"

"Does it really matter now?"

"Yes, it matters." She pinched back the tears brimming her eyes.

"I have to get out of here." Mel took off out the door.

Her heart thundered as she watched the only woman she'd ever really loved walk out of her life. "Mel, please." She choked as she chased her in desperation.

She spun around and put up a hand. "No. Don't." Her eyes were wet, pleading. Then she was in her car and gone. She'd left her in the parking lot again, only this time, with good reason.

Tony brushed past her and swung back around to look at Izzy. "You can't just let her leave. You can't let Dana mess with her like that. Go after her."

"It could be true."

"What the hell? You really slept with Dana?"

"When I saw those tabloid pictures of Mel, I just lost it. I went to a bar and got really drunk."

"Jesus, Izzy."

"I'm not proud of it, Tony. I don't even remember it." She rubbed her face. "When I woke up, I felt like a freight train had hit me."

"Yeah. A freight train named Dana."

The past few days with Mel had been like a dream come true. Each night they'd fallen into each other's arms and made love in wonderful bliss like they were life-long partners. Now because of her stupidity, it was all gone.

The hurt in Mel's eyes was excruciating. She'd gone from the warm, fun-loving woman she'd seen over the past few weeks to a fragile ball of emotions. It killed Izzy to know she'd been the one to make it happen. She'd torched the only real relationship she'd ever wanted. Wanted? Yes. She wanted everything with Mel.

Mel stood on Nancy's doorstep and raised her fist to knock. She'd already gone back to the beach house and collected all of her things. She eyed the unfamiliar Lexus sedan parked in the driveway and realized she should've called first. She'd just turned to go back to her car when she heard the door pull open.

"Hey, where ya going?" Nancy must have seen her through the kitchen window.

"I'm sorry. I should've called."

"Don't be silly. You don't have to do that." Nancy swung the door open wide to let her in.

"But..." She glanced back at the car in the driveway.

"Lauren's in the den working. She's staying here. We're trying it out." Nancy gave her a sheepish grin. "I was just making some tea. You want a cup?"

"Sure. Why didn't you tell me this morning?" She dropped her purse into a chair in the living room, then followed her into the kitchen and perched on a stool at the breakfast bar.

"I wasn't quite sure where it was going." Nancy took another cup from the cupboard and dropped a tea bag in it before filling them all with steaming water.

"And?"

"And it's going really well. She moved a few things in last week."

"Wow. How unobservant have I been?" She shook her head as she noticed the changes in the living room. A mix of vibrant throw pillows on the couch and chairs, a pillar candle on the coffee table, and a framed photo of Lauren and Nancy on the entry table. The changes were subtle, but they were there.

"Well, you've been wrapped up in your own little fairy tale lately." Nancy lifted a brow and tilted her head.

"That's done."

"What do you mean, done? This morning you were over the moon about her."

"I broke it off." Mel couldn't stop the quiver in her voice.

"But you were so happy. What the hell happened?" Nancy rushed around and threw her arms around her.

"She slept with her."

"Her ex?"

She nodded "That weekend we were in LA, she slept with her."

"How do you know that?"

"I went to see her, like we discussed, and Dana told me." She rubbed her forehead. "It all makes sense now. When we got back from LA, she wouldn't return my calls. I thought it was because of the pictures with Rick."

Nancy took her hand, led her into the living room, and sat with her on the couch. "Are you sure it's true? Did you ask Izzy about it?"

She nodded. "She didn't deny it."

"I'm so sorry, Mel. You probably don't believe this, but I wanted you two to work out. I could see how freaking crazy you were about her."

"I don't know what the hell I was thinking. I have no claim on Izzy, and it was pretty clear Dana doesn't have any intention of letting me have any." By then she was sobbing uncontrollably, doubting the pain in her heart would ever go away. She wasn't just crazy about Izzy. She was in love with her.

"Oh, honey. Come here." Nancy pulled her in close.

"Hey, did you forget about the tea?" The voice became louder as Lauren entered the living room.

"The tea is in the kitchen. Sorry. I got a little sidetracked." Nancy rubbed Mel's shoulder. "You remember Mel, don't you? She's going to stay with us tonight, okay?"

"Of course." She pulled her brows together. "Anything I can do?"

"No. Nobody can fix this, but thanks." Mel sat up, and Nancy handed her a tissue. She wiped the tears from her cheeks and blew her nose.

Lauren headed into the kitchen. "I'll get the tea. Milk, sugar?"

"Just sugar. Two in mine, one in hers," Nancy answered.

A few minutes later, Lauren brought in their two cups of tea, then went back to the kitchen to fetch her own. "You want me to call in an order to the Chinese place we had deliver before?"

"That sounds great, honey. The number is on the fridge."

Mel noticed the sweetness in Nancy's tone and couldn't help but smile. She was glad Nancy had finally found someone. She wasn't going to spoil it with her problems. "I should go."

"Oh, no, you don't. You're staying right here with us."

Nancy's cell phone rang on the counter and she got up to answer it. "Hello."

Mel heard the immediate change in her tone. She was all business. "Yes, she's here." Mel caught her gaze as she glanced over at her. It was Izzy. "I'll tell her. Not that it will help." She pinched her lips together. "Sure, bye." She pressed her finger to the phone and slid it back on the counter.

"She wanted to make sure you were all right." Nancy took Mel's hand between hers. "I know it doesn't help, but she also said she's sorry."

"You're right. It doesn't help."

The conversation was sparse during dinner, and Mel barely touched her noodles. Lauren and Nancy cleared the dishes while Mel went out to her car and got her bag. When she came back in Nancy was sitting on the couch, and Lauren was sitting in the chair adjacent to it. Mel put her bag in Nancy's spare room and came back out to the living room. Nancy patted the spot next to her.

"We were just talking in the kitchen about what happened and well…we realized that was the weekend when Lauren and I first met, right?"

"Right."

"Lauren overheard us talking and gave me her card." Nancy glanced over her shoulder at Lauren and gave her a soft smile.

Lauren picked up where Nancy left off. "You were talking about your husband possibly blocking your divorce, I believe." The attorney in Lauren came out. "You were still married at that time, and technically, you and Izzy weren't even together yet. Correct?"

Mel nodded.

Nancy's gaze floated around the room as she seemed to search for the right words before locking her gaze back on Mel's. "So do you really think you should hold that against her?"

"Before I left, she told me she wanted to be with me."

"But *you left*…and then after we got back, you kind of fixed her up with me." Nancy turned to Lauren, who'd raised her brows. "It was purely platonic. I knew they were in love. I just had to make her feel it," she added quickly.

"She should've told me." Mel pushed the words out softly. "I shouldn't have had to hear it from Dana." *I'm talking about trust here.*

"Yes, she should have." Nancy patted her on the thigh. "But please think about it before you write her off. I've never seen you as happy with anyone as you were with her."

Nancy was right. She *had* left her standing there in the alley, heart in hand, slashed raw and bloodied in a million pieces. *How can I hold anything against her after that?*

CHAPTER TWENTY-FOUR

Close to a month had gone by in what seemed like a milli-second. Fall had moved out as quickly as winter had swept in with deluges of rain, bringing the long-missed blanket of green back to the dried, brown mountains of Marin County. The days had been dark, painful, and lonely, only reminding Izzy of what she wanted in her life but couldn't manage to capture. She didn't know if it was her loneliness getting to her or sheer fatigue.

She'd gone all in at the restaurant, earning herself a Best Chef, West Region nomination by the James Beard Foundation. The JBF Awards were the Oscars of cooking, and business had been off the charts since the announcement. Gio had moved into a full-time chef position, and they'd had to hire a couple of new sous chefs and wait staff to keep up.

When she'd received the card of congratulations from Mel, even though it was purely professional, her heart constricted a bit. Unable to throw it away, Izzy had filed it under a stack of books in the bookcase. She didn't have time to think about what she'd lost or speculate on what she could've had with Mel. But with the one thing she wanted most in life out of reach, the award felt meaningless.

Izzy was now the chef she'd always dreamed of being, but outside of the restaurant and her family, she had nothing else to show for it except pure exhaustion, which was what she needed. She didn't have time to dwell on what she was missing, to acknowledge she had no one to come home to, no one to share it with. No time to miss the woman with whom she'd fallen hopelessly in love.

Izzy rolled over and cringed at the red numbers on the clock. It was finally almost seven. She'd woken many times during the night, just as she had every night since Mel left. She fixed her gaze on the AC/DC T-shirt lying wadded in the corner of the chair. She'd thought she'd gotten rid of all the reminders. She'd even bought new sheets and a new down comforter. Twisting to get out of the tangled sheets, she reached over, picked up the shirt, and pressed it to her nose. Mel's faint scent still lingered in the cotton. Tears flooded her eyes. "Damn it, Izzy." This was exactly why she avoided getting this close to anyone. Getting emotionally involved with someone only set her up to get hurt, and this time the pain was excruciating.

Tossing the shirt back onto the chair, Izzy made her way to the kitchen. She glanced at the coffeemaker in the corner and took the French press from the drain board. Even though she wasn't using it, she couldn't bring herself to get rid of such a nice piece of kitchen equipment, no matter who had given it to her.

Izzy knew it was over. Even though she'd called Mel a number of times, Mel had never answered and hadn't returned her calls. She wouldn't beg. If Mel couldn't find it within herself to forgive her, Izzy would leave her alone.

Mel arranged various vases with flowers around the house. Nancy and Lauren were having their first party together, and soon women of every kind would be roaming the house and backyard. They both thought it would be a good way to get Mel back into socializing. But Mel had no desire to socialize, especially with single women. It had been weeks since she'd seen Izzy, and from what she'd read, Izzy had gone on famously without her. Mel had seen the nomination for the James Beard Foundation and was sure Izzy was too busy to miss her. When she'd read the announcement, Mel had wanted to go straight to the restaurant, take her in her arms, and tell her how proud she was of her. She'd actually found herself taking a detour now and then past Bella's on her way home. The parking lot was always packed. She'd thought twice about sending the card but knew she should do something to acknowledge the accomplishment. She'd burned through a full box of cards trying to keep her message warm yet impersonal.

She heard the doorbell ring. "You want me to get that?"

"Would you mind? It's probably the food," Nancy shouted from the kitchen.

Mel pulled open the door and let it thud loudly against the wall behind it. "What are you doing here?"

Dana stepped back. "You ordered food from Gustoso?" She lifted the bags she was holding.

Mel left her standing on the porch and went to the kitchen. "You ordered food from Gustoso?"

"Yeah. They're one of our clients."

"Since when?"

"It's the nouveau Italian place I told you about."

"What the fuck, Nancy. That's Dana's restaurant."

Her eyes went wide. "Oh, shit. I didn't know."

"Where do you want the food?" Nancy heard the voice from behind Mel and peeked over her shoulder.

"On the counter is fine." She slid open the screen door to the backyard and pulled Mel out on the deck. "Lauren, honey, Mel's going to help you out here while I take care of the caterer."

The old wooden ladder squeaked as Lauren turned. "Not necessary. I'm almost done." She hooked the wire of the light string around the hook hanging from the corner of the arbor.

"I'm sure you can find something for her to do for a few minutes." Nancy pulled the glass door closed as she stepped back inside.

"What the hell was that all about?"

"Izzy's ex." Mel's voice faltered. "She's the caterer."

The ladder wobbled as Lauren jumped from the third step down to the redwood deck. "Seriously?"

Mel only nodded, feeling choked by emotions she thought she'd finally started to overcome.

Lauren peeked through the glass door into the kitchen. "She's nothing special."

"I know how attractive she is. Thanks for trying." She glanced back at the house and caught Dana's outline through the glass door. She squeezed her eyes closed.

"Probably just a good lay." Lauren folded the ladder up. "I could use some help moving a few of the chairs out under the tree." She motioned her over to a pile of folded chairs leaning against the house. "Be careful. The yard is still kind of squishy from the rain. I'm really glad it cleared out, so people can actually come out here tonight if it gets too hot inside."

It had been raining for days but had finally let up early this morning. The gloominess had matched Mel's mood; she wasn't sure if she was ready for sunshine yet.

❖

The table decorations were beautiful. Flowers and candles were dotted in between the various trays of pasta, vegetables, and appetizers. At the end of the table stood a wide variety of red and white wines. Mel had already had a few glasses of the latter.

Mel watched Lauren put a spoonful of vegetable gnocchi onto her plate. The food was different than Bella's, but it wasn't half bad. Enjoying it felt like a betrayal.

Lauren bumped Mel's shoulder. "You should eat something. The food's pretty good."

"I know. I tried it. Eating it just feels wrong."

"Are you ever going back to Bella's?"

Mel didn't answer.

"You're the only one stopping you." Lauren put down her plate, poured herself a glass of wine, and refilled Mel's glass.

"I'm just not there yet." She glanced around the living room, which was scattered with single women. *I'm not there yet either.*

"You're considering it?"

She nodded. "I miss her."

One of the women joined them at the table. She poured herself a glass of wine and nudged Lauren. "Are you going to introduce me?"

Lauren glanced back and forth between them, then cleared her throat. "Sure. Mel, this is Erin. She's one of the attorneys at my firm."

"Hi." She stuck out her hand. "Nice to meet you, Mel." Her sparkling amber eyes squinted as she smiled. She reached up and tucked a strand of her shoulder-length blond hair behind her ear. Erin was nothing short of gorgeous.

Mel took her hand and shook it. "Nice to meet you too."

Nancy popped in next to Lauren. "Honey, can you help me for a minute in the kitchen?"

"I can help you," Mel offered.

"I think we can handle it." Nancy pulled Lauren away, ignoring the daggers Mel shot at her.

Erin immediately slipped into the spot Lauren had vacated. She leaned close and started probing Mel about her work. The woman had a beautiful smile and smelled like a mix of citrus and ginger. Mel gulped her wine. "You want to go out back? The sky is clear tonight."

"Sure." They stepped out the door and moved to the edge of the deck.

"What kind of law do you practice?" Mel asked as she leaned up against the pergola post. She remembered hearing Erin say something about corporate accounts, and then Mel zoned out, immersing herself in the beauty of the night sky. The Harvest Moon was long gone, and the Frosty Moon had taken its place. It was almost pink, the warm redness of the previous full moon fading into the cool, dreary season. She'd never thought much about the stars or the moon before she'd met Izzy, but that part of her life was over. She'd have to find the beauty in the stars on her own. A soft breeze crossed her shoulders, and she shivered.

"Are you cold?" She heard the voice faintly and emerged from her thoughts to find Erin watching her intently. "Take my jacket." She started to pull it off.

"No, I'm fine." She rubbed her shoulders and glanced back up at the moonlit sky, then back at Erin. She didn't want to feel warm and tingly right now.

"What are you thinking?" Erin asked.

"I was thinking how beautiful the stars are tonight." She gazed back up at the flickering diamonds in the sky. "Have you ever thought about the peaceful clarity they bring when you look at them?"

"Not really, but I have been thinking about how beautiful you are."

She felt Erin's fingers trail down her neck and shifted her gaze to meet her amber eyes. Then Erin's mouth was on hers. She hesitated at first but thought, what the hell? She had to start somewhere. She thrust her tongue deep inside, probing Erin's mouth, trying to lose herself in the kiss. She felt Erin's hands roam up her sides and broke away. Mel zeroed in on her eyes. Brown...not blue. *It's not over yet.*

"That was nice," Erin said.

"It was." *But not nice enough.* She smiled softly and held up her glass. "I need a refill." She rushed into the house, leaving Erin standing outside with a bewildered expression.

❖

Nancy felt a tap on her shoulder.

"Um, you have a hysterical woman in your bathtub."

"What?"

She looked down the hall. "Your friend, the one with the dazzling green eyes."

Nancy rushed down the hall, threw open the bathroom door, and slid the shower curtain back. Mel was in the tub with her legs dangling over the side. "Jesus, Mel. You couldn't just go into one of the bedrooms and lie down?" She turned back to the woman who'd found her. "Can you watch her a minute?"

"Sure. I could watch *her* all night."

Nancy grabbed Lauren from a group of people and pulled her down the hall. "I need your help with Mel."

Lauren drew her brows together.

"She's in the bathroom."

"Is she sick?"

She pushed past the woman standing by the door. "Not yet." She turned back to Lauren. "How did she get this drunk?"

Lauren chuckled. "We have a full bar, and you did surround her with single women."

"I thought she was past this."

Shiny, red-rimmed eyes peered up at Nancy. "I'm sorry. It's just everyone…" Mel snorted and sucked in a gasp of air. "Is so happy." She let out a sob. "I just couldn't take it. Why can't I be like that?"

"Because you're too fucking stubborn." Mel's feet hit the porcelain with a thud when Nancy swung them into the tub. She tried to pull her upright, but she was dead weight. She looked back at Lauren, who moved in to help her. "Come on. Let's get you out of there."

Mel heaved a big sob. "I don't want to be alone." Another sob spilled out. "Alone for Christmas…New Year's."

"You won't be alone, honey. We'll be here." Nancy stepped into the bathtub, wrapped her arms around Mel, and held her tightly as she and Lauren hoisted her out.

"You need any help?" the woman standing guard asked.

"Thanks. We got this."

Mel woke up in the morning with Nancy's arm draped over her. She squeezed her eyes shut, hoping she hadn't made a fool of herself last night. But her mouth tasted like cardboard and her head throbbed. She tried to slip out of bed quietly, but Nancy's arm tightened around her.

"How are you feeling, party girl?"

"Did I do anything stupid last night?"

"Besides the tub?" Nancy sat up and rested against the headboard. Mel winced and sat up next to her. "Besides the tub."

"No. But you sure have a lot of women interested in seeing you again. Apparently you kissed a few before you decided to have your breakdown in the bathroom."

"Oh my God." She pulled at the T-shirt she was wearing. "I didn't take my clothes off, did I?"

Nancy smiled and shook her head. "I did that after you puked all over yourself."

"I'm sorry, Nance." She leaned her head on her shoulder. "That probably wasn't the way you wanted to spend your night."

"It's okay." She kissed her on the top of her head. "But you're clearly not over Izzy."

She let her eyes slide shut. "I know."

Nancy got up and moved to the door. "I'll get you a Sprite. Then you're on your own. I'm going to go get into bed with my girlfriend."

It's time for me to go home and deal with my life.

❖

Mel's eyes burned. She'd been putting in twelve-hour days at the office in front of the computer screen and then going home to put in several more on her laptop before collapsing into bed. The only thing saving her was the six hours of sleep she was able to get due to pure exhaustion. She kept her mind busy both at work and at home. Most nights she fell asleep with the TV on so she wouldn't feel so completely alone.

She left work and drove to Bella's Trattoria and parked in the lot away from the building, but didn't get out of her car. It had been months since Mel had seen or talked to Izzy. Still, she couldn't get the feel of her touch out of her mind. She'd dealt with it by throwing herself into her work. It didn't help. She couldn't eat without thinking of Izzy. She couldn't sleep without dreaming of her touch, her warm wonderful mouth, her fingers inside her. Izzy filled her mind constantly.

Mel started her car without a clue where she was going. She just drove and found herself parked at the bottom of Tank Hill. She climbed to the top and settled on the edge of the rock where she and Izzy had sat when they were there together. The view was just as beautiful as she remembered, but it felt very different. She was alone. No matter how beautiful it was, she couldn't enjoy it because Izzy wasn't there to share it with. Izzy had told her how special this place was to her, and Mel had felt honored she'd shared it with her. The burnt-orange sunset was so amazing. Its vibrant orange glow and red flickering hues splintering the sky made her heart ache. As the sun dipped behind the zigzagged buildings of the city, a tear rolled down Mel's cheek. Would she be able to forgive her? Could her love possibly outweigh the pain of betrayal she'd felt?

❖

Mel stepped out of her car onto the cobblestone drive of her parents' house, walked up the dimly lit pathway, and pushed through the heavy oak door. Her condo had sold faster than she'd expected, so she'd put all of her furniture in storage and moved back home with her parents temporarily while she searched for a new place. Nancy had told her she could stay, but she couldn't very well move in with her and Lauren. Their relationship was new, and they certainly didn't need the complication of an old girlfriend in the house. When her mother had suggested she move into her old room, Mel agreed. At five thousand square feet, the house had more than enough room for Mel to have privacy, and she honestly appreciated the company. Her father had converted one of the rooms on the second floor to a home gym, and Mel had started using the treadmill in the mornings to clear her head.

She knew her mother would be in the sitting room reading by this time of night.

"Mel, honey, where have you been? Your friend, Nancy, called. She's worried about you."

Mel reached into her purse, took out her cell phone, and pushed the power button. When she'd seen Nancy's number pop up on the screen earlier, she'd turned it off. "I'll text her." She used both her thumbs to type a message and tossed the phone back into her purse.

"You look a little disheveled."

"I've been up at Tank Hill doing some thinking. Have you ever been there?" She propped her shoulder against the doorway.

"No. I can't say that I have."

"It's beautiful. The view is absolutely breathtaking." She walked across the room to the window and took in the moon. It was almost full tonight. "After that I drove to the beach."

"The beach? What on earth were you doing there at this hour?"

"Thinking."

"You know I don't like to interfere in your life, dear, but you haven't been yourself lately, and you don't look well."

"I've just been busy at work, Mom."

"This is more than that." She patted the spot on the couch next to her. "Come. Tell me what's got you so upset."

Mel did as her mother instructed and took the spot next to her. "If someone you loved made the biggest mistake of their life, would you forgive them?"

Her mother skirted the question. "The answer to that lies within your heart. Do you love her enough to forget about whatever it is she's done?"

"How did you know?"

"I may be old, but I'm not blind, dear." She covered Mel's hand with hers. "I just want you to be happy."

Mel was stunned. When had her mother become so progressive? A huge weight lifted from her shoulders. "I think I can be really happy with her. I just have to get past something."

"You were happy there for a little while after you divorced Jack."

"I was very happy."

"But I can see that's somehow changed. Can you get back to that happiness?"

Mel sat quietly for a minutes. "I do want to. I just don't know if I can."

"You're only hurting yourself by not forgiving her."

"You say that like it's easy."

"Just think about it, dear. I haven't seen you that happy *or* this sad in quite some time." She squeezed her hand and then got up. "I'll fix you something to eat, and then I want you to go up to your room and get a good night's sleep. We'll have a nice breakfast together in the morning."

Mel didn't argue with her mother. She followed her into the kitchen and ate the grilled-cheese sandwich she'd cooked for her. When she was done, she went up to her old room and crawled into bed, thinking of how her life had changed over the past year. It had become full of love. She'd begun to anticipate a future filled with adventure, to plan a life with the woman responsible for making her see it.

And now Izzy had become a stranger. Her mind longed to hear her voice, and her body ached for her touch. The depth of Mel's aloneness weighed heavily in her chest. She hugged her pillow tight and sobbed into the cotton case. She would never be that happy with anyone else, but she didn't know if she could bury the pain of betrayal tormenting her.

CHAPTER TWENTY-FIVE

Izzy wandered out of the hospital elevator and down the hall to the cafeteria. Coffee would be her only savior today. Lots of it. She hadn't slept well in months, not since she'd seen or talked to Mel. *Why does love have to be so fucking complicated?* She slapped her hand to the wall. "What the hell is wrong with me? I was never gonna do this again. I can't do this again." She sighed and dropped back against the sterile-white cinder-block wall, catching a woman's stare as she passed. Pointing a finger to her temple, Izzy made a circular motion. "Late for my appointment." The woman gave her a tentative smile and hurried down the hallway. *You think I'm crazy. You should meet the rest of my family.*

Squeezing her eyes shut, she remained glued to the wall, remembering the first time she'd brought Bella here. After they took her into the Intensive Care Unit, the nurse wouldn't even let her in the room to see her right away. The nurse had led Izzy and her father to a waiting room filled with people, most of whom were exhausted. Some were sleeping, some were pacing, and some were just staring off into space. She shivered. Being here, in this hospital, unnerved her, and she knew it terrified Bella.

She opened her eyes. The hallway was full, people hurrying in both directions. No one acknowledged her as they passed. None of them seemed to notice the fear invading her thoughts. Hell. No one even made an attempt at eye contact. She supposed all of them were dealing with their own problems. God, she hated this place—too big, too impersonal.

She popped away from the wall and headed back to her mother's room. Izzy didn't think she could take much more of this, knowing the days to come could be even longer and more exhausting than the previous had been. She never wanted to experience this again. She could do nothing to help Bella and hated herself for bringing her here, for being so selfish. She should be at home in her own bed with people she loved caring for her. Izzy felt totally helpless and was going through it all alone. She was too stubborn to ask anyone for help, especially not the woman whose heart she'd broken. The woman she wanted to call the most.

Next week, when this flare-up subsided, she would take Bella home and let her enjoy the holidays in her own home, surrounded by the people she loved. No more sterile white walls, surgical gloves, beeping monitors. She'd had enough of that. They all had.

❖

Mel stopped at the nurses' station to say hello before pulling open the sliding-glass door to Bella's room. The curtains were already open on the floor-to-ceiling windows that covered one side of the room. Bella had commented before that the view of the pond was a beautiful sight in the morning.

Bella was asleep, so Mel moved around the bed and sat in the chair. She studied the lines in her face. She'd definitely passed her beautiful features on to her eldest daughter. The high cheekbones, the small delicate nose, the dimples that made Mel shiver whenever Izzy smiled.

The weight in her chest lingered, just as heavy as it had been since she found out about Dana. The trust she'd forged with Izzy had been shattered. She thought about what her mother had said about forgiveness. Could she possibly file it away and move forward? After what she'd been through with Jack, Mel didn't know if she had the strength to do it again. She let out a heavy sigh and flipped through a week-old copy of *People* magazine to occupy her mind. The caption read SEXIEST MAN ALIVE, and the familiar face of her childhood friend stared back at her. If the public only knew he had a wonderful, loving male partner at home, he might not have ever made it to the cover.

Bella shifted, and Mel saw her eyes begin to flutter.

"Hi there, sweetheart. How are you today?" Mel asked softly. Bella smiled. "Not too bad."

"That's good then, isn't it?" She grinned as she inched closer to the bedside.

Bella smiled at her for a minute, as though formulating what to say. "Have I told you how much I enjoy your visits?"

"Yes, you have. But I think I enjoy them more."

"Are you sure you're not one of my daughters?"

"Not lucky enough for that, I'm afraid."

"Maybe a daughter-in-law." She raised her brows. "With a beautiful girl like you, that could easily be arranged."

"That's very sweet of you, Bella, but I'm steering clear of commitment for a while." She responded to the offer the same way she had daily for the past few months. Bella had been trying to set her up with one of her children since she'd first started visiting.

"I have a couple of lovely daughters also."

Mel chuckled softly. "Yes, you do." *There's one in particular I need to erase from my heart, but it doesn't look like that's going to happen anytime soon.*

"Well, which one is it going to be then?"

"Bella. Stop." She reached over to squeeze her hand, but realized she hadn't washed hers when she came in. "Be right back." She popped up and went to the sink.

"You don't have to do that."

"That's not what the nurses say, and I'm not taking any chances." She rubbed the empty space on her ring finger. The tan line had almost faded entirely. Izzy flashed into her mind again, and her stomach dropped. For the past few weeks, no matter what Mel did, she couldn't seem to get Izzy out of her thoughts. *Chances...maybe I should be taking more of them.* She pumped the soap dispenser and lathered up. After drying her hands, she sat back down and took Bella's hand. "Now, what's on the agenda for today?"

"Would you mind reading to me for a while?"

"I'd love to." She took the true-crime hardback book from the nightstand, found where they'd left off, and laid it in her lap before taking Bella's hand again.

Mel had just finished reading the first page of chapter nine when the glass door pulled open, and Izzy slipped in. Dressed in black jeans, flip-flops, and a turquoise V-neck T-shirt, she looked tired and had lost some weight, but she was just as gorgeous as Mel remembered.

"Hi, Mom." Her brows pulled together as she slid her gaze from Bella to Mel and back to Bella again.

"Hi, sweetheart. I didn't expect you back again today."

Neither did Mel. Emotions sparred back and forth within her. Happiness, anger, sadness, then anger again.

"Lunch was slow. I got my dinner prep done early." She turned her gaze back to Mel and held it there. "I didn't think I'd see you here," she said softly.

Bella spoke up. "She comes to see me every day."

"What?" Her eyebrows flew up.

"Don't act so surprised. I told you about her. This is my friend, Mary Elizabeth."

"She's the woman you've been trying to—"

"Introduce you to," Bella said eagerly.

"Huh," Izzy mumbled, and Mel thought she spotted a slight smile cross her lips. "Mary Elizabeth." The name rolled slowly from her lips as she smiled at Mel and then grinned briefly at her mother.

"I told you she was beautiful."

"Yes, you did." She nodded and smiled. Those damn dimples captivated Mel again as Izzy returned her gaze to her. "Can I talk to you outside for a minute, Mary Elizabeth?" The name rolled deliberately off her tongue this time.

Even with the smile masking her face, Mel knew from the steel in her eyes it wasn't a request. "I'll be right back," Mel said, letting Bella's warm, frail hand slip out of hers before crossing the room to the door.

"I'll put *Animal Planet* on for you while we're gone." Izzy found the bedside remote and switched on the TV before following Mel out.

"What?" Mel growled, knowing she was in for an emotionally draining clash.

"Not here." Grabbing her hand as she passed, Izzy pulled her through another door and then out the exit. She kept walking until she made it to the farthest tree next to the small pond behind it. Mel yanked her hand away, and Izzy spun around with fire in her eyes. "Mary Elizabeth? That's a fine Catholic name." She lifted a brow and crossed her arms across her chest.

"It's my given name," Mel responded, crossing her arms across her chest to match Izzy's stance.

"Where did Mel come from?"

"If you must know, my little brother couldn't pronounce Mary Elizabeth, so he called me Mellie. As I got older it seemed a little adolescent for the professional world, so I shortened it to Mel." She bobbed her head mockingly as she spouted the information.

"That was convenient." Izzy didn't make any attempt to hide the sarcasm in her voice. "Am I the only one you've hidden that tidbit of information from?"

Anger bubbling inside her, Mel planted her hands on her hips. "You can't honestly believe I was trying to deceive you." She pressed her lips together into a thin smile.

Izzy raked her hand through her hair. "No. I don't believe that." Izzy's voice was soft and genuine. "Why didn't you tell me you've been visiting my mother?" She stroked a small, heart-shaped cut that had been carved deeply into the tree trunk long ago.

"It wasn't important."

"The hell it wasn't." The attitude roared back.

"Listen, Izzy, just because you and I can't get along doesn't mean I'm going to stop seeing Bella."

"You are if you're doing it to get to me. I won't have my mother used that way." Izzy backed her up against the tree.

"I think you're mistaking me for someone else." Izzy shifted uncomfortably, and Mel knew she'd caught her vague reference to Dana. "My seeing Bella has nothing to do with you. I was visiting her before you and I became friends. I'm not going to stop just because we're not anymore."

Izzy cocked her head. "So we're no longer friends?"

"Hell. I don't know what we are," Mel shot back in a more hostile tone than she'd intended. "All I know is we're not what we were."

"That's the way you want it, isn't it?"

"Not really." Mel's voice softened.

Izzy planted a hand against the tree on either side of her and moved closer. Mel could feel her warm breath on her lips. God help her, she wanted desperately to kiss them. "But you said..." Izzy's words were barely audible. Mel flipped her gaze from Izzy's mouth to her innocent blue eyes, seeing the vulnerability in them.

Mel stared into the deep pools of blue. She couldn't think with her this close. "We both said a lot of things." She steadied herself against the tree, her mind hazy. She didn't know what to think anymore. "For God's sake, Izzy. I need you to keep your distance." Mel slipped under her arm and hurried to the edge of the pond.

Izzy pushed off the tree and followed her. "You don't talk to me for months, and now you tell me you're not okay with it?"

Mel watched the ducks dipping their heads in and out of the water. "Are you still seeing her?"

"I was never seeing her." She took in a deep breath and blew it out. "You know, when I first met you all I wanted to do was get in your pants."

"And?"

"And then I got to know you." She studied the ground. "Now I've hurt you."

"That's a fucking understatement."

Izzy's head snapped around at her choice of words.

She watched a family of ducks swim across the pond. "Why Dana?"

"It was the night I saw the tabloid. I got really drunk. I mean, carry-me-out-of-the-bar drunk." She raked her fingers through her hair. "The last thing I remember is the bartender telling me the wine bottle was empty. The next morning I woke up next to Dana and had no idea how I got there." Her soft blue eyes were glassy and filled with regret. "Will you ever be able to forgive me?"

"You shouldn't worry about that right now. Bella's sick. You need to take care of her."

"You didn't answer my question." Izzy moved closer and took her hand, stroking the back of it with her thumb. "Can you forgive me for being such a fucking idiot?"

Mel tried to shake the jolt afflicting her midsection. "I…" She pulled her hand away and slapped it to her neck, trying to rub away the unwanted tingle rushing it. She hadn't expected her feelings for Izzy to remain so strong. "I need more time, Izzy."

"I guess that's the least I can give you." Izzy leaned forward, pressed her cheek to Mel's, and held it there for a few minutes. "You can see Bella anytime you want," she whispered in her ear before backing up and turning toward the lake.

"Thank you." She was back. The warm vulnerable, compassionate woman she'd met that first night in the alley behind the restaurant. "You deserve someone better than Dana."

"You think so?"

"I do."

"Someone like you?"

Mel's insides quivered, and she shot out a breath. "What makes you think I'm any better?"

"You visit my mother every day. She likes you. Bella's a very good judge of character, you know." Izzy turned to face her, capturing her gaze. "And even after...you're still here." She reached up to brush her thumb across Mel's cheek but pulled back, letting her hand drop to her side. "You're notches above Dana."

Mel's cheeks flushed, and Izzy spun around and headed back to the hospital.

"Izzy, wait." Mel ran to keep up with her.

Izzy didn't slow as she slipped through the electronic doors, almost running into them as they opened. She rushed down the hall, pulled open the door to Bella's room, and went straight to the windows.

Mel glanced at Bella and saw she was asleep before continuing on to the window, moving in behind Izzy. She fought the natural urge to snake her arms around her waist. Instead, she put her hands on Izzy's arms and squeezed. "There's nothing you can do to change the fact she's not going to be around forever." Mel eased her forehead to Izzy's back. She closed her eyes and took in a deep breath. The scent of lemon and verbena filled her head. She'd missed it desperately.

"I'm so sorry I hurt you, Mel." Izzy's voice cracked as she turned into Mel's arms and looked into her eyes. Mel could see the strained emotion in them. Then came the tears. She pulled her in, holding her closely as Izzy sobbed into her shoulder. This felt so right. Being here, holding Izzy, comforting her. The woman she loved. *The woman she loved.* Fear tore through her. Did it really matter that she'd slept with Dana? She tensed. *Will I ever be able to trust her again?* Suddenly she couldn't stop her own tears. *What am I going to do?*

At the sound of the glass door sliding open, Izzy immediately let go of Mel and turned back to the window.

"Hey," Angie said.

"Hey." Mel wiped the tears from her face. "How are you?" she asked, trying to deflect attention away from Izzy.

"Good. How's Mom?"

"About the same today, I'm afraid," Mel said, watching Izzy intently as she crossed the room to her sister.

Angie sat down next to the bed and held Bella's hand. "She looks so frail."

"This has taken a lot out of her," Izzy whispered. Standing behind Angie, she leaned down and kissed the top of her head.

"I don't like seeing her like this."

"I know, honey. None of us do. The doctor said once she gets the transfusion, she should be better. Then we can take her back home." Izzy seemed to have compassion for everyone but herself.

Mel glanced at her watch—almost six. She didn't want to leave. But she had a meeting she couldn't miss.

Izzy must have seen her check the time, because her disposition changed immediately. "You have someplace to be?"

"I have to meet a client." *A client that may change her mind if I don't lock the deal in now.*

"Then by all means, go." The attitude was back again.

Mel let out a heavy sigh and pulled her lips into a solemn smile before pushing out through the door.

CHAPTER TWENTY-SIX

Doug bumped Angie with his shoulder. "That girl from class is staring at us."

Angie snapped her focus to the blonde who seemed to be studying the two of them intently. "What the hell? She sure is," she whispered back at Doug. "Whaddaya think's up with that?"

"I don't know, but here she comes."

"Hey, Doug." The blonde looked right past Angie and gave him a smile.

"Hey." Doug sat up straight and grinned.

"Seriously?" Angie hit him in the ribs with her elbow.

"Ow, that hurt." His attention snapped back to Angie.

"Good," she said before looking at the blonde, who had conveniently slid into the chair adjacent to Doug. "What's up?"

"It looks like both our groups are working on restaurant websites. You want to collaborate on a few ideas?"

Doug smiled real big. "Yeah, su—"

Seriously. Angie gave him another shot to the ribs. "What kind of restaurant is it?"

"It's kind of nouveau Italian."

Doug tilted his head toward Angie and said, "That means modern."

Angie scowled at him. "I know what it means, Doug." She turned her attention back to the blonde. "What's the name of the place?"

"Gustoso."

"That's—" Angie stomped on his foot this time. "Knock it off, will you," he squealed.

"How'd you guys come up with that place?"

"We couldn't find a business. So the instructor gave it to us."

"It wasn't on the list she gave us."

"Yeah. I know. They were all taken."

"Wow." Angie jammed her papers into her book and slapped it closed. "Are you coming?" she asked Doug as she popped out of her chair.

The blonde seemed totally baffled. "So do you want to work together?"

"It's a competition, remember?" *Dumbass.* Angie headed across the library.

"Sorry. We gotta go. I'll talk to you tomorrow." Doug jogged to catch up with Angie, who was already on her way out the door and down the steps to the parking lot. "Hold up, will ya?" He pulled the key from his pocket and hit the unlock button. The car chirped and the lights flashed.

"What are the fucking odds of that?" She pulled open the car door and tossed her books into the back. "My sister's gonna flip."

Angie rushed into the kitchen and told Izzy how Gustoso's website had been offered to one of the teams as a project assignment in class.

"That can't be true. Mel wouldn't do something like that."

"Call her." Angie yanked the phone from the wall and handed it to her. "Ask her yourself."

Gio chimed in. "What's that saying you told me, Iz? Nothing worse than a woman screwed?"

"It's scorned, smart-ass," Izzy said, narrowing her eyes. She hung the receiver back on the cradle. "Tony, can you handle the kitchen for a while?"

"Sure."

She took off her chef's coat and tossed it on the counter before slipping on a chambray shirt over her tank top. No matter what Izzy had done, she'd never thought Mel was the vindictive type. She wouldn't try to purposely hurt Izzy's business. There had to be some sort of explanation.

Izzy blew by the receptionist and pushed open the door to Mel's office.

"Hi," Mel said, popping up out of the chair behind her desk. She seemed surprised to see her.

The receptionist followed her in. "I'm sorry. She wouldn't stop."

"It's okay." She rounded her desk. "Do you want to sit down?" Her emerald-green eyes sparkled as she motioned toward the club chairs in the corner of her office.

"No thanks. I'll stand."

"Okay." Mel leaned back against her desk, planting a hand on either side. "This is a coincidence. I was going to come see you this evening."

"Oh? What about?"

"I need to talk to you about Gustoso."

Izzy held back, waiting to see what Mel had to say. "Go on."

"That's where I went the other night when I left the hospital."

"So it's true." She watched Mel's mouth drop open, then close again. "Angie told me you have one of the groups in her class working on a website for them."

Mel's forehead puckered as she shifted her weight. "Yes. But—"

"Is Gustoso one of your clients?" She pushed forward.

"I guess you could say that."

"Did you know about it?" She tried to tamp down her anger, but it was getting more difficult by the minute.

"Not until after it was assigned to the group. Nancy chose the clients for the class."

"What the hell, Mel? That's Dana's place." The words came out louder than Izzy intended, and Mel's face hardened.

Her eyes had turned cool green. "You never told me the name of the restaurant, and you said it wasn't Italian."

"That's not the point. Why would you create a website for a restaurant that could pull my business?"

"I can't turn away every restaurant because they might be your competition."

"Why not?"

"That's bad business, Izzy."

"And you care more about your business than you care about me."

"That's not true."

"Apparently it is, or you wouldn't have taken Gustoso on as a client." Mel didn't respond but pinched her lips together. "Wow." Izzy rubbed her forehead. "I know I hurt you, Mel. But I didn't think you'd be so bitter."

"Angie's designing a wonderful website for Bella's." She moved toward Izzy, who backed away. "The site the other team is creating will never compare."

"But it will when you're done with it."

"Izzy, Gustoso isn't your competition. I—"

Izzy put up a hand. "Any restaurant is my competition."

"I don't know what to say."

"It is what it is." She shrugged. "It looks like neither one of us is innocent in this mess." She pulled open the door and took off.

Mel listed the details on the whiteboard as she and Nancy brainstormed ad ideas for the new hardware-store contract they'd acquired. Business had been booming, and she was thankful she'd decided to bring Nancy on as her partner.

The phone rang, and Mel reached across her desk and picked it up. "This is Mel." She leaned back against her desk.

"Hi, honey."

"Hi, Dad. What's up?"

"It's your mother, dear. She's had a heart attack."

Adrenaline rushed through her, and she shot to her feet. "Is she okay?" She held her hand to her stomach.

"I'm afraid not. It happened some time during the night. When I tried to wake her, she was already gone."

She let the phone slide from her hand and dropped to her knees. *No. No. Not her.*

"Mel? What is it?" Nancy picked up the phone, and Mel could vaguely hear only her side of the conversation.

"Hello, Mr. Collins. It's Nancy."

"Oh my God. I'm so sorry."

"Is there anything I can do?"

"Yes. I'll take care of her."

Mel sat, crumpled to the ground in a zombie-like state. She'd just spoken to her mother on the phone yesterday. "I was supposed to have dinner with her last night, but she said she was feeling flu-ish and went to bed early. I should've checked on her."

"Honey." Nancy put her arm around her shoulder. "The doctor said it was a massive coronary during her sleep. You couldn't have done anything."

"But if I'd checked on her, maybe I might have seen something."

"No, honey. You wouldn't have. Your dad was in the same bed with her and didn't even know."

"I need to see him."

"Okay. I'll take you."

Mel touched the end button on her cell phone and set it on the table. It immediately rang again. She picked it up but didn't answer it. She just couldn't do it anymore.

Nancy took it from her hand. "Hello."

"No, she's lying down."

"I'll let her know." She touched the red button and disconnected the call. "That was Rick." She slid the phone back onto the table. "He wasn't very happy when I wouldn't let him talk to you."

"Thanks. I really didn't need to deal with him right now. He's been in real mega-prick mode lately."

Nancy gawked at her like she was startled by the foul comment coming out of Mel's usually proper mouth.

"I'm sorry. I shouldn't be that way."

Nancy pulled her lips up slightly. "No, you're spot-on. He is a prick."

Mel let out a laugh, which quickly turned into a gurgling sob. Nancy wrapped her arms around her, holding her closely. Mel dreaded the days to come. When this part of the ritual was over, she would be the one to make the arrangements. She was stronger, more responsible than her brother Mike.

She dried her eyes and sat in the living-room chair silently while her dad told her how he'd rolled over to wake her mother and she wouldn't stir. How he'd called 911 and when the paramedics arrived they hadn't even tried to administer CPR. How she'd looked so peaceful, like she hadn't felt the slightest twinge of pain. How he'd wanted them to leave her there long enough for Mel and Michael to come say good-bye, but they wouldn't.

She watched her father, his head cradled in his hands. How would he survive without her? Who would take care of him now? He certainly wouldn't let her; that would show weakness. She watched Mike as he sat beside him and knew he would tend to him for the time being. At least until her father reached a place where he could accept her for the daughter she was, not the daughter he wanted her to be. Mike was the golden boy. He could do no wrong in her father's eyes. While her father ignored all of Mike's imperfections, he always spotted Mel's. She'd never been able to live up to his expectations.

Her mind wandered to the day she'd come home from college so excited to tell him how well she'd done that term. During dinner she'd told him she ranked third in her graduating class. He'd looked up from his plate just long enough to ask who the other two students were. She remembered the sting like it was yesterday. Even though she owned her own business and made a very good living, he had an innate way of making her feel inadequate.

She popped up off the couch and moved toward the terrace doors but stopped at her mother's chair and picked up the plaid throw she'd often used to keep her legs warm. She held it to her nose, warming herself with her mother's familiar scent before wrapping it around her shoulders. She couldn't take any more of this. She needed some air.

Nancy followed Mel out, keeping a close watch on her. Mel was sure Nancy thought she was going to lose it any minute. She was numb. Her mother was her rock, her source of strength when things got tough. She had no idea how she was going to live without her.

"Bella's," Angie said as she picked up the phone and pressed it to her ear. "She can't come to the phone right now. Can I help you with something?" There was a moment of silence. "Just a minute." Izzy craned her neck to see Angie wave the receiver at her. "It's Mel's friend, Nancy. She says it's important."

"Get her number and tell her I'll call her back."

She put the receiver back to her ear, and her expression told Izzy something was wrong. She pulled it from her ear and covered the mouthpiece. "Mel's mom died."

"What?"

"Her mom...she had a heart attack and died this morning."

Izzy left what she was cooking on the stove and took the phone from Angie's hand. "Where is she?"

"I don't know," Nancy said. "I checked her office, my place, and a couple other places I thought she might be, but I can't find her. I hoped maybe she'd come to see you."

"She hasn't been here."

"I'm worried about her, Izzy. She's acting strange. Like nothing happened."

A rush of panic swept through her. "I'll call you back." She spun around and took off out the back door. She could think of only one other place Mel could be. She sped down the highway pushing eighty, ignoring the horns as she weaved in and out of traffic. Izzy would never forgive herself if anything happened to Mel.

Relief washed over her when she spotted Mel's car in her driveway from down the street. She pulled into the driveway, threw the car into park, and hopped out of the Jeep as it jerked back and forth from the sudden shift.

She pushed the door open. "Mel," she shouted. No answer. She felt the cool breeze rush through the house and crossed the room to the back door. No sign of Mel on the deck. She saw the shoes on the deck, the jacket on the railing, and rushed down the pathway to the beach. Mel was sitting in the water with her knees pulled up against her chest. The waves lapped at her legs as the ocean foamed around her body.

Shit! Izzy ran to the water. "Mel, honey, it's cold out here. Let's go inside."

Mel didn't move. She sat staring at the ocean as the sun slowly dipped behind the horizon. Izzy sat down next to her in the frigid Pacific water, matching her position. Her feet numbed immediately.

"The tide...it wasn't...this high...when I got here." Her lip quivered as she spoke.

"You're shivering." Izzy put her arm around her. She was ice-cold, almost hypothermic. "Let's go inside." Mel turned and stared blankly into Izzy's eyes. "Come on. We need to get you warm." Izzy helped her up and wrapped her arm firmly around Mel's waist as they trudged through the sand and into the house.

Mel trembled uncontrollably as Izzy led her to the bathroom and took her into the shower fully dressed. As the warm water ran down

Mel's back, Izzy held her tightly against her until the trembling stopped. Neither one spoke as Izzy removed Mel's clothing and then her own. She washed her tenderly before drying and wrapping her in a towel. Izzy wrapped herself in a towel too, led Mel into the bedroom, and sat her on the bed. She pulled a thermal shirt and sweatpants from the dresser drawer and handed them to her. "Can you put these on?"

Mel nodded.

She took a long-sleeved T-shirt and pajama pants from the drawer for herself and slipped them on. "I'm going to take care of our clothes. Be right back." When she came out of the laundry room, she saw Mel drift across the deck to the railing. She grabbed the throw from the couch, went outside, and wrapped it around Mel's shoulders. Standing at the railing next to her, they watched the ocean waves ebb and flow. "I'm so sorry, Mel," she said softly.

Izzy's cell phone rang. She touched the screen and pressed it to her ear. "I've got her. She's fine." She ended the call without giving Nancy a chance to say anything. "Everyone's worried about you."

"Why do you love me, Izzy?" Mel said, turning to look at her.

"You have such a pure heart, Mel. You make me feel like I can be so much better than I am."

"If only that were true." Mel scoffed and shook her head. "Are you a religious woman, Iz?"

"I believe in God, but I can't say I spend much time in church."

"Do you pray?"

"On occasion." *I prayed the whole way over here I would find you okay.*

"I stopped praying." Mel's eyes filled with tears. "I stopped praying and now she's gone."

"Oh, Mel." She took her by the shoulders. "Your mother didn't die because you stopped praying."

"Then why did God take her?" she asked, softly. "My mother prayed. Each and every day she was able, she went to church. She lit candles for people who had passed and prayed for those of us who were still here."

"I think he takes the best first."

Mel pulled her lip up and shot out a breath. "She was the best." Her vivid green eyes clouded with tears.

"Yes, she was." Izzy dried the tears rolling down Mel's cheeks with her thumbs. *She gave me you.*

Mel gave her a look she wasn't familiar with before she fell into Izzy's arms. "I don't know what I'd do if I lost you."

"I'm not going anywhere."

"You could get hit by a bus tomorrow."

"I won't cross any streets tomorrow."

"You could die in a plane crash."

"I'm not flying anywhere." With Mel still clinging to her, Izzy lifted Mel's chin to look into her eyes. "Nothing is going to happen to me."

"I can't live without you, Izzy."

Izzy had waited so long to hear those words. She pulled her in close and held her. "You don't have to, baby. I'm right here."

After the service, Izzy drove Mel back to the house she grew up in. People would be coming to pay their respects—to eat, to drink, to remember Cecilia. Many people would be there. Cecilia was well loved in the community for her philanthropy as well as her loving personality. Mel was so numb by this point, the false smile she'd been giving was a reflex. She would paste it on for as long as she had to socialize with both friends and strangers. People she hadn't seen in years. It wouldn't be easy. She glanced at her brother and father. Not for any of them. She didn't know if she could get through it. All she wanted was to lock herself in a room away from all these people. She glanced over her shoulder and spotted Izzy, who hadn't been more than five feet away from her all afternoon. Somehow, just knowing she was there gave Mel inner strength.

The steady stream of people hadn't stopped, and when Jess came through the door, no one seemed more surprised than Izzy.

"What are you doing here?" Izzy asked, stepping in front of Mel.

Mel was warmed by her protective stance. "It's okay," Mel whispered into her back, then slid under her arm to remain as close as she could to Izzy.

"I'm so sorry about your mother," Jess said, empathy choking her voice. "I need to talk to you." Her gaze slipped from Mel to Izzy, then back to Mel. "I'm sorry to do this here, but I just found something out I think you should know."

"Okay. Let's go back outside and talk." Izzy motioned to the door. Jess stayed put. "Mel needs to hear this."

"What is it?"

Jess rolled her lip in and bit it. "What Dana told you when you came to see her...about her and Izzy that night. It wasn't true." She hesitated. "You *were* at the bar all night drinking, and she *did* take you home, but nothing happened between the two of you. I was there too. I helped get you out of the car and inside. You were totally passed out. We both stayed that night."

"But when I woke up—"

"Yeah, that." She shifted her weight to her other foot. "We left at the same time in the morning. I had no idea she went back and tried to make you think you and she..." Jess shook her head and slid her gaze back Mel. "I'm so sorry. I just found out about this."

"Thank you for telling me." Mel uttered, still holding on to Izzy.

"Well, I'm gonna go." Jess rocked back on one foot. "If there's anything I can do for you, I mean anything at all, please let me know." Jess turned and stepped back out the door.

Izzy led Mel over to Nancy, then followed Jess out the door and down the steps. "Thank you for that."

"It's the least I could do, considering all the trouble I caused you. I picked up her phone the other day and saw all the texts she's been sending. I didn't realize she was trying to destroy your life."

"So, are you done with Dana?"

"Yeah. I don't know what I ever saw there."

"I know exactly how you feel."

"Well, for what it's worth, I am sorry."

She turned to go, and Izzy called after her. "Hey, Jess. Maybe we could talk later in the week and work out some kind of compromise about the restaurants? I'd much rather be allies than enemies."

"I'd like that. But I have a new partner to deal with now. Dana sold her share to some corporation. I have no idea what's going to happen."

"A corporation? Really?"

Jess nodded. "I should know more next week. Give me a call."

"I will." She waved and watched Jess walk down the street to her car.

Mel met Izzy at the door as she walked back into the house. "Are you okay?"

"I'm so sorry about all that. I just can't believe Dana could be so cruel."

"She's the one who should be sorry. You're not responsible for her actions. Remember?"

"But I am responsible for my own." She searched Mel's eyes. "I am truly sorry, Mel. If I hadn't gotten so drunk that night, none of it would have ever happened." Izzy threaded her fingers through her hair. "What a big fucking mess I made of everything."

"It's all right," Mel said.

Izzy stroked Mel's arm. "I must have been some kind of idiot to let that woman into my life."

"Really, I'm okay." Mel gave her a soft smile. "As long as you are."

"Look at you. All this going on and you're worried about me. Let's go back inside and get some food in you."

"I'm not really hungry."

"Did I ask if you were hungry?" Izzy took her hand and led her inside. "Now you can pick something I made." She motioned to the array of pastas on the dining-room table. "Or we can go into the kitchen and you can take a chance on something of your own making." She smiled. "I hear you cook a mean omelet."

"I'll stick with the safe stuff today, if you don't mind." She picked up a plate. "But I will give you a rain check on the omelet."

Izzy gave her a soft smile. "I'll take you up on that."

"Please do." She cupped Izzy's face in her hand, stroked her cheek with her thumb.

"I'm seeing a bit of optimism here. What happened to the pessimist?"

"She's tired today." She set her plate on the table.

Izzy wasn't surprised when her strength gave out and Mel fell into her. She held her close, stroking her hair. Food wouldn't help now—pure comfort was what Mel needed. She glanced up at Izzy, who was watching her intently.

"You okay?" Izzy uttered softly.

Mel nodded against Izzy's chest.

Izzy knew she was lying. The woman Mel respected most in the world, the rock in her life, was dead.

❖

Later that evening, when Izzy took her home to the beach house, Mel headed straight into the master bedroom, then turned abruptly. "I've got to get my bag out of the car." Izzy could see by her bloodshot eyes, she was drowsy already.

Izzy pointed at the dresser. "Second and fourth drawer. T-shirts and sweats."

"Thanks." Mel tugged the drawers open, took out the clothes, then stripped off her dress and pulled on one of Izzy's over-sized T-shirts.

Izzy took a shirt and a pair of athletic shorts from the dresser as well. "I'll get your bag." She started to leave, then turned back. "Are you sure you'll be all right?"

"Yeah, I'm fine. Just tired." She crawled into the bed and under the covers.

"I have a little work to do on next week's orders, but I'll be right down the hall if you need me." Izzy pulled the door to, leaving it open just a crack before going into the spare room to change.

Izzy took off her suit jacket and hung it in the closet along with her slacks and blouse, then flopped back onto the bed to pull on the shorts and T-shirt. She was headed into the bathroom to wash her face when she heard Mel let out an agonizing sob. Work would just have to wait. She pushed open the door, crawled into bed with Mel, and wrapped her in her arms. Mel's sobs vibrated against Izzy's chest as she clung to her. Izzy's heart constricted. Nothing she could say or do would make this any better.

CHAPTER TWENTY-SEVEN

Mel glanced at the clock. Fifteen minutes had ticked by since the last time she'd checked. It wouldn't be light until close to seven. She hated turning the clocks back for daylight saving time in the fall. The days seemed to get darker and drearier. She'd managed to get a few hours of sleep, but they were restless. Mel studied Izzy's face in the glow of the moonlight. She'd almost forgotten how lovely she was when she slept. The smooth, olive-toned skin; the thick, naturally shaped eyebrows that relaxed perfectly above her eyes; full, pink lips that pulled easily into a smile when she woke; the slight scar on the bottom of her chin Mel loved to kiss. She ran her finger across the scar, remembering the story she'd told her from her childhood about the surfboard accident.

Quietly slipping out of bed, she went into the living room and grabbed the blanket from the couch on her way out to the deck. She wrapped herself in the blanket and took in a deep breath, letting the saltiness of the sea air fill her nose. The sound of the waves stirred thoughts of Izzy. Mel wanted her, needed her. She longed to see the world the way Izzy did. She lowered herself onto the lounger, pulled her knees up to her chest, and closed her eyes.

Mel felt the soft brush of Izzy's fingers on her cheek and opened her eyes to see her deep-blue eyes. With a swipe of her finger, Izzy motioned for Mel to move forward, and she slid down behind her, wrapping her with her body. The sun was still elusive. Muted yellows, oranges, and pinks melted into the sea.

"Tell me what you see, Izzy."

"I see the promise of daybreak as it tickles the rhythm of the sea and the stillness of the sky. It's neither here nor there yet. It's the temperance, the vaporous haze. It entrances us, keeps us wanting more. A quiet consciousness to help us indulge in its beauty."

"I love the way you see the world, Izzy. I want to spend every day for the rest of my life seeing it through your eyes."

"That's good, because I want to spend every day for the rest of mine sharing it with you."

"Really?" She turned her head to face Izzy.

"Yes, really." Izzy brushed Mel's lips lightly with hers. "I've wanted that since the first night you came home with me."

Mel sank back into Izzy and squeezed her. She was right where she wanted to be, where she should've been all along. Her mother had seen what Mel couldn't. She had everything she needed right in front of her. Her name was Isabel Calabrese.

"Are you working today?"

"No. I thought I'd stick close to you. Is that okay?"

"I'd like that."

"I need to call Tony later. Jess told me yesterday that some corporation bought Dana out of the restaurant."

"I bought it."

"What?"

"I'm the corporation." She twisted around to face Izzy. "The day after we saw her at the wine tasting, I called Mike and had him prepare an offer."

"Why?"

"I was being selfish. I knew if Dana was still in the restaurant business she would always be showing up in the same places as you. It's probably not the best investment. The reviews haven't been all that great. Apparently the food is good, but the manager is a bitch." She let her lips tip up slightly.

"Sell it to Jess. Let her have it."

"I can't. It's not mine to sell."

Izzy pinched her brows together.

"When I bought it, I had Mike form the corporation in both of our names. Thomas Calabrese LLC." Izzy gave Mel a look she hadn't seen before, and she thought maybe she'd done the wrong thing. "I love you, Izzy. I want you to be happy. It's yours. No strings."

"Except the one big string that connects my heart to yours." Izzy brushed a strand of hair from Mel's forehead. "I can't believe you did that."

"Do you still love me, Izzy?"

"I've tried my damnedest not to." She brushed Mel's cheek with her thumb and pulled her lips into a contented smile. "But I can't help it. I do love you, Mary Elizabeth."

Mel thought she'd never hear those words again. She grabbed her face and kissed her. Slowly, softly, tenderly. It was the most wonderful kiss ever with the most wonderful woman she'd ever known.

Izzy had met with Jess earlier in the week, and they decided to serve a few signature dishes in each restaurant to tie them together. They would still keep their separate names and styles of cuisine, but now they would be sister restaurants connected in a subtle, yet distinct manner. They hadn't worked out the staffing yet, but Jess would need some help once they made the announcement about their partnership, and Izzy was going to have to replace Angie now that she'd received the internship at Mel's firm.

As Izzy sat at the table next to Tony showing him her plan to bridge Gustoso with Bella's, she could see he was apprehensive about the partnership.

"I think I need to step out here at Bella's and let you run things for a while. I'm going to help Jess get Gustoso back on its feet. Once the clientele has been established and business has stabilized, I think we should move Gio over there to work with Jess. He can do his market testing and bring in new dishes there before we try them here."

"What about the JBF nomination?"

"Does it really matter if I win? The nomination has brought in more business than we can handle."

"But they're coming for your cooking."

"No. They're coming for the food, which you and Gio can prepare just as well as I can."

He gave her a blank look. "You've never said that to me before."

"What? That you're a great chef? You've taught me everything I know, Tony. I may have learned to step up the recipes in culinary school, but you taught me the basics." She squeezed his shoulder. "I could've never gotten the nomination without you. In fact, I feel kind of guilty accepting it. We're a team. We always have been."

"A team." Tony nodded slowly and his smile widened. "A team that is going to bring Jess and Gustoso into the family."

❖

Mel skipped down the steps of the building where she worked. She was ready for a celebration tonight. Instead of going straight to the restaurant, she drove home to change out of the navy suit she'd put on this morning. She thought about throwing on a pair of jeans as she clanked the hangers together, looking through her closet, but it was such a beautiful night. It would be ninety degrees in the kitchen, so she should wear something light. She came across a red spaghetti-strap dress and smiled, remembering the last time she'd worn it.

When she had first started going to the restaurant, Izzy rarely came out of the kitchen, but one night she'd hand-delivered the crème brûlée Mel had ordered. At the time, she was trying to decide what color dress to wear for a wedding she and Jack were attending that weekend. When she'd asked him which color he thought she should wear, Jack didn't answer. When she'd persisted, offering him red or blue, he'd said either one would do.

It wasn't the kind of answer she was looking for, so she'd been a little disappointed with his lack of interest. She remembered the sound of Izzy's voice clearly as she said, "Wear the red. It brings out your eyes." And then she simply smiled and headed back into the kitchen. Mel was flattered at the compliment and a little surprised she'd even noticed her eyes.

She remembered thinking red was a little flashy for a wedding, but she wore it anyway, and somehow she felt sexy and more confident than she had in a long time. She should've known then why Izzy had noticed her eyes, but she'd been too self-involved to pick up on it.

"Red it is." She slipped the dress off the hanger and pulled it over her head. Gazing at her reflection in the mirror, she grinned. Her eyes weren't all it was going to bring out tonight.

❖

RESERVED FOR PRIVATE PARTY. Mel smiled at the sign hanging on the door of the restaurant. She pushed it open and squealed at the sight of all the balloons and streamers scattered throughout the room. The tables were decorated with flowers, candles, glitter, and confetti. The room was beautiful.

"What do you think?" Angie said.

"I think it looks awesome. Izzy is going to be so surprised."

Angie smiled at the compliment, then eyeballed the tables across the room. "Dougie, can you move those tables against the wall for the cake?" She pointed from the tables to the wall and then turned back to Mel. "You know Izzy is going to complain about the cost. She thinks someone else is paying for this."

"Someone else is. Me."

"You know what I mean."

"I know, but this was the only way I could get away with it. Otherwise she'd be here working all night, and there's no way I'm going to let her work on her birthday."

"Tony has most of the food prepared, and Izzy should be here soon."

"How'd he get rid of her?"

"He sent her to get the cake." She pinched her lips together. "She wasn't happy about that."

Nancy came streaking out of the kitchen and across the room to pull Mel into a hug. "She'll freak when she finds out the party's for her." Lauren followed right after her. "You're going to be in so much trouble."

They all turned and admired their work.

"I know, and I love it." Mel wrapped her arm around Angie's shoulder. "You know it's not easy to pull something over on your sister." She glanced around the restaurant. "Are your mom and dad here yet?"

"They'll be here soon. Aunt Julia and Uncle Rennie are bringing them."

"And the rest of the family?"

"By the time she gets back, everyone should be here."

"Great. Let's hope she hasn't figured it out."

Nancy and Lauren helped Angie and Mel put the finishing touches on the tables.

"What color tank did she wear today?"

"Black."

"I figured, but that will go with anything." She grabbed a shopping bag from the bar. "I don't want her to have to wear that chef's coat all night." *Although she does look awfully cute in it.*

"Did you bring a zippered hoodie?"

"Nope. I bought her a nice black silk blouse to wear over her tank instead." She pulled it out of the bag, held it up, and they all nodded in approval.

"That will be a nice birthday present," Angie commented.

"This is just for the party. I got her something else for her birthday." She reached into her bag, held the small velvet box in her hand, and smiled at Nancy and Lauren. They'd both helped her pick out just the right ring.

❖

Izzy pulled her Jeep into the alley behind the restaurant and popped the back hatch. Then she turned the knob to the back door—locked. Thinking it was strange, she pounded on it and shouted to Tony, then went back to the SUV.

The door swung open, and both Tony and Gio pushed through the screen door, letting it slap back into place.

"Why's the door locked?"

"Some kids were messing around out here earlier."

"Did you tell them to get lost?"

"Was gonna, but they were just riding their skateboards down the loading dock."

"You're such a softie, Tony."

Gio chimed in. "I wish I'd had a place like this to ride my board when I was a kid."

"You think that would've kept you out of trouble?"

"Maybe." He shrugged.

"Well, then, all right. That's enough reason for me. Let them ride whenever they want."

Gio chuckled to Tony. "Iz is getting a little mellow in her old age."

She glared at him.

"Oh. That's right. I almost forgot. You're adding another year today, aren't you?"

"You'd better have bought me something good." She winked at him.

"How about you take the day off tomorrow? Then you and Mel can do something fun," Tony said.

"That's my plan."

"Oh, yeah? What are you gonna do?"

"I'm not sure yet."

"If nothing else, you could always explore the beach."

"I guess." *Or just hang out in bed and explore Mel.* The thought made her grin as she slid the oversized cake box across the tailgate and picked it up. Tony tried to help her, but she waved him off. "Can you get the roses out of the backseat for me? They go on top of the cake."

Gio rushed around her and held the door open.

Tony retrieved the roses. "What do they call this color?"

"Salmon. It's my favorite. Apparently the customer likes it too."

"I didn't even know you liked roses, sis," Gio said.

"Every woman likes roses." She glanced over her shoulder at Gio and winked. "Don't ever forget that." She slid the cake onto the center island and opened the top of the box.

Tony broke off the stems as he handed her the rosebuds, and she meticulously put them in place. Now that she looked at it, she had to admit it was a beautiful cake, but Izzy had been a little put out this afternoon at having to go get it. She could've made them a delicious Italian cream cake.

"Is everything set up in the dining room?"

"Yep. Just waiting on you."

"What time is the party?"

"Reservation was for seven, but a few people came early to decorate."

She glanced at the clock on the wall; it was almost six thirty. "Well, I guess we'd better get this in there."

"Here, let me help you." Tony slid the cake off the counter and into his arms. "Can you get the door, Angie?"

"Already on my way." She pushed the kitchen door open. "From the amount of food they ordered, it looks like it's gonna be a hell of a party."

"Let's hope so." Izzy turned, facing Tony as she backed through the door.

After they stepped through the doorway, Angie directed them to the table against the wall, where Izzy centered the cake and smoothed the tablecloth.

"Surprise."

The sound nearly knocked Izzy off of her feet.

"What the—" She spun around and was engulfed in the arms of her mother and father.

"Here. Take that coat off." Angie handed her the silk shirt and waited as she put it on.

"Where is she?" Izzy searched the small crowd of familiar faces but couldn't locate the one she was looking for.

Angie pointed to the corner of the room. "At the bar." Before Izzy could move, Angie touched her elbow. "Don't be mad. She worked really hard on this."

She spotted Mel sitting on the stool at the end of the bar, dressed in a red dress that hugged her every curve. She stared at Mel's lips, tripped across her breasts, and landed on the long, lean legs she loved to be wrapped in before she swept back up to beautiful emerald-green eyes that locked with hers. The all-too-familiar feeling danced in her belly. She was stunning.

"I'm not mad." She smiled. *How could I be mad at that vision of loveliness?*

After giving a few hugs and hellos, she headed her way, and Mel gave her a sultry smile.

Izzy trailed her finger down Mel's arm as she leaned near and whispered in her ear, "I love this shirt, but I feel a little underdressed."

"Oh, really? Well, just so you know, *I'm* hoping to feel that way later." Mel gave her a steamy stare over her glass as she sipped her wine.

A red-hot jolt of arousal shot through Izzy like a lightning bolt. "You'd better stop that, or we're going to have to leave early." Izzy took the glass from her hand and drank. "And don't have too much of this." She lifted the glass, looking at the legs of wine as they flowed slowly to the bottom of the glass.

"You either." Mel poured another glass of wine and clinked it against Izzy's. "Happy birthday, baby."

"Thank you." She pressed her lips gently to Mel's. "Can't we just sneak out now?"

"And disappoint all these people?" Mel's lip pulled up as she slid her finger from the base of Izzy's neck to the neckline of her tank. "But save your energy. I don't plan to get much sleep tonight."

"God, I love you." Izzy's mouth covered Mel's in an urgent, demanding kiss that left her in a pool of anticipation.

"Love you more," Mel said breathlessly against her cheek. "I have one more gift I'd like you to open." She set her wineglass on the bar before retrieving the small velvet box from her clutch and handing it to Izzy.

Adrenaline raced through Izzy as she flipped her gaze from Mel's eyes to the box and back again. "What's this?"

"I love you, Izzy, and I want you to be my wife," Mel said, and everything else in the room disappeared for Izzy. She saw nothing except Mel's sparkling green eyes as she fumbled to find a place to land her wineglass. She swept Mel off the barstool into her arms and kissed her completely. It was the most amazing kiss ever—soft, demanding, and sweet all wrapped up together. She didn't want it to stop. Mel had beaten her to the punch, but she'd made her the happiest woman in her little part of the world.

When they finally parted to take a breath, Mel quietly gazed at Izzy, her eyes glassy with emotion. It took her a minute to realize Mel was actually waiting for an answer. "Yes, I'll marry you."

Mel took the diamond-embedded band from the box and slid it onto Izzy's finger. It was a perfect fit. Then Mel gave her one more heated kiss before whispering in her ear. "Now go mingle."

"Not sure I can after this." All she wanted to do now was spend the whole evening alone, wrapped up with Mel.

"You have to. Your mother's waiting to see it on your finger. She's already going to be mad because I didn't ask you in front of everyone." Mel ran her finger down the side of Izzy's face, tucking a strand of hair behind her ear.

Izzy kissed her again softly, then took in a deep breath and growled before she reluctantly turned and headed to where her parents were seated. Her mother's smile was wide, and Izzy knew Bella would take credit for Izzy's happiness. But that was okay, because she was, indeed, extremely happy.

EPILOGUE

Mel Thomas sat at the bar staring across the room at her other half. The grin she saw on Izzy's face told her she'd been successful in her quest. The birthday party had been a total surprise.

Adrenaline flooding her veins, Mel enjoyed the way her heart was pounding. Her body surged with desire when Izzy looked her way and she took in that dimple-pricked smile. God, she loved that smile. If anyone had told her six months ago she could be this happy, Mel would've flat-out called them a liar.

During the last two years of her dwindling decade-long marriage, her life had been far from perfect. Happiness hadn't often been in her thoughts. If she hadn't had her work, getting through each day would've been an absolute chore. But then something wonderful had happened—no, someone wonderful had happened, and her reality had changed. She was jarred back into active living, leaving behind what had become, for her, a meager existence.

It was almost six months ago to the day that Mel had begun falling in love again. She hadn't known it at the time, but that day was a new beginning, the launch of a journey to self-discovery. It might have been a rocky voyage, but it was one she would never regret riding out.

Some people might call it a mid-life crisis or even some sort of life epiphany. But, remembering Bella's story, Mel simply called it finding where the light glows.

THE END

About the Author

Dena Blake grew up in a small town just north of San Francisco where she learned to play softball, ride motorcycles, and grow vegetables. She eventually moved with her family to the southwest where she began creating vivid characters in her mind and bringing them to life on paper.

Dena currently lives in the Southwest with her partner and is constantly amazed at what she learns from her two children. She's a would-be chef, tech nerd, and occasional auto mechanic who has a weakness for dark chocolate and a good cup of coffee.

Books Available from Bold Strokes Books

Forsaken Trust by Meredith Doench. When four women are murdered, Agent Luce Hansen must regain trust in her most valuable investigative tool—herself—to catch the killer. (978-1-62639-737-8)

Her Best Friend's Sister by Meghan O'Brien. For fifteen years, Claire Barker has nursed a massive crush on her best friend's older sister. What happens when all her wildest fantasies come true? (978-1-62639-861-0)

Letter of the Law by Carsen Taite. Will federal prosecutor Bianca Cruz take a chance at love with horse breeder Jade Vargas, whose dark family ties threaten everything Bianca has worked to protect—including her child? (978-1-62639-750-7)

New Life by Jan Gayle. Trigena and Karrie are having a baby, but the stress of becoming a mother and the impact on their relationship might be too much for Trigena. (978-1-62639-878-8)

Royal Rebel by Jenny Frame. Charity director Lennox King sees through the party girl image Princess Roza has cultivated, but will Lennox's past indiscretions and Roza's responsibilities make their love impossible? (978-1-62639-893-1)

Unbroken by Donna K. Ford. When Kayla and Jackie, two women with every reason to reject Happy Ever After, fall in love, will they have the courage to overcome their pasts and rewrite their stories? (978-1-62639-921-1)

Where the Light Glows by Dena Blake. Mel Thomas doesn't realize just how unhappy she is in her marriage until she meets Izzy Calabrese. Will she have the courage to overcome her insecurities and follow her heart? (978-1-62639-958-7)

Escape in Time by Robyn Nyx. Working in the past is hell on your future. (978-1-62639-855-9)

Forget-Me-Not by Kris Bryant. Is love worth walking away from the only life you've ever dreamed of? (978-1-62639-865-8)

Highland Fling by Anna Larner. On vacation in the Scottish Highlands, Eve Eddison falls for the enigmatic forestry officer Moira Burns, despite Eve's best friend's campaign to convince her that Moira will break her heart. (978-1-62639-853-5)

Phoenix Rising by Rebecca Harwell. As Storm's Quarry faces invasion from a powerful neighbor, a mysterious newcomer with powers equal to Nadya's challenges everything she believes about herself and her future (978-1-62639-913-6)

Soul Survivor by I. Beacham. Sam and Joey have given up on hope, but when fate brings them together it gives them a chance to change each other's life and make dreams come true. (978-1-62639-882-5)

Strawberry Summer by Melissa Brayden. When Margaret Beringer's first love Courtney Carrington returns to their small town, she must grapple with their troubled past and fight the temptation for a very delicious future. (978-1-62639-867-2)

The Girl on the Edge of Summer by J.M. Redmann. Micky Knight accepts two cases, but neither is the easy investigation it appears. The past is never past—and young girls lead complicated, even dangerous lives. (978-1-62639-687-6)

Unknown Horizons by CJ Birch. The moment Lieutenant Alison Ash steps aboard the Persephone, she knows her life will never be the same. (978-1-62639-938-9)

Divided Nation, United Hearts by Yolanda Wallace. In a nation torn in two by a most uncivil war, can love conquer the divide? (978-1-62639-847-4)

Fury's Bridge by Brey Willows. What if your life depended on someone who didn't believe in your existence? (978-1-62639-841-2)

Lightning Strikes by Cass Sellars. When Parker Duncan and Sydney Hyatt's one-night stand turns to more, both women must fight demons past and present to cling to the relationship neither of them thought she wanted. (978-1-62639-956-3)

Love in Disaster by Charlotte Greene. A professor and a celebrity chef are drawn together by chance, but can their attraction survive a natural disaster? (978-1-62639-885-6)

Secret Hearts by Radclyffe. Can two women from different worlds find common ground while fighting their secret desires? (978-1-62639-932-7)

Sins of Our Fathers by A. Rose Mathieu. Solving gruesome murder cases is only one of Elizabeth Campbell's challenges; another is her growing attraction to the female detective who is hell-bent on keeping her client in prison. (978-1-62639-873-3)

The Sniper's Kiss by Justine Saracen. The power of a kiss: it can swell your heart with splendor, declare abject submission, and sometimes blow your brains out. (978-1-62639-839-9)

Troop 18 by Jessica L. Webb. Charged with uncovering the destructive secret that a troop of RCMP cadets has been hiding, Andy must put aside her worries about Kate and uncover the conspiracy before it's too late. (978-1-62639-934-1)

Worthy of Trust and Confidence by Kara A. McLeod. Special Agent Ryan O'Connor is about to discover the hard way that when you can only handle one type of answer to a question, it really is better not to ask. (978-1-62639-889-4)

Amounting to Nothing by Karis Walsh. When mounted police officer Billie Mitchell steps in to save beautiful murder witness Merissa Karr, worlds collide on the rough city streets of Tacoma, Washington. (978-1-62639-728-6)

Becoming You by Michelle Grubb. Airlie Porter has a secret. A deep, dark, destructive secret that threatens to engulf her if she can't find the courage to face who she really is and who she really wants to be with. (978-1-62639-811-5)

Birthright by Missouri Vaun. When spies bring news that a swords-woman imprisoned in a neighboring kingdom bears the Royal mark, Princess Kathryn sets out to rescue Aiden, true heir to the Belstaff throne. (978-1-62639-485-8)

Crescent City Confidential by Aurora Rey. When romance and danger are in the air, writer Sam Torres learns the Big Easy is anything but. (978-1-62639-764-4)

Love Down Under by MJ Williamz. Wylie loves Amarina, but if Amarina isn't out, can their relationship last? (978-1-62639-726-2)

Privacy Glass by Missouri Vaun. Things heat up when Nash Wiley commandeers a limo and her best friend for a late drive out to the beach: Champagne on ice, seat belts optional, and privacy glass a must. (978-1-62639-705-7)

The Impasse by Franci McMahon. A horse packing excursion into the Montana Wilderness becomes an adventure of terrifying proportions for Miles and ten women on an outfitter led trip. (978-1-62639-781-1)

The Right Kind of Wrong by PJ Trebelhorn. Bartender Quinn Burke is happy with her life as a playgirl until she realizes she can't fight her feelings any longer for her best friend, bookstore owner Grace Everett. (978-1-62639-771-2)

Wishing on a Dream by Julie Cannon. Can two women change everything for the chance at love? (978-1-62639-762-0)